Praise for *The Dollmaker*:

"A fantastic book, revealing a zone of wonder and a world of truth" Andrew O'Hagan, author of *The Illuminations*

"Elegant, beautiful and subtly scary" Daniel Kehlmann, author of *Measuring the World*

"Mesmerising, richly layered and wholly original – worthy of a modern Grimm" Andrew Caldecott, author of *Rotherweird*

"A masterful and multi-layered haunted toyshop of a novel" Tony White, author of *The Fountain in the Forest*

"Beautifully written and deeply strange" Leaf Arbuthnot, *Sunday Times*

"Unsettling, intricately constructed and teasingly elliptical" Stephanie Cross, *Daily Mail*

Praise for *The Rift*:

"Beautifully told, absorbing and eerie in the best way" Yoon Ha Lee, author of *Ninefox Gambit*

"It leaves the reader looking at the world anew. Dizzying stuff" Anne Charnock, author of *Dreams Before the Start of Time*

"A lyrical, moving story" *The Guardian*

"Moving, subtle, and ambiguous" *Booklist*

"A wrenching read, offering a 'missing person' story with more depth and emotion than the plot normally allows" Barnes & Noble SFF blog

"One thing you won't find in this brilliantly ambiguous book is the truth, but so long as you don't read it expecting a definitive explanation, you definitely won't be disappointed." Tor.com

Praise for *The Race*:

"A unique and fascinating near-future ecological SF novel. Buy it!" Jeff VanderMeer, author of the *Annihilation* trilogy

"Literate, intelligent, gorgeously human" Alastair Reynolds, author of *Revelation Space*

"An ingenious puzzle-box of a narrative that works both as a haunting family saga and as a vivid picture of a future worth avoiding" *Chicago Tribune*

"Enticingly mysterious... akin to the best alternative history fiction" *Publishers Weekly*, Starred Review

"A novel of tender nuances, brutality, insight and great ambition" Tor.com

Also available from Nina Allan:

the RACE
the RIFT
the SILVER WIND
the DOLLMAKER

NINA ALLAN

RUBY

TITANBOOKS

Ruby
Print edition ISBN: 9781789091724
E-book edition ISBN: 9781789091731

Published by Titan Books
A division of Titan Publishing Group Ltd
144 Southwark Street, London SE1 0UP

First edition: September 2020
1 3 5 7 9 10 8 6 4 2

A CIP catalogue record for this title is available from the British Library.

Printed and bound in CPI Group (UK) Ltd, Croydon CR0 4YY

To my mother, Monica Allan

CONTENTS

B-SIDE

The thought of telling Lennox was unbearable. As Michael came out of the sports hall it was Lennox he thought of, his skimpy eyebrows, the round spectacles that always reminded him of Leon Trotsky. Lennox had warned him many times that believing you could win at chess and assuming it as a given were not the same thing. Now, when it really mattered, Michael had let all his teacher's advice fly out of the window. His mistakes had been shameful and stupid and he had lost the tournament. He had let the old man down.

The only mercy was that Lennox had not been there. There had been a hospital appointment, something he couldn't get out of. Michael had been disappointed when the old man broke the news of this – now it seemed like a gift from the gods. For some moments he felt consoled, safe in the knowledge of his teacher's absence. But in the time it took him to walk from the hall foyer to the school gates he recognised the stay of execution for what it was: not a reprieve but a postponement. Lennox would find out what had happened soon enough.

"There's no escaping disappointment in chess," Lennox had told him. "Failure is there as a safeguard. Use it properly and it will help you improve. Losing to a better player can be more valuable than any number of victories against weaker opponents. It is only in losing that you find out who you are and what you are made of. This is something you will have to learn the hard way if you are serious about becoming a grandmaster."

Michael had listened and nodded in agreement but the truth was he hadn't believed a word. He had known disappointment before in small things, things with no connection to chess. He thought he understood how failure would feel but really he hadn't a clue, he saw that now. True disappointment had nothing to do with missing a school trip to Lapland or losing your iPhone. True disappointment made you question your whole idea of yourself. It ate you alive from the inside, like one of the necrotising parasites in *The Puppeteer*, the film starring Ludo Henry and Ruby Castle. Michael would watch anything Ruby Castle was in, although it was her horror films he liked best. His mother told him he shouldn't watch so many horror films, that they would give him bad dreams, but while it was true that Michael did sometimes have nightmares, none had compared with the horror of what had just happened to him in broad daylight.

The parasites in *The Puppeteer* were spread by monkeys in a carnival sideshow, wide-eyed lemur-like creatures dressed in red blazers that had a talent for stealing money out of people's pockets. Ruby Castle played the monkey trainer. Michael had read she did all her own stunts. He wondered what it was about carnivals and circuses that made them such popular settings for horror films. There were the freaks, of course, but it was not just the freaks. Mostly it was the sense that nothing was exactly as it appeared. The carnival people had a special way of speaking, not another language, but a tone of voice. They told you what you wanted to hear. They talked you into deceiving yourself.

Michael had loved the fair when he was younger. Most of all he had loved the dodgems, his father's arms around him, his plaid shirt spicy with the scent of tobacco. Each time they bumped another car Luis Gomez had laughed unstoppably and so had Michael. It was the only time he remembered them sharing a goal.

• • •

His rival's name was Douglas Coote. Michael had spotted him as the main threat immediately, though they hadn't been drawn together until the knockout stages. There were forty other competitors but it had only ever been about the two of them. Coote's eventual opponent in the final, an overweight senior from Bexley Grammar, had resigned the game in less than half an hour.

Coote was nervy and thin with hazel eyes. He had the habit of clearing his throat after each move, sipping incessantly from his water glass. What hurt was not so much that he had won, but that he was good. Michael imagined an alternative scenario in which their positions had been reversed. He saw himself shaking Coote's hand, congratulating him on a fine game and shyly suggesting they get together sometime and go through some openings. The picture was so plausible Michael found it difficult to relinquish. He began to walk faster, scuffing his trainers against the tarmac. He was anxious to get away before the others started coming out of the hall, pushing and chattering and conducting excited post-mortems of the various games. As he passed through the gates and into the road he felt a surge of relief. The appearance of Jackson and Pullen caught him off guard.

"What are you doing here on a Saturday, Gomez? Old Lennox keep you chained to your desk?"

"Shut up, Jackson," Michael said. "Bugger off." He mumbled the words, blurring their edges, affecting the language he knew Jackson and Pullen would best understand. He wasn't about to run he didn't want to hang around arguing with them, either. What Steven Jackson wanted was an excuse for a fight. It would be foolish to give him one. Michael hunched his shoulders, hugged his bag to his chest and tried to push past. Jackson and Pullen weren't normally dangerous. They took the piss out of his glasses and his skin colour, his closeness to Lennox, but they had never pushed their abuses further than verbal taunts. There were times when Michael thought they might even be afraid of him.

"What's the big hurry?" said Jackson. "Had a row with your boyfriend?" He made a grab for the strap of his bag, which Michael had left dangling. "He's an ugly bastard though, isn't he, old Lennox? I'd have thought that even Specky Gomez could do better than that."

Michael scowled. It occurred to him that *they might know*, that they had learned about Coote's victory and had come to torment him with it. He knew this was unlikely – what Jackson knew about chess could be written on the back of a postage stamp – but Michael hated them to make fun of Lennox. On any other day he would have ignored them anyway but his failure at the tournament had worn away at his defences.

"Get lost, moron." He yanked on his bag strap, snatching it from Jackson's grasp. Jackson looked down at his hand while Pullen started doing his inevitable chimpanzee impression. Michael's heart sank. Gareth Pullen was a weakling and a coward but he and Jackson together still made two against one.

"Who are you calling a moron, you frigging queer?" There was a red, painful-looking stripe across Jackson's palm. Michael felt laughter coursing through him, threatening to burst forth. He forced it back down.

"You," he said. "You're a fucking moron."

He swung his bag at Jackson, catching him a walloping blow to the side of the head. He was surprised how good it felt, how delicious, to lose control. He told himself he was doing it for Lennox, but even as Jackson came for him he knew his action was payback for Douglas Coote.

"I'll kill you, you fucking geek." Steven Jackson surged forward, his right fist aiming for the centre of Michael's face. Michael ducked away to one side and almost tripped over. At the same moment Pullen cannoned into him from behind. Michael went down like a sawn-off tree, sprawling full-length on the tarmac. As he fell he noticed Jackson's nose was bleeding. Hot gravel sank its teeth into his palms.

He scrambled to his knees but Jackson shoved him backwards and he was on the ground again. Pain flared in his side like a struck match and he realised Gareth Pullen must have kicked him. He was frightened but also furious. He knew he had brought the whole thing on himself.

"Who's the moron now then, you spastic?"

"Frigging geek."

Jackson was kicking out also, not at him, Michael realised belatedly, but at his schoolbag. It skidded away from him across the tarmac. Michael lunged after it, wondering at his own stupidity. Pullen threw himself on top of him, pinning him flat. An image rose in his mind: a can of Terminator insect spray with its famous cockroach logo. The cockroach was on its back, legs flailing as the poison dissolved its insides. Michael's grandmother always kept a can of Terminator under her sink just in case. Grandma Lisa was generally fearless but she had a horror of large insects.

Michael forced himself forward, dragging himself across the tarmac with the full weight of Pullen on top of him. His knees whimpered with every movement but he knew if he didn't throw Pullen off there would be worse to come. He tugged his right hand free and removed his glasses, tucking them inside his shirt. Somewhere far above him Pullen was making the chimp noise again. Then suddenly the weight was lifted. Michael gasped as his lungs reinflated. He realised someone must have got Pullen off him. As to who his rescuer might be he had no idea.

"What's going on?"

A man's voice, one he vaguely recognised but could not place. Michael squinted upwards, trying to establish if he was still in danger. Someone was gripping Pullen by the elbow and Michael realised with a shock that it was the man Lennox sometimes had staying with him, the man he had introduced to Michael as his nephew. Michael tried to recall his name but it wouldn't come, and he wondered if in fact he had ever known it. The nephew was old, forty years old at least, his greying hair pulled into a straggly ponytail. He had a scar across one cheek, a hard white seam that followed the arc of his right eye socket like a line of stitching. He was wearing jeans and old trainers, like Michael, and a leather biker jacket that hung awkwardly on his narrow shoulders. Once, when Michael had gone to the bathroom in Lennox's flat, he had caught sight of the nephew sprawled on the divan bed in Lennox's spare room. His shoes were off, and there was a ragged hole in one of his socks. He had seen Michael and said hello, but that was all.

Jackson was tugging on Pullen's other arm. Pullen hung suspended between the two of them like a lump of meat.

"Get off him, you pervert, or I'm calling the cops." Jackson's face had turned a fierce shade of red. His acne stood out like rivets.

"That works for me, I'm sure they'd have some interesting questions. Shame they've got better things to do really, isn't it?" He let go of Pullen's arm and gave him a shove. Pullen flew backwards into Jackson, who staggered under the impact and almost fell. "Sod off before I lose my temper."

"Sod off yourself," Jackson said. "There's a mighty queer smell around here." He turned abruptly and marched off down the road. Pullen slouched along after him, rubbing his arm.

"Are you hurt?" asked Lennox's nephew. He touched Michael lightly on the shoulder. His grey eyes were the colour of rain.

"I'm OK," Michael said. He bent down to retrieve his bag. He felt inside, checking his books, his computer chess set and his mobile phone. All seemed undamaged.

"I'd better be going," he said. He replaced his glasses. "Thanks for helping me."

"I was hoping you'd come back to the flat. Lennox asked me to meet you today – that's why I'm here. He has something he wanted to give you. It won't take long."

Michael hesitated. He had never been alone with the nephew but if Lennox had sent him then it must be all right. Going to Lennox's flat would also put off the moment when he had to go home. His mother would be fine but he dreaded having to explain things to his father. His mother didn't care about chess, or at least she cared about it only insofar as it affected Michael. Luis Gomez pretended to be an expert. His questions were painfully embarrassing. He would be upset at Michael's defeat without having the least idea of how to assess its importance. He would try to buck Michael up. The thought of this was more awful somehow than the thought of his father angry, which never happened anyway.

It had been Luis Gomez who found Lennox in the first place, who arranged for Michael to be enrolled at the school where he taught. It was Luis Gomez who paid for the extra lessons. Michael could not bear the thought of his stricken face.

"Will Lennox be there?" Michael asked.

"No," said the nephew. "He's still at the hospital."

"OK," Michael said. The man made him nervous but he was always uneasy with strangers. "But I can't stay long."

They stood at the bus stop and waited. There was a bus from

outside the school that would take them right to Lennox's door. Michael had travelled on it often, though never with Lennox. Lennox was always waiting for him at the flat when he arrived.

"I lost," Michael said. In his head the words resounded like death knells. Let loose in the open air they seemed slightly less terrible.

"I know," said Lennox's nephew. "I could tell by your face."

"Do you play?" Michael said. It was a relief to talk about it, he found, which was also surprising.

"I used to. Just a bit," the nephew said, then laughed. Michael wondered what was funny and decided it was probably him.

• • •

Lennox lived in Kidbrooke, in one of the council blocks. The bin store stank of piss and the lift was often out of order, but the flats themselves were all right and Michael supposed Lennox had been lucky to get one. From Lennox's living room you could see all the way to Greenwich and the river beyond.

Lennox's nephew's name was Colin Wilkes.

"I'm not really his nephew," he said. "Lennox made that up so he didn't keep having to explain things. Lennox hates talking about his private life. You must have noticed."

"Who are you, then?"

Wilkes shrugged. "I've known Lennox since I was your age. We might as well be related." He dug around in one of the kitchen cupboards and brought out a frying pan. "I'm going to do some eggs. Would you like some?"

Michael nodded. The mention of food made him salivate. It felt odd to be in the flat without Lennox, though Lennox never talked much even when he was there. Usually he would sit reading the paper while Michael worked on a chess problem. When he was done with the news he would bring Michael a cup of tea and a plate of Tuc biscuits with cheese. The problems he set were sometimes difficult, sometimes not. Occasionally they would be impenetrable, the lines of logic knotted together like the tag ends of embroidery silk at the bottom of Grandma Lisa's sewing basket. The proper word for such a problem was *abstruse*, Lennox said. When he encountered an abstruse problem Michael felt a tense, tingling excitement in the pit of his stomach, as if he were a paratrooper about to leap out over enemy territory. Lennox said that what counted was not the number of problems he solved but his manner of approaching them.

"The answer is already within you," Lennox insisted. "It is simply a matter of locating it."

Never once did he tell Michael how good he was. It was as if he took his gift entirely for granted.

The table Michael sat at to do his chess problems was topped with blue Formica. A piece of the Formica had been snapped off, leaving an oatmeal-coloured space shaped like the map of Argentina. Argentina was where his grandparents came from.

Lennox slept in a narrow iron-framed bed with a tatty horsehair blanket instead of an eiderdown. The things in Lennox's flat were shabby and old, but Michael liked them. He knew that by themselves the chipped mahogany tallboy and the faded chintz curtains might be considered ugly, what his grandmother would have called *poverty-stricken*, but Lennox's presence somehow made them all right.

He went to the bathroom to wash his hands, carefully soaping the grazes on his palms. It stung but his skin felt better afterwards. He took off his shirt and ran his fingers carefully over his ribs. There was some soreness when he breathed in, but otherwise he seemed unhurt. He leaned forward, examining his face in the mirror. There was a cut on his cheek but it was shallow and had already started to scab over. Michael thought of the scar on Wilkes's face, that puckered white line. It looked as if someone had tried to gouge out one of his eyes, the kind of thing that only happened in horror movies. He wondered what had happened to Wilkes, and where Wilkes went when he wasn't at Lennox's flat.

He put his shirt back on and stepped out into the hallway. He could smell onions frying, cooking oil – food smells. Michael's stomach rumbled. He caught sight of Wilkes through the open doorway, in front of the stove. His leather jacket was slung across the back of one of Lennox's dining chairs.

"What did you mean when you said Lennox doesn't like to talk about things?" Michael asked.

"I didn't say things, I said his private life," said Wilkes. "Let's have some music on, shall we?"

He turned the heat down under the frying pan and came through to the lounge. Michael noticed he had taken his shoes off. He was wearing the tartan slippers Lennox usually kept beside his bed.

Wilkes flipped back the grooved laminate lid of Lennox's ancient stereo system and began flicking through the records on the shelf beneath. All of Lennox's music was on vinyl. There were a couple of classical LPs, but most of the records were jazz albums from the forties and fifties. Michael liked the look and feel of them, the old photographs on the covers, the faint mustiness, like the smell inside a junk shop.

Of the music itself he knew nothing. On the wire CD rack at home in the kitchen they had the Eagles' *Greatest Hits*, the soundtrack to *Out of Africa* and an album by a band called Marmalade. There were various other CDs that had come free with newspapers and magazines, but his parents hardly ever listened to music. His mother preferred the political documentaries they had on the radio and his father preferred to watch cricket. It had been Michael's Grandpa Felipe who was musical. According to Michael's father he had owned hundreds of records: tango music and classical symphonies and jazz albums like Lennox's. Felipe Gomez had come over from Argentina soon after the war and opened a grocery store in Brockley.

"He could add up whole columns of figures in his head, just like that," his father told him. "It's him you take after."

Felipe Gomez had died when Michael was three. There was a photograph of him holding Michael as a baby, but Michael had no memory of him at all. At least he had his grandmother, Lisa von Pelz, with her crazy German accent and her bug spray and her amazing and terrifying stories of Nazi spies. Of all the family it was Grandma Lisa who indulged Michael's passion for horror movies. But she understood chess and numbers as little as his father did, and Michael couldn't help wondering what his Grandpa Felipe had been like. Also, Lisa had got rid of all Felipe's records. She claimed they were taking over the house.

"What do you reckon?" said Wilkes. "Which do you prefer, fusion or bebop?"

"I don't know anything about jazz," said Michael. "You choose."

Wilkes made a tutting sound, striking the back of his teeth with the tip of his tongue as he sorted through the records. Michael didn't like the casual way Wilkes handled Lennox's possessions, although he supposed Wilkes believed it was his right. He was masquerading as Lennox's nephew, after all.

"You'll like this," he said at last. "This is a classic."

He lifted a record from the stack and held it out. The sleeve, like most of the rest, showed a black-and-white photograph of the singer and then the title, red letters on a white background. The singer's name was one he recognised, Billie Holiday, although he couldn't have said for certain whether he had heard her sing before. In the photograph Billie had her hair tied back off her face with a silken ribbon. She looked very young, almost childlike, and reminded Michael of Lynette Berger, who sat next to him sometimes in maths class. Lynette had a wooden pencil case with a sliding lid with a silver propelling pencil and a mean-looking architect's compass inside. Her parents came from Mozambique. Michael sometimes found himself staring at the nape of her neck, at the gleaming white arc of her shirt collar, at the silky wrinkled line where her hair met her skin.

She had once asked Michael if his mother came from Mozambique, too.

"No, from Nigeria," he replied, praying like a madman that he wouldn't stammer as he sometimes did when he got nervous. "She was born in Lagos."

Lynette smiled and turned back to her work. It had been his first and so far only contact with a girl he liked the look of and it had been exhausting. On the whole it seemed safer to be in love with Ruby Castle. It would be difficult to make a fool of yourself in front of a dead girl, even for him.

The title of the record Wilkes had chosen was *Santa Fé Nights*.

"There are some rare tracks on here," Wilkes said. "Even the title track is rare, because Holiday only recorded it once, in some tin-pot studio in Mexico. It was released as the B-side to one of her later singles with Lester Young, but other than that the only place you can get it is on this album. The tune is actually a tango by Ariel Ramirez. He was born in Santa Fé."

He slid the disc out of its sleeve, holding it carefully by the edges. He placed the record on Lennox's turntable and lowered the stylus. There was a faint crackling and then the music started, a blowsy saxophone over a rhythm line of piano and bass, and then Billie's keening vocal, a sound so open and pleading it made your stomach hurt.

Michael felt hot and then cold. He recognised the music instantly from the soundtrack of *American Star*, the film starring Ruby Castle and Raymond Latour. He had never consciously known the woman singing was Billie Holiday, but the track itself was familiar to him as the music from the ballroom scene on board the *American Star* cruise liner, just before the ship ran aground off the island where the monsters were. The legend was that it was while they were filming the ballroom scene that Ruby Castle and Raymond Latour fell in love. A year later, Ruby Castle had murdered Latour in a jealous rage when he refused to leave his wife for her. Ruby in the ballroom scene was transcendental. She was thirty-eight years old and, as the critics said, at the height of her powers. Those who had written about the film seemed to agree that the impact of the sequence was increased by the painful knowledge of what was to come, not just in the film but in Castle's life. Some even seemed to enjoy this, to revel in the prospect of Ruby's tragedy, but Michael felt his heart break for her each time he saw it.

The scene was famous, at least among horror fans. Michael was amazed Colin Wilkes hadn't mentioned it when he put on the record. He even wondered if Wilkes was playing some kind of game with him, if he knew about Michael's crush on Ruby Castle and was trying to show him up. He couldn't imagine how this could be – Michael had never admitted his feelings to anyone. But he wouldn't put it past Wilkes to have found out somehow. The man was strange. The way he had turned up just in time to save him from Jackson and Pullen, for instance. The way he had guessed about what had happened with Douglas Coote.

The words *guardian angel* flashed through Michael's mind, piercing its trembling surface like an azure dart. He kept staring at Wilkes, waiting to see if anything would happen, but Wilkes seemed almost to have forgotten Michael was there. He stood at the kitchen counter dishing up the food, his body swaying slowly in time to the music.

"Lennox loves Billie Holiday," he said. He opened his eyes, fixed Michael with his steel-grey gaze. "You do know he's dying?"

Michael stared at him.

"He might not even come home from the hospital," Wilkes continued. "He's known for weeks but he didn't know how to tell you. That's what I meant when I said he hates to talk about his private life."

Wilkes brought the steaming plates to the table. He had found an oven mitt somewhere, a long yellow gauntlet. There was corned beef hash and fried bread, a golden mound of scrambled egg. Michael gazed at it dumbly. Wilkes sat sideways in his seat and began to eat, lowering his head towards the food, shovelling egg into his mouth with the back of his fork.

"He said he'd see me next week for the lesson," said Michael at last.

"He has liver cancer."

There was a long silence, filled with the rich scents of corned beef and onion. Michael still wanted the food but he felt it would be wrong to touch it. He resented Wilkes for spoiling his meal. He experimented with the idea that Wilkes was lying, but the experiment refused to take off.

"Look," said Wilkes. He got up from the table, scraping his chair noisily against the linoleum. "He told me to give you these."

He disappeared into Lennox's bedroom and came back with a brown paper bag. Inside the bag was the carved wooden chess set Lennox had told him once belonged to Nicolai Maslanyi, Lennox's own well worn copy of Turati's *Great Chess Openings*, and a book that was called simply *Chess* by a writer named Stefan Zweig.

"He gave me a copy of that once, too," said Wilkes. "I read it so many times the covers fell off."

"I can't take this," Michael said. Mostly he meant *Great Chess Openings*, which Lennox rarely let out of his sight. The gift seemed like a sign, Lennox's way of telling him that Colin Wilkes was speaking the truth. A hard lump came into his throat. He realised he wanted to fight Wilkes, to knock him to the ground and start kicking him the same way Gareth Pullen had laid into Michael.

"I'm sorry to spring it on you like this," Wilkes said. "But maybe it's for the best." He licked his fork and wiped his mouth on his sleeve. "You won't believe me, but I learned to play chess by watching it on television. I grew up in a council care home. They used to show the British chess championships on BBC2 back then. One of the housemasters noticed my interest and encouraged me. Before long I was beating everyone I played and they didn't know what to do with me. When Lennox came along it was like being reunited with a long-lost father. I was like you once. I loved him, and I lived for chess. The only problem was that I wasn't good enough, not for the world circuit anyway. When I began to lose it almost killed me. I had no idea how to live in the world, and Lennox could never admit that he had failed. Eventually we stopped talking about it. He's cared for me like his own son but I sometimes think it would have been better if he'd put me out on the street." Wilkes paused. "I envied those wankers today. I envied them their simple-mindedness. When I saw what they were doing to you I almost kept walking. I wanted them to teach you a lesson, you see. I didn't want you to end up like me."

"I won't," Michael said. "It was just that one game."

"That's exactly what I would have said. Aren't you going to eat your corned beef?"

Michael shook his head. Quite suddenly he didn't feel hungry. "I have to go home."

"Did you like the record?"

Michael nodded, his mind far away.

"I have it on CD. I can burn you a copy if you like." Wilkes put his hand on Michael's shoulder. "I don't like you leaving like this."

"I have to go," Michael said, getting up. "My dad will be worried about me."

"I'll be sticking around for a while if you want to talk. You know the number."

Michael nodded. The lift was broken again so he used the staircase. He did not look back.

• • •

The sun was setting, the clouds along the horizon a candyfloss pink. It would soon be dark, Michael realised. He thought about catching the bus then decided to walk. Wilkes's news had shaken him badly. He needed time to think. It was not just Lennox's illness, it was the other things, too – Wilkes's suggestion that his gift might not be sufficient to fulfil his ambition, the kind of fear you didn't dare contemplate in case it came true. Until today Michael had never doubted his talent. But first there had been Douglas Coote and now there was this.

What he wanted was to talk to Lennox but Wilkes had told him that Lennox was dying and might never come home. Michael suddenly realised he didn't even know which hospital Lennox was in. He came to a standstill, wondering if he should return to the flat and ask Wilkes about visiting hours. Then he realised he had left Lennox's gift behind, the chess set and the books. He longed for these things, as if they somehow represented Lennox himself. He ached to go back, but both his father and Lennox had warned him never to hang about the estate after dark. Michael made up his mind to telephone Lennox's flat as soon as he got home. If Wilkes was still there he would pick up. He had even suggested that Michael should call him whenever he wanted.

He struck out across the heath. He had read that Blackheath Common was once haunted by highwaymen and that the vast oak forests of Shooter's Hill once stretched all the way to the English Channel. Not now, though. Oxleas Wood was where families went for picnics on Sunday afternoons, and the heath itself was just a patch of rough turf, spread out like a blanket across the ground between Blackheath and Greenwich. People flew kites there, and walked their dogs. At night the main pathways across the heath were illuminated by electric light. Michael never felt he was in any danger, although it was true that once it was dark the heath seemed bigger, slipping back a little in time perhaps, to when it really was a heath instead of a park.

He began to pick up his pace, heading for the part of the heath where he could cut across the road then down Crooms Hill and into Greenwich. There were two men on the pathway ahead of him, strolling side by side and deep in conversation. Michael walked a little faster, thinking he would overtake them, but just as he was about to go past, one of them edged over, blocking his path. The movement appeared casual but Michael sensed it had been deliberate. The other man laughed briskly, and once again Michael suspected it was him they were laughing at. He had a bad feeling, the same as when he knew Pullen and Jackson were in the vicinity. He wanted to shake off these men, to get far away from them. He would run if he had to, but his ribs still hurt from the beating earlier. He knew he wouldn't get far.

Michael stepped off the pathway and on to the grass, meaning to bypass them that way, but there was more of a rise than he thought. He tripped to his knees with a hard thump. Fresh pain jolted his ribs, filling his mind with memories of Jackson and Pullen.

You've had it now, you moron, he thought. Only this time, he was talking to himself.

"Oh Lord, are you all right?" said one of the men. "Can we help at all?"

The men were standing at the edge of the pathway, looking down at him. The one who had spoken was closest. He had an educated voice, what Jackson would call posh, the vowels round and lugubrious as in a play by Shakespeare. He sounded nothing like Jackson or Pullen, which ought to have been reassuring but for some reason was not. With Jackson you knew the worst you would get was a good kicking. This man seemed more dangerous than that, though how and why that should be remained unclear.

"I'm fine," Michael said. He pulled himself to his feet, meaning to get away immediately and as quickly as possible. The other man grabbed him by the arm.

"Oh look, it's the little chess boy," he said, peering at Michael down his elongated nose. "We were looking for you." He moved to one side slightly, drenching himself in light from a nearby streetlamp. He wore a long dark coat, knee-high lace-up boots with diamanté buckles. His face was thin and pale, and his voice was terrifying, with the same knife-edge of sarcasm teachers used when they were about to give you detention. Only it was worse somehow even than that, because it was a voice he knew.

The man was Aeneas Lascombe, from *The Puppeteer.*

"Eh, *niño,*" said Lascombe's companion. "You hurt?"

He had a thick Spanish accent and Michael felt outraged, imagining that the man was making fun of Michael's own father. Then he got a proper look at him and realised he had been mistaken. The man, smaller and wirier than Lascombe but no less awful, was Gara Brion, the Guanche restaurant owner in *American Star.* He was wearing his spider-god costume, the same yellow cloak and papier-mâché mask he had worn for the island fiesta scene. As Michael watched he performed an extravagant cartwheel across the grass, the yellow cloak billowing in the twilight like an amber sail.

Aeneas Lascombe still had Michael by the arm. His grip was not painful exactly but it was firm enough to make Michael feel he could not escape it. He took a step backwards, hoping Lascombe would let go and after a moment he did, the pale fingers gliding off him, cutting the silken twilight like nacreous knives. They left trails of whitish light behind them, a phosphorescent glimmer that was gone almost before Michael realised it was there.

"I need to get home," Michael said. His lips felt numb. He listened to his own words with a kind of distant interest, as if they were part of a programme on the radio.

"That's perfectly all right," said Lascombe. "We weren't intending to detain you. Only we have something of yours, I believe? We thought you might need it."

He reached inside his coat and drew out a small package. It was the brown paper bag he had left behind at the flat, the bag that contained the chess set and the books. In spite of his terror Michael found himself reaching for it. The paper crackled, and Michael could feel the hard wooden edge of the box that held the chess pieces. The box was beautifully carved, and opened flat to make a chessboard.

"You should take better care of your things. Especially presents. Presents are beneficence in physical form. They should be treated with respect."

"Yes, I know." Michael found he could no longer think straight – he was simply reacting to each new and terrible moment as it arrived. Reason told him these men must be actors, that this was some sort of masquerade, but at the same time Michael knew that this was not so. These people *were the characters*, the people Angel Garcia and Ludo Henry who played them in the movies had represented. Knowing that Aeneas Lascombe and Gara Brion were imaginary made no difference – Michael knew it was the truth. The inside of his head felt weightless, as if he might float up from the ground at any minute, drift away across the heath and into the night.

"If our business is concluded, we really must fly," Lascombe said. "It's a shame we can't stay and chat." He folded his arms across his chest and inclined his head. "Think about where you're headed, won't you? You might not realise it yet, but success – fame – brings in its wake its own cruel and special form of captivity." He turned his eyes away from Michael then spread his arms, seeming to take in the whole heath, the coloured lights burning from the bars and restaurants at its fringes, the tall spire of All Saints' Church that was Blackheath's main landmark. "I'll wager there's not one player or scholar or prodigy that does not at some hour of the day or night wish for the harlequin life of the varmint, the abject failure, the vagabond." Lascombe grinned, showing the gold-capped tooth Michael remembered so well from the film. "Of course, travelling with the circus I can have both."

Gara Brion laughed like a loon, gathering his spider cloak closely around him then unfurling it like a bat's wings. He gave a deep bow, an illusionist accepting his applause, then threw something on the grass. Michael saw it was a pair of shoes, Colin Wilkes's tatty Adidas trainers. The lace of the left shoe was missing. Michael bent down to pick them up, then realised he already had his hands full with the chess set and the books.

"I wouldn't bother if I were you," Lascombe said. "He doesn't need them. Not any more." His voice had grown fainter, Michael realised. By the time he turned back towards them, they were already gone.

Michael ran. He didn't stop until he reached the edge of the heath, the bright arcs of car headlamps moving slowly along Shooter's Hill Road. He crossed at the lights then turned, looking back the way he had come. Beyond the immediate glare of the lights the heath was dark and inscrutable, a hole in the luminous fabric of the world.

A bus was just stopping. Michael leaped on to it, swiped his Oyster card and collapsed into a seat towards the rear. The back of his throat was burning and tasted of iron. He was still breathing hard, as if his body had not yet caught up with the fact that it was now at rest. He pressed his face to the window, shielding his eyes against the reflection. He saw the road, and more cars, the lights of Greenwich. Already the details of his encounter with Lascombe were beginning to become confused inside his mind. He closed his eyes and leaned back in his seat. He stayed that way until he arrived at his stop. He got off the bus, looked both ways along Trafalgar Road. There were plenty of people about. It was Saturday, Michael remembered. Greenwich on a Saturday night.

I won't see them now, Michael thought. *That kind of stuff only happens when you're by yourself. That's horror movie rules.*

He realised he hadn't thought about the chess tournament in almost an hour. He walked the short distance to his home. His mother opened the door as he came up the path.

"Where on earth have you been? The headmaster phoned. We've been worried."

"I'm not a kid, Mum."

"You're thirteen years old, Michael. That means you're not an adult yet either. You might at least have switched on your phone."

"You have to switch it off. It's a chess tournament."

"I meant afterwards."

Michael felt bad. He had forgotten that the phone was off. It had never occurred to him to switch it back on again.

His mother was wearing skinny jeans and one of his father's plaid shirts. Michael thought she looked good whatever she wore. Her name was Micaela. Michael had been named after her.

"I'm sorry," he said. "Where's Dad?"

"Driving around the streets looking for you." She mock-cuffed him then ruffled his hair. She walked away along the hallway and a moment later he heard her on the phone to his father, telling him he could come home. He hung his bag on the coat rack and went through to the kitchen. Micaela Gomez was bending down, taking something out of the oven. As he entered the room she straightened up, wiping her hands on her jeans.

"Are you OK?" she said. "I mean really?"

"I'm hungry," he said. He remembered the corned beef hash that Wilkes had made and he had not eaten. It seemed like ages ago.

"The headmaster said you seemed upset."

The idea of Bassett calling his home seemed composed of equal parts glamour and shame. Quite suddenly Michael felt exhausted. He wanted to be alone in his room with his chess books and his computer and his film DVDs. More than anything he wanted this day to be over and done with.

"I'm fine," he said. "I'm going upstairs for a bit."

"Wash your hands while you're up there," said Micaela. "Supper's nearly ready."

Normally the darkness of familiar places did not bother him, but this evening he turned on the landing light, just to be sure. The house felt steady and quiet. Michael found it reassuring and somehow miraculous that his mother had continued preparing the supper as usual, believing and trusting in his return.

He went into his bedroom and sat down on the bed, his body still aching from all the running and falling. Everything was exactly as he had left it that morning – only he and the world had changed. He was contemplating this fact, wondering whether he should try calling Wilkes immediately or wait until after supper, when he noticed that not everything about his room was the same, that something had been added to it in his absence.

The shelf above his desk, which normally carried only a jar of pencils and his current homework projects, now also held a medium-sized parcel. The parcel was square and wrapped in gold paper. Michael stared at it stupidly, wondering what it was and how he should deal with it. It was not Christmas or his birthday. There was certainly nothing to celebrate. The parcel seemed out of place, a carol singer at a crematorium.

Michael lifted it down from the shelf and placed it on his desk. It was surprisingly heavy. He stroked the shiny paper then edged his nail under the Sellotape and tore it off.

Inside was a wooden box. Michael thought it might be mahogany, though he was no expert in these things. The box's front panel was made of glass. When Michael looked inside he saw the box contained a model of two people sitting at a table, playing chess. The room they sat in was furnished like an old-style parlour, with a Persian rug and a standard lamp, a miniature sideboard with a tiny crystal decanter. It reminded Michael of Queen Mary's dolls' house, which they had watched a documentary about once at school, though he understood that this construction was not a static model but a clockwork automaton. The two figures were exquisitely made, the hands and faces finely detailed. Michael thought they were probably made from wax. One was a hunchback, dressed in an embroidered silk waistcoat and velvet breeches. In spite of his misshapen body he was strikingly handsome.

The other figure was Colin Wilkes. The scar on his cheek had been exaggerated slightly, giving him the look of someone accustomed to violence. He was wearing miniature copies of Lennox's tartan slippers.

Michael stretched out his hand towards the ornate winding key. He gave it three or four tentative twists, then turned it steadily until he could feel the spring was fully loaded. When he released the key, the lamp came on and the hunchback and Colin Wilkes came grindingly to life. Their movements were slow and jerky, and Michael could hear the clockwork beneath the brass panel. The hunchback opened the game with the Sicilian. The Colin Wilkes figure followed this with an error so basic it made Michael gasp. Wilkes's error allowed the hunchback to play Levenson's Ruse, a trick move that inevitably led to mate in five.

The box was a minor miracle. While the game was in progress it played a tune, which Michael recognised immediately as *Santa Fé Nights*. At the end of the game the two figures froze, then snapped back to their original positions. The music ended in a final flourish and then fell silent. Wilkes's grey eyes seemed to fix on him, pleading. Michael could think of nothing more humiliating for a chess player than being forced to fall for the Levenson Ruse over and over again into eternity. It was grandmasters' hell.

Michael gazed at the motionless figures. Their features were so lifelike that after a while it became unsettling to look at them. It was difficult to believe that under their clothes they were just an assemblage of tin plate and clockwork. It was difficult to believe the box existed, even when it was standing right in front of him. He stretched out his hand, meaning to wind the key again, but at that moment his mother started calling from the foot of the stairs.

"Michael, the food's on the table."

He ducked into the bathroom, ran his hands briefly under the tap then went downstairs. His father had returned. Michael saw him exchange glances with his mother, and knew she had made him agree not to question Michael about the tournament.

"Did you like your present?" Luis Gomez said instead. His face was falsely bright, overeager in exactly the way Michael had known and feared it would be.

"It's great, Dad. It's amazing."

"It plays a real game, you know. Levenson's Gambit."

Michael almost retorted that a cheap trick like the Levenson would never be dignified with the title of gambit but stopped himself just in time. "I know, Dad, I saw. But you shouldn't have. It must have cost a bomb."

His father's face fell. "It was meant to be a surprise. For after the tournament."

"But I didn't win, Dad. I don't deserve it."

"Michael, you know we're proud of you whatever," said Micaela. "You'll win the next one. Now eat this before it gets cold." She placed a shallow bowl in front of him, filled with the bean and chorizo stew that was their Saturday night favourite. He marvelled at the calm confidence of her statement. *You'll win the next one.* Michael knew she believed this as completely and unquestioningly as she had believed he would arrive home safely that evening. He felt himself grow suddenly lighter, the bright balloon of his thoughts bobbing up from his head, primrose-coloured and translucent and free. He listened to his father make a few tortured remarks about the weather then gave him what he wanted and told him about the game.

"I was stupid," he said in the end. "I underestimated Coote. I won't make the same mistake again. I'll learn from what happened. That's what Lennox would say, anyway, and I believe him."

Saying Lennox's name out loud made his stomach churn. Could Lennox really be dying? On the plus side, his father looked much happier.

"Would you like to watch a film after supper?" he said. "You could bring down one of those monster videos of yours?"

Michael couldn't help smiling. He knew his father couldn't watch a horror film without switching on every light in the house. "No, Dad, that's OK. I want to go over the game."

Luis Gomez put on his serious face, a look that was always tinged with anxiety.

"I don't want you sitting up till all hours," said his mother. "You should give chess a break for this evening."

"Don't worry, Mum. I won't be up late."

He lingered on the stairs for some moments, listening to the voices of his parents and their quiet laughter as they moved about the kitchen, clearing the dishes and putting things away. He loved to hear them when they were alone together, the secret and intimate pulse of the life they shared. He knew he was never far from their thoughts, but he also liked the way they became something else when there was just the two of them, something fierce and private that he could never enter or be a part of. Knowing this made him feel less responsible.

Back in his room, these matters receded as if they had never been. It was the box he had to think about now. His parents had never set eyes on Colin Wilkes. They didn't even know he existed. The horror and strangeness of the automaton would not have been apparent to them. For them the box was nothing more than an extravagant toy and here again Michael was glad. Their worry and interference could only make things more complicated.

He wound the key, setting the mechanism in motion. He watched Wilkes and the hunchback go through their immortal motions. The more he looked at them the more it seemed to him as if they were hiding something, as if Levenson's Ruse was a ruse in more ways than one, a decorative cover for some other more elaborate game that was being played out behind the scenes.

Still, the horror of being defeated in that ridiculous way every time – who would choose that? Michael waited till the charade was over then wound them up again, unable to resist seeing the awful spectacle one more time. The music played, the tango rhythm turning the chess game to a stylised dance.

Santa Fé was in Argentina, where Grandpa Felipe was born and where Michael's grandmother Lisa von Pelz had emigrated with her family after the war. He felt he should ask Grandma Lisa about Santa Fé, although Michael was certain the place itself had nothing to do with what was going on here, that the tune was part of the joke, the *ruse*, to make it clear to him that whoever was pulling the strings knew everything about him and then some.

And who would be pulling the strings if not the puppeteer? For the first time since arriving home he thought back to his encounter with Aeneas Lascombe. It was Lascombe that mattered, Michael knew that. Gara Brion in his stupid spider costume had been so much stage dressing. Lascombe had been awful, as pale-faced and sinister as he was in the movie. Michael knew he could not exist in the real world. He was a projection, quite literally the figment of someone's imagination.

Could he himself have imagined Lascombe into existence? Was Lascombe the secret embodiment of all his fears?

But that still left the matter of Wilkes – Wilkes-in-the-box who had saved him from his tormentors only to warn him against the one thing in his life that mattered to him.

He had briefly thought of Wilkes as a guardian angel. What if he was the devil instead? A devil sent to tempt him away from the path he had chosen, into the same life of doubt and disillusionment that had reduced Wilkes himself to a mannequin in a glass box, playing out his own nightmare in an infinite cycle of games he could never win.

Michael shook his head in irritation at himself. The idea of celestial beings warring over his soul was absurd. Why would they bother with him? He was unimportant, at least thus far, a pawn in the game. He couldn't even win a county tournament.

He waited till the music stopped and then covered the box with one of the used shirts that lay in a heap on his bedside chair. He could not bear the sight of it any longer, the sight of Wilkes pleading with him not so much to save him as to *guess*.

He lay back on the bed, wondering if he should watch *The Puppeteer*, if the film might contain a clue that he had missed. He had the DVD after all, he had all of Ruby Castle's movies. He decided against it. He had the feeling that seeing that film tonight would be a bad idea. Michael closed his eyes, wishing more than ever that he could talk to Lennox. He had no intention of telling him about Aeneas Lascombe. If the old man really was ill then a horrible story like that would only worry him. But they could talk about chess. If Lennox was in a good mood he might even be persuaded to tell Michael about the time he had seen Nicky Maslanyi beat Garry Kasparov. Then everything would be all right, at least for a while. Michael climbed under the covers and fell asleep.

• • •

He was woken by Luis and Micaela coming upstairs. He switched off the bedside light and turned on his side. The luminous digits of his bedside clock radio were showing 23:30. Michael closed his eyes as his father eased open the door and peeked into the room. After a moment or two, the door eased shut again.

"He's fast asleep," his father whispered.

"He's worn out," said his mother. "I wish you wouldn't encourage him to take this chess thing so seriously."

They went into the bathroom and he could no longer hear them. After their bedroom door finally closed, Michael waited a further half an hour by his clock and then switched on his mobile, holding it under the bedclothes to smother its warm-up jingle. There were no text messages, but he was not expecting any. He queued the number of Lennox's flat from his contacts then pressed the call key. It was well after midnight, but he imagined that for a man like Colin Wilkes that would still be early.

Michael held the phone to his ear and waited, imagining the sound of Lennox's phone, ringing in consort in the empty hall.

THE LAMMAS WORM

The first time I saw Leonie Pickering she was standing beside the A419 just east of Cirencester. Someone had scrawled her name in square black capitals on the back of a torn-up cereal packet then fastened the cardboard label around her neck with a piece of string. There was no return address. She was wearing a yellow dress, soiled at the back with mud or excrement.

Her features were odd. I don't mean deformed, just strangely put together. Her skull was elongated, like the artists' impressions you see of Neanderthal people. There was a small ridge on her forehead, just above her eyebrows. Her eyes were a liquid black. Her frizzy dark hair looked a mass of tangles, matted together like a piece of old carpet. She seemed not to have a clue where she was.

It was early on a Sunday morning, well before nine, and the roads were quiet. We had played a ground in Marlborough the night before. Cirencester was our next stop and most of the other wagons were already there. I was bringing up the rear with Morrey Shyler and Piet van Aspen. Morrey was taking it slowly because his engine had developed a knock, and I was taking it slowly because I always tended to end up driving with Piet. Piet was moving at a snail's pace as usual, because that was the fastest his decrepit old jalopy would go.

Morrey braked so suddenly I almost went into the back of him. *Steady on, Morrey,* I thought, *what the hell do you think you're doing?* Then I saw the kid. She was standing at the edge of the road, staring out into the traffic like a dummy in a shop window. I hooted to warn Piet to slow down then pulled over on to the verge. As I switched off the ignition I saw Morrey jump down from his cab. He went straight up to the girl and put out his hand to her, the way you might do with a frightened animal. The girl's lips drew back from her teeth in a kind of snarl. She looked like an angry baboon.

She was tiny, no more than five feet tall. *Shit,* I thought, *she'll have his hand off if he's not careful.* I opened the door to get down.

"What's going on?" said Mae. She had been dozing in the seat beside me. Her blue eyes had a misty, faraway look as if she were still half in a dream.

"Just some kid," I said. "A runaway, I think. I'm going to help Morrey before he does something stupid. You stay here."

I wasn't in the habit of telling Mae what to do but for some reason the girl made me nervous. Mae leaned forward and peered through the windscreen.

"She doesn't look like a runaway to me. I reckon she's been dumped there."

"Perhaps," I said. I was sure she was right. I jumped down from the cab and went over to where Morrey was standing. Up close the girl was even smaller, and so skinny she looked half-starved. Morrey towered over her like a full-grown grizzly on its way to the hunting grounds. Morrey was a gentle giant, daft as a brush, but the kid wasn't to know that. She looked terrified.

"Back off a bit," I said to Morrey. "Give her some space."

I noticed she had no shoes on. Her feet were bony and narrow with high, graceful arches, the feet of a ballet girl. Her toes were longer than normal, more like fingers than ordinary toes. I put out my hand as Morrey had done, hoping to show the girl that I meant no harm.

"Are you hurt?" I said. "Can we give you a lift somewhere?"

The girl's lips pulled back in another snarl and I caught a glimpse of uneven yellow teeth. A second later she was flying right at me. I leapt instinctively to one side, my mind seething with visions of those crooked yellow incisors gouging into my flesh. She raced straight by me and underneath Morrey's trailer, going flat like a rat under a granary and tucking herself in behind one of the wheels.

"Well that's our morning cancelled," said Morrey. "Anybody fancy a cup of tea?"

I swore quietly to myself. I had visions of us stuck there for hours, trying to tempt the girl back out on to the roadside so we could drive on. Eventually I supposed we would have to call the police. I imagined them forcing the girl out with a cattle prod and then carting her off somewhere in the back of a cop car. I didn't like the idea of that. I rested my hand on the wheel-hub and bent down, hoping to see better, but there was just the rusty, diesel-smelling underside of Morrey's wagon and the humped dark unmoving shape I knew was the girl.

"What's happened? Has Morrey got a flat?"

Piet's voice made me jump sky high. In all the fussing over the girl I had forgotten about him.

"No such luck," said Morrey. "We've gone and got ourselves a luggage louse."

Luggage louse was an old company expression for stowaway. Piet edged closer to the trailer, toddling down the bank with that rolling, sideways walk of his. The grass was long and slippery and I was afraid he'd go flying.

"Let me see," he said. "Perhaps I can help."

Privately I thought the sight of Piet was only going to freak her out more, but I stepped back from the wagon anyway, giving up my spot by the wheel. I watched Piet peering into the darkness, wondering what he would make of it all. He had on his old jeans and one of the brightly coloured paisley shirts he liked to wear, a diminutive figure, shorter by a number of inches than the runaway girl.

"Come on," he said. "Don't be afraid."

Piet was about forty then, although like many dwarfs he had an ageless quality. His whole lower body was stunted, and in addition to this he had spina bifida. Mostly he could get about all right but he had pain flare-ups from time to time, pretty bad ones. The curvature of his spine meant he carried his head a little to one side. With his well-shaped mouth and high cheekbones his face was strikingly handsome. He had iridescent violet-coloured eyes. The public loved him, not just for the freakish contrast between his noble head and mangled body, but for his broad cockney accent, his dandyish clothes and his passion for gambling. Many people seemed to assume that a carnival was not a carnival if there wasn't a resident dwarf somewhere around, and Piet was the kind of dwarf they wanted to see.

Officially he was in charge of the funhouse. Unofficially he ran poker games into the small hours, relieving the local card kings of large sums of money. He had been with us for longer than anyone could remember. He never talked about his life before the company and none of the stories about him seemed to join up. My father told me that Piet had Dutch grandparents and that he had spent his childhood on one of the Rotterdam barges. But Vaska Kornilev's wife Marnie said that was all nonsense, and that Piet had grown up in a children's home attached to the London Hospital in Whitechapel. The Kornilevs were aerialists. They were both very close to my father before he retired.

"Piet never knew his parents at all," said Marnie. "Although he did have a sister. He was fond of her."

"What was she like?" I asked. I was endlessly curious about Piet. The idea that someone could erase their past and walk into a new life was fascinating to me.

"I couldn't tell you, love, I never knew her. I think she died when Piet was still in the home."

It was often difficult to tell what Piet was thinking. I guess he had grown so used to hiding his feelings that in a way he was always performing, even when he wasn't on stage. But I swear I saw something go off in him at the sight of

Leonie Pickering, some sort of inner explosion. He became incredibly still, and a light came into his eyes, the same as when he knew he was about to win an important hand at cards. Something must have happened in her, too, or at least she was less afraid of him than she had been of Morrey and me, because suddenly she raised her head and began inching forwards. As she emerged into the light she put a hand up to push back her hair. The hand was filthy like the rest of her but her fingers were long and delicate, finely made. Some of her fingernails were broken, as if she had been shut up somewhere and scrabbling to get out.

Gradually she straightened up, her black eyes never leaving Piet's face. The scrap of cardboard with her name on it was still fastened about her neck.

"It's all right," Piet said, very softly. "Would you like to have a ride with me in my van?"

Slowly he reached out his hand, and incredibly the girl took it, her long fingers wrapping themselves around Piet's short stubby ones like vine suckers around a beanpole. She looked down at the ground then, as if giving herself up to his charge. Piet set off back towards his trailer, leading the girl step by step along the verge as if she were a blind woman. Her dress flapped in the warm July breeze like a creased yellow flag.

"Bloody hell," said Morrey. "What do you reckon?"

"What I reckon is we're late already," I said. "Let's get back on the road."

I swung myself into the cab and started the engine. I was aware that Mae was eager to talk but I drove the rest of the way in silence. I couldn't get what had happened out of my mind. As we lined up to enter the ground it occurred to me that Leonie Pickering, in her smallness and her vulnerability, might well have reminded Piet of his dead sister.

Cirencester was a good pitch. The ground adjoined one of the main roads into the town. There were views of the Cotswolds. I parked the trailer, then left Mae to sort out our stuff while I went to help Vaska and Morrey with the marquees. I forgot about Piet for a while, though later on when I caught sight of old Jones doing his site inspection I thought it best to go and tell him about our strange visitor.

Jones's real name was Diccory Bellever. In his heyday and before he put on weight, he was famous all over Europe as an escapologist and wire-walker. The name Jones came from Davy Jones's Locker, and the near-miss Jones had had in his twenties when one of his routines had gone wrong and he sank to the bottom of the Solent, wrapped in half a hundredweight of steel chains.

"Can she do anything?" Jones said. "I mean, can she work?"

"I don't know," I said. "I doubt it. She's just a kid."

Jones sighed. "You know how I feel about carrying dead wood. The last thing we need is the cops on our backs if she's run off from somewhere. How old did you say she is?"

"About fifteen," I said. "I didn't really get a proper look at her." Actually I thought she was younger, but I didn't want Jones blowing a fuse. It was Piet I was thinking of, how he might react if Jones read him the riot act.

"Can you handle this for me, Marek? God knows I've got enough on my plate." Jones sighed again and folded his sinewy, still-muscular arms around the vast barrel of his stomach.

"Don't worry," I said. "I'll sort it." I wandered around the outfield for a bit then ambled over to Piet's trailer. There was no sign of Piet but I could smell cooking so I guessed he was inside making supper. The girl was sitting on the trailer steps under the awning. She was wearing one of Piet's vests and a pair of his corduroys. The trousers were too short for her and the shirt too big. The armholes gaped open, revealing the hollows of her armpits, matted with tawny hair, and her saucer-sized breasts. In front of her was a deep-sided bowl containing a generous helping of Boston beans and the paprika-seasoned potato cakes that were Piet's speciality. She was shovelling beans into her mouth with a spoon, her head bent low and her hair almost dragging in the food. She looked up at my approach and put both arms around the bowl as if she were afraid I might try and take it away from her. There was a crusting of potato on her upper lip.

A moment later Piet appeared in the doorway. He had a tea towel around his waist, and was holding a potato masher.

"Mark," he said. I am Marek Platonov, the knife-thrower. My father, Grigor Platonov, was a champion fire-eater. Mae and Piet have always called me Mark. "Would you like some latkes? There's plenty to go round."

"No thanks, Piet," I said. "I'll have my supper later, with Mae."

I wondered how Piet had managed to persuade the girl to remove her dress. Once when we were both drunk I asked Piet what he did for sex. He told me there was a woman he saw in London from time to time. I had assumed he meant a prostitute. Now I wondered if he saw Leonie Pickering as her replacement. The idea worried me – the girl looked so young – but I didn't see what I could do about it.

I chatted with Piet for a while then went to get changed. By the time I arrived backstage Ruby was already waiting.

"You're late," she said. "What's all this about a runaway?"

Ruby Castle and I are astrological twins. We were born on the same night but to different mothers, just fifteen minutes apart. We were inseparable as children and spent most of our teenage years thinking we were in love. But life doesn't always go the way you think it will. Ruby hooked up with Tolley and then I met Mae. Things were difficult for a while, but I don't think either of us ever considered breaking up our act. We had a connection on stage that was close to telepathic. You don't throw something like that away. What you do is bury the past the best you can.

"Just some weird kid," I said. "Piet's looking after her."

She gave me a look, as if she suspected me of not telling her the whole story. I shrugged my shoulders in silent denial and then it was time for us to go on.

It was a full house and a good crowd, and I was soon lost in the danger and the excitement of the strange craft that earned me my living. When I got back to the trailer I found Mae already in bed. She was reading *The Aspern Papers.* I could never understand Mae's addiction to Henry James. I had tried reading him, for her sake, but had found his writing turgid and deeply dull.

"In bed with another man again, I see," I said.

"Oh, Henry's the perfect gentleman," she said, smiling up at me. "All we ever do is sit and talk."

I took the book from her hands and laid it aside. She was wearing a pale silk slip that clung to her breasts and pooled in her lap like spilled milk. I undressed quickly and lay down beside her, sliding my hand up under the slip and between her legs. I caressed her until she came, and then I raised myself on my knees and entered her, climaxing almost at once.

We slept where we lay, in the warmth and salt-stickiness of our lovemaking. I woke once in the night, and pulled the sheet up over us. Mae's hair lay scattered across the pillow, turned silver by the moonlight creeping in between the curtains. In the instant before I fell asleep again I glimpsed in my mind the face of Leonie Pickering, her narrow lips drawn back from her discoloured teeth in a silent snarl.

• • •

After Cirencester came Stroud, then Tetbury and Malmesbury and Frome. Each time we arrived at a new ground the girl would jump down from the cab and run about like a child that disliked being shut indoors. She made no attempt to help us set up, but would sidle up to us as we worked, standing close by with her hands behind her back as if we were some fascinating new species of animal and she was afraid she might scare us away. It was unnerving at first but we soon grew used to her. For the first couple of days she was more or less mute, then suddenly she wouldn't shut up, though it was often difficult to make out what she was saying. Every now and then something would startle her and she would dash to find Piet.

She seemed devoted to Piet, yet she teased him too, pulling faces behind his back. Once I saw her dart out from behind some bushes and begin jeering at him in her high, excited sing-song voice, cupping her hands around her mouth to make a loud-hailer:

"Come on, Piet-Piet, you old slowcoach, you old monster!"

She leapt up on the fence, gripping the top bar with those extraordinary long toes of hers. She seemed light as dust, with all the natural balance and poise of a trained wire-walker. The spikes of her elbows cut V-shapes in the clear July air, and her top rode up, exposing a stripe of her flat dirt-brown stomach. I felt a rush of desire in spite of myself. Usually she gave me the creeps.

Piet bought her things, clothes mostly, but also the bright, gaudy trinkets she seemed to have a passion for: silver-backed brushes and mirrors, gilt snuffboxes, crystal animals. They must have cost a bit, some of them anyway, but what else did Piet have to spend his money on? Leonie guarded these presents jealously, counting and recounting them, glowering from under her eyebrows at anyone who came near.

Piet referred to her as "the kid" or "the hoodlum" and tried to make light of his attachment to her. He insisted he was only looking out for her because she'd had a tough life and deserved some TLC, but within a matter of days it was obvious not just to me but to everyone in the company that he was in love with her.

"The kid's special, Mark," he said to me. "She has talent. You'll see."

I dismissed his words, believing they were just another aspect of his infatuation, but in fact he turned out to be right. Leonie Pickering was special. She possessed the kind of talent you see once in a lifetime. She reminded each of us, in her way, of who we were.

She reminded me of my father, and my father's father, of the days when circus had really meant something. In the years before the war, when my grandfather was still performing, people would save for weeks to get a ticket to see him. They would talk about what they had seen for years to come. Leonie gave me a window on that vanished world. Sometimes I still dream about what I saw.

• • •

It was midweek, a Wednesday, and we were pitched up at Shepton Mallet. There was no matinee that day, so I decided to take advantage of the sunshine and go for a walk. On my way up the hill I caught sight of Ros, Ruby's sister, practising her bareback riding in one of the pastures. She had used some yellow rope to rough out a circle and her two horses, Gideon and Gilgamesh, were cantering around the perimeter in opposite directions. Ros was standing on Gilgamesh's back, her bare feet dusty with Tac. As the two horses passed each other she leapt in the air and somersaulted down on to the back of Gideon. Neither horse so much as broke his stride.

Rosalind was a tall girl, much taller than Ruby, with the flat-chested, well-muscled frame of the professional gymnast. She was five years older than Ruby and I, and because of that she had always seemed distant from us. On that day she was togged out in a pair of snagged ballet hose and an old running vest but she was still incredible to watch. She had worked with horses all her life, yet I could never help being impressed by her control over them, especially since Gideon and Gilgamesh were big beasts, rangy and full of mettle, with the narrow muzzle and intelligent eyes of the pure-bred Arab.

I stood and watched them, leaning against the gate with my eyes half closed against the glare of the sun. Suddenly I saw Leonie entering the field on horseback through a gap in the hedge. She was riding Pierrot, one of the two skewbald ponies that the Treacher twins used to pull their glass carriage. As I watched she leapt to her feet on the horse's back, then bent over backwards into a handstand. She was wearing a halter top and yellow shorts, the thin material pulled tight across her buttocks. The soles of her feet flashed white as plovers against the sky.

She made a whooping noise, somersaulting off Pierrot and landing on her feet in the grass. Ros called out to her and Leonie responded excitedly, but they were too far away for me to hear what they were saying. I realised Ros must have been training the girl. Just then Ros caught sight of me. She jumped down from Gideon and sprinted towards me across the field, long legs lithe as a deer's.

"Oh Marek, you mustn't spoil things. This was meant to be a surprise." She leaned on the gate, smiling broadly and smelling of horses and dry bracken. Golden freckles dusted the top parts of her cheeks.

"How long has she been doing this?" I said.

"Only a week. But she's a natural. I've never known anything like it."

We both turned to look at her then. Leonie stood with her arms around the horse's neck, her face resting against his withers. She seemed to be breathing him in. Pierrot whickered with pleasure, slapping flies away from his hindquarters with his tail.

"I won't say anything," I said. And I didn't, not even to Mae, though I didn't have to keep the secret long. Five days later, at Yeovil, Leonie's act was added to the bill.

At first she was just a warm-up for Ros. She didn't do anything too complicated, just a couple of turns of the ring and some basic tumbles. But what a carnival audience wants mostly is spectacle, the sense that they are seeing something extraordinary and preferably freakish. With her small size and her long toes Leonie Pickering was an immediate success. She wore a tiny sequined leotard and Pierrot wore a plume of pink ostrich feathers.

Old Jones came down to watch, prepared to be furious – he'd assumed we'd ditched Leonie Pickering weeks ago. He changed his tune quickly enough when he heard the applause.

For a while Ros seemed happy to regard Leonie as her protégée. But soon things began to change. Leonie's stunts became more daring and her act quickly became the main draw in the show. By the time we played the goth festival at Whitby I think Rosalind hated Leonie. Leonie made Ros feel she was getting old.

On the last night at Whitby, we got a fire going and Morrey organised his traditional hog roast. Piet had gone to bed early with some sort of stomach bug. He had seemed uncommonly tired in recent weeks. The kid left her things strewn about the trailer and made no attempt to clear up after herself. Piet was forever cleaning or preparing more food. I began to grow concerned about him. I knew that Piet, like many dwarfs, had a dicky heart.

"Oh cobblers," he said when I suggested he should get Leonie to help out more. "You're only young once." His violet eyes had their faraway look. His veins stood out in blue knots on the backs of his hands.

Leonie sat close to the fire. She gorged herself on pork, hunched over a pile of spare ribs with the juice running down her chin as if she hadn't eaten for a week. Yet she had eaten most of a chicken at lunchtime – I knew that because I had seen Piet cook it for her. No matter how much she ate she never seemed to put on weight. It was as if she had a tapeworm inside her. Once she had finished eating she slipped away, disappearing into the darkness. She never stayed anywhere long if Piet wasn't there.

I watched her leave, then after a few minutes I followed her. We were camped in a field set back from the cliff top, high above the town. Once away from the fire it was bitterly cold. There was no moon, but I could just about keep sight of Leonie as she hurried along. I moved quickly to close the distance between us then reached out and grabbed her by the elbow. She was wearing an old anorak, something of Piet's. My fingers slithered on the puffy plastic. She let out a scream but I quickly stopped her mouth with my other hand.

"It's all right," I said. "It's just Mark."

I took my hand away from her mouth. Her teeth were chattering with cold or perhaps it was fright. I pulled her towards me and unzipped her coat. I was already hard. She seemed to weigh nothing at all.

I gripped her head between my hands and forced my mouth down on hers, opening her lips with my tongue. Her flesh was cold. My first taste of her was sour, the tart acidity of unripe apples. But there was something behind it, a clogged stickiness, as if I were gulping mud, and in my nostrils the fetid odour of spoiled meat.

She was clinging to me eagerly. I pushed her away, wiping at my mouth with the sleeve of my coat.

"You're sick," I said. "What are you doing?"

Leonie laughed. "I'm seventeen," she said. "I can do what I want." She smiled her twisted smile, pulled her coat tightly about her and scampered away.

Could what she said be true? I didn't see that it mattered. I was horrified at what I had done, no matter her age, that Leonie might tell Piet or even Mae. I couldn't understand what had come over me. I was afraid she might have given me a disease.

• • •

I never looked forward to winter. It was then that I worried most about the future. Sitting in a Dalston laundrette on a Sunday afternoon, while freezing February rain lashed the pavement outside, I would start to think of my father's last years in a static caravan on the Isle of Sheppey and wondering what would happen when I lost my touch.

I went for long walks. When I became particularly restless I would get on a train and head out of London, calling Mae later from some down-at-heel boarding house in Lowestoft or Aberystwyth, reassuring her I would be back the following day.

I must have been hell to live with, and that winter was particularly bad. I felt constantly on edge, as if there was some urgent unfinished business I had to attend to. I lay awake into the small hours, Mae soundly asleep beside me, endlessly reliving those few brief violent moments on the cliff.

Piet always spent his winters in Norfolk, and this time Leonie had gone with him. I had last seen Piet in the service station on the Peterborough ring road where we stopped off for a final breakfast before going our various ways. Leonie stayed behind in the van. She seemed to have a dislike of public places. As I watched Piet heading for the A47 turn-off for Wisbech, I couldn't help asking myself how he and Leonie would occupy the long winter months.

"Do you think they'll be all right?" I said.

"He'll look after her, don't worry," Mae said, and we left it at that. I had avoided Leonie since Whitby, but now more than ever I wanted to know the truth about her, who she was and where she had come from. The obsession did not fade with time as I hoped it would. Instead it seemed to grow stronger and in the end I grew sick of myself. I told Mae I needed time away.

"I'm going stir crazy," I said. "Just a couple of days."

She smiled at me sadly. I hated leaving her, but I did it anyway. I packed an overnight bag and hitched a lift in a Ford Sierra. I was in Cirencester before nightfall.

I remembered the town as bustling, almost festive, but the arrival of winter had made it turn in on itself and I barely recognised it. The streets seemed dour and stark, the stone cottages huddled like beggars, the outlying fields where we had set up our tents reduced to a grubby wet pastureland.

I booked into a bed and breakfast on the Gloucester Road. In spite of the dreariness of the weather and of the place itself I felt curiously exhilarated. I realised how rarely I had the chance to be alone.

I slept better than I had in weeks and woke up refreshed. I was eager to explore the town. It was not the tourist sites I was interested in, the Norman arch nor St John's church nor the fine old buildings on Castle Street, but the corner newsagents and garage forecourts, the rows of terraced cottages with their untidy back gardens. The anonymous outskirts. I knew it was crazy but I couldn't help myself. I wanted to see where Leonie might have lived.

I walked for a couple of hours. The houses I passed were mostly well kept and respectable-looking and I quickly began to resent them for it. My eyes fastened keenly on any sign of dereliction or dilapidation: a rotting shed on an overgrown allotment, the torn mesh on a line of empty rabbit pens, a broken pane of glass replaced with cardboard in the window of an abandoned Morris Minor. Through the gaping doorways of old tractor barns I caught glimpses of rusting machinery. On a low-slung washing line outside a mouldering farmhouse a yellow dress flapped wetly in the chilly air. I kept feeling I was being watched, yet all the time I was walking I barely laid eyes on a soul. Finally it began to rain. There was nothing for it but to head back into town.

The library was housed in a modern building, which had recently undergone a refurbishment. As well as the main lending library there was a reference section where you could consult a selection of more specialised textbooks, or use one of the library computer terminals. I paid for an hour upfront and then logged on. I typed Leonie Pickering into the search bar, but none of the results it generated seemed relevant. I did a search for local papers and discovered that the main newspaper for the Cirencester area was the *Wilts and Gloucestershire Standard*. I clicked on the tab marked archive, then went back twelve months. I felt frustrated at first, with so much information to sift through, but I became engrossed in spite of myself and quickly sidetracked. The articles were mundane but they had the compulsive quality of any good soap opera. I was halfway through a story about the neighbourhood war that erupted over a dog-stealing incident, when the name *Pickering* leapt out at me from the article below.

It seemed that in the May of the year before a local man named Wilfred Pickering had been arrested for the murder of his grandson, Eric Quayle. According to the newspaper report, the boy was less than a month old when he died and he had been in the care of his grandfather at the time.

A later report stated that Wilfred Pickering had been acquitted. The report carried a photograph of Pickering leaving the courthouse together with a woman the paper named as Willis Quayle, Pickering's twenty-nine-year old daughter and the mother of Eric Quayle. The picture was out of focus, and the Pickerings were facing away from the camera. They could have been anyone.

I carried on searching, typing in *Wilfred Pickering* and *Eric Quayle* and even *Pickering murder*. I kept finding versions of the same articles in other newspapers, plus one further photograph of Willis Quayle. She had on the same belted mackintosh she had been wearing outside the courthouse. The photographer had made an attempt to capture her in close-up, but she had turned her head at the last moment, blurring her features.

I was no further forward. I could have paid for more time on the computer but it was late in the afternoon and I had had enough. For all I knew the Wilfred Pickering in the articles was a complete red herring. Pickering was a common enough name, after all. I closed down all my searches and put on my coat.

Outside it had stopped raining but it was beginning to get dark and the wind had turned bitingly cold. I realised I was ravenously hungry – I hadn't eaten since breakfast. I headed back towards the old part of town, where I knew most of the bars and restaurants were bound to be concentrated. The first pub I came to was called the Dog and Soldier, a narrow-fronted, dark red building with small windows. Not a particularly inviting prospect but I went in anyway. The place turned out to be deceptively spacious, a warren of side rooms and alcoves extending a long way back from the street. There was a log fire burning and a television set in one corner tuned to a football match. I heard relaxed laughter and the chink of glasses. The clock above the bar was showing quarter to six.

I ordered a pint and the chicken casserole from the bar menu then went to sit down. I felt very tired. I tried watching the football but couldn't summon up much enthusiasm for it. I wished I had something to read. Then I noticed there was a small bookcase just to the right of the television. The top shelf was stacked with magazines, *Woman's Own* and *House and Garden* and *What Car?* On the lower shelves there were some paperback spy thrillers and crime novels, also a clutch of guidebooks and town histories, most of them long out of date. None of them appealed to me. I flicked through the pages of one or two of the spy stories, trying to rouse an interest, but it all seemed too involved, too much of an effort, and eventually I settled on one of the guidebooks, a dusty red hardback called *Gloucestershire Myths and Legends*. The boards were cracked, and the book smelled as if it had spent a long time in someone's attic, but the chapters were short and I thought I could probably read through one or two of them while I waited for my food to arrive.

The book was not what I expected. I had prepared myself for something po-faced and old-fashioned, but the prose was clear and direct and the stories themselves were compelling. There was one about a primary school teacher who turned out to be a distant relation of the Pied Piper of Hamelin, and another in which the inhabitants of a village burned one of their neighbours as a witch. I supposed the book was meant as a gimmick, the kind of joke travelogue that was either funny or unsettling depending on the state of your nerves. It certainly kept me entertained.

There was one particularly gruesome story about a giant mythical land leech called the Lammas Worm. The book claimed that some of the more isolated communities in the steep wooded valleys around Stow had built a cult around the creature, that they kidnapped local girls and offered them to the worm in a kind of debased marriage ceremony. The offspring the girls gave birth to were monsters, man-worm hybrids of low intelligence and rapacious appetite. The mothers themselves were slaughtered, as much to conceal the crimes of the cult as to assuage the agony and madness that followed in the wake of what they had suffered.

I laughed nervously to myself as I read this, then jumped in my seat when the barman brought my food. The Dog and Soldier was evidently a popular place to go for an early supper, and I was glad to be surrounded by other people. Just as I was clearing my own plate the barman delivered two steaming platters of fish and chips to the men at the table next to me. The men were both large, with callused hands and ruddy complexions. They ate steadily and with intense concentration, as if they were engaged in some arduous task. They finished their food at the exact same moment then sat back in their seats, their beer bellies resting comfortably on their knees. One of them began setting up a game of chequers.

"I see they finally caught up with that Pickering chap," said one of them.

"I don't read the *Standard*," said the other. "Not since that new bloke took over the sports page. Gone right downhill, it has."

"They say he drowned the kid in a bucket like a newborn puppy. Deformed, which were why he drowned it, least that's what Pickering says. Put it out of its misery, see. You can't believe what you read though. Not the way the papers are these days."

"I suppose that's what you get for fecking your own daughter."

The two of them began to laugh, a soft companionable chuckle that rocked them back in their seats and hid their eyes in the flesh of their faces like currants in dough.

A wave of heat and nausea rushed over me, a sensation so intense I wondered if there had been something wrong with the food I had eaten. The two draughts players seemed to shimmer before me like a mirage. Their conversation had already begun to take on an edge of the surreal. I turned away, replacing *Gloucestershire Myths and Legends* on the shelf. When I turned back to look at them again they were so deeply engrossed in their game I found myself in doubt that they had ever spoken.

I reached for my beer. My hand was shaking, and my sweaty fingers left visible prints on the glass. In spite of the log fire and the massed body heat of the drinkers at the bar my teeth began to chatter. There was a sharp, dry tickling at the back of my throat, as if someone had given it a prod with one of my knives. I realised with a kind of dazed relief that the sickness and dread I was experiencing had nothing to do with the chicken casserole, or the book of horror stories, or even the prurient gossip of the two chequers players. I was going down with a cold.

I paid for my food and left. As I walked through the darkened streets my symptoms intensified, and by the time I got back to the guesthouse I was ready to crash. I don't often catch colds but when I do they lay me up badly. When I woke the next morning my nose was blocked with mucus and my throat was burning. All I wanted was to turn on my side and go back to sleep. Somehow I managed to get up, to keep moving. I didn't want to spend another night in Cirencester, no matter what. I bought some aspirin from a local chemist, swallowed three of the tablets there on the street then set off on foot towards the bypass.

I was lucky that day. In less than ten minutes I caught a ride from a frozen foods haulier who let me sleep on the mattress in the back of his vehicle all the way to Potter's Bar. I was home before dark. Mae was so preoccupied with feeding me chicken soup and dosing me with more aspirin she forgot to ask a single question about my trip.

• • •

I tried to forget what had happened, to put it all down to a fugue state brought on by the flu. But sometimes I would hear again the quietly contemptuous laughter of the two draughts players, remember the book with its dented covers, and a feeling of panic would engulf me. I drowned the panic in tedium. The blank grey stasis of late February and early March that normally left me tense as a wire now soothed me with its sameness, its repetition. Once I was fit again I found work on a building site and later in a canning factory. In the evenings I sat on the sofa with Mae in front of the gas fire and read detective stories. Around midnight we went to bed and made love. Gradually I realised I was happy, that I was glad it was just Mae and me. I wanted things to stay the way they were. I awaited the start of the season with something like dread.

On the weekend of the spring equinox we gathered as usual at Stevenage for the off. When I first saw Leonie I didn't recognise her. The frizzy hair was combed smooth, and she had lipstick on. Her jeans and T-shirt were spotless and, most extraordinary of all, she was wearing shoes. She smiled at me, and I could not tell if that smile was meant as invitation or mockery. I felt like shaking her. The peace of the past two months were gone as if they'd never existed.

"Mark!" Piet came hurrying across to where we were standing on the outfield, moving with that lopsided, twisting gait of his that always reminded me of a brandy bottle rolling downhill. Normally he would greet me with a high five, or by punching me playfully in the stomach. On this occasion he put both arms around my waist and hugged me as if we had not seen one another for many years.

He raised his head then and looked at me and I saw his violet eyes were shining with elation. He kept tugging at my shirt cuff, and I realised he was trying to show me something.

"We've got something to tell you," he said. "Leonie and me. We're married."

He thrust out his hand, eagerly displaying the gold band. I saw then that Leonie was wearing a ring also, a matching band in the same yellow gold but narrow as wire.

"They had to make it specially," Piet said. "The jeweller didn't have anything small enough to fit her." He raised her hand to his lips and kissed the ring. Leonie's painted mouth twitched in a half smile.

"Silly old monster," she said quietly. She touched the back of Piet's head with her other hand then wandered off to where Morrey Shyler was getting ready to load the ponies. She laid her face against Pierrot's neck then nuzzled him behind the ear. She stood for a while, watching Morrey fill up the haynets, then went inside Piet's trailer and closed the door.

"She's pregnant," Piet said suddenly. His face filled up with a kind of earnest tenderness. I stammered my congratulations. I felt my stomach curdle and a chill went through me, as if cold hands had reached inside me and given my intestines a squeeze.

Once we were on the road I told Mae the news.

"I think it's wonderful," she said. "Piet is one of the angels. If anyone can help that girl it's him."

She glanced across at me as if fully expecting me to agree with her, but I said nothing and kept my eyes on the road. I hoped she was right, but I doubted it. In my heart I already believed that Leonie Pickering was beyond help, but I could not explain that to Mae. I was afraid that if I tried she would think I was insane.

• • •

I watched Leonie like a hawk. I was waiting for a sign, I suppose, something I could use to prove what she really was. My suspicions disturbed me so profoundly they kept me awake at night. And yet my desire for her only intensified. Sometimes when I made love to Mae I found myself imagining Leonie's tiny, bud-like breasts, her brittle clavicle, the ripe green stench of her. I imagined myself battering her so hard with my body that it broke her bones. I would come so violently then that it was like having a piece of me torn away. Sometimes there were tears on my cheeks. I would lie in Mae's arms, my breath coming in heavy gasps while she stroked my hair. Eventually I would fall asleep, waking the next morning to a foul headache, as if I had been drinking heavily the night before.

We had three full houses at Cambridge, and Leonie's picture was in the local paper.

"You're going to be famous, my sweetheart," Piet said to her. "We'll have to start keeping a scrapbook."

He seemed thrilled with the photograph, and carried it with him everywhere.

"Aren't you worried about her performing?" I asked him. I hoped he would know what I meant without my having to mention the pregnancy directly. He beamed like a schoolboy who had just been awarded a gold star for some improbable feat, a record-breaking tap dance, maybe, and shook his head.

"She knows what she's doing; you only have to look at her. She'll stop when she's ready."

I supposed he was right. We played Northampton and Rugby and Warwick, Coventry and Leamington and Worcester, then headed south towards Great Malvern and Tewkesbury. Leonie was on every night and usually did the matinees, too. Her act, as daring as ever, had become even more ambitious, her movements so quick and light you almost found yourself believing she was weightless. I saw her do things Ros had never attempted, not even when she was Leonie's age. Leonie loved being in the spotlight and she relished applause, wolfing it down the same way she wolfed her food. In the hours between performances she seemed oddly withdrawn. When she was not rehearsing she spent most of her time with Corinne Cooley, who ran the insect circus. Corinne was part Chinese, with long black braids that reached to the ground. She was very fat, and ponderous in her movements. She reminded me a little of the giant African land snails that had long been a favourite feature of her act. She never said much but she was kind, and Leonie seemed calm in her presence. The friendship seemed to benefit them both.

I dreaded our return to Cirencester. I was convinced the place was unlucky. On the evening we arrived there I tried to work out my anxiety in rehearsal. I had to practise without Ruby, who had injured her arm the week before, meaning I had to rejig most of our routine. The tension in me worked in my favour and I was throwing well, but even so my heart was not in it. Piet must have been anxious too, because I couldn't get rid of him. He stood and watched me, congratulating me on every throw, even the easy ones, until I finally gave in and asked him what was on his mind.

"Do you think I should talk to her?" he said at once. "Try and explain where we are?"

"I think it's best we don't make an issue of it," I said. "Just carry on as normal. It's no big deal."

I was trying to reassure myself as much as him. In all our months on the road, Leonie had displayed no curiosity about the towns we visited or the distances we travelled. Time seemed to have no meaning for her beyond the immediate moment. She was like an animal in this way. I looked across at her, sitting with Corinne on the back steps of Corinne's caravan, looking at fashion magazines. She seemed perfectly happy. It never occurred to me that the trouble I had been anticipating might come from outside.

No one saw the boy arrive. It was a beautiful evening, warm and filled with the scents of wood smoke and dry grass. Morrey and Vaska had a quoits match going and I remember hearing the Treacher twins' accordion. Leonie's scream came out of the blue. It was a dreadful sound, high and drilling. I thought at first it was one of the horses.

He was skinny as a daddy-long-legs, his narrow pointed chin shiny with acne, the back of his jeans jacket stained heavily with what looked like machine oil. His right cheek was horribly scarred, the hardened tissue bunching out of his face like a cancerous growth. I had seen a similar injury once before, in a lion tamer who had been mauled by one of his cats.

The boy's feet were bare. I noticed with slow astonishment his toes: long, almost prehensile, the same as Leonie's.

Leonie was backed up to the door of Corinne's wagon, cowering. Her hands were pressed to her face. Corinne stood off to one side in a slew of magazines. Her black, pinprick eyes looked completely blank.

"You're back, then," said the youth. "Dad's been asking."

His voice was unpleasantly nasal and for some reason I felt certain his clothes were squirming with lice. He darted forward and grabbed Leonie by the arm. Leonie screamed again then bit his arm, shaking her head from side to side like a dog.

"Get off me, you cow!" The youth shrieked and tried to pull his arm away, but this only seemed to make Leonie hang on tighter.

She thrashed out wildly with her tiny fists, raining down blows on his chest and lower abdomen. I dived in behind her and locked my arms about her waist, trying to pull her backwards and away. It was the first time I had touched her since Whitby. Her body was stiff as a rail and she reeked of fear. As I struggled to restrain her, Vaska and Morrey came dashing over and laid hold of the bawling youth on either side. By our joint efforts we managed to separate them. The youth clutched at his injured arm and blood flowed down between his fingers in streamers of red. He tried to turn on Morrey, but Morrey was triple his weight and twice his height – no contest. Morrey grabbed him by the hair and tugged, forcing the boy's face up towards him.

"You can see you're not wanted, son, so bugger off. If we catch you round here again we'll feed you to the lions."

Someone laughed, Tolley, I think. Morrey and Vaska marched the boy as far as the road and turned him loose, giving him a push and a shove by way of encouragement. I saw him standing there, a dishevelled stick figure, his long arms trailing. He should have been pathetic, comical even, but something about him made my hair stand on end.

"I'll tell Dad what you did, you dirty bitch," the boy screamed. "Don't think you've heard the last of this."

He turned then and ran, his bare feet slapping the concrete. I was left holding Leonie. Her body had relaxed a little but she was shaking so hard it was difficult to keep hold of her. Her dress was glued to her back with sweat, and gradually I realised that the acrid stench boiling off her was not just body odour but that she had wet herself. There was a damp patch on the ground between her feet.

It was then that Piet appeared, his chest heaving from the effort of running. Leonie moaned at the sight of him and threw herself into his arms. They huddled together like frightened puppies. The rest of us stood around awkwardly, not knowing what to do.

"Who was that?" Piet said to her at last. "Who frightened you, sweetheart?" He stroked her head, his pudgy fingers smoothing her ruffled hair. I saw his gold ring flash, catching the last of the evening sunlight.

"Aaron," Leonie stammered. "He's my brother."

• • •

Leonie didn't perform that night, but for the rest of us it was business as usual – the show must go on, as they say. I was exhausted by the end, but still I lay awake for some time, my ears alert to every sound. When I finally drifted off I slept like the dead.

When I woke the next morning my head felt muzzy and sore. I washed and dressed then went outside. I saw Piet at once, standing at the edge of the ground and looking down towards the town. I walked over and stood beside him.

"How is she?" I asked.

"Much better," he said. "But I've told Jones she's not going on tonight. It's too much of a risk, with that bastard around. Especially in her condition."

I nodded in agreement, though I felt more than ever embarrassed and disquieted by the mention of Leonie's pregnancy. She was still not showing at all, and I could not help remembering that when I grabbed hold of her the evening before her belly had been hard and flat as a child's.

"Tell Mae I've gone into town," I said at last. "I need to stretch my legs. I'll be back in an hour."

I think I had some insane idea of returning to the Dog and Soldier, of hunting down the two draughts players and demanding they tell me what they knew about the Pickerings. It wasn't until I reached the High Street that I realised all the pubs would still be closed. I wandered aimlessly through the streets, trying to gather my thoughts. Once I thought I saw Aaron Pickering, slipping away from me between the houses, but as soon as I set off in pursuit he disappeared.

There was no sign of him that day or the following morning. We packed up and set off for Stroud. Leonie stayed in the trailer, and I did not see her again until five days later, when we arrived at Melksham. I was shocked at the state of her. Her hair was a mess, and her skin had a greyish cast, as if she were sickening for something. The worst thing was that her grace appeared to have left her. There was a clumsiness in her step, and she held her arms awkwardly away from her body as if her sides were bruised.

I thought her circus days were over, but I was wrong about that. She didn't perform at Melksham but at Frome she went on for the matinee. I watched her go into the ring, half-convinced she would fall and injure herself, but once she was in front of the audience her confidence returned. Her performance was tight and spotless and appeared secure. When she did not appear in the main performance I presumed she was tired, that she had spent the evening resting in the trailer. But later as I returned to the van I saw a dark shape moving swiftly between the wagons. I thought at first it was a fox or a stray dog, but suddenly it made a dash for Piet's trailer and I saw that it was Leonie. For a moment she looked straight at me, her tiny face pale in the security lights, her black eyes hard and glittering. I took a step towards her, but she went inside the van, disappearing so suddenly it was as if she had melted through the door. I wondered where she had been. She never usually went far without Piet.

"She's seeing him, I know she is," Piet said to me a day or two later. We were at Warminster by then, and the summer was ripening, the fields around the camp heavy with corn. I thought at first Piet was talking about some love rival, some lad she had met in the town. When I realised he meant her brother I knew at once it made a hideous kind of sense. The thought that Aaron Pickering had been with us ever since Cirencester, shadowing us, spying on us, perhaps even stowing away in one of our wagons, filled me with horror. I told Piet he must have got it wrong.

"She can't stand the guy," I said. "You saw what she was like."

I didn't tell him that I had already been a witness to one of Leonie's midnight escapades, but from that moment on I saw Aaron Pickering everywhere, or imagined I did, and my thoughts dwelt on him constantly. He disturbed and repulsed me, as an infected wound repulses, or a seething mass of maggots on a garbage heap. I couldn't get him out of my mind.

We continued travelling south and west. The nights were hot and humid, the trailers like ovens. At Yeovil, the dashboard thermometer reached thirty-four degrees. I lay sleeplessly beside Mae, making futile attempts to get more comfortable. I heard thunder in the distance, but it was a dry sound, like an old man coughing, and did nothing to dispel the heat of the day. I lay twisted in the sheet, my mind turning in exhausted circles. I thought Mae was asleep. When she spoke to me out of the darkness I jumped a mile.

"I know there's something wrong, Mark. I wish you would tell me."

"It's nothing," I said. "It's this heat, that's all. I can't sleep."

I laid my hand in the small of her back. I wanted to make love to her but my thoughts and the sweltering heat had sapped my strength.

"I think we should talk," she said. "I know there's something." Her voice was heavy and slurred. A couple of minutes later we were both asleep.

We were awakened by Leonie screaming. There was the crash of breaking glass and then, unbelievably, a burst of wild laughter. Mae started to get out of bed but I told her to stay where she was. I threw on a pair of jeans and raced outside.

The door to Piet's trailer was open, and as I ran towards it I saw a man emerge. He was completely naked, his scrawny body white against the surrounding darkness. He started down the trailer steps but then tripped and fell headlong. In the light from Piet's old carriage lantern I saw that it was Aaron Pickering. His back was a mass of scars, as if he had been beaten on repeated occasions with a nylon rope or a cat o' nine tails. As he picked himself up off the ground I saw that his groin had been shaved. His penis hung stunted and flaccid like a limp white worm.

Our eyes met and he grinned. Then he was on his feet and racing away. I was after him in a moment but he had a head start on me and unlike Pickering I wasn't used to running in bare feet. It was clear to me almost at once that I wasn't going to catch him. I stood at the edge of the ground, breathing in painful gasps and trying to work out which way he had gone. In the light of the single streetlamp the road was empty. It was as if the youth had simply vanished into thin air.

At that moment there was a flash of lightning so bright it was as if daylight had momentarily been restored. The thunderclap that accompanied it was loud enough to make me cover my ears. There was a moment of complete hiatus, as if the universe itself was holding its breath, and then the heavens opened. I was saturated in an instant, the torrent coming down so hard it was like standing beneath a waterfall. The ground gave up its heat with a hissing sigh.

It was a moment of insanity, of joy. I felt flooded with an intense vitality, a kind of pagan exhilaration. My skin prickled and my heart rate increased. The smell of wet grass was intoxicating. It was as if every cell in my body stood rampant, confirming its allegiance to the earth.

I wanted to run and shriek, to roll in the bracken, to give myself up to the night. It was only the sight of Piet that stopped me, that brought me back to myself. He had tried to run after Aaron Pickering but had fallen down. He lay on the soaking ground, his violet eyes overrunning with rain and helpless tears.

"I woke up and he was there in the bed with us," he wept. "He was lying on top of her. I threw the water glass at him. I didn't know what else to do."

He tried to get to his feet but couldn't get any purchase on the slippery ground. He was still crying, and his tiny body was beginning to shake with cold. I knew that Piet's lungs were not of the normal capacity, that colds and chills were more dangerous for him than for other people.

"We can worry about all that later," I said. "Let's get you out of the rain."

Some of the others had appeared by this time but I waved them away. I didn't want to talk about what I had seen. I caught Piet under the arms and lifted him. He was surprisingly heavy. I supported him towards his trailer but when we got there we found the door locked and all the curtains drawn. I rattled the door handle and called Leonie's name but the noise of the rain drowned everything out. I toyed with the idea of fetching my hacksaw and cutting my way in but decided that would probably make things worse.

"She's had a bad scare," I said to Piet. "She'll need to calm down. Come over to our place, at least until the morning. You need a change of clothes, for a start."

I looked down at him and for the first time I noticed he was still in his pyjamas. By the time I got him back to our trailer Mae already had the kettle on. She gave Piet some towels to dry himself and found an old dressing gown of mine for him to put on. I took the cushions off the sofa and made up the foldaway bed.

"Try to get some sleep," I said to Piet. "You'll see her in the morning."

He hadn't spoken a word since his outburst about Pickering. He looked more miserable than I had ever seen him, shrunken somehow, and it was not just that my burgundy dressing gown was way too big for him. It was as if the stuff that made him Piet was leaching away.

Mae hung his sopping clothes over the drier in the bathroom and made him a cup of sweet tea. Once we were sure he was asleep we went back to bed.

"Has that boy gone for good, do you think?" Mae said. Her face was tight with anxiety, and suddenly I had a raindrop-bright memory of the first time I saw her, all by herself, hanging around the entrance to the funhouse and eating a chocolate ice cream. I had known I was in love with her before we exchanged so much as a single word.

"I don't know," I said at last. She seemed better after that. Perhaps it was because she knew I was no longer lying to her.

The next day dawned bright and clear, with that particular apple-crisp freshness that only comes in the wake of a summer storm. The sky was high and infinite and blue.

Piet's trailer was deathly quiet. I had the feeling Leonie was gone, that she had run off in the night, but I didn't like to say as much to Piet. I left him with Mae while I went and did my morning practice with Ruby. We worked in silence for a while, going over the routines we intended to use in that evening's performance. Suddenly Ruby turned to face me. She had a knife in her hand, one of the antique Savitskas that had belonged to my father. She was in her tracksuit bottoms, with her hair pulled back from her face in a black bandeau.

"What's been going on with Piet?" she said. "What have you done? I bloody well want to know."

Her eyes flashed, sharp as the knife, yet what I read in them was hurt, for whatever secrets she thought I was keeping from her, for the summer as it passed its zenith, for the way our lives had diverged, long ago and inexplicably, the way a road does when it suddenly splits in two.

"I've done nothing," I said. "I don't know what you're talking about." I bowed my head, refusing to meet her eyes.

If I get free of this it's over, I thought suddenly. I felt heartsick and somehow in peril, and I knew then that I was finished with the company. It was as if, peering through the dust-streaked windscreen of my old trailer, I had unexpectedly glimpsed the shape of another life.

"I've been offered a job," Ruby said suddenly. "I'm going to leave the show at the end of this run."

I stared at her, open-mouthed. I could hardly believe what she had told me, not because the idea of her leaving was impossible to contemplate but because what she said was so close to what I'd been thinking myself just a moment before. For a moment I felt our old closeness, our odd twin-hood, and wondered why we had ever thought we could be apart. I felt an ache in my chest, the deep dull hurting that comes when, for an instant, you see all the other choices you might have made. I started towards her but she folded her arms across her chest and turned away.

"Don't, Marek," she said. "There's no point."

"What kind of job?" I said. "What will you do?"

"A theatre in Shoreditch. They've offered me a place in their new rep." She shrugged. "It's not much money but I can get by and at least it's a start. At least I'll be a real actress and not a circus freak. It's what I've always wanted to do, Marek, you know that. If I don't take this chance now I'll be stuck here for ever. Haven't you ever felt you could be more than you are?"

I thought of how I had felt during the storm, with the lightning flashing and the rain pouring down. For those moments I had felt like a god, as if the world had been created for my personal pleasure. I had come close to feeling like that on stage a couple of times, but never with such raw intensity, and I knew now that I was tired of the whole business.

Ruby leaving was like fate, just one more piece of the jigsaw. She must have seen the change in me because she let me hug her. Her hair smelled like sweet hay, like nettles. For no reason at all I found myself remembering our eighth birthday, when Marnie Kornilev had baked Ruby a cake in the shape of a castle. It was covered in pink icing, and had windows made of caramelised sugar. I ate so much of it I made myself sick.

• • •

The day passed in a kind of dream, the sun arcing across the sky like a blowtorch slowly cutting through a steel bulkhead. When it got to five o'clock and there was still no movement from Piet's trailer I had a quiet chat with Vaska and we decided to break in. I used my hacksaw to cut around the lock then eased my hand through the hole and opened the latch.

The wagon lay in semi-darkness, and there was a bad smell, rancid butter and rotten vegetables. Except for the faint buzzing of a fly trapped in the narrow corridor between a curtain and the window glass the place was eerily silent. I looked cautiously about, prepared to find squalor and chaos, but there was just Piet's living room, with the ancient Ultrabrite television in the corner and the reproduction Audubon bird prints on the walls. A half-finished cup of coffee stood on the draining board in the kitchen area but apart from that it was spotless.

I went into the bedroom. The sheets were torn back from the bed, and I saw shards of glass glittering like tiny daggers on the carpet – the remnants, I supposed, of the broken water glass. The rancid smell was stronger here, and although the room appeared as empty as the others I knew it was not. Somehow I could sense her presence, tugging away at me like the pull of a tiny fish at the end of a line. Or perhaps it's just hindsight that makes me think this. Most likely it was just that I refused to believe she had escaped without my knowing.

"What shall we do?" said Vaska. "She's gone."

I shook my head, willing him to be quiet. I knelt down and peered under the bed but there was nothing there. Then I crossed to the wardrobe and opened the door.

Leonie was crouched inside, folded so tightly into the narrow space that my first confused impression was that this was not Leonie herself but some clever imitation, a shopkeeper's mannequin made to look exactly like her. She was hugging her knees, the tiny face upturned, a white blank space in the greenish forest of paisley shirts and velvet jackets. She was holding something of Piet's, a lemon-coloured silk waistcoat, clutching it between her fingers as if for support. She had on some brief garment, a slip or camisole, stained in patches with a dark viscous substance that looked like treacle. The rancid smell was close to overpowering.

My heart knocked in my chest like a hammer on stone. I seemed to hover above myself, observing my own actions with a keen intensity as if I might be asked questions about them later. As I stood there trying to decide what to do, Leonie suddenly unfurled her limbs and came out of the wardrobe, shooting between my legs like a spider through a crack in the wall. I could not believe the speed with which it happened. One minute I was looking right at her, the next there was just the wardrobe's velvety interior, the terrible smell.

"Catch her!" I yelled.

I heard Vaska roar uncomprehendingly behind me but it was already too late. I bolted past him, striking my elbow painfully against the door handle. I saw Leonie ahead of me, in the square cupboard-like space between the kitchen and the tiny bathroom. I lunged at her, grabbing at the back of her camisole, but the shiny material slipped through my fingers. She flung herself out through the door of the trailer, which foolishly I had not thought to close.

She ran hunched over as if protecting her stomach then staggered and went down on all fours. Her hands were splayed, her outstretched fingers clawing the dirt. The bright daylight made her garment transparent, and as she righted herself again I saw that she was naked beneath it – the narrow hips and child's breasts, the dark tuft of hair between her legs all clearly visible. Her belly, once so flat, seemed to have become enormous overnight. It swung before her, quivering grotesquely, the pale skin criss-crossed with blue, veins pulsing in her flesh like living wires.

She looked back at me once, her face blank with terror as if it was not me she saw but some vision of hell. Then she gathered herself and ran on, making for the ragged copse of beeches at the edge of the field.

I went after her at top speed, yelled out for Vaska to follow. At the back of everything, as if from some far distance, I could hear Piet crying.

• • •

We kept looking for several hours, tracking back and forth through the fields and copses and the small tracts of woodland in the immediate vicinity of the camp. In the end it was too dark to see and we had to stop. As we retraced our steps to the wagons I caught sight of something white glimmering in the grass, a scrap of cloth from Leonie's camisole. Part of me did not like to touch it, but I picked it up anyway.

As soon as it got light we carried on with the search. I had barely slept, kept awake most of the night by the sound of Piet's agonised weeping.

It was Morrey who found her. She was lying in a shallow ditch at the edge of a small stand of sycamores, half in and half out of one of the old poacher's shacks that were common in the area as a hiding place for illegal snares or simply as a protection from the rain. An obvious place, really. I don't know how we had missed it the night before.

She lay with her face to the ground and half covered in leaves. Her legs were drawn up under her, the filthy smock torn almost in two. The tops of her thighs were slathered with congealed blood and some other substance, a greenish-yellow mucus that stank like bile. I knew without having to touch her that she was dead.

"Where's the child?" said Vaska, stupidly.

"God knows," I mumbled. "A fox must have taken it."

I don't know if they saw what I saw, the narrow track through the vegetation where something had dragged itself free of Leonie's body and crawled away. The leaves had been pushed aside, revealing the brown earth beneath, and over it a silvery encrustation, transparent and brittle as ice, some kind of solidified slime. It crackled when I touched it, breaking into glistening pieces like spun sugar.

I moved about noisily, kicking up twigs and leaf litter, covering up the traces the best I could.

"Are we going to call the police?" said Morrey.

"Are you mad?" I said. "They'll keep us here for weeks."

We walked back across the fields. None of us spoke. The sun was up by then, and I realised it was the first day of August, Lammas day. My grandmother Dmitra used to say that any child born on Lammas day was a sign of good fortune for the whole community, but she was funny that way, a great believer in old proverbs and superstitious rituals. My father always insisted it was a lot of nonsense.

"Don't believe a word of it, son," he said. "The old ways are done for."

• • •

Piet became very ill. Someone came to take him away, a stocky and rather taciturn man who claimed he was Piet's older brother. We heard later that Piet died in a hospital in Amsterdam, of complications following a heart attack.

I thought how strange it was that Piet had a family that cared about him after all. It made all the years I had known him seem unreal, as if his time with us had been a fantasy of his own making, a kind of dream-projection. I worked on until the end of the season. I thought at first that would be difficult, though it turned out not to be. People said I was on fire, which made me smile and think of my father. I gave everything in those last months, with a kind of desperate joy, and it seemed as if nothing could go wrong for me, that I could not make a mistake, the kind of perfection that only comes when you no longer care.

I told no one about my plans, but I think Ruby guessed. We went weeks at a time without really speaking, though we performed together as well as ever.

On a freezing January morning Mae and I left our old life behind. I drove the trailer to a campsite in Leigh-on-Sea, where I had booked a berth for the rest of the winter. It would give us some time to think, if nothing else.

Mae settled quickly. She signed on to a computing course at the local college, and soon found work as a receptionist at a private health practice. I worried about her adjusting to a desk job but she said she liked it, she liked hearing people's stories, that in some strange way it reminded her of the company.

For a while I earned money as I had always done in the off season, working on building sites and in factory compounds, getting by but without any particular aim for the future. In the end I took up a new trade as a sales rep for a pharmaceuticals firm. It was Mae, in fact, who found me the job. I thought at first that I would hate it, but I quickly learned that there was an art to selling potions, a kind of showmanship I became fascinated by and that, I suppose, reminded me also of the company. The job also gave me freedom to travel, and I found there was enough of my old life in my new one to keep me satisfied.

My usual patch was the Home Counties, the old fortress towns of the south coast, the rural hinterland of Kent and Essex, the outer suburbs of South East London, but occasionally something happened to take me further afield. About eighteen months after I first landed the job, the representative for the South West region fell off a ladder whilst painting a window and broke his arm. He was off work for a couple of months, and his beat was temporarily split between the rest of us. It meant some extra driving but I didn't mind. It was late July when I happened to drive through Yeovil. I had no calls to make there but it had been a busy day and I decided to stay the night. I enquired at several bed and breakfasts but there were no vacancies. Eventually a pub landlord took pity on me and let me sleep in his spare room for a nominal fee.

"What's going on?" I asked him. "Why are you so booked up?"

"It always gets like this when the carnival's in town," he said. "It's the Lammas fair. But you're not from around here, are you, so you weren't to know."

I ate a meal in the pub, and afterwards I set out walking across the fields. It was a perfect summer's evening, the sky high and transparent, the sun setting behind the trees in an amethyst haze. I found the place easily, as if my feet still carried a memory from the time before. I was expecting the old shack to have been torn down, or blown away, but it was still there, its boards even more warped and weathered but otherwise the same. As I approached I saw that the lower branches of the trees had been hung with ribbons and paper decorations, stars and lanterns and other, more mysterious shapes. The walls of the shack had been chalked all over with a series of symbols, or letters in a foreign alphabet I did not recognise. In the doorway of the hut an assortment of food had been laid out on some squares of rush matting: summer berries and plantains, three golden plaited loaves of Lammas bread.

It was a still place, but somehow not quiet, and I was anxious to leave. As I turned away something bright and shiny caught my eye. I reached out my hand, grasping at the empty air, and found myself holding a small glass ornament. It was star-shaped, about the size of a fifty pence piece, and had been tied to a twig with a piece of nylon thread. I brought it closer to look at it properly, and it was only then I saw what was embedded at its heart. It was a small grub, or insect, with a long segmented putty-coloured body and six multi-jointed amber-coloured legs. Its legs were flung out to either side, as if it had died while trying to escape.

I had never seen anything like it before, and did not wish to again. I left the glass star where it was, and hurried away.

THE GATEWAY

After what happened in Heiligendamm, I would have forgiven Thomas Emmerich for cutting off all contact with me. Instead he chose to stay in touch in spite of everything, at least until the war made it impossible. After that I lost sight of him for fifteen years. I told myself it was for the best, that it was time to let the past be the past. But then something extraordinary happened and I began searching for him again. It took me months to find him. I began to think he must be dead, when suddenly one of my enquiries turned up a lead.

Thomas Emmerich was alive, a patient at a nursing home in Friedrichshafen on the north shore of Lake Constance. I sent a telegram to say I was coming then booked my flight. Less than three days later, I was unpacking my suitcase in a hotel room overlooking the lake. I washed and changed then set off for the nursing home, which I discovered from one of the hotel porters was just a short tram ride away. I was anxious to see Thomas that same evening. I could still scarcely believe my friend was here, and that I had found him.

There was a uniformed care worker on the reception desk, sorting a stack of mail into various piles. She seemed determined not to admit me.

"Visiting hours are over," she stated briskly. She was young and pretty, with shiny brown hair and blue eyes. She claimed my telegram had never arrived.

"But I'm an old friend of Herr Emmerich's," I said. "I've come all the way from London to see him."

She hesitated then seemed to relent, saying that if I waited a couple of minutes she would take me upstairs to his room.

"He's out of danger but he's been very ill," she said. "He may not recognise you."

This possibility had never occurred to me. Even in the depths of despair Thomas's mind had always been clear as glass. The woman's words shocked me deeply but I didn't want to let my feelings show.

"I wouldn't be surprised if he didn't," I said. "We haven't seen each other since before the war."

She nodded, as if that much were self-evident and then went back to sorting the mail. I wandered about the reception area, taking in the vase of purple irises on the reception desk, the high shine of the parquet flooring, the comfortable-looking armchairs. It was more like a rest home than a hospital, one of the high-class sanatoria you read about in novels by Arthur Schnitzler or Thomas Mann. I wondered how Thomas had ended up here, what was wrong with him. He had always been so fit and healthy.

The woman on reception finished her mail-sorting then straightened her cap and marched off towards the main staircase. I broke out of my reverie and hurried after her. She led the way upstairs, then along a carpeted corridor to a room on the first floor. She knocked softly and then opened the door. My heart was thumping, and I realised I was preparing myself for the worst, some blank-eyed, drooling figure in a grubby smock. But the man in the room was just Thomas. He looked older, of course, but I would have known him anywhere.

He was sitting in a reclining armchair beside the window, a woollen blanket draped across his knees. He was very thin and his features, always gaunt, now looked cadaverous, the skin stretched tightly across his temples like cellophane wrapping. His eyes were closed. His emaciated hands, the fingers bunched together with arthritis, twitched on the blanket.

"There's a friend here to see you, Thomas," said the care worker. She bent down and smoothed the blanket. "I'll leave you two comrades together, shall I? I'm sure you have a lot to talk about."

She glanced at me as if in warning, then left the room. I went to stand beside Thomas's chair, taking in the view from the window, a soothing vista of beech trees and sun-striped lawns. I looked around the room, hoping to see something I recognised, some reminder of the old Thomas, but there was just the simple pine bed, its down quilt folded back to air the mattress, a hand basin behind a tiled partition, the four walls painted a restful cream. There were pictures on the walls, bland watercolours of mountain scenery and lakeside views, not the kind of thing Thomas would have chosen. I reached out to touch his shoulder. His eyes opened at once.

"Andrew," he said. "My God, Andrew." His voice was faded to a dry whisper but the words themselves were perfectly clear.

My heart leaped as he spoke my name and giddy relief flooded through me. The nurse had been wrong – Thomas Emmerich knew me after all. Whatever misfortunes had befallen his body there was clearly nothing wrong with his mind.

"I'm here," I said. I hunkered down beside his chair.

"I thought you were dead." A smile trembled on his withered lips.

I laughed quietly and touched his hand. "You're a fine one to talk," I said. "It's taken me an age to track you down." I sat down on the edge of the bed. "What happened? Why are you here?"

"That's a long story." He began to cough, a dry, racking cough that seemed to shake him deep within his bones. There was an empty glass on the windowsill. I took it across to the basin and filled it quickly with water from the tap. Thomas drank it in sips, holding the beaker carefully in both hands. "I've had pneumonia, but the doctors tell me I'm clear now," he said at last. "It's just this cough. I can't seem to get rid of it. I'm terribly behind with work."

I couldn't help smiling at that – still the same Thomas, the same driven personality. I had once joked that even if he were condemned to death Thomas would still be making notes about the experience on his way to the gallows. Looking at him now made it clear that this was no laughing matter. I had been closer to the truth than I would have liked.

"Is Hermine here with you?" I asked him. It was the question that had been in my mind all along.

"Hermine left me before the war. I don't know where she is."

I fell silent. I was shaken by the news but not surprised. There had been nights during the Blitz when I had drifted close to madness, imagining that the destruction and terror were some kind of cosmic retribution for the lies I had told my friend, for the wrong I had done him. I was too old to fight, and spent the entire war typing reports in a basement room of the War Office. I saw the bombs falling on London, and watched our own aircraft setting out to wreak havoc on Germany with a kind of numb despair.

I couldn't get past the idea that somehow it was all my fault. I felt like a dead man, or a man in a dream, able to see but not touch. Even when the war ended the feeling stayed with me. The world had moved on at last, but I remained rooted in place.

Then the miracle happened and colour and light began seeping into the world again. I understood at once I had to tell Thomas, to tell him everything, but I hardly knew where to begin. I was so wrapped up in my own thoughts that when Thomas spoke again it made me jump.

"I have something for you," he said. "It's in the cupboard. I had a feeling you might reappear." He chuckled softly to himself and pointed at the bedside cabinet. I noticed that his hand was shaking.

"Do you want me to open it?" I said, and he nodded. I knelt down by the bed, slid back the bolt that secured the door of the cabinet and reached inside. There was a stack of papers, a bundle of typed foolscap, and on top of that a sealed white envelope.

"Just the envelope, don't worry about the rest of it," said Thomas. "It's the book I've been working on. You can always read it later, if you like."

I got to my feet, holding the letter and feeling confused. I had assumed I was the one with the story, but Thomas had beaten me to it. I was about to ask him what was going on when the care worker reappeared. She entered the room without knocking, carrying a tray on which rested a tall tumbler of what looked like milk and a shallow bowl covered with a napkin.

"Supper time, Thomas," she said, pointedly. She set the tray on the small wheeled invalid table at the end of the bed then stood with her arms folded. She was obviously waiting for me to leave. I was about to protest, to insist that we needed more time, but one look at Thomas's face changed my mind. His lips were pale; his eyelids drooped as if desperate to close. The short meeting had clearly exhausted him.

"You see what we're up against here?" he said. "We're under strict orders to get better." He tried to smile, but this only resulted in a fresh bout of coughing.

"Get some rest," I said. "I'll come back tomorrow."

"You might leave it a day or two longer," said the care worker. "It's dangerous to his health if he's overtired."

Thomas winked. The gesture reassured me, although I kept being shocked at the sight of him, the hollow cheeks, his hair, once black and vigorous, now flopping against his shoulders in limp grey wisps. We were the same age, give or take a couple of months, but Thomas now had the look of a much older man. I felt a sharp pang of guilt that I had let him slip out of my life when he had so obviously been in need of my friendship. I was determined things would be different from now on.

I took out the small spiral-bound notebook I always carried in my breast pocket and jotted down the number of my hotel.

"I'm five minutes down the road," I said. "If you need anything just call." I tore off the sheet of paper and placed it on the tray between the beaker and the napkin-covered bowl. "Goodbye," I said to the nurse. I hoped she would relent and give me a smile but her pretty rosy mouth remained firmly set.

I walked slowly back down the hill. The sun was setting, and the breeze that rose up from the lake was pleasantly cool. The tram, when it came, was full of tourists in their bright summer clothes. Closest to me sat a young English couple, the woman's cheeks pink with sunburn, the man in a smart linen suit just a little too tight for him. Each time the tram swayed they pressed closer together. The man read out the street signs in a comically inept attempt at a German accent, blundering against the unfamiliar syllables like a blind man on an obstacle course. The woman put her hand to her mouth and tried not to laugh. I watched them, feeling touched by their innocence, their obvious excitement at being together in a foreign country. The man was too young to have fought in the war and I was glad.

Back at my hotel I ate a light supper on the terrace then retired to my room. I opened the windows, flooding the room with the aroma of pine trees and the laughter of the children playing in the park across the road. I tore open Thomas's envelope, then settled myself on the bed and began to read

My dear Andrew,

I don't know how much of this letter will make sense to you. Perhaps none of it will, although I tend to think rather the opposite. I have always believed that you lied to me about what happened to Claudia, or that you did not tell the whole story, which amounts to the same thing. Let me say at once that I do not blame you. I know you well enough to know you would not have lied without good reason. I might well have done the same in your position. I want you to know I have never stopped being your friend.

You know me well enough by now to understand that I am by nature a solitary person, that although I always enjoy the company of close friends such as yourself I am most comfortable when alone. Perhaps it is this that made me a writer. Perhaps it is the other way around. In either case it is for this reason I have decided to write down the story of the years since last we met, rather than to recount it to you face to face. I tell myself this is because I am happiest when committing words to paper, although I can almost hear you retorting that in fact it is because I do not like to be interrupted. Most likely both statements are true. The main thing is I do have faith we will meet again, and that you will read this letter. There will be time enough to talk then, I am sure.

Edgar and Oskar Gelb were the two sons of Adalbert Gelb, a blacksmith and cooper living in the town of Wernigerode, in the Harz Mountains of Eastern Saxony. Edgar was born in 1820, his brother Oskar two years later. Both boys grew up strong and healthy, and from an early age they enjoyed helping their father in his workshop. When they were not hanging around the yard, they were off exploring the blue-green wilderness of mountain and forest that formed the background to their childhood and adolescence. They were devoted to each other, but did not mix much with other children. When they did seek company it was the company of adults, Axel Abendroth, for instance, the old hunchback who scratched a living quarrying for rough amethysts and peridots on the Brocken, or Gisela Singer, the mother of Ilse the Idiot, who some people claimed was a witch.

When Edgar Gelb was fourteen he fell into a ravine, badly bruising his spine and breaking his right leg in three places. He eventually made a good recovery, but was confined to the house and yard for several months. Being indoors was torture for him. What brought him through it was teaching himself to make things out of wood. The objects he produced were clumsy to begin with, but as he increased in skill the carved animals and toy soldiers and latched strongboxes took on beauty and weight, becoming at last an expression of his yearning for the mountains.

Oskar saw what he was doing and was curious. One evening, after a fishing trip, he sat at the table in the stone-flagged kitchen and put together an oaken pencil box with the image of a pike carved into the lid. A businessman from Rostock, who had stopped off at the yard to have a stone removed from his horse's hoof, happened to see the box and asked if he might buy it. This is where Claudia's story really begins.

I don't know how to write about my daughter. In the years since she was lost to me I have come ever more to realise how little I knew her, how this tiny being was more of a mystery to me than the great artists and scholars I have earned my livelihood and some reputation from writing about.

I read a line of Hölderlin and see my daughter sitting in the dirt, gently prodding a beetle with a blade of grass.

I stumble in my ham-fisted way through the piano transcription of Julius Reubke's great organ sonata, and think of Claudia asking me in a serious voice why the devil has the same name as a box of matches.

My whole life has been about words, yet I do not have the words to describe how losing her has altered my life. I feel I let her down, that I took her for granted. I assumed she would always be there for me to enjoy. When she stopped being there I learned some terrible things about myself. One of the things I learned was that I had stopped living in the world, I had constructed a narrow closet, a place where I could secrete myself and get on with transcribing the past. I had forgotten what the present felt like. Suddenly it was all around me, fleshly and intrusive and terrifying. I felt soiled by pain, molested by it. I felt I would never regain my dignity.

Another thing I learned was that my wife and I had stopped loving one another. You hear of couples forced apart by personal tragedy or financial hardship, but in our case it was nothing so honourable. The feeling was simply gone, as if a switch had been thrown, cutting off the current of emotion. And it was not the loss of Claudia that did this to us. Rather it was as if our daughter had been the one thing that held us together, the reflective mirror in which each saw the face of the other, dazzling and delighting us into believing we were a family. With the light of her removed, we saw ourselves for what we were: two separate individuals who happened to have a child together. Whatever else there had been between us had disappeared long ago.

I knew Hermine felt the same. Almost from the first moment of Claudia's disappearance we regarded each other with a kind of numb horror. I would have tried to comfort her, if she had let me. As it was I felt only relief that she did not.

In the end she turned for comfort to Martin Foerster, of all people. The idea that she and I had once confided in one another, dreamed of a future together, shared a bed – the concept became fantastical, like something once experienced in a dream.

Foerster was a bad enemy to have but without intending it he did me a favour. His Gestapo friends ruined my health, but as luck (strange word!) would have it, it was because of them that I ended the war on the right side of the Iron Curtain.

As soon as I was sufficiently recovered I continued in my search for Claudia.

The Gelb brothers presented a problem for the would-be researcher. In their own way they had been famous, but that fame had never reached beyond the boundaries of their own profession. There were no photographs, no letters, none of the usual paraphernalia of biography. But I relished the challenge because it gave me the sense that I was doing something, and bit by bit I managed to uncover their story, though whether more by luck or experience I would not like to say.

The most vivid account of the brothers that I was able to find was written by the circus impresario Louis Touissant as part of his memoirs. "They are ugly," he wrote, "but with that peculiar species of ugliness, so secure within its own identity that it confuses the onlooker into believing that what he beholds is beauty, or at least something like genius. They are not twins, but they resemble one another extremely, so that often they are mistaken for twins, each with the same narrow diamond-shaped face and flap-like ears, the same full-lipped lopsided mouth, the same pale-lashed eyes the colour of unpolished topaz or weak tea."

Perhaps it was their ugliness that made them concentrate all their energies into their work. Within two years of Oskar's first sale to the Rostock merchant, the Gelb brothers had established their own workshop. In less than five they were making more money than their father. Gradually they turned their attentions from domestic work – the carved armoires and whatnots and blanket chests that had established them in their profession – to the more valuable theatre commissions that eventually made their name.

Their work was controversial, certainly. The heavily worked, rococo style of their carving led the drama critic Felix Shapiro to describe them as "the masters of infernal excess". A children's puppet theatre in Lübeck was forced to temporarily close, because the newly installed Gelb masks and stage screens frightened some of the children so badly they later required the attentions of a doctor. But others saw the brothers' creations as playful fantasies, delightfully imaginative pantomimes of miraculous escape and grotesque transformation that conjured the very essence of the Harz.

The brothers did not mind either way. Their very controversy made them more money, and the money they earned tempted them to ever more extravagant acts of creation. Their art reached its apotheosis in the great carnival funhouses, the so-called *Paläste*, which were so time-consuming and expensive to produce that less than a dozen were ever completed.

About three years into my research I came across an article in a journal of stage magic that claimed the Gelb *Paläste* were a hoax and had never existed. Some readers wrote in to refute this, but none had actually seen one of the palaces for themselves. I had seen one, but I did not write in. I supposed that people would continue to believe what they wanted to believe, regardless of any evidence to the contrary, and I had no wish to draw attention to myself.

Because of my experiences with the Gestapo I became eligible for a modest invalidity pension. The money made no difference to my overall lifestyle, but it did mean I could afford to travel more. I began scouring museum brochures and auction catalogues, searching for works, any works, by the Gelb brothers. I travelled to see the pieces wherever I could, sometimes many hundreds of miles. I tracked down one of their bottomless cabinets to a private collection in Strasbourg, and then followed that up with a trip to the headquarters of the Magic Circle in London to see a set of interconnecting "rooms" that had been part of the stage apparatus of Barnaby Gardner, famous as an illusionist during the 1890s. While I was there I had the good fortune to strike up a conversation with one of the sub-curators of the collection there. He told me that one of the northern goose fairs still used a Gelb carousel. He insisted it had originally been made for the great circus patriarch Caleb Castle, the grandfather of Ruby

Castle, the famous film star. I travelled north to Nottingham to see it. I don't know how much truth there was in the Castle provenance, but the twenty-four carved wooden stallions were indisputably the work of the Gelb brothers.

Gradually the business of research, so familiar to me and so beloved, began to work its own magic, and the book became an end in itself. I occasionally wondered what my publisher would make of it, whether there could possibly be any appeal to the reading public in this convoluted tale of two uneducated artisans from the eastern provinces, but I didn't let such minor considerations distract me. What mattered was that I was working, and therefore alive.

The war had been over for five years before I found what I had dreamed of finding. I already knew from my research that one of the Gelb *Paläste* had burned flat in the Cologne circus fire of 1938, and one more had been destroyed in an air raid on Antwerp. There were rumours one had been shipped to the United States by an obsessive collector of magical memorabilia, that still another *Palast* continued its rounds with a carnival company in Romania.

That should have left half a dozen, but I was unable to trace any of them. I began to lose hope, to imagine that the Gelb funhouses had gone the way of the freak shows and the dancing bears and the levitating magicians, that like so much of old Europe they had simply disappeared into the past.

Then one day my luck changed, as luck often does one way or another. It was a sweltering day in mid-June. I was waiting to catch a train at the Gare du Nord, browsing the newsstands and wishing I could get out of the heat when suddenly there it was, my luck, staring out at me from the cover of a magazine. It was the first photograph I had ever seen of one of the Gelb *Paläste*, and for all I knew the only one then in existence. I bought the magazine at once, hardly daring to look at it, half-convinced the image would change or disappear once it was in my possession. It didn't, though, and there were more photographs as an accompaniment to the main article. It turned out there was to be a landmark show of German folk art in the East German city of Naumburg, of which the Gelb *Palast* would form the main exhibit.

It was my first journey east since the war. In those early days, before the Berlin Blockade, West Germans were able to visit the East without too much difficulty – so many of us had relatives there – but you had to cite a reason for going. In order to avoid unnecessary delays I got in touch with the curator of the museum where the exhibition was taking place, and arranged for her to extend a personal invitation. Naumburg seemed a sad place to me, pallid-faced and withdrawn, a community doing its best to come to terms with some private disaster. I was surprised by the number of Russian soldiers on the streets. The museum curator, whose name was Gilda Klemmer, told me quietly over coffee that the town was now a Soviet garrison.

The *Palast* had a room to itself, dimly lit and with a greenish cast, suggestive of a woodland glade. The Gelb funhouses gave the impression of being solid, immovable structures but this was a deception, of course –they were built in sections, each to the same basic pattern. The interior walls were made from sanded oak. They could be slotted together in any number of possible configurations, rather like the sections of corrugated cardboard that form the divisions between the bottles in a case of wine. An experienced crew could unload and assemble the components in a couple of hours. After that it was just a matter of fitting the mirrors and the carved facades. One of the things I had not yet been able to discover about the Gelb brothers was the identity of their mirror maker. The glass was of a distinctive and unusual character. It had a greenish tint, like pond water, and from certain angles its gleam was flat and opaque, like that of jade. When viewed from a distance, though, it appeared to still be liquid, slipping downwards through the air like a waterfall in slow motion. From the books I had read on the subject I knew already that glass is in fact still a liquid, that it is only its dense viscosity that enables it to keep a stable form. Whoever had made the Gelb mirrors had managed somehow to highlight that property, to quantify it, to persuade the glass to reveal its true nature.

The door to the mirror maze had been closed off, but a glazed round spying aperture had been carefully opened in one side, allowing a partial view of the mirrored interior. I put my eye to the glass, and at once the outside world seemed to slide away. In its place there sprang into being a luminous domain of angles and planes. Before me was a gleaming corridor, its length an infinite perspective of marsh-fire light. I knew what I was seeing was simply a variation on the common optical illusion produced by placing one mirror facing another, but I was dazzled and somewhat troubled by it nonetheless. It seemed to me suddenly that the *Palast* was more than just wood and glass. I saw before me, reconstructed, the living and dangerous essence of the Gelb brothers' phantasmagorical imagination.

I fancied I could feel its force, driving its luminescent tunnels into the fabric of existence as a steel drill bites into a block of masonry, the *Palast* simply a gateway to this realm as the brain is simply a gateway to the mind. I fancied I could feel myself slipping into the uncharted dimensions beyond, layers of imagined reality folded closely together like a nest of black silk scarves inside a hatbox.

The mirrors clouded over and then clarified, and as I gazed into their depths I gradually became convinced that what I saw there was not a greenish distorted reflection of my own face, but something else entirely, a landscape of low hills and muddy fields, some derelict buildings half-hidden amongst the trees…

• • •

I stopped reading. I felt defenceless and cold, as if I had suddenly been divested of all my clothes. Thomas's words brought everything back to me. I remembered the line of a child's footprints in the snow, the beams of searchlights, the dogs barking. I saw these things, remembered them as if it were yesterday, with all the memories I had acquired since falling away into the darkness, as flat and as easily disposed of as a pack of cards.

• • •

"There's as much anarchy as order in German culture," said Thomas. "You foreigners like to think of us as boring, all straight lines and clean parade grounds. But we're all a bunch of misfits, really. Did you know that some of the first freak shows originated in Germany?"

"Daddy, please let me go to the freak show," Claudia clamoured excitedly. "Uncle Andrew said he'd take me."

"Only if your parents agree," I said hastily.

"There are no freak shows any more, my child. The English won't let us have them. They believe it's in poor taste. But if you'll settle for a ride on the Ferris wheel I'm sure we can come to some arrangement."

"She's too young," said Hermine. "Thomas, I don't want her going. You know what I said."

She addressed her words to her husband, but it was me she was looking at, the familiar little frown line between her eyebrows. I kept silent, not wanting to be caught in the crossfire, although the outing to the carnival was something I had been counting on. I had assumed Hermine would be coming too, that it would finally give us the chance to be alone together. Thomas wouldn't be going anywhere for a while because of his sprained ankle. He could hobble about the house but that was all.

"Don't be silly, Min," he said with a smile. "Andrew will take good care of her. Unless she gets mixed up with the freaks and carted away, that is."

He made a playful grab for his daughter, who had been sitting cross-legged on the carpet beside his chair. Claudia squealed and stuck out her tongue then squirmed away. She had her mother's bright blonde hair, but her facial features – the strong jaw-line, aquiline nose, and the cocoa-brown eyes – made her the image of her father. Thomas sometimes made references to his Jewish roots, way back on his father's side. Thomas always seemed amused by his ancestry for some reason, but I couldn't help noticing the way Hermine frowned each time he mentioned it.

"You can't be Jewish if your mother wasn't," I had heard her say on more than one occasion. "The father's side doesn't count."

But for the moment, at least, it was the carnival that concerned her.

"You know I don't like those places. The drinking."

She sounded tense still, but I could tell she was softening. I didn't know if she had actually changed her mind, or if it was simply that she didn't want me to see her rowing with Thomas. Ever since she had written to me, breaking off our affair, my emotions had ricocheted between relief and despair. I had returned to Heiligendamm as soon as I could, but from the moment I arrived Hermine had made it impossible for me to be alone with her. A part of me at least was not sorry. The situation was complicated and I dreaded a confrontation. Thomas was my friend, after all. I had few other friends, if any, that I valued more.

"Andrew will have her home by nine-thirty, won't you, Andrew?" Thomas said.

"I want to stay out till midnight," pleaded Claudia. "It's not a proper carnival unless it's dark."

"Don't push your luck, young lady. It's half-past nine or nothing at all." Hermine twisted her rings, the diamond Thomas had given her when Claudia was born and the opal that had belonged to her mother. The ring I had given her myself, the piece of Baltic amber in its gold setting, was not in evidence. I could see she was suffering, in spite of the cool demeanour she had affected. My heart clenched as I thought of the way it had been the previous summer, the rambles along the beach, the first stirrings of love between us. Our walks, which had begun as simple strolls along the promenade, had extended further and further until eventually we were walking several miles each day, far beyond the boundaries of the town and out into the pale wilderness of sand dunes and couch grass beyond. On the final morning of my visit we left Claudia with friends in the town, and set out along the beach to a place we both knew and had silently agreed upon, a rest-pavilion halfway between Heiligendamm and Kühlingsborn and at sufficient distance from both to be largely unfrequented. We secured the door with a broken-off branch and then made love.

Afterwards we walked back again, mostly in silence. As we approached the first of the white stone buildings that marked the western outskirts of the town, I found myself in a state bordering on shock. Part of Hermine's attraction for me had always been what I thought of as her remoteness, the mysterious inner life she nurtured through books and paintings but kept carefully hidden from intruders. Because of this remoteness, I had been unsure whether she had genuinely wanted to consummate our relationship or if she had consented because she imagined it was expected of her. The fierceness of her passion had knocked me sideways. I was due to leave first thing in the morning, a fact that now seemed cruel beyond imagining.

What Hermine herself was thinking I had no idea.

"We'd better hurry," she said at last. "Claudia will be wondering where we've got to."

From then until the end of my visit we were never alone. We wrote to each other later, of course – over the course of the next six months I must have received some three dozen letters from her. I had hoped the letters might contain some of the heat of our one sexual encounter but I was disappointed. The tone of the letters was dreamy, distracted, and rather than the great love I imagined we shared she wrote to me mainly of the oyster catchers on the dunes, the collection of quartz pebbles she was making with Claudia, a new opera by Richard Strauss.

I looked forward to these letters because they were at least a link with her, but in other ways they confounded and frustrated me. I longed to arouse her somehow, to provoke her to a more direct expression of emotion. In the early spring I managed to arrange a trip to Rostock, and with considerably more difficulty I managed to persuade Hermine to spend most of a day there with me. We booked into one of the anonymous hotels along the harbour front, places used mostly by commercial travellers and merchant seamen, and there occurred a repetition of what had happened out in the dunes the summer before. I felt that this time there must be some difference in her, some letting down of her guard, but I felt her withdraw from me almost in the very moment of her climax.

"Can't we at least talk about this?" I said as she put on her clothes.

"Talk about what? I cannot leave Thomas, I will not. And I could never live in England. I would die there. I would become stupid and timid and plain. It is foolish even to think about it." She inhaled sharply, and for a moment I thought she was going to shout at me, or burst into tears, but whatever the impulse had been it was quickly controlled.

In any case I knew she was right. I hated to think of her in England, even in London where people were used to foreigners, and anti-German sentiments were less apparent. There were other things, too. I had been in love before, yet I had always drawn aside from fully committing myself. I enjoyed the life I led and had no wish to change it. The idea of having to contend with someone else's moods and desires on an hour-by-hour basis filled me with panic.

There was also the question of what would happen to Claudia. I was not exactly surprised when, a week or so after our meeting in Rostock, I received a letter from Hermine, stating that she wanted to end our affair. I saw the sense in it, I welcomed it even. But that did not stop me from dropping everything and making arrangements to travel to Heiligendamm for the upcoming Whitsun holiday.

Thomas seemed delighted that I was coming. He wrote to me by return, telling me he had sprained his ankle jumping down onto the beach from the sea wall, and that a good dose of my invigorating company was just what the doctor ordered. I felt certain that where my relationship with his wife was concerned he remained in complete ignorance.

• • •

I was clever at school, and I think my parents rather hoped I would take advantage of that by going into law or the civil service. Instead I became a dealer in antiquarian books. It was something I stumbled into when I first came down from Oxford, trading out of the back bedroom of my rented flat in Clapham. It was meant to be a stop-gap, something to tide me over while I looked for a real job, but that wasn't the way things turned out.

I first encountered Thomas Emmerich when he wrote to me ordering a particular edition of Hölderlin I had advertised. He mentioned in his letter that he was working on a new biography of the poet. I slipped in a note with the book, wishing him luck with his research. This was where our friendship began, and it was not long before Thomas invited me to visit him in Germany. Claudia was just a baby then, and Hermine did not register with me particularly, partly because she seemed so shy and partly because I was involved with a woman in London at the time. It was only later that I began to realise I was attracted to her.

Sitting there once again in the Emmerichs' living room, I felt irritated that my feelings of nostalgia and regret over my affair with Hermine were intruding on the pleasure I always felt at seeing Thomas again. I scarcely even thought of the effect it might have on him, were he ever to learn what had happened. It was as if the two relationships were in entirely separate compartments.

"Would you like me to see to Claudia's supper?" I said. "You're looking tired." They were the first words I had spoken to Hermine directly since I arrived.

"No." She inhaled sharply, seeming to dismiss me exactly as she had done in the hotel room in Rostock. "I'll do it. You stay and talk to Thomas. He needs cheering up."

She seized the child's hand and led her away. Once they were out of the room Thomas turned to me with an apologetic smile.

"Don't let Hermine upset you," he said. "We've been trying for another baby, only nothing seems to be happening. It's left her feeling a little out of sorts." He sighed, and leaned back in his chair.

I felt a painful surge of jealousy, something I had not been prepared for. I was beginning to think my coming here had been a mistake.

"Is it true, what you said about the freak shows?" I said, changing the subject. "Were they really a German invention?"

"Doktor Himmelfahrt's Cabinet of Wonders and Abominations," said Thomas. "Ferdinand the Goat Boy, the Monster Brothers, the Wesendonck Twins, the Human Fish Tank." He grinned. "They were famous all over Europe, in their day."

"What on earth was the Human Fish Tank?"

"One Heino Kretschmar. He could swallow six live goldfish and then vomit them back up into their bowl, completely unharmed."

"You're making that up."

"Would I lie to you?"

I laughed aloud, and then Thomas ordered me to break out the brandy. We stayed up talking long past midnight, just as we had always done. I fell into bed just after two, my mind pleasantly blank, a distant rushing in my ears like the sound of the sea.

• • •

I woke around six, feeling badly dehydrated and with a powerful headache. I stumbled downstairs, thinking I would make myself a cup of tea, only to find Hermine had beaten me to it. She was bending to light the stove, wrapped in a Chinese silk dressing gown that I knew was Thomas's. The thin material clung to her body, revealing the delicate curves of her buttocks and the long, straight back with its protruding vertebrae. When she saw me she started with fright.

"What are you doing here?" she said. "It's so early."

"I'm feeling a bit hung over, I'm afraid," I said. "We polished off most of Thomas's brandy last night."

I smiled sheepishly, doing my best to make a joke of it. My head was throbbing. If I had longed for a meeting with Hermine then this was the worst timing possible. All I wanted was to get back to bed.

Hermine frowned. "Thomas shouldn't drink like that, the doctor said so."

"What do you mean, the doctor? What's wrong with him?"

"There's nothing wrong with him, apart from the ankle. It's just that he's not as strong as you might think."

She turned her back on me, running water into the kettle. I wondered what we were doing, going on about Thomas all of a sudden. Just as before, I felt tense with frustration at the way she seemed able to cut off her emotions.

"Hermine," I said.

She whirled round so swiftly that I took a step backwards. Her face, which a moment before had appeared so calm and indifferent, was now pale and fraught, her grey eyes hardened to a steely brightness. Her anger seemed barely contained.

"What do you mean by coming here?" Her hands were shaking. "How could you do this to me?"

"I had to see you," I insisted. "I needed to. I don't want things to end like this. If only you would let me talk to you, let me explain."

"There is nothing to talk about. I thought we agreed."

I wanted to protest that I had agreed to nothing, that the decision had been hers alone, but I managed to stop myself. There was no point in getting caught in the familiar and depressing cycle of blame and counter-blame. Such arguments were always futile.

"Can't we at least spend some time together?" I said. "Later on today, I mean?"

"I don't think so. I'm taking Claudia to see the Modersohns. We won't be back until this evening."

"Well then, what about the carnival? Claudia would love it if you came with us."

I thought the mention of Claudia would ease the tension, make the idea of being together seem less threatening, but Hermine's reaction was strange. She seemed to turn inward, hugging her sides and shivering all over, as if a cold draught had passed through the room.

"I wish you wouldn't take her to that place."

"It's just a bit of harmless fun. She'll be quite safe."

"You do not know that. They are not good places."

"Hermine, what on earth are you afraid of?"

"Ach." She bent her head and stared at the ground, as if she had become tired of looking at me, strands of her hair hanging loosely about her face. “I know it is silly, but when I was a small girl I had a bad experience. I went to the carnival at Goslar with a friend and her family. Soon after we arrived I became separated from them in the crowd. There were so many people, all pushing and laughing, and the more I tried to find my friend again the more I seemed to be lost. The carnival ground went on for ever. The rides and sideshows had sounded thrilling when my friend had described them to me, but now I was alone they seemed different, not like amusements at all.

“I knew the worst thing I could do was panic, but then a fat man with smelly breath and shiny red spots on his face grabbed me by the shoulders and asked if I wanted to go for a ride with him. I couldn’t help it, I just ran. It never occurred to me that I should stop and ask for help, that someone in the crowd might be friendly. All the adults seemed like the fat man, either frightening or dangerous or both.

“I ended up hiding in one of the tents. I could smell *Bratwurst*, and frying onions, and I thought perhaps my friend might be there getting something to eat, but it was just another part of the carnival. There were clowns in stripy trousers, asking the children to come up on to the stage. Some farm boys who had probably had too much beer to drink started pulling the children out of their seats. They made them go up on the stage, even the ones that didn’t want to, even the ones that were crying. One of them spotted me and pushed me forward, and suddenly I was up there, right next to one of the clowns. It whispered something into my ear, only with all the shouting and crying I couldn’t hear what it was saying. I moved a little closer, trying to find out what I was supposed to do, only then I noticed something awful: the white make-up on the clown's face went all the way down his neck and inside his clothes. I saw then it wasn't make-up at all, and neither were the swollen nose and bushy red eyebrows and hair. The clown's hands were huge, like the great Bavarian hams my mother always ordered at Christmas, and it smelled nasty, bitter, like a back alleyway that cats have been using as a toilet. When it opened its mouth to smile at me I saw its teeth were bad, and that they were the wrong shape, narrow and pointed like a rat's teeth. Some of them were broken off halfway down.

"It sounds crazy to say it, but I was overcome with terror. The idea came into my head that the clown didn't just want me to be in the show, that he wanted to keep me for ever. And not just me, but all the other children too. I flew across the stage and down into some kind of storage area behind. It was pitch black, full of ropes and packing cases and all kinds of other rubbish. I tripped and fell, bumping my head.

"The next thing I knew there was a woman in a purple headscarf slapping my face, and someone was making announcements through a loud speaker. After a couple of minutes my friend's father appeared and we all went home. I felt dreadful because I had ruined the evening, but in some part of myself I knew things could have been much worse; I knew I'd had a narrow escape. I've never told anyone what happened that night, not even Thomas. I was afraid he might think I was mad."

She looked up at me and tried to smile. Her grey eyes were wary, but the anger in them seemed to have dissipated. I longed to hold her, but I knew all at once that whatever had been between us was over. I thought perhaps that was for the best.

"You were just a child," I said softly. "Getting lost like that, of course you were frightened."

"I don't want anything like that happening to Claudia."

"I won't let her out of my sight."

She seemed not to hear me. "It's strange, you know. Thomas has spent most of his life writing about madness, but he doesn't really believe in it. It's just an idea to him. He makes me feel so lonely sometimes."

She set the kettle down on top of the stove.

"I'll leave here tomorrow," I said.

"If you like. It doesn't matter now, either way."

I felt chagrined by her matter-of-factness, but I knew she was right. In whatever roundabout way, we had said everything that needed to be said. All that remained now was the slow journey back to neutrality, to a place where both of us could feel convinced that our brief and pointless affair had never happened.

She made me a cup of tea and I returned to my room. I lay in bed with the curtains half closed, sipping my drink and considering my options. I had planned to stay in Heiligendamm for a week. Now I decided I would leave the following day. I would say I had received a telegram, calling me back to England. I might even hint that the sender was a woman. It would be easy.

I let my mind drift, listening to the sounds of the house. At first there was just Hermine, her footsteps passing softly back and forth downstairs. Then I heard Thomas, hobbling along the landing to the bathroom. At one point Claudia said, "Where's Uncle Andrew?" very loudly outside my door, but Hermine immediately told her to be quiet. I waited until I heard them leave the house then washed and dressed and went downstairs.

"So it is Herr Rip Van Winkle himself," said Thomas, looking up from his newspaper. "Someone had a heavy night, by the look of things."

"It's your fault, you torturer," I said. "You and that Courvoisier."

The breakfast things were still on the table, the usual spread of ham and smoked cheese and fresh rolls. Seeing the food made me ravenous. I took a roll from the basket. Thomas made a fresh pot of coffee and we went outside.

The house stood just a short way inland, divided from the main hub of the town by a narrow stretch of woodland at the foot of a low line of hills. The garden extended some hundred feet from the rear of the house, with a splendid view of the rooftops and the sea beyond.

Heiligendamm is Germany's oldest spa town, famous for its ducal palace and its sandy beaches. It was an idyllic spot, yet curiously isolated. Staring out across the Baltic towards Denmark, I sometimes experienced a sensation like vertigo, convinced at least temporarily that the vast mainland of Europe behind me had ceased to exist, and there was nothing left in the universe but the scatter of white buildings along the shoreline, sunk in past glories, dreaming of an Enlightenment that had been promised but never materialised.

"It is almost too beautiful, really," said Thomas. "It makes you forget what's going on in the rest of the world."

It was as if he had read my mind. I supposed he was referring to the food riots and the wave of political murders that had swept across Berlin in the run-up to the recent elections, the increase in support for the National Socialists. Away from the cities these problems were less evident, although when I had changed trains at Hamburg it had been impossible to ignore the unemployed labourers begging at the station entrance, the National Socialist graffiti defacing the newspaper kiosks.

"Are you worried?" I said.

"People are starving," he said. "There is violence on the streets like we have never known, and yet the government just sits there, mouthing platitudes. Of course I am worried. I am worried they will dream up another war, just to save their political skins."

"But Germany can't fight a war. The economy is ruined."

"What better way to get it back on its feet again?" He threw up his hands. "Andrew, you are a man of intelligence and compassion but it is impossible for you to grasp how we Germans are feeling. There are many who believe that Germany was used as a scapegoat, forced to take the blame for a war that was not the sin of one country but of many, that the Versailles treaty arose not out of a desire for justice but out of fear and jealousy and old-fashioned spite. There are thousands of young men out there, waiting for someone to give them permission to take revenge. I am afraid it will not be long before someone does."

It sounded like madness to me, but I couldn't find the energy to argue about it. Instead I distracted Thomas with questions about his latest writing project, a study of the Austrian occult novelist Gustav Meyrink. From there we passed on to other subjects, other writers, and before I knew it the morning was halfway gone. After lunch I left him to work and walked into town. The time spent alone with Thomas, the simple remedies of good food and fine conversation, had helped to settle my mind, and by the time I had descended the mile-long footpath that ran from just below the Emmerich house to the *Kurhaus* end of the beach promenade, I had decided to forget the lie about the telegram. To leave so soon would be bound to hurt Thomas's feelings and might even arouse his suspicions. I could manage an extra day at the very least.

I strolled along the front, enjoying the crisp astringent breeze that flowed off the Baltic, the sight of the young women in their floral dresses taking an afternoon turn along the jetty. Some went arm in arm with their mothers or grandmothers, and others were in the company of young men. I felt a twinge of envy for those young men, thinking of my walks with Hermine the summer before, but on the whole I was relieved to be on my own.

On the way back to the house I took a detour out towards the level area of parkland and surrounding fields where the carnival was being set up. Heavily muscled carnies, their naked torsos gleaming with sweat, wielded mallets and hauled on guy ropes. A straggling line of ex-army trucks and high-sided wagons, some of them draped with brightly painted tarpaulins, stood parked beneath the trees. Groups of spectators clustered close by, laughing and jostling and eating fried fish out of paper cones. Children ran about unchecked, pelting each other with handfuls of sawdust and straw. These people were very different from the genteel tourists I had seen on the promenade, rougher and less sophisticated, but the jokes, though bawdy, seemed mostly good-natured, and there was nothing to suggest the disorder was out of control. The sense of anticipation was palpable. I felt sorry that Thomas's injured leg had got in the way of him enjoying the outing with us. The carnival, with its brash colours and bohemian characters, was the kind of spectacle he revelled in.

By the time I got back to the house Hermine and Claudia had already returned. Hermine's behaviour was relaxed, sunny, almost mischievous. She appeared happier than I had seen her, really, since the start of our affair. It was Claudia that seemed oddly shy.

"She's afraid you won't like her dress," Hermine said. She put her finger to her lips and smiled. "She chose it especially."

The revelation made me feel a little sad. Claudia had always seemed entirely without vanity, unconscious of her gaucherie and innocent of conventions in a manner I found touching. I supposed that worrying about her appearance was just a sign she was growing up, but I felt a pang of regret all the same.

The four of us had supper together, and then Hermine took Claudia upstairs to help her get changed. When they reappeared, Claudia had swapped her plain cotton sun dress for a lilac silk shift, with pearl buttons up the front and a lace collar. She shifted from foot to foot, shoulders hunched forward, obviously waiting for my approval. She was tall for her age and slightly gawky, something the finely made dress only seemed to accentuate. The lilac colour clashed oddly with her complexion, although it would have suited her mother perfectly.

"You look lovely," I said. "Like a carnival queen."

I felt fiercely protective towards her suddenly. I wanted nothing in the world to hurt her, least of all some careless word of mine.

"Half past nine at the latest," said Hermine. She glanced at me briefly then looked away. She touched the top of her daughter's head, stroking the fair hair smooth with the flat of her hand. Claudia gazed up at her and smiled.

"Why don't you come with us, Mummy?" she said.

"Oh, you don't need me really," said Hermine. "Mothers spoil the fun."

These were the last words they exchanged.

• • •

The carnival ground was packed.

"Stay close to me," I said to Claudia. "I promised your mother I'd look after you."

The sun was setting. The horizon glowed a saccharine pink, the colour of famished hydrangeas. Claudia gripped my hand tightly but her eyes were everywhere.

"I want to go on the roundabout. Can I, Uncle Andrew? It's so beautiful."

The carousel was enormous, a tumult of wooden horses and flashing lights. We went over and stood in line. When the contraption ground to a standstill I handed Claudia a coin and told her she should give it to one of the carnies once she was on board. I watched her scoot across the grass, her pale hair flashing white in the electrical glow. She smiled and waved from the back of her painted stallion, calling to me through her cupped hands, but the wheezing groan of the calliope drowned her out. The air was filled with strong aromas, burnt sugar and frying onions and underarm sweat. When the ride was over Claudia leaped down and came running, her features submerged in patterns of coloured light.

"Uncle Andrew, that was wonderful!"

She seemed lit from within, as if a part of her previously dormant had been brought to life. Her fingers were grubby with grass stains, and I noticed there was a grease mark on the hem of her dress.

"What would you like to do next?" I said. It was difficult not to be infected by her excitement.

"I want to go on everything."

I laughed. "We'll see," I said. I kept a close watch on her, anxious in case the crowds and the noise were proving too much for her, but she seemed perfectly at ease. I had always thought of her as a nervous child, intense and introverted, like so many precocious youngsters happier in the company of adults. She was a passionate reader. She loved Jules Verne and Alain-Fournier, the macabre tales of Hoffmann and Kleist, and it was easy to forget she was only nine. Now and unexpectedly she was showing a different aspect of her character, more extrovert and more childlike. Her normally pale cheeks flared like carnations. In the purple dusk beneath the Chinese lanterns she suddenly looked as beautiful as her mother.

"Let's see if there's a ghost train," I said. Claudia squealed and hid her face in my jacket. I bought a cone of fried fish and some honeycomb from one of the refreshments stands. Memories returned to me of my boyhood in Nottingham and the annual goose fair. My friend Stephen Black, nicknamed Blackie, had devised a foolproof strategy for playing the machines in the penny arcade and won a jackpot so huge we had needed a hessian bag to carry it home. Blackie later became a civil engineer, a designer of road bridges and railway tunnels. I hadn't been back to Nottingham in years.

"This is the best night of my life," said Claudia. "I don't want it to end."

She sucked sugar from her fingers, and in a peculiar moment of recall I saw Hermine in the hotel room in Rostock, licking icing from one of the Genoese sponge cakes we had left over from our picnic. I could feel myself blushing – luckily it was too dark for Claudia to notice. I went with her on the swing boats, and a terrifying whirligig called the Endeavour. I had better luck on the shooting range, where I managed to win her a stuffed lion cub. When eventually I looked at my watch it was ten past nine.

"Time to go," I said.

"Just one more ride, Uncle Andrew, please?"

She looked up at me, her brown eyes pleading, and I fumbled in my pocket for more coins. "Just the one then, and I mean that. You choose."

It was then that I saw Hermine. She was walking quickly, slipping purposefully through the crowd and obviously in a hurry to get somewhere. She was facing away from me but with her long back, her bright hair, and her firm stride there was no doubt in my mind that it was her.

Claudia put her hand on my sleeve. "I want to go in the mirror maze," she said. I gave her the coins and told her she mustn't be long.

"Aren't you coming with me?" she said.

"No. I don't like mazes. They scare me."

She laughed delightedly and darted away. I hardly noticed which direction she took. My eyes and my attention were all on Hermine. I was anxious not to lose sight of her in the crowd.

She had braided her hair. It stuck out around her head like an elaborately woven mesh of silver wire. She was wearing a long silver coat, embroidered with poppies. In the garish light from the stalls they looked like splashes of blood. The coat clasped her figure closely and, my overheated mind told me, tenderly. Its hem swished to and fro as she walked, giving tantalising glimpses of silver stilettos.

I could hardly believe what I saw. Hermine's usual style of dress was simple and plain. I would never have guessed she had items like these in her wardrobe. Then suddenly the truth crashed in upon me: she had another lover, and was on her way to meet him. All at once everything made sense – her coolness towards me, her decision to end our relationship, her angry reluctance to discuss anything. It could only mean she was in love with another man.

My equanimity vanished in an instant, replaced by a tumultuous mixture of anger and grief. If I thought I had come to terms with the situation I had been wrong. I felt foolish to the point of rage. I knew I had to have it out with her, at once. I began to hurry after her, pushing people aside like so many stuffed dolls. Dimly, as if on a cinema projection, I saw a child's carton of popcorn go flying, the pale kernels scattered upon the ground like thrown confetti. A boy screamed in cartoonish outrage, his mouth a round black "o". I passed him by with scarcely a thought. The only thing that mattered was keeping track of Hermine.

I increased my speed until I was running, but somehow she was able to stay one step ahead of me. The carnival ground was huge, much bigger than I had realised, and I kept passing strange attractions I hadn't seen before. The thought that I was leaving Claudia further and further behind barely penetrated my consciousness.

I caught up with Hermine by the ice cream stands. I reached out my hand, grabbing her by one delicate, poppy-clad shoulder. I had a stitch in my side, and was sweating. The girl whirled round, her violet eyes enormous with fright. I saw at once that she was not Hermine. There was a passing likeness, as to a cousin perhaps, or a younger sister, but there the resemblance ended. A stupid mistake.

Her full lips were slightly parted. She was staring at me fearfully, as if she had fallen into the clutches of a madman.

"I'm most terribly sorry," I said. "I mistook you for someone else."

I let go of her shoulder. I tried not to think what a sight I must look, my face red and blotchy from running, patches of perspiration staining my chest. She gave a brief laugh and turned away, obviously anxious to pretend the incident had never happened. It was only then I remembered Claudia. Dull panic sped through me. When I could bring myself to look at my watch I saw it was half-past nine.

By now it was completely dark. I tried retracing my steps, but nothing seemed familiar. When I asked the way at one of the fried fish stands the vendor gave me directions to the first-aid station, but either he had given me false information or I had gone wrong somewhere because when I got inside the tent there was some kind of show in progress. Three orange-wigged clowns, their shoulders muscular beneath their lemon-striped vests, were chasing a little girl around a stage. The clowns were shrieking with laughter, trying to capture her in what looked like an enormous butterfly net. It was difficult to tell if the girl was laughing or in tears.

I stepped back into the night. I felt disorientated and desperate to the point of madness. I pushed onward through the crowd, a treacherous inner voice informing me at every step that I was wandering in circles, that in another minute I would find myself back by the ice cream stands, no nearer to finding Claudia than I had been before.

I found the mirror maze completely by chance. My eyes would not believe it at first, but then I began to notice other things I recognised: the swing boats, a sausage stand manned by a dwarf in a bright green livery. The maze was built of wood, faced on all four sides with elaborate carvings. An ogre in a belted kaftan stood on guard at the entrance.

"Have you seen a little girl?" I said to him. The words came out in an incoherent rush. The doorkeeper stared at me blankly. His forearms were tattooed with matching skulls. "She came in here about half an hour ago," I insisted. "She was wearing a pink dress."

"I'm not a policeman, brother," said the ogre. "I don't keep a count of them. So long as they pays their money I lets them in."

The vast face shut down again. I tried to go past him but the ogre grabbed me by the collar. I struggled feebly in his grip like a fish on a line.

"If you're going in then you'll need a ticket, same as everyone else," he said. His indifference to my situation increased my panic. I hunted frantically through my pockets, remembering I had given all my small change to Claudia. Eventually I located my wallet. I snatched out a note and flung it at him, then hurried past him into the maze.

I became disorientated almost at once. From the outside the Mirror Palace looked no larger than an average-sized cricket pavilion, but once through the entrance it was like passing into some glimmering, limitless space, a shimmering infinity of mirrors. The mirrors had a murky, greenish cast, and initially appeared to give no reflection at all. I peered into first one mirror and then another, expecting them to reveal to me my inner compacted dwarf, my spectral attenuated giant as the mirrors in the funhouse at the Nottingham goose fair had done, but all I saw was the blurry, greenish outline of my normal-sized features. I failed to see the point of it.

It was only as I penetrated deeper into the maze that I realised things were not as they seemed. The mirrors seemed to glow with a peculiar internal brightness of their own. A clever lighting effect, most likely, though I was at a loss as to how this had been achieved. My reflection seemed to come and go in the glass, as if on the surface of water that had been disturbed. When I moved in to get a closer look I imagined

I saw another reflection behind it, the shadow of someone peering over my shoulder.

I spun round anxiously but there was no one there, just my own face staring back at me from another mirror. The effect was unsettling and, unlike that of an ordinary mirror maze, not at all entertaining. I pressed onward through the corridors, vaguely wondering why there were not more people in the maze, why I appeared to be so thoroughly alone. I turned corner after corner, occasionally encountering dead ends but more often the reflective, quicksilver gleam of another gallery. The silvery tunnels seemed endless, and although I knew this was merely an optical illusion I started to wonder how I would ever find my way out again.

I rounded another corner and felt a breeze blowing, the unmistakable smell and texture of outside air. I was surprised by how cold it was. When I had first entered the maze the night had been gentle and warm. The floor of the tunnel was strewn with debris: leaves and twigs, sweet wrappers, even a pine cone. But there was no sign of Claudia. I knew there was nothing for it but to hunt down someone in charge and get them to put out a call for a missing child. It seemed insane now that I had not thought of this in the first place. I had already wasted valuable time.

Then I noticed something strange, a line of footprints coming towards me, into the maze. The prints were fresh, ringed with moisture, as if someone with wet shoes had passed through the tunnel only moments before. I knew this was impossible. If someone had come this way I would certainly have seen them. I moved cautiously towards the exit, realising only then how quiet it was, the strident cacophony of the fairground entirely vanished. The closer I came to the outside the more the mirrors in the gallery wall seemed to be losing their brilliance. When I touched one it felt rough, as if its surface was pitted by acid. About six feet from the tunnel's entrance the mirrors gave way entirely to brick.

Stars glimmered in the blackness of the night. I was standing in a dimly lit alley. The tunnel I had emerged from appeared to be the side entrance to a squat two-storey house, built of grey stone and in a state of advanced dilapidation. I saw there was snow on the ground. In the place where I was standing a confusion of overlapping footprints had reduced it to slurry.

I took a step forward, looking both ways along the street. To the left there were more houses, a green cross sign hanging outside a pharmacy, a bicycle chained to a lamp post. To the right, iron railings, the dark hump of what looked like a monument of some kind or a water fountain, beyond that only blackness. I went a little way along the street, holding my arms out to keep my balance on the slippery ground. At the next lamp post I stopped and looked down. The mass of footprints around the tunnel entrance had thinned to a single line, leading away from me and further into the snow. The footprints were small and narrow, a child's prints. I shivered with cold.

The alley soon petered out into a rutted dirt track. The track ran across open fields, their covering of snow gleaming blue-white beneath the light of the moon. I could see tyre marks on the snow, which seemed to indicate the recent passage of some heavy vehicle. I walked along in the tyre tracks, following the line of footprints and trying to avoid the deepest patches of snow. The footprints were blurred now because of the unevenness of the ground, yet still I felt certain they were Claudia's. I tried not to think about how frightened she must be, or how cold. If I could only find her quickly then all would be well.

The rutted path passed through a copse of barren trees then widened into a no-man's-land of slag heaps and builder's rubble. Directly in front of me was a steel perimeter fence, held up by concrete stanchions and topped with barbed wire. Stranger still, the band of air between me and the fence seemed to quiver, to ripple, to be in some manner visible, as a heat haze over August fields is visible. There was a low hum, as of drowsy insects, and I realised the fence was probably electrified.

The footprints ended just in front of the wire. They did not peter out or become obscured by snow but stopped dead, as if they had passed through an invisible door. I bent down and touched the last print, its outline particularly crisp, not like a real footprint but a plaster cast of one, the kind the police make from the footprints at the scene of a crime. The melting snow numbed my fingertips. I waved my hand around slowly in front of my face, testing the barrier. I felt a discharge of static, the faint pricking of pins and needles as if the air itself were electrified, and once again I had the sense of something invisible being revealed, a material echo of objects that did not exist. I realised then that I could hear sounds, faint but clear: shouts and the barking of dogs, a rapid burst of gunfire. I *felt* rather than saw a searchlight beam rend the darkness.

I quickly lowered my hand and the silence returned. Somewhere in the far distance I heard a train ratcheting over rails, the shriek of a vixen in the dark undergrowth. I remained immobile, hugging my sides and feeling the cold bite into the exposed skin of my face. I was more afraid than I had ever been in my life, yet I did not know how much my terror had to do with the palpable malignancy of the place, or with the fact that I did not know if it was even there. I had the sense of being close to an abyss.

I turned to retrace my steps, forcing myself to walk and not to run. A new terror had seized me: that I would return to the darkened alleyway to discover my return route had vanished, leaving me to freeze to death in an impossible world. But these fears at least were to prove unfounded. As I staggered in under the stone lintel I noticed there were two sets of footprints leading into the maze now instead of one. The earlier prints were beginning to dry. The new ones, my own, were shiny with melted snow. The strange thing was I could see at once that both sets of prints had been made by the same person. The size of the prints, and the patterning on the shoe sole made it impossible to doubt it.

I scrambled back through the maze. As I had anticipated, it took me a long time to find my way out, and by the time I emerged on the other side my shoes and socks were dry. The night was sweet and warm, the carnival still in full swing. Above the general din I heard the clang of a bell, the signal for the roller coaster to begin its ascent. I felt a sharp pang of grief, that Claudia and I had not had time to take a turn on the roller coaster. I imagined her face, the bony features so like her father's. It was half-past eleven. I wondered where Claudia had got to, a question that would haunt me for twenty years.

• • •

I do not like to dwell on my return to the Emmerich house. A sense of unreality consumed me, as if I were still in the maze, as if everything that had happened since my encounter with the false Hermine had been part of a nightmare. As I climbed back up the hill it occurred to me that I need not return at all, that I could keep walking until I reached the station at Bad Doberan, where the mail train would be leaving for Hamburg at ten past five. I had a diamond-clear image of myself, sitting in the buffet car drinking hot coffee and reading the morning papers as if nothing had happened. Had it not been for the certainty that I would be arrested within a matter of hours I think I really might have left that way. As it was I stood in the hallway with Thomas and the real Hermine and waited for the police to arrive.

"I watched her go into the maze," I said to Thomas. "I didn't take my eyes off her."

I had tried several times to explain, to rehearse my story: Claudia had gone into the funhouse and never come out. I comforted myself with the knowledge that this was at least a version of the truth. Later on I chastised myself for maintaining a delusion.

"Don't tell me any more," said Thomas. "The more you repeat the story the less immediate it will seem. That could make you forget things, some vital detail. It's best to wait until the police are here. Then you can tell them."

He was curt, dismissive, not remotely the Thomas I knew. He seemed not to want me near him, and one look at his face made it obvious there was nothing I could do or say that would improve the situation. Hermine seemed to draw into herself entirely. She went to the kitchen to make coffee but poured it down the sink before anyone could drink it, a terrible smile twisting the corners of her lips. She spoke not a word to me. I think that for a couple of hours she was insane.

The search went on for days. Suspicion centred on the carnival, at least at first, although as time went on the police began to think Claudia must have been taken by someone in the crowd. After the initial bouts of questioning no one seemed interested in me. The ogre guarding the mirror maze remembered me, because I had tried to get in without paying. His statement backed up my version of events, and in the end I started to believe my own story, if only because it was more plausible than the reality.

I stayed on in Heiligendamm for most of a week and then I went home. The police said they had no further need of me, at least for the moment, and that I was free to go. Thomas offered to escort me to the station – he was down to one crutch by then – but I told him he should stay with Hermine. I thought that would be the end of our friendship but I was wrong. Less than a fortnight after my return to London there was a letter from him, apologising for what he called his brutal treatment of me during the last days of my stay. I wrote back, enclosing a review notice I had clipped from *The Times* of a lieder recital by the bass baritone Ernst Schwabe, of whom I knew Thomas was a fan. The first few letters were rather awkward, but within a couple of months our regular correspondence had resumed. The following year he wrote to ask if I would like to spend Christmas in Germany with him and Hermine. I found a reasonable excuse not to, although

I took the opportunity to ask after Hermine. In the days following Claudia's disappearance Hermine had spoken fewer than two dozen words to me, and I'd had no contact with her since returning to England.

"Hermine has plenty to occupy her," Thomas wrote. "She has joined our German Culture Appreciation Society. She has made some interesting friends."

I didn't know what to make of that, although the ironic tone of Thomas's letter was unmistakable. I wondered if he was concerned that his mail might be opened. I read the newspapers, like everyone else, but I was well used to anti-German propaganda and uncertain of how much of it I should believe.

Thomas issued several more invitations for me to visit but I always declined. The truth was I couldn't face the thought of seeing him. In letters it was possible to stick to neutral subjects, to keep more personal matters at a distance. In person this would not be so easy. Reading between the lines I had become aware that Thomas blamed himself for what had happened to Claudia, for not being there to look after her when she needed him most.

I did not know if I could look him in the eye. Also I did not want to see Hermine.

But finally, in the early spring of 1936, I wrote to Thomas telling him I was due to travel to Brussels to attend a book fair, that there was the possibility of coming on to Heiligendamm afterwards. I deliberately left things open, but the enthusiasm of Thomas's response meant I did not have the heart to disappoint him. I paid extra for a sleeper berth, hoping for some peace and quiet on the journey east, but my rest was rudely interrupted at the German border when a dozen or so military policemen boarded the train.

"Damned insolence," muttered my travelling companion, a French perfume salesman on his way to visit relatives in Leipzig. "You can't go anywhere in this country nowadays without having a gun poked in your face."

One of the troopers entered our compartment and asked politely if he could see our papers. He was very young, fresh-faced and chubby-cheeked, the brown uniform sitting upon him stiffly as if on its first outing. He examined my passport briefly and then handed it back.

"Welcome to Germany," he said. I chose to take his greeting at face value. Looking back on it I am forced to admit I wanted to believe the situation in Germany had been exaggerated, that nothing had changed. What I had not anticipated was how little I wanted to be in Heiligendamm. As I made my way up the hill towards the Emmerich house I felt overcome by sadness, by foreboding, and by a weary sense of resignation. I wished I had kept the door closed on the past.

Thomas embraced me like a brother. I found I couldn't take my eyes off him, not realising until that moment I had expected never to see him again. He asked if I was hungry, and I told him I had eaten on the train.

"Hermine meant to have lunch ready," he said. "But she has a friend with her at the moment. She tends to lose track of time when he's around."

He smiled an odd smile, as if he were mocking himself. I waited for him to explain, to say more, but he hurried me up the steps and into the hall.

"Do you think you could manage without me, my friend, just for half an hour? There's some work I need to finish, then I'm all yours. Your room's made up, of course, the same as always."

I encouraged him to take his time and went upstairs. I laid my suitcase on the bed then crossed to the window. There before me was the Emmerichs' garden, the sloping green lawns, the last of the spring crocuses, and beyond them the cool grey shimmer of the Baltic, known to the Germans as the *OstMittelsee*. I could also see Hermine, sitting on the bench beneath the lilacs. There was somebody with her, a man.

I washed then changed my shirt and went outside. The sea glimmered dully, like mercury, and I could hear Hermine laughing. She looked up sharply as I approached and I saw she was blushing. She looked thinner, her features harsher somehow. Her bright hair showed an undertint of grey.

"Andrew," she said, getting up. "I hope you had a comfortable journey. This is Martin Foerster, the president of our cultural society. Martin, this is Andrew Allingham. He's a friend of Thomas's. He's come all the way from London to see us."

Foerster rose also. He grasped my hand briefly and then released it, as if it were not to his liking.

"That's a very fine watch you are wearing," he said. "Not one of those Jew boy bankers, are you?" He laughed, trying to make a joke of it. I wondered if he greeted all his new acquaintances in a similar fashion.

"As far as I know we're Presbyterians," I said. "The watch belonged to my father."

"You speak excellent German."

"I had an excellent teacher," I said. "He was originally from Breslau."

I thought it best not to mention that the teacher in question had been Nathan Goldfarb, the brother of the kosher butcher who lived down our street.

"And how do you like our town?" said Foerster.

"Very much indeed," I replied. "I always enjoy my visits here."

Foerster fixed me with his strident blue gaze then turned away, granting me a glimpse of himself in profile. He was a man of extraordinary physical beauty, of medium height, but with a posture so straight and upright he appeared taller. His features were so perfect in their refinement one might almost have believed them to be fashioned by Bernini or Michelangelo. Foerster's skin appeared delicately transparent, its pallor intensified by the contrast with the deep, velvety blackness of his uniform. His flaxen hair was combed to a platinum shine. I glanced across at Hermine, trying to engage her attention, but she refused to look at me.

"If you will excuse us," she said. "Herr Foerster and I have things we need to discuss. For the society's next concert, you understand? Martin is a wonderful organist. He has been kind enough to play for us on several occasions."

Foerster took her arm. They walked briskly away together across the lawn.

I returned to the house. Thomas was in his study surrounded by papers.

"Who is that awful man?" I said. "How do you put up with him?"

"I do my best to ignore him," said Thomas. "We don't have much in common."

He smiled a wan smile. I noticed there were bags under his eyes. All at once I felt guilty, that not once in all my letters had I been courageous enough to ask him how he really was. Seeing Hermine with Foerster had made me feel contaminated, as if my former love for her had made me complicit with the Michelangelo in the black uniform. I experienced a brief urge to tell Thomas about my affair with Hermine, to have everything out in the open, but I quickly suppressed it. I realised it would be a selfish act, cathartic for me maybe but presenting my friend with yet another emotional crisis he would have to deal with. Besides, the thing was dead. In the face of all that had happened since it could hardly matter.

I asked Thomas instead what he was working on.

"Something new," he said, and smiled. "I don't want to say too much at the moment, but I think I might be on to something exciting."

He seemed almost like his old self again and I was glad. I sat down in the ancient plush armchair by the window, feeling relaxed for the first time since I had stepped off the train. There was a book on the windowsill, a slim green-covered pamphlet containing the morphine-induced, war-torn elegies of the Austrian poet Georg Trakl, who had died, like Keats, before he reached the end of his third decade.

"I wouldn't let our friend out there see you reading that." Thomas nodded towards the window. "He thinks lily-livers like Trakl are bad for the nation's morale."

Both of us began to laugh. I turned the pages slowly, my mind filling up with Trakl's terrifying yet incandescent images: the shattered face of a dying soldier, starving women begging for scraps of offal at the gates of an abattoir, the clammy blue-black air of an October dusk. I gazed out at the sun-dappled lawn. I did not know it then, but I was seeing the Emmerichs' garden for the last time. The Baltic glimmered in the middle distance, a narrow band of tempered steel. All at once I found myself wondering what we would all be doing in ten years' time.

"Why didn't you go into the mirror maze with her?" said Thomas suddenly. "You went on all the other rides together."

The blood seemed to freeze in my veins. Thomas never spoke of Claudia in his letters, and I had been more than happy to believe he had decided it was better for both of us not to reawaken painful memories. Now I wondered if he had been playing me along all these years, waiting for me to make a mistake. My mind raced, wondering what I should tell him. Yet in the end I stuck to my story, the story I had invented and come to believe.

"I'm not keen on confined spaces," I said. "I told Claudia I would wait for her outside."

Thomas was quiet for a moment. I could hear the strident, bugle-bright screams of the herring gulls dive-bombing the tourists out on the jetty. "These mazes were known as *Paläste*," Thomas said at last. "I've been doing some research on them, actually. The first was made for an amusement park in Hanover. It went on display in 1881."

He began moving papers around on his desk. I sensed he was waiting for me to say something, but I did not trust myself to speak. It was typical of Thomas to try and *work* himself through his grief, but I couldn't help thinking his newfound interest in carnival funhouses could not be good for him.

"I hardly remember what it looked like," I said finally. "It was dark by then and all I could think of was Claudia. I felt like I was going out of my mind."

He glanced up at me sharply, then reached into his breast pocket and took out a pipe, one of the sour-faced meerschaums he collected, and lit it with a gold cigarette lighter. Blue smoke rose up, together with the sweet smell of tobacco.

"Let's go out," he said. "We can have lunch at the Rivoli."

I returned to England the following day. Thomas came to the station to see me off. We continued to write our letters, but finally the war came, bringing our correspondence to an end.

Fifteen years later, in a hotel room overlooking Lake Constance, I listened to the sound of children playing in the park and thought of the young couple I had seen in the tram, who would have been children themselves when the war broke out. For the first time I wondered what Thomas had been through during those years. I carried on reading his letter, finally beginning to realise how much I had missed him.

I kept in touch with Gilda Klemmer. She was intelligent, and I found her company sustaining. She was some five years older than me, but this did not worry me in the least. She was the first woman I had been attracted to since Hermine.

On the day I first met her in Naumburg she was wearing thick square-framed East German spectacles she told me she hated. I had a pair made up to her prescription by an optician friend of mine in Frankfurt, who assured me they were the latest style. Gilda seemed delighted with the result. She sent me a photograph of herself wearing the new glasses, and asked if my visit to her humble museum had been productive. I replied that it had, and said that I was also interested in visiting the folk museums at Wernigerode and Drei Annen.

"That should be simple to arrange," she wrote. "I have contacts with most of the provincial museums." She asked also if I would like to meet up with her in Wernigerode. "It is a beautiful place," she wrote. "And I happen to have some holiday owing." I told her I would like that very much.

I wasn't certain what I was looking for in Wernigerode. I hoped I might be able to track down some of the Gelb brothers' early work, the wardrobes and bureaux that had been their livelihood before they turned exclusively to the production of magical apparatus. Mainly, though, I wanted simply to be in the town, to walk the streets they had walked, to eat a meal at their favourite inn.

And I suppose if I am to be honest I have to admit also that I was looking for Claudia. I had the illogical conviction that if she were still to be found anywhere in this world it would be here. I imagined myself catching sight of her, a young woman now, crossing the square in front of the Rathaus or coming out of a bookshop on the Sperlingsallee. I would know her at once, by the mole on her cheek, her unaffected smile, her way of walking, shoulders drawn forward as if shielding her thoughts from outside intrusion. Mostly, though, I would know her because she was a part of me, and somehow I knew that bond would still be intact. I imagined it so clearly, that moment of first seeing her. The thing I could not imagine was what came next.

And of course it was nonsense anyway, because I did not find her. The town was just a small town in eastern Germany, wrapped up in its own affairs. Its only miraculous quality was that its picture-postcard prettiness seemed as untouched by the war as by the new political arrangements that followed in its wake. Surprisingly little had changed, although Adalbert Gelb's original smithy had become a car repair workshop, and Gisela Singer's tumbledown cottage had been demolished to make way for a hotel.

In an unlikely stroke of happenstance this turned out to be the hotel Gilda had booked us into. She had not said anything to me about the sleeping arrangements, and I had not asked, but I was gratified to discover on arrival that she had reserved just the one double room.

She was a tender and generous lover, and patient with my silences. She seemed content for us simply to be together, and displayed no overt anxiety about the future. I had told her about my book on the Gelb brothers, but not the reason I had initially been compelled to write it. I was afraid if I did she might think I was mad.

On our last evening together in Wernigerode I broke down in tears, confessing I'd had a daughter who had been abducted, many years ago before the war, and that she had never been heard of again.

"You must hope," Gilda said to me. We were in bed at the time. She stroked the hair back from my face and kissed my eyelids. "You must simply keep loving her, and never give up the hope that she is still alive."

My other friends and acquaintances had all, after what

they no doubt considered to be a suitable interval, advised me gently that I should try to forget, to move on with my life, all the usual things people say. Gilda's advice was so at odds with this, and so closely in accordance with my own feelings and desires, that I began in that moment to know I could love her as well as be content with her, that I would continue with the relationship in the face of all difficulties, with the eventual aim of bringing Gilda to live with me in the West.

She had arranged with the curator of the Schlossmuseum for a professional photographer to come to the museum and make some slides. The museum owned just three pieces by the Gelb brothers: a blanket chest, a gentleman's wardrobe, and a buffet sideboard. The last was a vast nightmare of a thing, its densely carved side panels depicting the Walpurgisnacht Witches' Sabbath in horrifying detail. I found the images unnervingly brutal, depictions of hell on earth as dark as anything I had seen in Bosch or Goya. It was difficult to imagine that the piece had ever found a welcome in someone's home.

Gilda seemed fascinated by it. "It's like a microcosm of Germany itself," she said. "A company of devils and madmen and plaster saints, all locked in a violent argument that never ends."

I thought it was an extraordinary image, and an apt one. I was still thinking about it when my train pulled out of the station the following day. As if the protracted border controls were not enough, my journey home was further complicated by having to change trains at Nordhausen, where the curious narrow-gauge railway that straddled the Harz came to an end. There were some signalling delays en route, which caused me to miss my connection. Rather than wait on the windy platform I decided to eat some lunch in the station buffet. The buffet had the atmosphere of a factory canteen, the customers crammed tightly together on wooden benches. Serving women in green checked overalls stood behind stainless steel troughs containing industrial quantities of goulash and pickled cabbage and fried potatoes. Huge tea urns puffed clouds of steam. I bought a ticket from the machine at the entrance then queued up to collect my food. I realised with some surprise that I was hungry. I found a place at one of the tables and began to eat. The tall plate-glass windows gave me a view of converging railway tracks and crumbling engine sheds, an overgrown siding banked with bramble and yarrow and blocked by the decaying corpse of an ancient piece of rolling stock that looked like it had been there since before the war. My neighbour, a man still young but with the sunken eyes and sallow skin that point to a lifetime of bad experiences, kept darting glances at me between mouthfuls.

"You're not from around here, are you?" he said at last.

"No I'm not." I wasn't sure what he meant, whether he was simply passing on his supposition that I was not native to Nordhausen, or whether he was trying to make some wider political point. He was wearing an old army greatcoat. As he reached for the hunk of bread on the side of his plate I was unable to help noticing that he had two fingers missing from his right hand.

"You're from the West. I can tell by your clothes."

I remained silent, not wanting to get involved in any discussion of our respective politics. The man hunched forward over his food, scraping every last remnant from the bowl and then wiping it clean with his bread as if he had not eaten a proper meal in some time. I assumed he must have fought in the war – he would have been the right age for it – but looking at his patched shoes and dirty hair I had the feeling that the battle was still being waged. Something was burning inside him, something private and deep.

"What do you do?" he said suddenly. His hollow cheeks were blotched with stubble, and his blue eyes blazed with a feverish brightness.

"I'm a writer," I said. "A literary biographer. I write books about other writers."

I thought this might shut him up, but instead it seemed to galvanise him. He gripped the tabletop with both hands, the taut veins bulging beneath his skin.

"Are you here to write about us?" he said.

I felt immediately alarmed. If this man were to accuse me of spying it could lead to all kinds of problems, not just for me but for Gilda.

"Not at all," I said hastily. "I'm researching nineteenth-century art."

He grabbed hold of my sleeve and drew me towards him. I caught the pungent reek of onions and sauerkraut, mixed with the fermented odour produced by bad teeth.

"What good is that?" he whispered. "You have to let people know what happened here."

His tangled blonde hair, pulled back from his face by an old bootlace, made me think of Hölderlin in his tower. I had argued in my book that Hölderlin's poems made sense of his madness, granted to the lunatic unravelling of his life a martyred magnificence. I wondered now if the man himself, day after day in his incapacity, might not have appeared to others as a pathetic nuisance.

I hated myself for these thoughts, but there they were.

"I'm not sure what you mean," I said to the man.

"I have their names. Their names are all I have, that's all I could save of them. I was a poet once, but I burned all my poems. I promised I wouldn't write again until I had passed on the names."

He felt for something under the bench, a filthy rucksack with one of its straps broken. He reached inside, dragging out a battered sheaf of papers.

"Here they are," he said. "You're a writer, so you'll know what to do."

I looked down at the topmost sheet. It was headed by a single line of type, executed on a machine that had evidently been missing its "e" and "m" keys: *Peter Knollhardt kitchen porter KZ Mittelbau-Dora 1944–45 his story.* Beneath the line of type was a list of names. The list ran for over five pages, and did not seem to be in any kind of discernible order, alphabetical or otherwise. The names were mostly Polish and Russian, but I noticed some French names among them and some German. The list began with Guillaume Depierre and ended with Michael Halkin. It occurred to me I had known a Halkin at school in Potsdam, but his name had been Dieter, not Michael.

"I talked to them," he said. I supposed he must be Peter Knollhardt. "We weren't supposed to, but I did. I asked them their names. It was all I could do." He moved his fingers across the paper. Dirty marks on the once-white surface suggested the gesture was habitual. I studied the names in silence, repeating them in my mind and thinking that names, even when spoken in isolation, had a rare kind of poetry all to themselves.

"Are you telling me there was a camp here? Is that it?" I found the word "camp" hurt my throat, seeming to catch in my gullet like a rusty fish hook. Beyond the simple practical problems of how we might meet, Gilda and I had not discussed politics. I hadn't told her where I spent the war nor had she asked. I guessed this was something our generation might never be able to talk about, not properly. It would be for those that came after us to try and make sense of things.

Instantly I thought of Claudia, and became filled with the ridiculous notion that if I did whatever it was that Knollhardt asked of me then she might be found.

"Yes, there was a camp," Knollhardt said. "It was less than a mile from this town. All you need to do is follow the track." He pointed through the window, down towards the railway lines. He spoke slowly, haltingly, as if the act of handing over the names had drained all other sentience from his mind.

"And you worked at this camp?" I said.

Knollhardt nodded. "I was in prison for forging a passport. I was better off than the Jews and Russians, though not by much. It was my job to distribute the food. The food in that place was terrible, not fit for pigs."

We sat in silence for some moments. It had the same pregnant quality, the same wakefulness as the silence I had experienced once, long ago and far away, in the wake of a minor earthquake that had struck our resort during a boyhood holiday in Turkey.

"Could you take me there? To where the camp was?" I said at last.

"I'll never go back. But I can show you the way."

I got to my feet. I hardly knew what I was doing, only that I meant to keep faith with this man, Peter Knollhardt, and his story. I wondered how long he had waited, hanging around the station canteen in the hope of waylaying someone, some Westerner, who would be willing to carry his list of names across the border. I supposed he had been waiting since the war. There would not be many tourists in a place like this, the dingy little town of Nordhausen, dominated as it was by the Korn brewery and the railway terminus. All at once even the railway terminus seemed sinister, darker than it should be, like something conjured from the Gelb brothers' fiendish imagination.

Even those who came to Nordhausen willingly, on business or to visit relatives, would be bound to shy away from a man like Knollhardt, with his list of names and his missing fingers and his smelly breath.

At least I didn't do that, I thought. *At least I listened.*

We left the station by the front entrance and walked along the tracks for about a kilometre. When we came to a small level crossing Peter Knollhardt came to a standstill, resting his backpack beside him on the dusty ground.

"You cross the lines here," he said. "Just keep heading north. It's not far."

He touched my shoulder and tried to kiss me on the cheek but I drew back, shying away from the contact. I was afraid he might have lice. He stood with his head bowed, as if considering, then thrust his wad of papers into my hands.

"Take them with you," he said. "Get them away from here."

I slipped the papers inside my jacket then stood in silence, not knowing what to say. Knollhardt extended his hand, the left one, the one with all its fingers still intact. I took it for one brief moment then walked away, following the narrow pathway that skirted the trees. After a hundred metres or so I looked back. Knollhardt was still standing there, his knapsack slung over his shoulder from its single strap. When he saw me looking he waved. I waved back and then went on. The next time I turned to look for him he was gone.

I could see the foothills of the Harz in the distance, the gentle slopes mottled with pallid sunlight. Closer to Nordhausen the land was flatter and bleaker, a featureless hinterland of gravel tracks and marshy fields. I followed the path for what seemed like a long time, apparently going nowhere. I had just started to wonder if any of it was real, if Knollhardt had been making a fool of me, when suddenly and without warning I came to the boundary of what had once been the Nordhausen concentration camp.

The original wire fencing was still in place, but it was no longer electrified and had been breached in a dozen places. Beyond the wire was grass, yellowish and unkempt. The grass was crisscrossed at intervals by rutted tracks, partially obscured by nettles and flanked by loose mounds of builders' rubble. Flints glimmered in the exposed earth. A macadam strip, what had been the camp's main thoroughfare, divided the ground in two from east to west. Narrower roadways ran off it, capillaries to the main artery. Huddled against the horizon were a group of brick buildings, derelict and blackened by fire.

The sense of desolation was all-pervasive, sucking at the heart and mind like a cosmic leech. I had known the feeling before, but only in nightmares. I was not surprised that Peter Knollhardt had found himself unable to return there.

I looked down at his papers with their list of names. I guessed there were about two hundred names in all, a sizeable number, although I knew even then that they must be only a tiny percentage of the men who had been imprisoned here. A part of me was tempted to let them go, to relax my fingers and allow the next gust of wind to whip the papers away, but a deeper instinct told me I should hold on, that the men were my comrades now, and like it or not I was responsible for their safe passage.

I sensed that Claudia was nearby, that she applauded my decision. The feeling comforted me, there in that place, even though I knew it was just wishful thinking.

I hunched my shoulders against the wind and walked back to the station. I supposed the people of the town all knew about the camp, although there would be few of them anxious to discuss it. I wondered about Peter Knollhardt, where he had come from originally. I imagined the war had picked him up like a piece of flotsam, ripping him out of his old life and depositing him in Nordhausen with as little care as it had washed me ashore in Friedrichshafen. It was only later I discovered that the lines of force which drew us together were perhaps stronger than I had thought, and that the places we had ended up in shared a similar history.

Friedrichshafen, a moderately sized town on the north shore of Lake Constance, had been the birthplace of the Graf Zeppelin. The Mittelbau-Dora labour camp at Nordhausen, one of the many "suburbs" of Buchenwald, had been where Wernher von Braun had perfected his design for the V2, the rockets launched against London. Thousands of men had died at the Mittelbau camp. The work on the rockets was carried out within a network of tunnels, the longest of them stretching for over a mile. The men had been confined underground for months at a time. Many never saw daylight again.

Via a series of circuitous leads I also discovered that one of the administrators at Nordhausen, a captain in the SS named Martin Foerster, had been transferred there when his previous posting at Rostock had suddenly been made redundant by Allied bombs. He had not worked at the camp itself, but in the town. He had given several organ recitals in the Nikolaikirche.

Foerster fled the American advance with just days to spare. The things he left behind were distributed among the foreign journalists and the top brass of the invading army. Among them were a modest stash of gold Austrian thalers, a small watercolour sketch by Lovis Corinth, and an antique writing desk of an unusual and rare design. Someone had seen fit to photograph the writing desk, most likely because of its elaborate carvings. From the photograph I was able to identify it at once as the work of the Gelb brothers.

I wondered if these were the tales we would tell ourselves now, that instead of the witches and werewolves of the Brocken our collective dreams would for ever be filled with escaped war criminals, the blood spilled on factory floors, and a nightmare of endless tunnelling. I felt Foerster's ownership of the desk as something obscene, and for some weeks and months after my return from Wernigerode I even considered abandoning my book on the Gelb brothers. I felt their work was dangerous, an embodiment of a deeper darkness, of the heresy and thwarted idealism that seemed to run like a strand of barbed wire through the richly shimmering fabric of German art. I had never been blind to that madness. I had spent the greater part of my career defending it. Only now we had seen what happened when it ran out of control.

When the photographs arrived from the Schlossmuseum I felt tempted to destroy them. The pictures of the sideboard in particular disturbed me. It seemed to me they might be contaminated.

"You sound tired," Gilda said, when I spoke to her that evening on the phone. A week later I fell ill with my first bout of pneumonia.

I recovered, and once I was better I went on with the book. Each time I visited a library or a bookshop in the course of my research I kept an eye out for the work of Peter Knollhardt. Three years after my visit to Nordhausen my patience was rewarded. On the counter of one of the more radical bookshops in West Berlin I spotted a small, stapled-together pamphlet of poems entitled *Harz-Songs*. Peter Knollhardt's name was on the cover.

"We don't have many copies," said the bookstore's proprietor. "Because they're privately printed. But he is making a name for himself."

I supposed that "privately printed" was the coy West German way of saying the pamphlets were samizdat, illegal. I bought a pamphlet and went to read it in a nearby café. The poems were stark, simple lyrics, mostly based around everyday objects: newspapers and shop windows, a kitchen table bathed in sunshine, a pair of boots. Several of the poems, about horses, seemed to contain veiled allusions to the war and its aftermath. Two or three dealt with the poet's relationship with a young girl with fair hair and brown eyes. In some of the poems the girl was spoken of as if she were dead, but in another, the final poem in the sequence, Peter Knollhardt had written about the girl in the present tense, as if he expected to see her again at any moment.

• • •

By the time I finished reading Thomas's letter it was growing dark. I switched on the bedside lamp then stood up to close the curtains. The park across the road was empty and silent. I leaned on the windowsill and looked out towards the lake. It lay like a sheeted mirror, shrouded in dusk. I felt badly in need of a drink. I took the water glass from the night stand and poured myself a generous measure of the single malt I happened to purchase at the airport. I had bought it with the idea of sharing it with Thomas – he had always been a whisky lover – but I thought that under the circumstances he would not mind me opening the bottle without him.

The letter had shaken me deeply. I now understood that the sinister encampment I had glimpsed on the other side of the mirror maze had been an evocation or recreation – or to be more exact a *pre*-creation – of the labour camp that later existed at Nordhausen. The camp had been in the town's future already, the particles of its potential existence first pricking the time-fabric then massing and spreading, coalescing around reality like the mould spores on a slice of week-old bread.

The *Palast* had been the gateway. The Gelb brothers had formed few personal attachments in their strange lives, but they had loved their native soil with unyielding passion. The outlet for that passion had been their work, their carvings and cabinets the most perfect expression of a sense of place that was at first extraordinary, but had finally become monstrous. This had been the true nature of their genius. I wondered how many others had stumbled upon it unawares.

But what of Claudia? Thomas had sensed her presence in that place, and Peter Knollhardt had written poems about her. The barren camp ground on the outskirts of Nordhausen no doubt seethed with ghosts. Claudia was part-Jewish, the child of a dissident and perhaps both Thomas and Knollhardt had imagined the worst. But I had reason to believe she was still alive.

I rejoiced at the end of the war, like everyone else, but as peace tightened its hold it came to seem more and more like an anticlimax. It is strange how war grants life a purpose. There is always some new headline, some new outrage. Even if one's only involvement in a war consists in disapproving of it there is still an impetus, a vigour, a sharpness and intensity of experience that all too often gets leached away from a life lived during peacetime.

I took up my trade again, taking out a lease on a small shop in Battersea. I had lost touch with most of my clients during the war years, but soon they returned, even bringing new ones with them. Within a year or two I was more than breaking even. I began to travel abroad again, and it was during one of these trips that I met the woman I almost married, an English teacher by the name of Rowena Browne. She was holidaying in Pisa, where I was attending a book fair. We were attracted to one another immediately. The relationship soon deepened, and at the end of a year I was nerving myself up to propose when Rowena dropped her bombshell: she had recently received a letter from her older brother, asking her to go and join him in Australia.

"He says the opportunities out there are fantastic," she told me. "They're desperate for teachers, apparently. I'd be earning three times what I'm being paid here."

I told her she should go. I could see the hurt in her eyes, and I have no doubt that if I had asked her then and there to marry me she would have agreed, even if it meant staying in London. But after only a moment's hesitation and a muted sense of regret I saw the brother's letter as a godsend, an opportunity for immediate and painless release from a situation I had unconsciously been wanting to escape.

I had the sense of having crossed a great gulf, only now I had reached the other side there was nowhere to go. The other life – the old life before the war – felt like my real life. What

I had now seemed dull and two-dimensional by comparison. Everything had changed around me, only I had stayed the same. I knew I was looking for something but the thing itself eluded me. I could never have guessed that she would eventually find me.

It was a Friday evening in late October, and I had been visiting an exhibition of Dutch still life paintings at the Royal Academy. The day was overcast, chilly with the foretaste of winter. By the time I emerged on to Piccadilly it had started to rain. I took shelter in the entrance to the Burlington Arcade, watching the traffic roll by while I waited for the rain to ease off. The light was almost gone, the sky a bruised purple, the pavements shone bright as mirrors beneath their varnish of rain. A flotilla of taxis, shiny as seals, cruised slowly down the thoroughfare towards Green Park. Damp commuters, made headless under black umbrellas, swarmed towards glowing red buses.

I seemed to feel the city breathing her long, juddering exhale, the faint snoring of an ageing noblewoman, ravaged now, her joints arthritic, her tired flesh reeking of talcum, the broderie anglaise that trimmed the cuffs of her nightgown soiled with food stains that would no longer wash out. She dreamed of her youth, that faded glitter, a bubble of saliva bursting on her lower lip. Her violet eyes, still magnetic, scuttled to and fro under wrinkled lids.

She turned over in her sleep, white hair banked upon the pillows. My heart contracted in my chest. Tears sprang from the corners of my eyes. It was as if for those few moments I had sensed the world turning. I felt heady with anticipation.

A taxi drew up at the kerb. The door opened and a woman stepped out. She was wearing a fur coat, a blue-grey chinchilla. There was a stiff breeze blowing but the coat still looked incongruous in the London drizzle, suited to a much harsher climate.

The woman had no umbrella. She looked both ways along the street, as if uncertain of where she was. She glanced back in the direction of the taxi but it was already gone. The rain continued to fall, drenching the high plush collar of the lovely chinchilla coat. The hurrying commuters jostled her, pushing her from one side of the pavement to the other. Strands of her straw-coloured hair clung wetly to the nape of her neck.

I stepped forward, opening my umbrella. The woman turned, sensing my approach, her lips parted in surprise. She had strong, almost masculine features, the fair hair making a striking contrast with her deep-set brown eyes. High on her right cheek was a small white scar, perfectly round, the ghost of a full stop. I knew, immediately and without any doubt, that I was looking at Claudia Emmerich.

"Do I know you, sir?" she said. She spoke English perfectly, with no hint of a German accent.

"No, madam," I replied. "But you looked as if you needed some assistance."

"This is my first time in the city." She seemed to hesitate, as if grasping for memories that eluded her. "My father had a friend from London, but I do not know what became of him."

"Is there anywhere I can take you?" I said.

"The Ritz Hotel," she said at once. "I am supposed to meet my husband there. He said it would be easy to find." She looked down at herself, laughing softly as if she had only just realised the indignity of her predicament. She was standing in a rain puddle. Her smart black boots were already soaking wet.

"It *is* easy to find," I said, laughing also. "It's just across the street. You were almost there."

I took her arm and began steering her along the pavement towards the traffic lights by Green Park Underground. The rain had become less insistent, but I kept the umbrella open, liking the way it forced us to stick close together. The word "husband" echoed inside my head as I walked along. I realised I was jealous of this husband, whoever he was. I had believed the capacity for such emotion had long since died in me. I was amazed and slightly amused to find I was wrong.

We came to the Ritz, too quickly. A liveried porter stepped forward as we came inside.

"This is Mrs—" I began, breaking off almost at once. I could not say *Emmerich*. It was, after all, no longer her name.

"Mrs Kleinfuhrt," said Claudia. "I am meeting my husband here."

Another doorman came gliding forward. He glanced at me suspiciously, as if I had wormed my way in under false pretences. "Mrs Kleinfuhrt," he said obsequiously. "We've been expecting you. Your husband has been delayed. We've reserved a place for you in the tea lounge until he arrives."

She looked momentarily at a loss, then all at once she brightened again. I thought how curiously naked her face still was, the emotions passing across it like clouds passing across the face of the sun. She was still the same intense, precocious child.

"Would you stay with me?" she said. She snatched at my hand and then quickly let it go again, as if afraid she might have transgressed some social code. "Have some tea with me, please. It would be nice not to be alone. Travelling is often so tiring, especially in winter."

I felt my heart leap with delight. "I would love to," I said. "It would be a pleasure."

The porter took our coats, looking daggers at me all the while. Beneath her furs Claudia was wearing a plain grey travelling dress in finely woven tweed. It was simple, but so well-fitting and elegant I knew it would have been expensive. This Kleinfuhrt was doing well, then. I felt jealous all over again. I had not been for tea at the Ritz since my days with Rowena. When the trolley was wheeled over Claudia clapped her hands in delight.

"So English!" she said. "My husband never stops telling me about these English teas. He was in London for a while, before the war, though he was only a child at the time."

"What does he do?" I asked. "Your husband?"

"He is a diplomat," she said. "An envoy." She said the name of a place I had never heard of, a jumble of harsh diphthongs and spiky consonants. I presumed it was one of the new Balkan republics, the peripheral post-war nations whose boundaries were still being established.

"Do you like the life?" I asked her. "I've always thought it must be unsettling, being on the move all the time."

She frowned, reminding me for just an instant of Hermine. "Actually I don't mind that. In many ways I like it. I enjoy seeing different places. In any case, I am used to travelling.

My parents died during the war, so I was moved around quite a lot."

I drew in my breath. I longed to ask her questions, to discover what she believed to be the truth about herself, but some deeper instinct warned me this might be dangerous.

"Shall I be mother?" she said. She poured the tea. The teapot was white porcelain, scattered with flowers. "Isn't this beautiful?" she said. "It reminds me of the house I grew up in."

She looked down at her plate and I wondered which house she was remembering, the graceful villa with the tall windows and sun-speckled lawns overlooking the sea at Heiligendamm, or some other place, a place I did not know and most likely never would.

"I don't even know your name," I said suddenly.

She darted me a glance, her eyebrows raised, questioning, just the trace of a smile on her lips. For the first time since we came together in the street she seemed completely aware, not just a charming and unusual woman but an intricate and acute intelligence. I knew then that she *knew*, that she was playing the same game I was, that she might even have come to London looking for me.

I knew I would lose her again, and soon. Claudia and I had been allowed to glimpse each other, like two passengers on trains that had stopped by chance at the same station on opposite platforms, but soon those trains would go their separate ways. I raised my hand to silence her, meaning to make some light-hearted joke about preferring the identity of my lady friends to remain a mystery, but as it happened there was no need. The damned porter appeared again, bearing a folded sheet of notepaper on a silver tray. He gave a stiff little bow, presenting the note to Claudia and somehow conspiring to smirk at me as he did so. I felt like kicking him.

"My husband has just arrived in reception," Claudia exclaimed, folding the note in two again and secreting it in her handbag. "You must come and meet him. You could have dinner with us. Please say you will?"

"I wouldn't dream of it," I said at once. I got to my feet, almost knocking over my chair. "You've had a long and tiring day, and you want to be alone with Herr Kleinfuhrt. I couldn't possibly intrude. But thank you for a most delightful tea."

I had no wish to meet this man, this Kleinfuhrt she had married. I wanted him to remain as he was, a name on a sheet of paper, the eternally awaited Godot who never actually enters upon the stage.

As for Claudia, it was enough simply to know she was alive, and happy. I knew I would not see her again.

"You are a very kind man," she said. "Very – knowing." She extended her hand to me, and I took it. She was wearing three rings: a gold band and a clump of diamonds I presumed were Kleinfuhrt's, and one other, a piece of Baltic amber set in gold. The ring I had once given to Hermine.

I brushed her fingers with my lips and said goodbye. I left by the side entrance, taking a short cut across Green Park. It had stopped raining, but the night air felt bitter and raw. I was halfway to Victoria before I realised I had forgotten my coat, that I had left it behind at the hotel. I cursed and flagged down a taxi to take me home. The next day I began my search for Thomas.

• • •

I poured myself another scotch, then began to read Thomas's letter again from the beginning. The next day I would return to the hospital and we would talk. I did not know, exactly, what I meant to tell him. Mainly that I had seen his daughter and she was safe. I hoped he would be able to believe me. I hoped also that the news might help him get well again. As for myself, I felt like I needed a holiday. If Thomas's health improved I could suggest we went hiking together in the Harz Mountains. As bait I had Heinrich Heine, who had journeyed through those same mountains as a youth. From what I had read it seemed he had spent as much time brawling in the local taverns as writing poetry. I knew Thomas would love that story. He was invariably excited by such things.

LABURNUMS

Christine tried to ignore Amma at first but she kept coming back. So long as she remained at a distance, hovering on street corners and in shop doorways, Christine could at least pretend to herself she had been mistaken. Seeing her up there on the cinema screen was somehow much worse. There could no longer be any doubt it was her.

The film was called *The Comet*. It was Richard Twycross who insisted they see it, who had chosen it as that week's selection for what he liked to refer to as their "film club outing". Richard was the chief design editor on the kitchens magazine where Christine worked as a copy editor, and with whom she had been briefly involved two years before. He fancied himself as a bit of a film buff. He seemed more than usually excited about *The Comet*.

"The print was lost for ages, years and years," he enthused. "It normally only gets shown at festivals. Goodness knows how the Electric got hold of it."

The film was the story of two female trapeze artists, one an American who had dropped out of high school, the other a Russian who defected from the Moscow State Circus and was known as the Comet. The two women were deadly rivals, each intent on outshining the other. The rivalry gradually escalated, beginning with minor acts of petty sabotage but culminating in a chain of events that ended with a circus fire. As the big top blazed against the night sky, the Comet fell from a ladder and broke her back. She was rushed to hospital but died soon afterwards. When the American learned the Russian had not survived her injuries she committed suicide, hurling herself sixty feet from the road bridge spanning the river beyond the town.

The actress playing the American had the statuesque, alabaster looks of a young Diana Dors. The girl playing the Russian was small and dark, the ghostly double of Christine's old school friend Annemarie Kovacs.

As they trooped out of the cinema at the end of the film Richard was loudly protesting that it was the wrong movie, a film of the same name perhaps but not the one he had been thinking of at all. The others appeared not to care – they had enjoyed the film anyway.

"At least it had a plot," said Piers Corswell, who worked with Richard on layout. "Unlike most of the arthouse bollocks you foist on us." He laughed his booming laugh. *Foist* was a very Piers word.

"You could have warned me, Richard," said Rachel Evans. Rachel was head of advertising. "I'm terrified of heights. I had to keep looking away."

"It was the wrong film, I've already told you. I've never seen it before in my life." Richard sounded impatient. Christine knew he didn't like Rachel. Because she was shallow, Richard maintained, but Christine suspected it was because he had once asked Rachel out and she turned him down. She listened to them bickering, but distantly, as if the conversation was going on in another room. She was still unable to believe what she had seen. When Richard asked if she was coming to the pub with them she started as if he had struck her.

"Not tonight," she said. "There's some work I need to finish." She walked with them as far as the Landseer then turned left into Lancaster Road, walking home the long way down Ladbroke Grove. She loved the Grove, the raddled tenements at the Kensal Green end, the tall white villas at the Notting Hill end, graceful as ocean liners, gliding sedately down the hill towards Holland Park. Christine had always thought of the Grove as London's spine.

Buses sped both ways along Notting Hill Gate. Christine waited at the lights then crossed the road. She wondered briefly if she should call in at the supermarket then decided against it. There was some leftover goulash in the fridge – that would have to do.

When she got home she fixed the supper, then left her mother watching *Newsnight* and went upstairs. The poem she was working on was called 'Laburnums', an extended drama in four parts that described a woman returning to the city after a long absence. She had imagined it as a blank verse epic about the goddess Persephone and her love for the old man, Hades, though Christine supposed that really it was about herself and Matthew Cleverly. She went to bed late, long after the midnight news. She lay awake in the darkness for some time, listening to the radio and wondering why she had started seeing Amma everywhere all of a sudden.

• • •

The next day was a Saturday. She ate breakfast at the Greek café she liked off Pembridge Road then walked along to the North Kensington Library on Ladbroke Grove. The reading room was quiet but never oppressive, and now that her mother no longer went out Christine preferred to work away from the house as much as possible. She spent the morning going over the first canto, which had Persephone emerging from the underground station at Kensal Green. Persephone's name in the poem was Penny Parker, a woman approaching middle age, slightly overweight, wearing a tatty old herringbone coat that was missing its belt.

Christine had shown some of the poem to Matthew. Not much, just the good parts, the sections that seemed most complete. The fear that he would find her work naïve, immature, lacking in some way was something that haunted her constantly. He would sometimes suggest minor corrections, but she was never able to draw much from him in the way of more general criticism. He had once compared her love of poems that told stories with the narrative sequences of Horace and Virgil, but Christine could not work out if he liked what she was doing, or if he thought her work was derivative and old fashioned. His own poems were densely allegorical. The *TLS* had hailed him as the true successor to Eliot, but another critic had likened reading him to stumbling into a copse of blackthorns ringed with barbed wire.

Matthew Cleverly was not widely read. The only book of his that had enjoyed a measure of popular success was *The High Wire and Other Transgressions*, the cycle of poems about the life of the film actress Ruby Castle, who was serving a life sentence for murder. Matthew had famously visited Ruby Castle in prison over a number of months, though *The High Wire* did not appear until ten years afterwards. The poems in *High Wire* were looser in structure than much of Matthew's other work, and in spite of their violent imagery they were more approachable, or so a lot of people seemed to think. Most commentators believed Matthew had been in love with Ruby Castle, that it was his obsession with her that ended his brief second marriage. Christine had never asked Matthew about Ruby. She liked to think his interest in her had been abstract, platonic, a concern for the rights and wrongs of her incarceration, though she knew also that Ruby was beautiful, and supposed she was being naïve.

Matthew Cleverly was eighty years old now and suffering from Parkinson's. He used a wheelchair most of the time. Christine knew she loved him, but was uncertain of what that might mean in practical terms. He had come into her life ten years before, when she sent him a fan letter care of his publisher. To her amazement, Matthew had replied, eventually inviting her to stay with him at his home in West Mersea. Christine tried not to think too much about the difference in their ages, but as Matthew grew older the forty years that separated them inevitably began to take on a harsher reality. She was shocked now by the extent of his infirmity. She still thought of him as the robust sixty-year-old who had written *The High Wire*.

His output had slowed since then, although the poems that did appear were as fine as anything he had written when he was younger. She was constantly amazed at his insights, though when he likened her own poetry to the Roman epics she felt something close to dismay. She had always avoided talking to him about her own past, and so he could not know that she had been familiar with whole swathes of Catullus and Ovid before she knew that Auden and Eliot and Lowell even existed. She remembered how shocked she had been when she discovered that not all poetry had originally been written in Latin. Christine sensed it was still a disappointment to her mother that she had eventually come to prefer her own language, even for reading the classics. She liked Emily Wilson's translations best, the rattling street rhythms that made Homer sound like Kerouac or Bukowski. Christine's mother thought they were coarse, but that only made Christine admire them even more.

Matthew knew her mother had been a teacher, but that was all. Christine left Rose out of her letters as much as she could.

At twelve-thirty she broke for lunch. On her way out of the library she saw Amma standing in line at the reception desk waiting to have some books stamped. She was wearing a hat with purple feathers around the brim and patent leather knee-high boots with very high heels. The clothes were very Amma-ish, the kind of flamboyant garments Amma had always lusted after and that she was forbidden to wear. Amma once told Christine about how her father went into her room once when she was at school and measured the heels of all her shoes with the retractable steel tape measure he used for work. Any that were over an inch went straight in the bin.

Amma stood with her back turned, a small stack of books piled in front of her on the wooden countertop. She had never been what Rose would call a serious reader, but she had a greedy appetite for books nonetheless, horror stories and crime thrillers mostly, the kind of novels Rose poured scorn on at every opportunity.

Christine edged towards the doors, desperate to get away without Amma noticing her. She was not frightened, exactly, just uncertain of what might happen. Amma's was the first ghost she had encountered and she wasn't sure what the rules were.

"Do you believe in ghosts?" she had once asked Matthew in one of her letters. "Have you ever seen one?" He replied that he had never seen a ghost as such though he had often sensed their presence, so he supposed he must believe in them to an extent. In typically Matthew fashion, he did not ask her why she had asked. She supposed he knew she would tell him when she was ready.

She decided to go home for lunch. The radio was on in the kitchen, tuned to a musical quiz programme that Rose and Christine sometimes listened to together. Rose was in her sitting room, her writing table strewn with the notes and the half-finished draft of the essay she was writing for the St Margaret's quarterly magazine. St Margaret's was the girls' grammar school in Holland Park where Rose had taught Latin and Roman History for twenty years. The only ties she had with the school now were these quarterly essays. She worked on them for most of the year in a continuous round, furious diatribes against the demise of Latin as a classroom subject or reminiscences of her time at Magdalen that seemed to Christine like confused dispatches from another age. She wondered how many people actually read them.

"Did you remember to pick up a loaf?" Rose asked. "We're almost out."

"There's enough for lunch. I'll pop into Waitrose and get some fresh on my way home this evening."

"You're going out again, then?"

"Just for a couple of hours." Quite suddenly Christine felt very tired. She looked around at Rose's sitting room, at the Coalport cream jug and the Minton beggar maid in the window niche, the beaded footstool with its neat stack of the current week's newspapers, the framed reproduction of Jan Mijtens' *The Lute Player* over the fireplace, things that originated not from Rose's brief time with Christine's father in Camden, but from her parents' home just outside Oxford. People had often remarked on how much the woman in the Mijtens painting looked like Rose herself, and Christine had no doubt that this was why Rose was so fond of it.

I'm so tired of these things, Christine thought. *I can hardly bear to look at them any more.*

They had lunch in the kitchen. Christine heated some soup – asparagus – which they ate with the remains of the bread. The flat felt airless and overheated. Rose complained constantly of feeling cold, most likely because she went out so rarely. Christine remembered the many Sundays and school holidays throughout her childhood when Rose had taken her to exhibitions and museums and parks all over London. She had been an energetic walker and Christine often had to run to keep up with her. Then, not long after her retirement, Rose had been mugged on her way home from a concert. She seemed to make light of it at the time, though the months following saw dramatic changes in her behaviour. She started refusing to leave the house unless Christine went with her. She lost a lot of weight very quickly, acquiring a hollow-boned, bird-like frailty. Her eyes became feral and evasive, like the eyes of the bag ladies Christine had seen dumpster diving round the back of Pizza Express.

At home, her horn-rimmed glasses on a chain around her neck, her thin fingers grasping the onyx barrel of the antique Parker pen she always wrote with, Rose still had the air of a latter-day Hypatia. Her former pupils came to visit her sometimes, Judiths and Joannas in their twenties and early thirties who now worked as arts administrators or conference organisers. They presented Rose with leather-bound editions of *The Odyssey* and chattered away insatiably about the old days.

Christine had never been one of them. In spite of the reduction offered to teachers they had been unable to afford the fees for St Margaret's, and Christine had attended one of the North Kensington comprehensives, a fact Rose had always regretted at copious length.

"That friend of yours rang," Rose said. She smeared butter on a piece of bread with the end of her knife. "That man."

Christine felt her muscles tense. "What man? Do you mean Richard?" Rose had met Richard Twycross, just once – Christine brought him back for coffee after they'd been to a film at the Coronet. Rose and Richard had been so uninterested in one another that Christine could not now remember what they had talked about.

“Not him. Do you still see him? I mean that old man you write to in Essex.”

“I work with Richard, Mum, of course I still see him. Did Matthew say what he wanted?”

She tried to keep her tone light, not wanting to betray her emotions, but she felt her anxiety rising, her breath tight against the roof of her mouth. She wondered why Matthew had called the house number and not her mobile, then remembered her mobile had been switched off all morning. If she left it on while she was in the library there was always the danger that Rose would call, demanding to know when she’d be home.

“He didn’t want anything. Just asked if you were there and when I said no he said goodbye and put the phone down. You never said he had a stammer. I could barely make out what he was on about.”

“He doesn’t have a stammer, Mum, he has Parkinson’s. I told you.”

“Oh.” Rose cut her bread into three diagonal slices then picked up the middle piece and began to eat it. She still looked like the Mijtens girl, even now her hair was grey and her cheeks had hollowed out. Christine remembered Rose once telling her that she had left Christine’s father the same night she discovered he was no good. Looking at her steep forehead and upright posture Christine found herself believing it, although why her father had been no good she had never discovered. As a child she had longed to know about him, but had never dared ask. Now she was older, she had a horror of revealing herself that was hard to shake off. Rose had a way of making everything she did seem small and futile. Some years ago, before Rose's agoraphobia had become fully entrenched, Christine had given her a book of Matthew's poems, though so far as Christine knew she had never read it. Rose had no interest in modern poetry. The subject, like so many others, had become a silence between them.

"If it's important I'm sure he'll call back," Rose said. She cleaned her knife on the last of her bread and then laid it aside. The radio had moved on from the music quiz and was now playing Chopin mazurkas. Christine felt goose bumps rise up on her arms. The first time she heard Chopin had been at Amma's. Amma's mother Beatrice had loved Chopin. She used to play piano records in the apartment almost incessantly, the way Rose now played the radio.

Before returning to the library Christine took a detour via the telephone box on Campden Hill Road. It was unusual for Matthew to call out of the blue. The phone was difficult for him because his hearing was going – he hated having to ask her to constantly repeat herself. That was why they still communicated mostly by letter. The phone box on Campden Hill Road was one of the old ones, well insulated against street noise and with clearer reception than she usually got on her mobile. She dialled Matthew's number and waited. She knew that if Matthew was in another part of the house it would take him some time to answer, but in the end the line cut out with no reply. He must have gone out, Christine supposed. There was a woman who lived nearby, Elaine Riley, who often took Matthew for a walk along the seafront in his chair. The thought of Elaine Riley made Christine feel tense again, though she knew this was foolish. Elaine Riley was a nurse – it was ridiculous to be jealous of her. She supposed she should feel grateful. At least Matthew was getting some fresh air. His health was always worse in winter, because of the damp.

She replaced the receiver in its cradle. On her way back up Ladbroke Grove she stopped outside one of the junk shops near the Westway flyover, looking for some small keepsake or curiosity she could send to Matthew. She flicked through the box of old postcards on the rickety camping table at the store's entrance, in the end buying just the one, a faded black-and-white snapshot of a girl on a beach. In the background of the photo there were beach huts and plastic buckets, a woman asleep in a deckchair. The girl was skinny with a mop of dark curls. She reminded her of Amma.

It was Amma's father who had loved the seaside.

"He never saw the sea until he was eighteen," Amma had told her. "Now he's constantly bundling us off on day trips to Eastbourne or Brighton." Christine had gone with them once. She remembered Gregor Kovacs running down the beach in his swimming trunks with Amma standing upright on his shoulders. His hard hands gripped her ankles, the veins bulging like tightened ropes beneath his skin. Amma spread her arms wide like aeroplane wings, screaming with laughter. Later in the afternoon Amma stripped herself naked and dashed into the waves. Her father dragged her out of the water and hit her twice around the head, hard enough to knock her off her feet.

"Teach yourself some modesty or you'll end up a whore." He turned his back on the sea and cracked open a beer.

"I hate him," Amma said to Christine, later. They were on their way back to the station. The pavements were still hot enough to burn their feet, the hotels along the seafront glittering the hard, pristine whiteness of some unreachable dream-city. "If I could kill him and get away with it I would."

"You don't mean that," Christine said.

"Yes I do. You'd feel the same if you had to live with him. You don't know what it's like."

Slipping the photograph into her bag, Christine wondered again why Amma had started appearing to her all of a sudden. In Amma's horror novels, the dead came back to avenge themselves on the living, but Christine couldn't imagine Amma wanting revenge, at least not on her. Perhaps she was trying to tell her something. She remembered the first time it had happened, at the supermarket about three weeks ago, when she had suddenly noticed Amma standing in front of her in the checkout queue. Christine had dismissed the incident, mainly because her mind had been elsewhere. Earlier that afternoon she had received an email from Emily Baxter at Nova Press, telling her that Nova wanted to publish a collection of Christine's poems.

In the years since her mother's illness, Christine had often wondered if it was possible to take a wrong turning and end up living a life that was not your own. Standing in the supermarket queue with her pasta and her Stilton and her packet of bean sprouts, Christine dared to wonder if by some miraculous turn of fate she had managed to find her way back again. Amma had turned towards her then, just briefly, and Christine had caught a glimpse of her familiar profile, the sharp, straight nose, the long lashes loaded with kohl. There was nothing in Amma's basket but a jar of coffee.

• • •

The day after she'd first seen Amma, Christine stayed late at work. She wanted to draft an email to Emily Baxter without having to listen to Rose moving around in the room below. She told the others it was because she wanted to put the finishing touches to next month's lead article on Philippe Starck.

"Are you sure you're OK, Chris?" asked Rachel Evans. "You look tired."

Christine smiled. She felt grateful for Rachel's concern. Rachel was nice, sympathetic. Christine thought she would probably even have believed her about the ghost.

"I'm fine," she said. "It's just these dark evenings, you know? I always hate it when the clocks go back."

"I know what you mean," Rachel said. "I'm the same." She smiled back at her and said goodnight. Christine waited until she heard the bottom door slam shut then logged on to her emails. She had already acknowledged Emily Baxter's original email, expressing her delight that Nova wanted to publish her work. Now she wanted to give Emily more details of her current project. She wrote her an outline of 'Laburnums' and suggested that if Nova were willing to wait until it was finished, the poem could form the centrepiece of the collection.

When Christine read the email through it struck her as tentative, almost apologetic in tone. She went over it again, replacing some of the might haves and perhapses with would likes and shoulds. She was on the point of pressing send when her mobile rang. Christine sighed, certain it would be Rose demanding to know why she was late, but when she glanced at the incoming call sign she saw it was Matthew.

She picked up at once.

"Are you all right?" she said. "I tried to call you back on Saturday but you were out."

"Don't worry," he said. "Your letter arrived this morning." The line was heavy with noise, crackles and gasps, though Christine could not tell if this was the sound of Matthew's breathing or static interference.

"With the photograph?" she said. "Did you like it?"

"I liked it very much. You should write about it."

"Do you think so? I will, then. I did wonder about it." She sensed he was straining to catch her words. "Do you want me to call you back on the landline? I'm here by myself in the office, so it's nice and quiet."

"No, Chrissie, please don't trouble yourself, you'll need to get home. I wanted to tell you, though. My son was here at the weekend. He wants me to sell the house."

"But you love the house."

"I know. But Mark seems to think I can't manage."

Mark Cleverly had grown up in Scotland with his mother, the painter Ruth Annis. Matthew had been married to her once, a long time ago, though he had told Christine the marriage had been a disaster. Mark was in his thirties now, working on the oil rigs. He came down to visit his father once or twice a year. Matthew's house was a tottering Victorian terrace, the twelve narrow rooms spread precariously over four storeys. Matthew had had a stairlift fitted, giving him access to the first floor with its views of the estuary, and that was where he mostly lived. The upper floors were badly neglected. Christine suspected he hadn't been up there in years.

Matthew had lived in the house for more than three decades. It was where he had written *High Wire* and *Canetti's Dwarf*. Christine couldn't imagine him being happy anywhere else.

"It doesn't matter what Mark thinks. What do you think? Do you want to move?"

"I don't think I could stand it, Chrissie. I wouldn't be able to work with all that upheaval."

His words were beginning to slur. It sounded like he'd been drinking, but Christine knew it was a side-effect of the Parkinson's. The medication controlled the worst of the symptoms, but his speech always started to deteriorate if he was worried or upset.

"You didn't agree to anything, did you?" she said.

"No. I told him I needed time to think about it."

She felt relief wash over her. "I'm glad to hear it. You should forget about the house now, at least for tonight. You sound exhausted."

"I am, a bit. But I feel better now."

"I'll write to you tomorrow, Math. I love you."

Christine broke the connection before he could reply. She sent her email to Emily Baxter then shut down her computer. It was ten past eight already – Rose would do a mental. Christine hurried south towards Notting Hill Gate, then on impulse she changed direction, walking along Westbourne

Park Road towards the Landseer. She did not often go to pubs but she could not yet face the thought of going home.

The bar was fairly full, but not as crowded as it would have been on a weekend. Christine ordered a whisky at the bar, a Teacher's – the Landseer did not run to a single malt. She took her drink to a corner table and sat down. Matthew's news troubled her deeply. In spite of what she had said to Matthew, she knew Mark Cleverly was right, that it was only a matter of time before the house became untenable. When that happened Matthew would be forced to move into a warden-assisted flat, or a bungalow on one of the new estates. If that happened he would wither away and die. And Christine would be left feeling that in some intolerable way it had been her fault.

She sipped her drink, thinking about how it would be if she were to move into the top two rooms of the house in West Mersea, the attic rooms with their windows overlooking the estuary, their rain-coloured south-facing light. She imagined herself bringing buckets of hot water up from the kitchen and scrubbing down the ancient dust-caked floorboards, the warm blonde grain of the pine gradually revealed.

A single she recognised came on the jukebox, one of the heavier rock bands from the eighties. Amma had been crazy about that song. It had been in the charts the year they were due to take their O levels.

She downed the rest of the whisky and went outside. It was well after nine. She pulled out her phone to call Rose then put it away again, unable to bear the thought of speaking to her before she had to. As she turned the corner into Ladbroke

Grove she saw a woman emerge from a doorway just ahead of her. Her stilettos tapped on the pavement, the lamplight gilding the gloss of their patent leather. Otherwise the street was empty. Christine began to run. She recognised the house the woman had come out of as Mrs Lempicka's, where Amma had been made to go for piano lessons twice a week. When she thought she could get away with it she bunked off, and they spent the hour wandering the streets, hanging around the Portobello Market or lounging under the trees in Holland Park, where Amma would smoke the black Russian cigarettes she filched from her father's stash behind the soup tins in the Kovacs' kitchen.

Amma talked endlessly of running away. She talked about joining the circus, of packing her leather miniskirt and Velvet Underground tapes into a rucksack and vanishing into the night.

"Don't you ever want to change the way things are, Chris? To say no to people, to tell them to fuck themselves? Don't you ever want to make everyone sit up and take notice?"

"What, by pinching your father's cigarettes and running away with the circus?"

"Oh, I don't know." Amma rolled on her back, peering up at the trees through the lattice of her fingers. "Don't be like that. You're such a killjoy. I'm just fed up with people telling me what to do."

By people, Christine knew, she meant her father. Gregor Kovacs was a building contractor, a short swarthy man with heavily muscled forearms and hard, intelligent eyes. He had always been strict, Amma said, but he became worse after Amma's sister Georgia married a German banker and swanned off to Frankfurt.

"Dad went nuts," Amma told her with a grin. "He hates Germans."

Georgia was ten years older than Amma and Christine had never met her, though there were pictures of her all over the Kovacs' flat. The Kovacs lived in Fremont House, a large 1950s block just north of the Westway and to the east of the Portobello Market. Their apartment was a sprawling assemblage of rooms on the third floor, the windows curtained with heavy plush fabric, the walls covered in dull green wallpaper with a geometric pattern. Amma swore the paper had been there since the building went up. The first time she went there Christine stared in amazement at the mess and clutter of Beatrice Kovacs' sitting room – the piles of old magazines, the ruby-stemmed wine goblets in their dusty glass-fronted cabinet, the books crammed three deep on fibreboard shelving. So different from Rose's orderly assemblage of prized collectables. Shoved in against the far wall was the vast black bulk of Beatrice Kovacs' Bechstein grand, the top closed and covered with a quilted bedspread.

Beatrice Little had been a student at the Royal Academy until she met Gregor Kovacs and fell pregnant with Amma's sister Georgia. To get the piano into the flat the removal company were forced to remove the sitting-room window and winch the piano up on a crane from the street below. The instrument had been brought in a van from Beatrice's parents' home in Sutton. Every time she tried to play it the neighbours complained.

"Bloody thing," Amma said when Christine admired it. "I wish it were dead."

On Amma's last day at school she seemed unusually quiet. When Christine asked her what was wrong she said she'd had another row with her dad.

"Can I come back to your place this evening?" she said. "I can't stand the sight of him at the moment."

Christine hesitated. She had nothing planned for the evening exactly, except that she wanted to spend it by herself. She had been looking forward to doing some work on her translation of Ovid. She wanted also to write up her journal while the events of the day were still fresh. She knew that by the morning her memories would be different, set black and hard as tarmac, an approximation.

It was the last week of the summer term. The main road outside the school was being resurfaced. Everywhere smelled of pitch.

"You can if you like," Christine said finally. "There's some homework I need to get done, though."

"It doesn't matter," said Amma. "I'll go to the park instead. He'll probably have calmed down by now in any case."

Christine wished she hadn't made it so obvious that she preferred to be alone. She was afraid she had hurt Amma's feelings. She hesitated, thinking she should try and persuade Amma to come over anyway, but in the end decided to leave things as they were. She would invite Amma over tomorrow or at the weekend.

Amma did not turn up for school the next day or the next. When Christine telephoned the Kovacs' flat there was no reply. On the last day of term, one of the Berkley sisters came up to Christine in the playground and showed her a news report in the local paper.

"That's Amma's dad, isn't it?" she said.

There was a blurred photograph of Gregor Kovacs, and a short paragraph saying he had been remanded in custody following the unexplained disappearance of his younger daughter.

A week later he was released for lack of evidence. Police detectives had been over the Kovacs' flat three times but were unable to find anything incriminating.

There was still no news of Amma's whereabouts.

The summer was long, hot and dry. As the days drew on towards September, Christine began to range further afield. She rode the tube out to the dusty edge-lands of Greenford and Ruislip, Morden and Epping, where brightly lit, three-bit carnivals parked their wagons and trailers along the gravelly, litter-strewn boundaries of parched yellow fields. As the light faded from the sky she wandered among the sideshows and the whirligigs, telling herself she was looking for Amma but knowing she was trying to escape a world from which Amma was gone.

Rose was busy marking exams. She didn't show any curiosity about where Christine had got to.

• • •

"Amma," Christine called. "Amma, wait!"

The woman turned but seemed not to see her. She looked both ways along the street and then moved on, more slowly this time, standing still from time to time as if she felt uncertain of where she was. Christine ran to catch up, then fell into step beside her. She could smell Amma's perfume, the musky scents of sandalwood and patchouli. Her heart was pounding, and in spite of the chilly night air she found she was sweating.

"I'm sorry, Am," she whispered, as if to herself. "I didn't listen. I'm sorry. I let you down."

When they came to the next streetlamp the woman stopped walking and reached inside her handbag. After a moment or two she brought out a packet of cigarettes – Marlboros – and a square gold lighter. She drew a cigarette from the packet, leaning against the lamp post while she lit it. Her face blazed up cinema-bright in the long yellow flame.

They walked together as far as the crossing on Holland Park Avenue. As Christine turned left towards Notting Hill Gate, Amma glanced down at her watch then disappeared.

• • •

The house was in darkness. Rose was asleep in her armchair. The light from the streetlamp outside fell in a syrupy pool across her face. As Christine entered the room she opened her eyes.

"What are you sitting here in the dark for?" Christine said. "Why don't you put on some lights?" She drew the curtains and switched on the lamp. Rose blinked in the sudden brightness.

"I must have dozed off," she said. "Where have you been?"

"I had some things to do at work. Shall I make us some supper?"

"It's too late to eat. I'm not hungry now."

Christine felt herself stiffen with annoyance. "Well, I am," she said. "I'll heat up that shepherd's pie. It won't take long." She went through to the kitchen and switched on the oven, then covered the pie dish with foil and slipped it inside. When she returned to the sitting room Rose was watching the ten o'clock news. A financial analyst and a professor from the LSE were discussing the banking crisis. Christine perched on the edge of the sofa, trying to remember exactly how much money she had in her savings account.

Enough, she thought. *Enough for a while at least.*

"I've heard back from Nova Press," she said to Rose. "They've asked me to put together a collection."

Rose was silent. For a moment Christine thought she might not have heard her but in the end she nodded, slowly, as if reluctantly conceding a point in a political debate. "I don't suppose they pay much, do they? These obscure independent presses never do."

"The money's not the point. The point is that they like my work. At least it's a start."

Rose sniffed. "Most of the great poets died before they were forty. I suspect that if you were going to get anywhere you would have got there by now."

Christine felt rage well up inside her like a spring tide. She fought to control it. She hated to admit to anger in front of Rose. "What about Thomas Hardy?" she said. "What about Matthew?"

An image came to her of the laburnum tree in Matthew's stony and badly tended back garden. The tree was old and twisted but clung tenaciously to life, drawing what nutrients it could from the brackish soil. It had been spring when Christine was there last and the tree was in flower. Approaching the house from the seaward side it looked as if someone had thrown a pot of yellow paint against the wall. Colour exploding like a starburst, dripping in gleaming gouts to the pavement below.

"I mean the great poets," Rose said. "I mean the Romans."

"That argument is meaningless. All Romans died young."

It was the closest they'd come to a row in years. Christine fled to the kitchen before it could escalate. She began dishing up the shepherd's pie. The potato on top had gone dry, but the meat was piping hot, the gravy smelling richly of onions. Christine realised she was really was hungry. She suddenly found herself wondering what had happened to Beatrice Kovacs' Bechstein grand.

"Do you remember Amma?" she said to Rose. "Annemarie Kovacs, my friend from school?"

Rose looked up at her sharply. "What are you talking about?" she said. "The only Annemarie Kovacs I know is the actress. She was in *Phèdre* at the Cottesloe, years ago, then she went into films. I can't stand that American stuff."

"She must have the same name, then." Christine gathered the dishes together. The plates were flat-rimmed and white, with a border of orange nasturtiums, part of a dinner service that had belonged to Rose's mother.

I shall miss these plates when I go, Christine thought. The idea swam into her head without warning, bulky and implacable, like an aging cargo steamer entering the mouth of one of the great South American rivers. She left the plates to soak in hot water then went upstairs to her room. She was in bed by half past eleven and fell asleep almost at once.

She woke early and packed her things. The house was silent, the furniture rendered ghostly in the nascent half-light. Christine shivered. She placed the note she had written for Rose on the kitchen table.

Don't worry about me, it said. *I shall let you know my new address as soon as I'm settled.*

She opened the door to the street and stepped outside. She got on the tube at Notting Hill Gate and travelled east towards Liverpool Street station. The next train to Colchester was due to leave in twenty minutes. From Colchester, buses ran out to West Mersea every hour.

Christine telephoned and spoke to Rose every weekend, but she never went back.

STARDUST

In my country, 10 July 2029 is remembered by everyone as the date of the *Anastasia* space disaster. For me it has a double significance, because it was also the day my grandmother Sofie Pepusch was killed by her ex-husband on the Lunacharsky estate. These two events are not connected, although it has always seemed to me as if they were. Whenever they replay the film footage of the *Anastasia*, images so familiar and so much a part of our history they are invariably referred to as iconic, what I remember is the smell of burnt pancakes, my brother Nicky accusing the government of murder, my grandfather Marius standing in the doorway looking dishevelled like a character in a movie by Ingmar Bergman. These are the random snapshots of memory, relentless in their stark depiction of terrible things yet strangely consoling also because they are so familiar. *This is how it was,* they say. *Make of it what you can.*

I had already started to write, but it was the aftermath of that day that made me a writer. I felt the change happen, a discernible click, as if a key had been twisted inside me. Free choice had little to do with it. The day marked me out for its own purposes, throwing me off my feet and igniting me in its backdraft of misaligned passion and burning rocket fuel. You could say it scarred me for life.

• • •

Sofie Pepusch was Marius's second wife. She was forty-seven when she died, just five years older than my mother, Nadia. My real grandmother's name was Hillary Belova Dussek. She was an industrial chemist. After her divorce from Marius she emigrated to the West, cutting off her ties from all of us, including my mother.

Sofie was delicate, with spidery, colourless lashes and very fair hair. She was once a dancer with the city ballet, but was forced to give up her career because of illness. She went over to teaching instead. Even that was too much for her in the end, and at the time of her death she was working two or three days a week giving music and movement classes at the local primary school. On her days off she liked to wander around the city picking up junk, bits and pieces she found in waste skips and hoarded in cardboard boxes in Marius's flat. For my mother, as for most people, Sofie's rubbish-collecting was a mystery and an annoyance, but for Sofie it was obviously important, as if the objects she brought back with her were imbued with talismanic properties. I myself found the whole business fascinating. I occasionally tried following her on one of her foraging expeditions but she invariably gave me the slip.

Sofie was twenty years younger than Marius, although

her frail constitution and peculiar behaviour made her seem even younger. Nadia referred to her as the Princess Baglady, though she never repeated the nickname in front of Marius. My brother Nicky kept a photograph of Sofie in his desk drawer. I didn't understand this at the time, although I did later. The idea of Nicky secretly lusting after his grandmother was amusing and weird.

People said Sofie was shy, but what they really meant was that she was unknowable. She was the opposite of Hillary Dussek, with her resonant contralto voice and slate-coloured hair. She was the least violent person I have ever known, but there was a sense of the inevitable in the way she died. Nicky claimed she was a magnet for violence. I have often wondered, down the years, what made him say that.

• • •

The tenth of July was hot. The day of the launch had been declared a national holiday, and along with the rest of the country we were throwing a party to celebrate. As well as Marius and Sofie we had invited the Laverins from the flat opposite, and Spinka Vinograd who at that time was living in the municipal dormitory across the street. Spinka was a mathematics professor who had been sacked from his job for getting involved with one of his pupils. I liked Spinka because he always had time for me, even though I was only thirteen and useless at maths. I was also fond of his dog, Grisha, a black-and-tan dachshund with rhinestones on his collar.

I woke early, just before seven. The skylight in my room had no blind, and light poured down upon me like a waterfall. I turned my face into the pillow and tried to fall asleep again but my mind was too full. I lay on my back beneath the top sheet, my eyes lightly closed and relishing the fact that it was finally launch day. We had been told by our teacher that the launch of the *Anastasia*, the world's first fusion-drive rocket, was an event of *global significance* and we had all been tasked with writing an essay about it. I had kept a journal since my ninth birthday but I had started to become dissatisfied with penning a record of school trips and classroom feuds. I wanted something real to write about, something exciting, and the rocket launch had come at just the right time. Our teacher said we should take care to record the little things: what we had for lunch, what our families said and thought, personal facts we would most likely forget if we didn't write them down. Such things were important as *historical context*, the kind of details we all took for granted but would be fascinating in hindsight.

"It's *because* you take these things for granted that you forget them," Old Lensky said. "Time consumes everything in the end. Only things that are written down are saved. The whole of civilization is based on people writing things down. Think of yourselves as squirrels hoarding nuts."

Some of the boys at the back of the class sniggered at the word nuts. Margarita Masterkova, sitting beside me, blushed bright pink – one of the boys who had laughed was someone she fancied. Margrit was like that, always fancying somebody. When I asked Margrit what she was doing for launch day she said she would probably watch it on television with her brothers. What she was really looking forward to was the fireworks in the evening at the Glazunov Pleasure Gardens.

"There's going to be a funfair," she added. "And I have a new dress."

She said she was sick of the launch and would be glad when it was all over. "It's all anyone talks about these days," she said. "It's worse than the football."

Lying in bed and remembering the conversation I wondered if it, too, counted as historical context. I slid open my bedside cabinet and took out my journal. I read back over what I had written so far that week. I liked the way words could fix memories in place the same way a photograph could, only with the added dimension of feeling as well as fact. If you wrote something down you could keep it, take it out and look at it whenever you wanted to. I began to see what Lensky had meant about hoarding nuts.

At eight o'clock I heard my mother come out of her room and go to the bathroom, and I knew she was getting up early to make a start on the food. Cooking for other people always made Nadia anxious, but today it didn't matter because all she had to do was mix up the pancake batter. Once Marius arrived he would take over and everything would be all right. Marius loved to cook. I don't know if this was always so, or whether he had trained himself to become interested in food because neither of his wives were, but in either case he was good at it, and was able to produce large, appetising meals quickly and with a minimum of fuss.

I got out of bed, slipped on my trainers and went through to the kitchen. My mother was still in her dressing gown. The rim of her sleeve had dragged in the milk she was using to mix the batter and there was a frown line between her eyes.

I asked her what time Marius and Sofie would be arriving. I thought the mention of Marius might calm her down.

"I don't really know, darling. Soon." She rubbed her eyes with the back of her hand, leaving a dusting of flour on the bridge of her nose.

"Is it OK if we turn on the television?"

"You can if you like, I suppose. There won't be much to see yet, though."

I kissed her quickly on the cheek and then hurried away, glad to have escaped the kitchen before there was a crisis. Nicky had already moved the television from its usual place in the sitting room to the top of the sideboard in the dining room, where there was better reception and more room for everyone to sit. While Nicky fiddled with the controls I went to the window and stared out over the park. There had been no rain for several weeks and the ground was parched and yellow. On the far side of the scuffed grass I could see a woman walking along the gravel pathway towards the line of stubby trees that marked Auchinschloss's boundary with the Lunacharsky estate. Something about her seemed familiar and after a moment or two I realised it was Sofie. She was wearing a red kerchief and carrying the canvas holdall she always used for her rubbish collecting. I gazed at her thin ankles and her long feet in their schoolgirl ballerina pumps and wondered where she was going. The launch show would be starting at ten. It would be strange even for her not to be here in time.

I came away from the window and sat down on the floor next to Nicky. I thought briefly of telling him about Sofie but decided against it. In the past few days Nicky's focus had narrowed to exclude everything that didn't directly concern the launch and I guessed at this moment that would include his grandmother. He had finished adjusting the television and sat frowning at the screen. It was eerie, how closely he resembled our father.

"Look at her," he said. "She's terrified."

There was a woman on the screen, glossy-haired and slim and with the perfectly symmetrical features of a fashion model. Her interviewer was Sergei Bayan, the anchorman for the early morning news show. Each time he asked her a question she raised her hand to her mouth, as if she was trying to prevent her words from escaping into the studio.

"It must have been difficult having the mission postponed so many times," said Sergei Bayan. His gold tooth, an ugly imperfection that had nonetheless become his trademark, flashed in the studio lights. "Misha can't have been around much. Many women out there will be wondering how you coped with that."

The woman gazed into space and smiled. "Misha was in the air force when I first met him, so that's something you have to get used to. And they're such a great crowd on the base. We wives and girlfriends tend to band together when the chips are down." She smiled again, a tight-lipped anxious smile that looked more like a grimace of pain.

"Who is she?" I said to Nicky.

"That's Sonia Batushin. Mike Batushin's wife."

Nicky was sixteen then. He was my half-brother, the son of my father's first wife, Elena Mertens. Elena and Nadia both knew every bit as much as Sonia Batushin about having a husband in the forces. My father, Rodion, was a military surveillance technician, first in Afghanistan and then later in southern Chechnya. You say surveillance technician and people think you mean spy though actually he was with the bomb squad. Elena Mertens must have become fed up with the life in the end, because when Nicky was two she left my father for a mining geologist from Perm and took Nicky to live in a tiny village beyond the Urals. I always knew I had a half-brother, but I didn't get to meet him until the day my father brought him back to Auchinschloss to live with us. I was nine years old at the time. I wasn't told the reason, only that Nicky's mother was having difficulties and needed some time by herself to straighten things out. I was prepared to hate him, firstly because he was a boy but mostly because I had been forced to give up my own larger room to him and move into the box room. In the event we took to each other almost at once.

"Is Mike Batushin the captain?" I asked. I loved the way Nicky talked, his short clear-cut sentences, his use of American names. Misha Batushin was Mike, my father was Rod and my mother Nadine. My own name, Alina, was deftly transformed into Lin. Nicky himself was Nicky and never Kolya. Nadia used to grumble at him about this, saying he watched too many American cop shows, though in truth Nicky didn't watch much television of any sort. He liked the way the names sounded, that was all, the way Nicky was different from Kolya and yet also the same.

"Batushin's the co-pilot. Leo Stanislaus is the captain." He paused and turned to look at me. His expression was deadly serious, the expression of someone about to deliver bad news. I was surprised and a little afraid.

"What's wrong?" I said. Because of what I had seen earlier I had it in the back of my mind he was going to tell me something about Sofie. His answer came out of the blue, scuttling across the surface of the day like a rat across a starched white tablecloth. I contemplated it, fascinated and horrified.

"You do know that they might not come back?"

"What do you mean?" On the TV screen Sonia Batushin had been replaced by a cartoon rocket climbing steadily towards arcs of coloured lights that were meant to represent the layers of the Earth's atmosphere.

"I've been reading up on the old stuff," Nicky said. "Gagarin and everyone. Did you know that when Vostok 1 was launched everyone expected it to burn up on re-entry? Gagarin knew, but he went up anyway because he wanted to be remembered as a hero. The technicians at IKI compiled a dossier listing more than three hundred faults with Komarov's Vostok 8, but the Kremlin chose to ignore them and everybody knows what happened to Komarov. It's the same with the *Anastasia*. The fusion drive isn't ready. Kushnev wanted another six months for testing but they told him no. They're determined to go ahead with the launch whatever the risks because they're scared the Chinese will beat them to it if they don't. Sonia Batushin knows her husband is in the firing line. Even if she doesn't know for certain she guesses. You can hear it every time she opens her mouth."

A chill passed through me, starting in the base of my gut and sweeping up like a tide into the tense, tight place between my shoulder blades. Nicky had a caustic sense of humour and was often sarcastic, but the launch had obsessed him for months and I knew he'd never joke about the crew. I didn't know what had happened to Komarov, or even who Komarov was, but from the tone of Nicky's voice I knew it was bad. Nicky gleaned a lot of his information from the Western internet sites he hacked into. I had no idea how far these could be trusted, but I was sure Nicky would tell me nothing he didn't personally believe.

"Gagarin did come back though, didn't he?" I said finally.

"You know he did," Nicky said. "I'm just warning you, that's all. In case you'd rather not watch the launch, I mean."

"Are you going to watch?"

"I have a duty to watch. It's the one thing I can do for them. There are some things you don't have a choice in."

We sat in silence, staring at the flashing animated rocket. My stomach grumbled with hunger and once again I found myself wondering about whether I should tell Nicky about Sofie, but in the light of what he'd just told me it seemed even less important than before. I decided to put off the decision by getting dressed. I showered and put on the denim cut-offs and Metallica T-shirt I had bought off a stall at Piatkovskovo Market. Metallica was the name of a Western band from the dark ages before the second Cold War. I had never heard any of their music, but I knew the horned devil's face on the T-shirt would drive Nadia crazy so I couldn't resist it. I wondered about writing down what Nicky had said about Komarov and Sonia Batushin, then decided it would be better to wait and see what happened. In a *historical context*, writing off the mission before it happened was likely to make me look a fool.

The Laverins arrived just after ten. Peter Laverin was a research chemist who had once worked in the same government laboratory as my grandmother Hillary. His wife Aster was a teacher and had recently become friendly with Sofie. She had smooth and perfect skin the colour of cream. When she laughed or got upset about anything her cheeks went a kind of mauve colour, clashing with her hair, which was the harsh clear red of a grass fire. The Laverins had twin children, Stepan and Liza. They had the same colour hair as their mother, only cropped short. From a distance it looked as if they were both wearing identical red velvet caps. As their contribution to the party the Laverins had brought a salmon coulibiac, its glazed pastry top plaited to look like a corncob. I showed them through to the dining room and was still standing there in the hallway, holding the coulibiac on its oblong baking sheet when Marius arrived.

"Are you thinking of running away with that?" he said. "Only you'd better cover it up or you'll have half the neighbourhood dogs chasing after you like the Pied Piper of Hamelin."

He grinned and tweaked my nose. He was in his late sixties, but with his hawkish Georgian features and heavy mane of silver-white hair he was still outstandingly handsome. I loved him dearly but took care not to show it too much because I knew it would upset my mother. I understood from an early age that Nadia adored her father and the thought of being without him terrified her more than anything in the world. She was painfully jealous of Sofie, an emotion she tried to conceal by being extravagantly nice to her, showering her with little gifts and expensive pastries from the German baker in the centre of town. Whenever Sofie came to visit, Nadia would invariably retire to her room with a migraine afterwards.

"The Laverins brought it," I said to Marius. I broke off a corner of the pastry and popped it in my mouth. It was flaky and sweetly spiced and very delicious. Aster Laverin also liked to cook. "Where's Sofie?"

Marius frowned. "Isn't she here yet? She left the flat an hour ago. She told me she was coming straight here."

I drew in my breath, meaning to tell him I had seen Sofie in the park and that she had been heading away from the house instead of towards it, but somehow the moment passed. "She hasn't arrived," I said instead. "I thought she would be with you."

I looked down at the ground. Marius laughed and touched my cheek with the back of his hand. "Not to worry, Linnet. She'll be here as soon as she's ready. You know what she's like."

By that I took him to mean Sofie was more than capable of losing half a day deciding what blouse she was going to put on, or just standing in the street watching the trams go by. I nodded slowly, still not wanting to look him in the eye.

"I can take that, if you like." He lifted the coulibiac out of my hands and carried it through to the kitchen. I heard my mother exclaim joyfully at his arrival and drop something on the floor, a wooden spoon it sounded like. Her relief was palpable, spreading out through the apartment like an exhaled breath.

Soon after that Spinka Vinograd arrived and for a while I forgot about Marius and Sofie and my mother. I knew that Spinka liked me and enjoyed spending time with me, and the idea that there might be anything sinister in his attentions never occurred to me. Spinka was a friend of my father's and had been in our lives for ever. I thought of him as old but in fact he was about fifty, a pale, straight angular man with thinning hair. I was fascinated by the ring he wore, a large onyx in a claw setting that looked like something out of the Borgias. He carried the dachshund Grisha under one arm.

"Have I missed anything?" he said. He winked at me conspiratorially, as if the two of us had shared a thousand launches and could take it or leave it.

"Nothing yet," I said. "It's just Sergei Bayan." From the dining room I could hear the music that always accompanied a particular car advert, and overlaying that the voice of Peter Laverin as he attempted to lecture Nicky on the physics of the fusion drive. "Let's go to my room for a bit," I said to Spinka. "I want to talk to you."

My bedroom had been converted from a walk-in larder, and was so small the only place you could sit was on the bed. Spinka and I were squashed so tightly together that I could hear his breathing and smell his smell, a mixture of washing powder and cigarettes. Grisha turned in a circle then settled himself on the duvet and closed his eyes. His dark fur was tight and glossy, like the hair of a horse.

"I love your little cabin," Spinka said. "It reminds me of when I was in the navy."

"I never knew you were in the navy," I said. It was true. The idea of Spinka in uniform was scarcely credible. Before he lost his teaching job Spinka lived in a third-floor apartment on Catherine Street with views of the Glazunov Pleasure Gardens. I had never been inside the municipal dormitory – my mother had forbidden it – but Nicky had, because my father paid Spinka to give him extra maths lessons as part of his preparation for the VosTech entrance exam. Nicky said the hostel's rooms were like cells, scarcely bigger than mine and with bare brick walls, and that when he went to use the toilet he'd seen silverfish scuttling for cover between the floorboards.

"Don't get excited," Spinka said. "I was never a proper sailor. I did my national service and then got out. I worked as a radar operator."

That fitted. I found I could easily imagine Spinka hunched over some machine, a ream of incomprehensible calculations at his elbow.

"Did you ever have to fire a torpedo?"

He laughed. "Not once. I told you not to get excited. Why all the sudden questions, young Linny? I hope my secrets are safe with you."

He put a finger to his lips and made a shushing sound, then winked again to show me he was joking. I giggled and nudged his shoulder. I couldn't help it. Spinka always found ways of making me feel relaxed and silly and younger than I was.

"It's for my journal," I said. "We're supposed to write down everything we remember about the launch day. It's historical context." I paused. "Do you think the rocket is safe?"

He raised an eyebrow. "Have you been speaking to that brother of yours?"

I fell silent. The idea that Nicky and Spinka had actual conversations about anything other than maths and chess was new to me, and something of a revelation.

"Nicky told me they might not come back," I said finally. "The cosmonauts, I mean. He seems to think the fusion drive isn't ready."

Spinka sighed. "Space travel is dangerous. But so is all travel, if you think about it. No action taken is entirely without risk. And the crew are soldiers, they know what they're signing up for. Taking risks is what they're paid to do."

I nodded slowly, thinking of what Nicky had told me about Yuri Gagarin, that he had risked his life to be a hero, that it was what he wanted. But Nicky's words about the *Anastasia* still preyed on my mind. I thought of Sonia Batushin, smiling her glossy smile and looking as if someone was pointing a gun at her back. Even if Misha Batushin had signed up for the mission voluntarily, his wife had not.

"If you're still worried, look at it this way," Spinka said. "Do you honestly think they'd put the launch out on national television if they thought there was the slightest risk of it going wrong? Imagine how foolish we'd look. New York would have a whale of a time."

He laughed, and so did I. What he said made such perfect sense I couldn't imagine why I had not thought of it myself. I let out my breath with an audible sigh. I hadn't known until that moment how anxious I was.

"I saw Sofie earlier," I said in a rush. "She was walking in the park. Do you think I should tell Marius? He's been wondering where she is."

Spinka looked thoughtful, far more so than when I asked him about the *Anastasia*. "I wouldn't," he said in the end. "Sofie needs her space. She's had a difficult life. She'll be here when she's ready."

That was exactly what Marius had said, so I supposed it was OK. I couldn't see what was so difficult about Sofie's life, though. She lived in a large centrally heated apartment close to Auchinschloss Mansions. Marius's civil service pension meant she didn't have to work at all if she didn't want to. What was so tough about that?

"Did you know Sofie before?" I said. "When she was a ballerina?" The idea had not occurred to me until that moment but from the familiar way Spinka spoke about her it seemed a distinct possibility. This day was unusually full of surprising facts.

Spinka nodded slowly. I waited, hoping he would elaborate, but he didn't. "You're rather like her, you know," he said instead.

I snorted. "Sure thing," I said, sarcastically. Sofie had not danced professionally for years but she still looked the part. I was below average height with plump thighs and a stocky body and freckled arms. The idea of me and Sofie having anything in common was plainly ridiculous.

"I don't mean in looks," Spinka said. "I mean in spirit. You think about things, you worry. You're not like other children of your age." He leaned towards me, pushing back a strand of hair from my face and then gently brushing his fingers against the side of my neck. I felt myself go shivery, as if his hand was cold, although it wasn't. I shifted uncomfortably on the bed. There was a sour smell of mingled breath, and it suddenly seemed as if all the air had gone out of the room. I wished I could open a window but there was only the skylight. Marius had wired it shut because my mother was afraid of burglars coming over the roofs.

The dachshund Grisha was snoring loudly, his long body curled into a ball.

"I suppose we'd better go and find the Laverins and everyone," I said. "We don't want to miss the launch." My voice sounded unsteady and strange in my own ears, the voice of an actress in a TV soap opera. I eased myself down off the bed and slipped out of the room without waiting to see if Spinka was following. I felt something very peculiar had just happened. I wasn't sure whether it had to do with the way Spinka touched my neck, or the way he had encouraged me not to tell Marius something when I knew I really ought to. All I knew was that I didn't want to be alone with him any longer.

In fact there was still more than an hour to go before the launch. Marius was in the kitchen, stirring his saucepans and listening to Django Reinhardt on Nicky's portable stereo. The flat was filling up with the smells of borscht and zhavoronki, the spiced leavened bird-shaped buns that were one of Marius's specialities. Everyone else was in the dining room. My mother was dressed in the ankle-length black skirt she normally wore to concerts or to Nicky's chess tournaments and a short-sleeved purple top that clung about her shoulders and breasts. Her hair was loose and slightly damp. She was wearing the jade beads my father had bought her during a stopover in Hong Kong. Her chest and arms were freckled, like mine, only on her it looked all right, exotic rather than geeky. I noticed that Peter Laverin was staring at her, his mouth slightly ajar, a sleek lizard with its eye on a particularly juicy insect. Nadia appeared not to notice. The Laverin twins were crammed into a single armchair, making it difficult to see where one of them left off and the other began. With their short hair and needle-fine eyebrows I always found it hard to tell which was Stepan and which was Liza. They rarely spoke, not even to each other, though they got top marks for everything in school.

Sergei Bayan had vanished temporarily from the television screen. They were showing a feature about the inventor of the fusion drive instead, the same documentary that had been broadcast every night of the previous week. The scientist's name was Valery Kushnev. His wife's name was Anastasia, although everyone insisted this was a coincidence and that the rocket was named after the Grand Duchess Anastasia, who abandoned a life of royal privilege to fight for the Revolution. Many films had been made about the life of the Grand Duchess, cheesy historical epics repeated endlessly at Christmas and New Year. Mostly they were sentimental junk but there was one I loved with a passion called *Ash Wednesday*, with Svetlana Stankevich in the role of Anastasia. Anastasia was usually played by a blonde bombshell like Irina Kharkova or Olga Bogdanov. Svetlana Stankevich had straight brown hair and the little finger of her right hand was missing. She played Anastasia as a studious bluestocking who read books and wrote incendiary articles for foreign newspapers. I suppose I saw her as a role model.

Nicky called *Ash Wednesday* subtle propaganda and made fun of me for being taken in by it but he never cared much about movies anyway, not the way I did. In the weeks leading up to the launch he showed me articles he found online about the other Anastasia. Kushnev's wife was known as Stash. She died in a car accident when she was thirty-nine. Photographs of her showed a tiny olive-skinned woman with her hair cropped as short as Liza Laverin's. There seemed to be some mystery surrounding her death. Some of the articles said she had been driving the car. Others insisted she had been an unwilling passenger. Nicky insisted Stash Kushnev had been murdered.

"She was killed by the cops," he said. "Everyone knows but no one dares say anything in case they're arrested for sedition."

"Why would anyone want to kill her, though?" I asked. Nicky refused to answer, just gave me a look as if to say I should be able to work it out for myself, but although I thought a lot about what he had told me I still couldn't make sense of it. Stash Kushnev was once Stash Sokolova, an Olympic gymnast. Then she joined the space programme and married Valery Kushnev. Surely she had been useful rather than dangerous? I began to wonder if Nicky's enthusiasm for conspiracy theories was getting out of hand.

I sat down on the floor beside him. He was wearing jeans but his feet were bare: long, bony, high-arched feet that reminded me of Sofie's. Dancer's feet.

"Has anything happened?" I asked him. I spoke quietly, not wanting to be overheard. Spinka had come into the room behind me and was deep in conversation with my mother. Nicky was frowning, serious. I knew nothing existed for him now except the launch.

"Just more old stuff," he said. "The interviews Batushin and Stanislaus did after the Sevastopol try-outs. They're not showing live footage at all, not even shots of the launch site. It's a complete shutdown. They're scared in case anyone says the wrong thing."

"Perhaps it's to protect the crew," I said. "They must be sick of TV cameras."

Nicky gave me another of his looks, a deadpan sideways stare that I knew was supposed to tell me I should know better. Before I could say anything else Marius came through from the kitchen. He had a red tea towel tied around his waist and his big hands were pasty with flour.

"Has Sofie turned up yet?" he said.

My mother turned to face him, anxiety settling across her face like a pall of dust.

"Is she coming after all, then?" she said. "I was wondering if she'd decided to stay at home."

"She told me she was going to buy some flowers," said Marius. "She was meant to be coming over here straight afterwards."

"I saw her earlier," said Aster Laverin. They were the first words I'd heard her speak since she arrived. "She was crossing the road by the supermarket. I assumed she was on her way here." She paused. "She didn't have any flowers, though."

Aster sat very still, and it was difficult to tell if she was watching the television or staring straight through it. Peter Laverin was fiddling with a lone chessman he had found on the floor, a white rook from a set that was normally kept in the sideboard. He rolled the piece slowly between his fingers, neither confirming nor denying what his wife had said.

"She was wearing one of those granny scarves." One of the twins spoke up suddenly. I knew from her silver nose stud that it was Liza. "A red one."

Sergei Bayan reappeared on the TV screen, speaking from inside a life-size mock-up of the cabin of the *Anastasia*. My mother fidgeted in her seat.

"Can't you just call her mobile?" she said to Marius.

"I've already done that but it goes straight to voicemail. Either it's not turned on or the battery's flat."

I cupped my knees with my palms and stared at the floor. I knew that now was the time to tell Marius what I had seen – Sofie in a red kerchief, making her way across the park towards the Lunacharsky estate – but still I said nothing. I glanced quickly at Spinka but his attention seemed wholly focused on Sergei Bayan. I felt a surge of anger towards him. I had confided in him, hoping he would take charge but he kept on not doing it. I thought over what I had seen, trying to convince myself that the woman in the red kerchief might not have been Sofie after all, but replaying the images in my mind only seemed to make them clearer and more definite. I knew the Lunacharsky estate was supposed to be dangerous, the haunt of drug dealers and black marketeers. Nadia said the only reason we could afford our apartment was because of Auchinschloss's proximity to

Lunacharsky Park. The rent on a place this size in Drubetskoy or Ekaterinskaya would be three times as high. Auchinschloss was respectable but only just.

I had always found the precariousness of our social standing both shaming and thrilling. Sometimes at dusk, Nicky and I would kneel on the sofa with the curtains drawn, watching the lights come on in Revolutionary Heights and taking it in turns to spy on the block's inhabitants through my father's old binoculars. The Heights was built at the turn of the century to ease the city's housing shortage, but there was something wrong with the concrete and the towers were slowly decaying from the inside out. The stairwells were glass-sided, and so it was easy to see people going back and forth between the flats. Mainly it was just families carrying bags of groceries and lugging pushchairs but there were stranger sights: men with handguns hidden in their jackets, a *babushka* in bright green tracksuit bottoms with a child-sized monkey on her shoulder. Nicky knew all their comings and goings and had made them known to me.

I was forbidden to go near the Heights. Nadia said the estate was a terrible place, full of rapists and mutants, and refused to discuss it further. When I asked Nicky about this he said if were mutants living in the Heights it was the government's fault.

"The land they built on is toxic," he said. "It was all factories there once, and the chemicals leaked into the soil. The council insisted the site had been cleaned but they were lying. They poured in tons of concrete and hoped that would be enough to neutralise the residue, but the concrete absorbed the toxins instead. It's as if the whole estate has got blood poisoning."

"How could they have been so stupid?"

Nicky shrugged. "Money, of course – to clean the site properly would have cost millions."

I had never seen a mutant but I was forever on the lookout for them, my nerves strung tight with a guilty mixture of dread and hope. I knew Sofie was born in the Heights, or at least had spent some of her childhood there, which seemed to fit with her sickly constitution and tendency to weirdness. Most of the Heights kids in school had the same pale skin – skin that showed all the veins and that bruised at the slightest touch. Marius was fond of telling everyone that when he first met Sofie she was living above a chemist's shop in Red Lane, and when I looked up Red Lane on the map I saw it was a long meandering road that ran right through the heart of Piatkovskovo, winding up in the northern outskirts of Lunacharsky Park. As a place to live, Piatkovskovo was even dodgier than Auchinschloss.

I wondered what drew Sofie back to these districts, what reason she could have for going there. Marriage to Marius should have insulated her from her past, but still there were her illnesses, her rubbish-collecting, her incessant restlessness.

I saw again the long slide of her gait as she walked across the grass. Had there been something secretive about the way she was walking, something furtive? Suddenly it was not Sofie I was afraid for, but my grandfather Marius.

"Do you think you could dish up for me, Nadenka?" Marius said. "I'd better see where she's got to."

Marius rarely asked my mother to do anything, let alone take charge of food. The hall door slammed behind him and then there was just the sound of his footsteps, running downstairs. An uneasy silence descended. I felt weightless, spinning in space, which put me in mind of the four cosmonauts strapped helplessly into their cabin. I wished my father was there. I wished Nicky would make a joke and jolly Nadia along the way he usually did, but his attention was fixed on the TV screen.

One of the twins yawned and stretched like a little red cat.

The plates of snacks and pastries were already set out on the trolley. Marius had left the bowls for the borscht warming in the top part of the oven – all Nadia had to do was ladle it out. In the end Aster served the soup, while my mother hovered anxiously in the doorway.

"Don't get any on your blouse," she said. "Beetroot stains worse than anything."

She took over from Aster long enough to wheel the trolley through to the dining room. When she asked Spinka what he would like to eat he shook his head and said he wasn't hungry. Nadia's expression tightened.

"You have to have something" she exclaimed. "This is Marius's speciality."

"I'll have some later, perhaps." He sat on the couch and stroked his dog, his eyes on the screen. Peter Laverin ate his soup rapidly, hunched over, his spoon clattering against the rim of the bowl. Aster Laverin refused to look at him. She sat very still in her flowered silk blouse, darting furtive glances at my mother from beneath her long lashes. Nadia seemed to have forgotten the Laverins existed. She twisted her rings and shot glances at the door. The Laverin twins ate one lark bun after the other, staring fixedly at the television screen as if they were at the movies.

Nicky looked at his watch. "It's almost time," he said to me quietly. "Do you think they'll go through with it?"

I stared at him, incredulous. *How should I know?* I felt like saying. *You're the expert. Why is everyone so crazy today?*

"They have to," I said instead. "The whole world is waiting. They can't back out now." Suddenly it really did seem as if everyone in the universe had stopped what they were doing in preparation for the launch. Nicky grabbed my hand, squeezing my fingers so hard the knuckles cracked. After what seemed an age Sergei Bayan announced that the broadcast was going live to Alma-Ata. He flashed his gold-toothed smile and disappeared.

There was no commentary from the launch site, just a view of a desert landscape with the launch pad barely visible on the horizon. The picture was out of focus. I wondered if that was deliberate, if the images we were watching were even real. I tried to catch Nicky's eye but his gaze remained locked on the screen. I could feel him trembling. The sky over Alma-Ata was grey as porridge. The pale nose cone of the *Anastasia* seemed to merge with the clouds. The rocket's reflector panels had a plastic shine that gave the craft the appearance of a child's toy. It frightened me to think something so insubstantial might be launched into space.

It looked like rain in Alma-Ata. On the other side of the dining room windows our own day was scorching hot, the sky above the park and pavements a searing blue.

I didn't know what to think. The lack of any commentary made it impossible to tell whether the launch was going well or badly. It occurred to me that perhaps that very uncertainty was a clue, a signal we had moved from the broad thoroughfare of the life we were used to on to the narrow tightrope of the unknown. There was no one to describe what we should feel or think because nobody had worked that out yet. This was a feeling only silence could describe.

Nicky had told me Kushnev's fusion drive, once it was perfected, might one day help us send spaceships to other planets. But the toy rocket stranded on the barren plains of Alma-Ata did not seem capable of living up to these expectations. I thought of the men in the capsule, repeating their names in my head like a protective mantra: Mikhail Batushin, Andrew Silvestrov, Vik Lerner, Lev Stanislaus. Silvestrov, Nicky explained, had an American mother.

"He's a trophy pilot," Nicky said. "For pissing off the Yanks. They think Silvestrov should be flying for them, but it's us who have him." I didn't know whether to believe Nicky or not. I'd seen Andrew Silvestrov interviewed on TV loads of times and he didn't sound American at all. He was the youngest of the four crew and I liked to persuade myself I had a crush on him.

For a long time nothing seemed to be happening. Every now and then there was a burst of static from the television's speakers, the muffled sound of voices on what I presumed must be a radio link with the *Anastasia*. The playback was so distorted you could barely hear a word.

"That's Mike Batushin's voice," Nicky said suddenly. "He's talking to mission control." He gripped my hand even harder, making me gasp with pain, and then as if to confirm his statement the radio burst into clarity. "*Vanya, we're ready to go,*" I heard someone say. The five words chilled me to the bone. They sounded so final.

There was a dense, dull rumbling, like an explosion of dynamite in a stone quarry. A cloud of dust and steam obscured the launch pad and for a few seconds it looked as if the engines had failed to ignite. Then I saw the nose cone of the *Anastasia* gradually begin to rise above the launch tower like a blunt white fingertip. It climbed slowly, agonisingly slowly, and although Nicky had told me that the launch speed of a fusion rocket was many times the speed of sound, I could not rid myself of the idea that the craft was moving too slowly to escape the ground. Then at last I saw it rise, heaving itself clear of the launch tower like a clumsy flightless bird regaining its wings.

There was flame at its base, the conical comet tail of fuel burn-off I recognised from so many Saturday night space operas. I could hear Nicky's breathing, the quick shallow lisp of it. I glanced at him briefly, thinking how alone he looked, and how young, as if his fear for the men in the rocket had stripped him bare.

"My God," said Aster Laverin. "What's happening?" She was leaning forward, her lips parted, a bubble of saliva bursting at the corner of her mouth. She spoke dreamily, wonderingly, like a person recently awakened out of sleep. On the screen the *Anastasia* was gone. In its place was a falling light, white and vaguely star-shaped, like a Skyrider rocket in a First of May fireworks display. Nicky snatched his hand out of mine. He folded both arms across his chest and drew up his knees, his bare feet flat and defenceless on the polished floor.

I gazed at the screen, still too bemused to be properly horrified. I realised a curious thing: that our homework project to write essays about the launch had just been cancelled. When we went back to school in September, I knew all the teachers would act as if launch day had never happened. I promised myself in that moment I would write down everything I remembered, whether anyone told me to or not. *It's the one thing I can do for them,* Nicky had said. Suddenly and with a new awareness I understood what he meant.

After Lebed won the election in '45, film footage of the *Anastasia* started turning up on our screens more and more frequently. The picture quality had been digitally enhanced, showing how the first explosion tore the rocket apart, how seconds later the vacuum core of the detached fusion generator collapsed under pressure, exploding in a fireball that could be seen for many hundreds of miles. These are the images people remember, a false memory that endures because it renders the original footage comprehensible. The film we all saw is a blur, and hard to make sense of, as any televised execution would be hard to make sense of.

I could not take it in, that we had just seen four people die, live on television. They had been there and now they were gone. It seemed wrong to move or speak, because they could no longer move or speak. And yet at the same time the urge to shout, to run about, to dash down to Mr and Mrs Gromyko on the ground floor and ask if they had seen it, if they had seen it too, was all but insurmountable.

The television went blank for a second, then the Channel 1 test card appeared. After about a minute there was a loud blast of music and the test card was replaced by a war film called *Scaffold Point*. The lead actor was Ivan Lateef, who had starred in *Spies to Die For* and *Renegades*. Then Marius barged into the room. He looked terrible, his underarms dark with moisture and his hair plastered to his skull from running. Through the stink of his sweat I smelled scorched batter. The pancakes under the grill had started to burn.

"I can't find her anywhere," Marius gasped. To my horror he looked close to tears. "I've been back to the flat but she's not there either."

Nadia stared at him as if she'd forgotten who he was.

"What's wrong?" he said. "Did she call?"

"They're all dead," said Nicky. "They've been murdered."

"Who's dead?" said Marius. "What are you talking about?"

The Laverins all began speaking at once. The twins, Stepan and Liza, seemed galvanised by the tragedy. They spoke in identical sentences, only half a second apart, so that one twin sounded like an echo of the other.

"The rocket blew up."

"Blew up like a firework."

"It never even got off the ground."

They leaned forward in their seat, their green-gold eyes glittering like topaz.

"I knew it was going to happen," said Aster Laverin. "I felt it." She brushed at her neck, and I noticed she'd got borscht on her blouse after all, a bright red speck high on the collar, rusty and indelible as blood.

"Felt what?" said my mother. "The picture was awful. You could hardly see anything."

"The fusion drive must have exploded," said Peter Laverin. "It's the only explanation." He paused. "The Kushnev process is radioactive, you know. There's bound to be fallout. We're lucky it happened in the desert."

Only Spinka Vinograd said nothing. The dachshund moaned and paddled in its sleep. Nicky got up from the floor and walked out of the room.

I stared at Marius, at his damply flattened hair, the gleam of sweat in the "v" of his shirt.

"I saw Sofie," I said at last. "I saw her first thing this morning. She was in the park."

"Did she speak to you?" said Marius. "Where was she going?"

"I saw her from the window. She was heading towards the estate."

He gazed at me blankly then turned away, his arms limp by his sides. I felt guilty yet also relieved. Finally I had told him what I knew. My part in the drama, whatever it was, had been played out.

"I'll have to go out again," Marius said. "Peter Sergeich, would you come with me?"

Peter Laverin jumped as if his chair had been set on fire. "Don't you think we should stay where we are?" he said. "In case she comes back?" I realised with a queasy lurch that Laverin, with his proudly displayed social conscience and his fondness for instructing others in the ways of the people, was afraid. He was afraid to go on the Lunacharsky estate.

My eyes drifted back to the television screen, where Ivan Lateef was in the midst of an argument with his co-star over a woman. The camera alternated between the two men and then shifted its focus to the girlfriend herself, a young Ruby Castle, before she became famous for *American Star* and got involved with Raymond Latour. I had always thought Ruby Castle looked a bit like Sofie – the eyes mainly, that same navy blue colour. It was weird seeing Castle just then, as if Sofie was trying to send us a message through the film.

"*Stop it,*" Ruby Castle said. "*Both of you.*"

For one mad moment I almost believed she was speaking to Marius and Peter Laverin, or to me and Marius, or to Peter Laverin and me. Nadia and Laverin were just standing there, deactivated and listless as puppets with no one to pull their strings.

"*Don't,*" cried Ivan Lateef.

The co-star, Gunther Sternbach, drew a pistol from his belt and shot Castle dead.

I gasped and shut my eyes. I had seen enough murder for one day. When I next looked at the screen Gunther Sternbach was running away across the fields.

"I'll go with you," Nicky said. "Everyone else stay here." He reappeared soundlessly in the doorway behind Marius and I saw he already had his outdoor shoes on. Marius turned to him and seemed about to say something but before he could speak the entry-phone buzzed. The sound was so unexpected I jumped a mile.

"Here she is at last," my mother said. "Panic over." She pressed the button that unlocked the street door. Normally she would have asked visitors to identify themselves over the intercom – this time she didn't bother. I watched Ivan Lateef bending over the slumped body of Ruby Castle and listened to the thump of footsteps coming upstairs. The footsteps were heavy and loud and they sounded as if they belonged to more than one person. Whoever the caller was, it wasn't Sofie.

"What on earth's going on out there?" said Nadia. "It sounds like a herd of elephants."

Marius threw open the door. There were two uniformed officers outside, not the regular city constables but FSB men. One of them looked about forty. The other couldn't have been much older than Nicky. Mongolian features, his uniform so neatly pressed it looked fresh out of its box. He had a scar on one cheek, a raised white crescent that reminded me of the half-moon logo on Pelegaya biscuit packets.

The older officer flashed his ID, then asked if there was a Mr Marius Dussek present in the apartment. He sounded like a cop on a cop show.

"That's me," Marius said. "What's happened?"

"There's been an accident, I'm afraid. Do you know this man?" He produced a colour ID card and handed it to Marius, who held it by one corner like a soiled handkerchief.

"Yes, I know him. He's the piece of filth that used to be married to my wife. Could you tell me what this is about, please?"

His face was flushed bright red. I had never seen Marius looking so angry and the change in him terrified me. I sensed it would only take one more word and he would go off like one of my father's unexploded bombs. I didn't know Sofie had once been married to someone else – the idea was shocking and deeply fascinating. I regretted not being close enough to catch a glimpse of the photo on the ID card.

"I'm afraid your wife has been shot, sir. Could you come with us, please? We need you to identify the body."

"Body? You're saying she's been killed?"

"Please come with us now, sir."

Marius staggered backwards as if he had been assaulted, and I knew I had seen the last of his strength leaving him, that he wasn't going to fight after all. He stood there dumbfounded, idiotic in his defeat, his silver hair straggling over his collar. The stink of his sweat merged with the smells of charred pancakes and the outside air rising up through the stairwell, the familiar dusty aroma of a summer afternoon.

"I'm coming with him," Nicky said. "I'm his grandson." He spoke to the officer directly, meeting his blue-eyed stare with a look of defiance. The FSB man nodded slowly and turned to leave. After they had gone I went and stood by my mother's chair. She leaned towards me slightly but did not touch me. She clutched her jade necklace, twisting the beads between her fingers like a rosary.

"She's always been trouble," she said. "Dad was a fool to marry her and I told him so. She only ever wanted him for his money."

I remained silent, knowing from experience that Nadia would turn on me the moment I dared to ask a question. She would tell me to mind my own business then change the subject. But sometimes if you kept your mouth shut she would unintentionally tell you what you wanted to know.

"She was still in love with that bastard, you know," my mother continued. "They never know what's good for them, these people. It's always take, take, take."

I presumed the bastard was Sofie's ex-husband. I hoped Nadia might say more but she rose abruptly to her feet and went out of the room. Peter Laverin crossed to the window. He placed the chess piece he'd been holding on the sill and stood looking out over the park. I realised he was standing in exactly the same position as I was when I saw Sofie that morning. The idea that Sofie was dead still felt light years from any conceivable version of reality. Spinka sat as if moulded from stone. Only the Laverin twins seemed unaffected. They sat in their armchair, one arm each about the other's shoulders, polishing off the last of the snacks and watching *Scaffold Point* as if nothing had happened.

From the kitchen I heard the sound of running water. Aster Laverin was doing the washing up.

• • •

Nicky and Marius did not return until after dark. Spinka and the Laverins were long gone. After my mother and Marius finally went to bed I crept across the hallway to Nicky's room. He opened the door right away, as if he had been expecting me. He was dressed only in his underpants. I had never seen him naked before and the sight of him now – long legs and pale chest, tea-coloured nipples, the bulge in his pants – was embarrassing in ways I found myself unable to describe. The room was bathed in the silvery glow from his computer screen.

"I thought you were never coming back," I said. "It's been awful here. What happened?"

Nicky shook his head, and for a moment I thought he wasn't going to tell me anything either. Then he plumped back down on the edge of the bed, accidentally jogging his computer mouse. The cursor looped wildly across the screen then came to a stop.

"She was lying on a trolley," he said. "There was a sheet drawn up to her chin, held down with clips somehow. I kept wondering what she looked like under the sheet, how damaged she was. I couldn't help it. I tried to stop the thoughts but they wouldn't go."

He told me the worst thing about seeing Sofie dead was knowing she had been alive just a few hours before. "Her face looked sort of greyish. Like dough – I don't just mean the colour but the way dough keeps the shape of your fingers when you touch it. Like that. But it didn't really matter what she looked like, because you could see straight away it wasn't Sofie on the trolley, but some *thing*, some remnant. You could never speak to her or hurt her again, not even if you shook her and shook her until her bones cracked. She had been put out, like flicking a light switch. I kept thinking how strange it was, that she had ever been alive at all. She looked like she'd been dead for ever. Granddad sat on a plastic chair, holding her hand and looking like he expected her to wake up any minute. I don't know how he could bear to touch her."

"Did they tell you who did it?" I asked. "Who killed her?"

Nicky shrugged. "They took Granddad away for questioning, for hours – that's why we were gone so long. I sat in the hospital canteen with all the other walking dead. When Granddad came back he looked wiped out so I didn't ask him anything. The coffee there is foul."

He turned back to his computer.

"What are you looking for?" I said.

"Anything," he said. "Just proof that it really happened, I suppose. But it's hopeless even trying at the moment because there's some sort of shutdown. The moment I get a connection it's gone again. They must be jamming the signals."

I thought at first Nicky was still talking about Sofie. Then I realised he meant the *Anastasia*. What with everything that had happened since, I had more or less forgotten about the launch. I sat in silence, mesmerised by the continuous circular movement of the buffer sign. The window was open, but the day's heat still lingered in the corners of the room, itchy with the scent of grass. Nicky finally gave up on the computer and threw himself down on the bed, pulling back the sheet so I could climb in beside him. I heard the distant sound of traffic on Blacksmith Alley and one half-hearted catcall from the pavement outside. Other than that the flat was so quiet it was hard to believe we weren't completely alone there.

"What are you thinking about?" I said into the darkness. I thought he would say he was thinking about Sofie but his answer surprised me.

"Sonia Batushin," he said.

I saw Sonia Batushin once, years later, sitting beside her husband in a box at the Arbatsky Theatre. Sonia's second husband was the actor Vladimir Gladkov, who played Peter the Great in the long-running TV series. Sonia was still beautiful, and in spite of being older she looked more certain of herself. I wondered if she ever thought about that day in July when she sat on a vinyl couch in an airless television studio, looking so frightened it might have been her inside the rocket instead of her husband. I wondered if she still thought of that life as the reality – a reality couture clothing and a box at the Arbatsky and Vladimir Gladkov's private limousine let her forget for some of the time but never entirely, or whether the day of the launch now seemed so long in the past that the woman she had been then no longer existed.

Nicky put both arms around me, holding me along the length of my body and stroking the soft cup of skin in the small of my back. I could feel his cock, stiff against my left buttock, but he made no attempt to touch me intimately. I knew enough of the world to understand that others would condemn his behaviour if they came to know about it, but I was also perfectly certain Nicky would do nothing to harm me. I was simply glad of his warmth, of his need to have me close to him. It had been a strange day.

• • •

We woke early. The internet was back on, but the *Anastasia* homepage had been taken down, and the personal profiles of the four crew members had been erased from the main IKI website. None of the general news sites appeared to be carrying the story, and all the Western sites kept showing server errors. When Nicky turned on the television there was a lot of talk about the latest bomb attacks in Tbilisi but nothing about the exploded rocket or the four dead cosmonauts. Nicky spent the best part of an hour retuning the set, trying to pick up satellite broadcasts from London or Paris, but all he managed to get was an old episode of the German soap opera Nadia sometimes liked to watch in the afternoons and someone on a windy dockside in Gdansk talking about an upcoming music festival.

"Is it the fallout?" I asked him. "What Peter Laverin was saying? Is that why they've all gone quiet?"

I had no memories of the SILCO meltdown in Kolyma, but Spinka told me when that happened there had been no internal broadcast news for five days.

"After the dust settled they blamed a faulty satellite," Spinka said. "But in the meantime we were all in the back room with the curtains drawn, huddled round our shortwave radios scanning the airwaves for news like old-time resistance fighters. Quite exciting in its way, I suppose, so long as you didn't live in Kolyma."

Nuclear radiation was the only thing I could think of that might cause such a fuss, but Nicky shook his head almost at once.

"The *Anastasia* was a fusion rocket," he said. "They're clean, or at least that's the theory. This is about loss of face." He flicked through the TV channels one more time then gave up, leaving the television tuned to a film in which a woman in a feather boa drank coffee in the bar of a dingy hotel. "They'll come up with a story soon enough."

We sat together and watched the film. The telephone did not ring, and Nadia and Marius had still not surfaced. I felt peaceful and almost happy, though I sensed even then that these were borrowed hours, a temporary hiatus before the forces of change pitched all our lives and certainties into the whirlwind.

And the change was not long in arriving. By late morning there was a long article on the IKI site talking about what lessons could be learned from the disaster, and how the fusion drive was already being improved. The article included a fuzzy set of stills showing the *Anastasia* in the moments before the launch. Short obituaries of the four crew members described them as heroes. I thought Nicky would be pleased that the tragedy had been made official but he seemed dissatisfied, describing the article as a cop-out. I felt confused at first but I gradually began to get a sense of what he meant. None of the facts appeared to be missing but the way they were reported made it seem as if the disaster had happened months or even years before. The TV news reports were the same. By the time I went east to Tynda the *Anastasia* wasn't in the news at all.

• • •

The six weeks between Sofie's murder and the day I went to live with Kiril and Munia Sharpnes were full of tense hot days in which bad things seemed to happen by themselves. I still find it surprising how quickly we allowed ourselves to become divided. I tried to carry on as normal, reading in my room or going to Petersen's Ponds with Margrit and Kira, where we spread blankets on top of the railway sleepers and ground the rumour mill. I recorded these scenes in my journal, reproducing our inane dialogue as accurately as I could. I was comforted by the memory of these conversations, even though the subjects we talked about were of little consequence. None of my school friends so much as mentioned the launch, though I guessed Nicky and his friends talked of little else.

Nicky spent most of his time scouring the internet for more information about the *Anastasia*, though what more he hoped to discover I did not know. Marius more or less moved into our flat. At night he slept on a fold-down divan in my mother's room, the two of them talking together in low voices into the small hours. Sometimes they argued. One night they had a blazing row that ended with Marius smashing the bedroom window and Nadia disappearing into the night. I lay still with my heart thumping, unable to sleep again until some hours later I heard the hall door open and then softly close as my mother returned to the apartment. The following day they were preoccupied and tense, with each other as well as with Nicky and me. They were people I barely recognised and tried to steer clear of.

There was no news at all from my father. Nicky was the only person I felt I could trust.

"What's going on with them?" I asked him the night after the big row.

"It's the guy they arrested for the murder," said Nicky quietly. "He's been released on bail. Granddad's convinced the cops have been bought."

The man's name was Danilo Korchnoi and that was all I had been able to find out about him. As the long summer evenings began gradually to fade I would stand at the edge of the park, looking across towards the Lunacharsky estate and wondering what the murderer was doing right at that moment. Sometimes, if the wind was blowing in the right direction you could catch food smells coming from the flats, the scents of frying onions and summer bonfires, the screams of children as they rolled on the grass. The atmosphere of our own apartment was deathly and close and I longed to be free of it. Nadia cooked and cleaned but intermittently and when she spoke it was with an abstracted tone, as if she had to keep reminding herself of who we were. Marius had become an angry unapproachable stranger. The only escape was through my journal. I wrote about the Heights, making up stories in which bands of mutants prowled the corridors, and a washed-up private detective became obsessed with bringing Sofie's murderer to justice.

Sometime towards the end of August they broke the news: Nicky was to return to live with his mother. Marius insisted this was temporary, that Nicky would be back with us after Christmas.

"It's just until we sort ourselves out," he said. He looked away from us as he spoke, and I knew he was lying. Sofie's death had aged him in some ways but he had also become as volatile and unpredictable as a youth of twenty. A month before I would have believed anything he told me but that was no longer possible.

"What does Dad say?" I said. I was playing for time and I knew it.

"Your father isn't here, Alina. We'll have to manage without him." Marius told Nicky he should start packing.

Nicky's train was booked for 1 September. In the hours before his departure, he and I behaved as if we both believed he would soon return. I sat on his bed while he folded clothes into his suitcase, hooking my bare toes through the handle of the drawer of his bedside cabinet and sliding it repeatedly in and out.

"Stop it, Lin, you're driving me nuts," he said. Soon after that he left. Marius went with him to the station. I stayed behind in the flat with Nadia, unable to bear the thought of him waving goodbye. When I heard Marius push open the street door I went to my room. It was only then that I understood my brother was gone. Had I known at the time that I would see him again, even though it would be twenty years later and in a foreign country, parting might have been easier. As it was it was my first taste of heartbreak, bitterer than I could have imagined. I pressed my face into the pillow, trying to force back my sobs. Nadia came and tapped on my door but I ignored her. I wished she were dead, like Sofie. I felt both guilty and surprised at how much better this imaginary assassination made me feel.

I slept for a while, exhausted by my own emotions. When I woke it was late afternoon. The apartment was quiet – too quiet. I pulled on my trainers and slipped out of the flat, passing around the side of the building and then sprinting across the road to Lunacharsky Park. The sky was a washed-out blue. Hazy sunshine enveloped the Heights, turning the towers and concrete stanchions of the estate into the shimmering dream-world of struck-off cops and persecuted monsters I had constructed in my journal.

My shadow stretched before me across the grass. The summer was all but over. I ached for Nicky so badly I wanted to cry.

Suddenly I saw Spinka Vinograd coming towards me along the path. He was wearing a blue pinstriped blazer that made him look like a character in a stage musical. He had Grisha with him on a lead, the dog's long body undulating across the grass like a large brown caterpillar. I hadn't seen Spinka since the day of the launch and had no wish to speak to him now. I thought briefly about pretending I hadn't seen him, but when he smiled at me and waved I knew it was already too late. I stood still, allowing him to catch up with me, then bent down to stroke Grisha. The dog surged forward, trying to lick my hands and face. Grisha always seemed pleased to see me, no matter how much time had passed since our previous meeting.

"Hello, Linnet," Spinka said. "I haven't seen you about lately."

I mumbled something about being busy with Margrit, hoping that would be the extent of our exchange, but he seemed determined to prolong it.

"How are things at home?" he said. I gazed up at him, remembering how we had talked on the day of the launch. It seemed an age ago. Suddenly I longed for our old camaraderie.

"Awful." The word burst from my lips, landing hard and black on the ground like a lump of coal. "Nicky left today. They said he'll be coming back but I don't believe them." Tears slipped from my eyes. I wavered on the edge of the precipice, then began to cry in earnest, my chest hitching with tight-packed sobs. Spinka reached into his jacket pocket and pulled out a handkerchief. It was folded neatly in a square and light blue, exactly the same colour as the sky. For some reason this made me cry even harder.

"Come on, let's go back to my place," said Spinka. "I'll make us some tea." He put a hand on my shoulder as if to steady me. I tensed, remembering his odd behaviour on the day of the launch. I didn't like the idea of being alone with him in a strange place. On the other hand he was just Spinka and he was there. I needed someone to talk to and I had always felt I could tell him anything.

In the end it was thoughts of Nadia that decided for me. She had forbidden me to go inside the municipal dormitory, just as she had forbidden me to go near the Heights, or the old stationmasters' building out by the tram depot where Nicky and his friends went sometimes to smoke cigarettes and play chess. When it came down to it, the lure of going against Nadia proved stronger by some distance than my half-formed worries about what Spinka might want to do to me in his room.

"OK," I said. "Thanks." We walked off together in the direction of the hostel, the dachshund Grisha trotting happily along behind us. After Nicky's description of the cramped rooms and silverfish I was prepared for the municipal dormitory to be a squalid place, smelling of dereliction and old food. In fact it was simply austere. The hallways were uncarpeted, and our footsteps clattered noisily on the faded lino as we went up the stairs.

Spinka's apartment was tiny but well kept. There was a small kitchen alcove, with a sink and a two-ring hob. There were books everywhere. Spinka's bed stood in the corner behind a curtain.

"Make yourself at home," he said. There was a rickety wooden table with three mismatched chairs. I perched gingerly on one of them, watching while Spinka used a saucepan to pour water into a vast, dented stove-top samovar. In front of me on the table was a pack of playing cards, shiny and pliable with age, the court cards designed as characters from *The Arabian Nights*.

"Did your brother seem all right when he left?" Spinka said.

"He's fine," I said, and sighed. "He's always fine." What I meant was that Nicky knew how to look after himself, that so long as he had his books and a chess set he would survive. It felt good to talk about him with someone who knew him. In spite of the pain, it brought Nicky back to me, at least for a while. "It's Nadia and Marius I'm worried about."

"How do you mean?"

I shrugged. "It's hard to explain," I said. "It's as if we don't exist for them any more." Sofie's death had been shocking, like diving naked into the freezing water of Petersen's Ponds: for a second it was hard to breathe, and for some time afterwards the detail of the world stood out in knife-sharp clarity. The murder was awful but it was thrilling too, a fact I would admit to no one, not even Nicky. Like the catastrophe of the *Anastasia* it was *an event*. I had not been that close to Sofie and so in a sense I felt aloof from what had happened to her. I resented Marius for his suffering and I resented Nadia for being in thrall to him. In spite of the terrible rows they clung together more tightly than ever. I felt I had become invisible, no longer a part of them.

"Perhaps I should go and get myself murdered," I said at last. "At least that might get me noticed."

Spinka inhaled sharply and then laughed. "Oh, Linnet," he said. "Your mother loves you, so much."

I watched him as he moved about the room, trying to decide if he meant what he said or if it was just something he wanted me to believe. In my heart I knew he was right but I did not *feel* it. In some part of myself I sensed that this was the way it would always be with me and Nadia, believing but not feeling for the rest of our lives.

"There's more to this story than you know," Spinka said. "Drink your tea, and then I want to show you something."

He placed a porcelain cup in front of me. The tea wafted a flowery fragrance, very different from the black tea we normally drank at home. There was a plate of biscuits too, the chocolate wafers from the German bakery that Nadia always used to buy when Sofie visited. I scooped one from the plate and bit into it, washing it down with hot tea. The taste with the melting chocolate was delicious. The little room was warm and smelled of books. For the first time in many days I felt safe and comforted.

"This tea smells so good," I said. I closed my eyes, savouring its scent. "Where do you get it from?"

"I have a friend who gets it for me, from London. It's called Earl Grey. I'm glad you like it. Have a look at this."

He placed something on the table beside me, a Polaroid snapshot of a young couple sitting on the grass by the fountains in the Glazunov Pleasure Gardens. The man's hair was shaved close to his head and he wore a loose grey singlet of the kind often worn by men who had been in the army. He was holding a child in his lap, a little boy with dark blue eyes and wheat-coloured curls.

The woman in the photograph was Sofie.

"That man is Danilo Korchnoi," said Spinka. "The child is their son, Orel."

"I don't understand," I said. Sofie in the photo looked younger, happier. "Do you mean that Sofie is his mother?"

"Yes. Orel is almost ten now, but he's terribly ill. Many of the children born in the Heights have birth defects. Orel has a rare form of leukaemia. There's a treatment but it's expensive. Sofie never told me exactly what happened but I think Danilo was in prison for a while. Things were difficult for her and Orel. Marius came along at just the right time."

I remembered what Nadia had said on the day of the murder, about Sofie marrying Marius for his money. I felt suddenly dizzy, as if I had straightened up too quickly after tying my shoes.

"Does Marius know?" I said.

"He knew Sofie was married, but I don't think she ever told him about Orel."

"But why would Danilo Korchnoi want to kill Sofie?"

"He was furious with her for what she'd done. He wanted her to leave Marius and come back and live with him and Orel. Sofie said she would, but only once she'd saved enough money for them to move off the estate. It went on and on, round and round. I think in the end Danilo just lost his temper for a moment. He was that kind of man, I'm afraid."

"Did Sofie love him?"

"Yes, I think she did, very much." He paused. "She was fond of Marius and she was grateful to him but I know she felt like a ghost in that apartment. She missed Orel and she missed dancing. Sofie was the real thing, an artist. If it wasn't for her health she could have made it internationally. She was once photographed by Vernon Reade."

"Who's Vernon Reade?"

Spinka waved his hands as if to say it didn't matter, that wasn't the point. "An English photographer. He's dead now, I think, but he was famous in his day."

"How come you know all this?"

"I saw her dance a couple of times, in the old days, but I only met her properly after she got married to Marius. I think she saw me as a connection to her old life. She used to come here quite often. She didn't really have anyone else to talk to, at least not about the things that mattered to her. She was lonely."

I wanted to ask him if he had been in love with Sofie himself but it didn't seem right to. In any case I somehow knew it was unlikely.

• • •

A long time later, after I came back from Tynda, I ran into Margrit Masterkova on the street outside the old Mogilev department store. I had not seen her since I left the city and it was a miracle we even recognised each other. Once we got over the surprise we went to the Polish lunchroom on Tverskaya and ate a meal together. We talked mostly about school, the friends we had shared, the teachers we most hated. In the course of our conversation, Margrit happened to mention the girl Spinka Vinograd lost his job over.

"Milena Sacher," she said. "You must remember her. She was brilliant at maths. My sister always said she was a genius. A real genius, I mean, like Mozart or Wittgenstein. She left school suddenly, right in the middle of term. Everyone knew why but we weren't supposed to talk about it. I can't believe you don't remember."

"The name rings a bell," I lied. "What happened to her?"

"She killed herself. Not *then*," Margrit added hastily. "When she was at college. No one was surprised, really. She never had many friends."

"What happened to Spinka Vinograd?"

Margrit shrugged. "No idea. I expect he's dead by now, too."

She seemed to lose interest in the subject at that point, and started talking about a handbag she had just seen in Mogilev's.

"It's real Italian leather," she said. "Do you think I should go back and get it?"

I smiled and said she probably should. I realised what I had already begun to realise all those years ago, that Margrit and I didn't have much in common. We exchanged mobile numbers at the end of our lunch but I never called her and she never called me and we haven't seen each other since.

"Will you tell Marius about Orel?" I asked Spinka.

He looked surprised and a little upset. "Of course not," he said. "What on earth has Orel to do with him?"

"I was thinking Marius could help. With the hospital bills, I mean."

"Not everything is about money, Lin. Will you promise me you won't tell them?"

I nodded. I didn't know if his decision was the right one and I felt sorry for the sick boy but I didn't want to get involved. I had enough problems to think about already.

"Would you like to keep this photograph? I have others."

I thought it was strange of him to suggest it but I said yes anyway. "I should go," I said. "If I don't get home soon Nadia will have a panic attack." I smiled. "Thanks for the tea." I kissed him quickly on the cheek then clattered back down the stairs and into the street. I ate supper with Nadia and Marius then told them I was going to read in my room.

"You're not going down with something, are you?" Nadia said.

"Don't fuss, Nadenka," said Marius. "It's been a difficult day for all of us."

I lay on top of the covers looking at the Polaroid of Sofie and her family. Its colours had already started to fade, to go greenish around the edges, the way Polaroids do. I gazed at it for what seemed like ages then tucked it inside my journal for safekeeping. I have it there still.

• • •

The following week Nadia sat me down at the kitchen table and told me I was going to live with the Sharpneses. The Sharpneses were friends of Marius and they lived in the city of Tynda in Eastern Siberia.

"How long for?" I said. Tynda was four time zones away. I imagined it as a cold, bleak place lost in an endless wasteland of pine forests and armaments factories. The knowledge that I was being sent there made my head spin.

"A couple of months, that's all, perhaps a year. It depends how long this trial business goes on. You know how hard things are for your granddad at the moment."

"What about school?" I said. "All my friends are here. I don't want to go."

Nadia's mouth tightened and the familiar frown line appeared between her eyebrows. "There are perfectly good schools in Tynda and you'll soon make new friends. Don't be difficult, Alina, it's all been decided. I don't have time to sit here and argue." She sighed noisily and rubbed at her eyes. "Just think of it as a break from all this mess."

There was something in that, at least, and I resolved to make the best of it. I wrote to Nicky, gloating that I would be travelling on the BAM railway, something I knew he lusted after. With him in Perm and me in Tynda we would be further apart than ever.

I started packing that same evening. Three days later I was on my way.

• • •

I shared a compartment with three others: a Magyar woman and her daughter, and a man named Erich Jorgenssen who said he was a traveller in pharmaceuticals. The Magyar woman had coarse-grained ivory skin and huge green eyes the colour of bottle glass. In spite of the cramped conditions her clothes and hair and make-up were always immaculate. The daughter was about six. They chatted together quietly in their own language. I wondered what they were doing so far from home.

Erich Jorgenssen was six feet tall, with a florid complexion and fair hair. Everything about him was large. The railway company had allocated him the top bunk, and it was while correcting this error in judgement that we got talking. Even with all his stuff transferred to the bottom bunk the space was too small for him. The only way he could lie down was with his feet poking out at an angle and resting on his suitcase.

"Thank God it's not an aeroplane," he muttered, musingly. "I hate aeroplanes."

He had a strong German accent and a laugh that seemed to shake the whole compartment. I kept noticing the ring he wore, a gold band set with a square-cut yellow stone. He told me the yellow stone was called a citrine.

"That's the smart name for yellow quartz," he said. "It's supposed to help you in achieving your goals." He waved his enormous hand, spattering the carriage wall with gouts of sunlight. His fingers were like sausages. I was surprised he had found a ring that would fit him.

I liked and trusted Erich Jorgenssen on sight. When I asked him how far he was travelling he said he was going right through to Shanghai. This meant he would be with me as far as Tayshet, where I had to change on to the BAM for the final stage of the journey to Tynda. I felt pleased and relieved that I would have his company most of the way.

"You're very young to be travelling by yourself," he said.

"I'm almost fourteen," I said. "And my uncle will be there to meet me at the other end."

I did my best to sound confident, for my own sake as much as his, though the end of the journey was something I preferred not to think about. I quickly grew used to life on board the train, the small closed world with its predictable and comforting routines. With Jorgenssen to talk to I secretly began to wish that we could travel for ever, eating *khvorost* and playing whist, always moving but never arriving in an endlessly repeating circuit of the world. I had little idea of what awaited me in Tynda. Did the Sharpneses actually want me, or had they agreed to take me in grudgingly as a favour to Marius? Would I ever be allowed to go home? So long as

I stayed on the train such questions were suspended and therefore irrelevant. But the days moved inexorably onward. The journey that seemed insurmountable at its outset was soon closer to its end than to its beginning.

On the morning of the fifth day I awoke to find the familiar landscape of ploughed fields and birch forests had begun to give way to the wider horizons and arid scrublands of Western Siberia. Somewhere to the north lay the Urals, and somewhere further east was my new home. I pressed my face to the window, steaming up the glass with my exhaled breath. A little later Jorgenssen brought me tea and rolls from the buffet car. The rolls were slightly stale but the tea was sweet and hot. Jorgenssen heaved himself on to his bunk. He wore the same thing every day: shabby carpet slippers and a vast blue tracksuit which he sometimes augmented with a marquee-sized silk kimono. His pockets were crammed with a seemingly inexhaustible supply of chocolate bars and trinkets, playing cards, propelling pencils, and cigarettes in a flat gold case. There were other things, too: a leather-covered notebook in which he jotted things down at regular intervals, and also a small device with headphones that Jorgenssen said was an mp3 player. But on several occasions I caught him inserting tiny cassettes into the machine and I suspected it was used for recording rather than playback.

"What are they?" I asked him. "No one uses tapes these days."

"I am no longer a cool young rapper, in case you haven't noticed," Jorgenssen said. "You could say I came out of the ark."

I laughed happily, settling myself back against the cushions. "I bet you're a spy," I said.

"A very large spy, then. Which obviously would make it difficult to blend in with the crowd. I'll tell you a secret." He put one of his huge fingers to his lips. "I'm a train spotter. I write articles for *Trans-European*, which is a boring magazine for other sad unfortunates like myself. If you would rather not share my compartment now I'm sure a transfer could be arranged."

I laughed again. "I think I can cope," I said. "Just about, anyway."

We sat on our bunks and talked for a while, then went down to the observation car and watched the landscape scroll by, vast and inscrutable. After lunch we played a few hands of rummy then agreed to take a nap. When I awoke it was early evening and Jorgenssen was not in his bunk. I lay on my back and dozed, expecting him to return at any moment, but when an hour went by and there was still no sign of him I leaned over and asked the Magyar woman if she knew where he'd gone. I pointed at the empty bunk, not sure how well she understood me, but she simply shook her head and lowered her eyes. I was not too worried. I thought he had probably gone to the buffet compartment, and I decided to join him. I slipped down from my bunk and started along the corridor. The train swayed gently from side to side, a continuous and soothing motion I had become so accustomed to I normally only noticed it when it stopped. Outside the windows the sun was going down in a creamy cocktail of pink and yellow. The land below was already dark, its intentions hidden.

The first sitting for supper had just started and the buffet car was full. I looked around for Jorgenssen but there was no sign of him. After a minute or two I spotted someone I recognised, a Polish woman who was on her way to a music festival on Lake Baikal. I approached her table and asked if she happened to have seen Erich Jorgenssen enter the compartment. She finished the mouthful she was chewing, helped it down with a gulp of *sekt* then shook her head.

"The fat man? I haven't seen him, dear. And he's not exactly someone you would miss."

A woman sitting nearby stifled a laugh. I thanked the Polish woman and turned away. I was beginning to feel anxious. I left the buffet compartment and walked along to the observation car but he was not there either. I knew we had been due to stop at Krasnoyarsk, and presumably had done so while I was asleep, but I could think of no conceivable reason why Jorgenssen might have left the train there. If his travel plans had changed he would have told me. In any case, his luggage was still in our sleeping compartment.

My chest felt tight, and I realised I was on the edge of panic. I began to wander up and down the corridor, peeking randomly into compartments and luggage rooms, stumbling over cleaning equipment and discarded crockery, and on one occasion surprising a train guard with one of the sleeper attendants in the linen store. His white shirt was plastered to his back, his uniform trousers with their sleek red piping rippled in a pool around his ankles. I backed away quickly, my cheeks on fire, and went back for one final inspection of the buffet car. As I made my way along the corridor, the door to the men's toilets opened and someone came out. The train lurched and he almost bashed into me.

"Excuse me," said the man. "Sorry about that."

He had a voice I vaguely recognised. I glanced up at him, thinking he must be one of the waiters from the buffet car, but he was not. I could not place him at first, though he was definitely familiar. Then I realised it was Andrew Silvestrov, the youngest of the four cosmonauts on board the *Anastasia*, the one Nicky had referred to as a trophy pilot. He was wearing jeans and a plaid shirt, also spectacles, though whether he needed them or was wearing them as a disguise it was impossible to tell. He was slim and dark and shy-looking, just like in the photographs. He raised his hand to me in a half-salute then went off down the corridor.

I felt too stunned at first to move. I watched Silvestrov's back as he moved further away from me, the slight hunch of his shoulders, the way his shirt creased where it was tucked into the waistband of his jeans. His hands hung loose by his sides. There was a piece of sticking plaster around his left pinkie finger. I closed my eyes and then opened them again. Logic told me I was seeing a dead man, a ghost, yet he seemed too ordinary to be a ghost, too secure in his skin. He was as attractive in reality as he had seemed on television.

He walked to the end of the corridor, then through the automatic door that led to the next set of sleeper carriages. Quickly and without reaching any conscious decision to do so I began to follow him. I felt suddenly convinced that when I passed through the doorway I would find him gone.

I eased the door open, emerging on the other side just in time to see Silvestrov vanish into one of the sleeper cabins. I briefly caught the sound of other voices, a burst of laughter, then the door thumped closed. I was in a part of the train I did not know well, the three or four carriages near the front that housed the first-class sleeper cabins and the executive buffet car. I kept expecting a guard to appear and throw me out but none did. I crept along the corridor until I came to the door Silvestrov had gone through. I put my ear to the panelling and heard once again the sound of voices and muffled laughter.

I needed time to think but knew I had none. There was a luggage stow towards the rear of the carriage. I selected a battered-looking leather trunk and pulled it out into the corridor, aligning it with Silvestrov's doorway and then upending it. I prayed it would take my weight without bursting open. I climbed on top, almost bumping my head on the carriage ceiling. The cabin doors were solid wood but most had fanlights, glass panels designed for the purpose of admitting extra light. I knew that by standing on top of the trunk I would be able to see directly into Silvestrov's compartment.

All four of them were inside: Stanislaus, Batushin, Lerner and Silvestrov himself. They were seated around one of the pull-down tables, playing cards. I could see an open bottle of vodka and four shot glasses. Vik Lerner was smoking a cigarette. They were obviously having a good time.

I stood there transfixed, terrified one of them would look up and see me, yet unable to stop staring nonetheless. What got me moving was the sound of a door slamming further down the train. I had no idea if whoever it was was coming my way but I knew it was time I got out of there. I had seen the impossible, something no one was supposed to see. The outcome of being discovered would not be healthy.

It occurred to me that Erich Jorgenssen must have known about the four cosmonauts all along, that they were why he was on the train. I thought of the notebook, the Dictaphone with its tiny cassettes, and felt sick to my stomach.

I moved the trunk away from the door, trying to make it look as if it had wound up in the corridor by accident. I dived back through the automatic doors, walking the length of the next carriage and through a further set of doors as fast as I could. After that I felt safer. I slipped inside one of the rest rooms and locked the door, then waited until my heartbeat and breathing returned to normal. When I finally emerged I made my way quickly back to my own compartment. I hoped that when I got there I would find Jorgenssen, that my fears for him were unfounded, a stupid mistake.

I slid open the door. The Magyar woman was reading a story to her daughter from one of her picture books. They scarcely registered my arrival. Jorgenssen's bunk had been stripped and his baggage was gone.

• • •

My mind boiled with questions. If the crew of the *Anastasia* were alive then either the launch had been a hoax, or Silvestrov and the others were never on board. I knew from Nicky that there were such people as test pilots, fliers of exceptional skill and technical knowledge who were willing to take certain risks. Could the *Anastasia* have been manned by test pilots? What would happen to Batushin and his crew now that everyone believed they were dead?

One thing that seemed certain was that the fate of Erich

Jorgenssen and that of cosmonauts were linked in some way. Someone knew or suspected the truth and Jorgenssen had been sent to confirm it. Later on someone else had found a way to shut him up. Either that, or I had imagined the whole conspiracy.

I climbed into my bunk, pulled the curtain across and lay down. I felt utterly alone, more miserable than I had done since Nicky left. Finally I slept, and when I woke the following morning I made up my mind to pretend that Jorgenssen had got off the train of his own accord. I stayed mostly inside the compartment the rest of the way to Tayshet, leaving it only to visit the bathroom and the buffet car. In my journal I sketched the outline of a story in which Jorgenssen was an investigative journalist kidnapped by the FSB. My first version of the story had him shot in the back of the head and dumped beside the railway line. Later the same night I rewrote it, with Jorgenssen left wandering on the road outside a one-pump gas station on the outskirts of Novosibirsk. I imagined the sweat on his brow, a dried bloodstain on his collar from where somebody had punched him on the nose. They had left him there without any money. I wasn't sure what happened after that.

• • •

Kiril and Munia Sharpnes both taught Russian. Kiril Sharpnes was the son of Alex Sharpnes, who had been Marius's best friend at college. Alex came from Glasgow, in Scotland. Kiril's mother was from Ukraine. Kiril and Munia had no children of their own. I had never met any of these people, but when I saw Kiril Sharpnes, coming towards me across the chilly echoing foyer of Tynda's main railway station, I recognised him immediately from the photographs in Marius's album. He was a tall man and skinny, his coat sleeves riding up around his wrists. A strand of grey hair kept flopping forward into his eyes.

"Alina Rodionovna," he said. "Our Alya."

He smiled at me, and I thought I had never seen a more beautiful smile. I felt my eyes fill up with tears of gratitude, and I longed to say something to him in greeting, but when I opened my mouth to speak nothing came. My mouth felt dry as dust, as if I needed to cough. I didn't utter a word for the next three days.

• • •

Tynda started out as a mining settlement and ended up as a railway terminus and a centre for the logging trade. Aside from the theatre and the station and a handful of houses put up by fur traders and the original gold miners, most of the city's buildings were less than a century old. Alex Sharpnes brought his family to Tynda during the second Cold War because there was a shortage of teachers in the east and wages were high, which meant they'd be able to afford a larger apartment.

Where Tynda ended the wastes began. From my second-floor bedroom window I could see the tracks of the BAM railway line as they wound their way east through the city and towards Komsomolsk.

Munia was part-Yupik, a compact round-cheeked woman with slightly foreshortened limbs and slanted eyes. She showed me photos of herself as a child, a tiny snub-nosed girl in a fur jacket, holding a silver balloon to celebrate the fiftieth anniversary of Tynda's first international gas pipeline. A fortnight after my arrival she took me along to the High School Rosa Luxemburg, just a short tram ride from where we lived. I was given a seat next to a Yupik girl called Lita Berezovsky.

"Where are you from?" she asked me as soon as the bell rang. When I told her she frowned and grabbed my hand, holding it tightly between both of hers.

"You'll freeze when the winter comes," she said. "I'll make you some proper gloves."

When she smiled her eyes disappeared into her face, her eyelashes curled like feathers on the rims of her cheeks. Her braided black hair reached to her knees.

She lived not far from me, in a prefab bungalow that had been put up on a patch of waste ground by Lita's father. The Berezovskys ran a lunch room in town and were never home till late in the evening. Lita cooked all her own meals, throwing things together in a large frying pan with a casual enthusiasm that reminded me of Marius, the way he had been in the old days. Lita's bedroom was huge and untidy, littered with half-finished sewing projects and piles of foreign fashion magazines. We holed up there for hours, listening to the Western rap stations and gossiping about the teachers.

Lita was clever and trustworthy, and in time I came to tell her most of the reasons I had ended up in Tynda in the first place.

"Harsh gig," she said. "Do you reckon you'll ever go back?"

"I don't know," I said. "I don't want to go back now, anyway."

I liked living with the Sharpneses. I especially liked the calm and considerate way they treated each other. When

Munia renewed my tram pass after Christmas I noticed that her name, instead of Nadia's, was stamped on the back of the ticket as my next of kin.

Tynda became my home for the next eight years.

• • •

There was a teacher at the school called Viktoria Fulkina. Fulkina taught history and literature, and ran an after-school drama club. When she put a poster on the class noticeboard advertising a play-writing competition I thought I'd give it a go.

"What makes you think you can write?" she said to me when I approached her after class to ask for an entry form. I wanted to sink through the floor. It was as if she had perceived some fundamental weakness in me, had made the whole idea of me becoming a writer ridiculous and impossible. I found out soon enough this was just her way of testing my commitment. Later she did everything she could to help me succeed.

Fulkina was a gifted actor who had once performed in Moscow and Petersburg. I couldn't imagine what had brought her to Tynda. She wore a wedding ring, though most people seemed to believe that her husband was dead. She lived in a tiny one-room apartment in the old town.

For a long time I was in awe of her. It wasn't until my last year of school, when her theatre group were putting on a play of mine, that I finally plucked up the courage to ask her about her life.

"What happened?" I said to her. "Why here?"

I thought she might find my questions impertinent but she seemed amused.

"There are worse places," she said. "And the Siberian skies are bigger, don't you find?"

Later that same evening she asked me back to her apartment for coffee. She showed me some old press cuttings, photos of herself at seventeen in Ostrovsky's *The Storm*.

"It feels like another world now," she said. "Sometimes the life you need turns out to be different from the life you wanted. And Ostrovsky is always Ostrovsky, wherever you go."

She laughed, as if to make light of her suffering, though I sensed something behind her words, a ferocity that insisted even if a person's life is broken, her spirit remains unbowed.

In those moments she reminded me of Sofie. I wondered about Fulkina's wedding ring, and I wondered what had become of Sofie's son.

• • •

My name is Alina Maslanyi and I am a writer. The work I am best known for is *Stardust*, the play I wrote about the *Anastasia* disaster and that was turned into a Hollywood movie starring Diccon Wetherall as Mike Batushin. The play focuses not on the disaster itself but on its aftermath, and in particular its effect on the lives of the cosmonauts' wives. The whole of the second act takes place in Sonia Batushin's living room in Moscow, and imagines what might happen if her husband suddenly came back from the dead.

The play is dedicated to the memory of my grandmother, Sofie Pepusch. *Stardust* was banned in my country at first. When critics began discussing the play as a work of science fiction it was reinstated. The success of the film adaptation enabled me to write full-time. I am currently at work on a novel based on the life of my brother, the chess grandmaster and political dissident Nicky Maslanyi.

WRECK OF THE JULIA

I have never attached much importance to what happens in dreams. I tend to dislike any story that relies on a dream sequence to resolve the identity of the murderer or the missing father – it feels like cheating to me. How ironic then that when I came to think about telling my own story, I realised almost at once I had to start with the dreams. Not that the dreams explain anything – they are as mysterious to me now as they were at the outset. I have to talk about them, though, because they were the catalyst for everything that followed.

The dreams began soon after the plane crash. I slept badly those first few weeks. If I went to bed early I couldn't sleep at all, but if I stayed up late in an attempt to feel sleepier I fell unconscious in front of the television, only to rouse again in the small hours, wide awake.

I saw those empty early mornings as a vacuum between days, a period of time to be got through simply by lying there waiting for the minutes to pass. I was too tired to read, and I developed an illogical fear of listening to the radio in case it brought me news of another plane crash. I never did more than doze during those hours and strange though it might seem, given what I am about to tell you, I don't remember dreaming much either. I still think of that first dream as a watershed, so clear and so entire, arising from the depths of what had been my first decent night's rest since Eloise walked out of the bedroom and out of my life.

I was on board a ship, a great ocean-going liner, its vast flanks gleaming white, its three funnels pillar-box red. There was an atmosphere of intense, almost preternatural stillness, and I understood at once that although I had complete awareness of my surroundings I was there as an observer, not a participant, and that whatever was going on here could not harm me.

The ship had run aground and come to rest on a narrow spit of land, a tapering sandbank that in my hyper-lucid state I remember thinking resembled the tongue of a dragon. At the landward end I could just make out some greyish bushes, more sand dunes, a pebbly path. The sea that lapped the shore looked unbearably cold, the steely Prussian blue of northern waters. The ship lay tilted against the sky, a beached leviathan. Strangely it cast no shadow.

Some of the passengers had come ashore, and what I remember most clearly is that they were in evening dress, the women in strapless gowns, the men in tuxedos, their hair combed and brilliantined in the manner of 1950s movie idols. They huddled beneath the prow of the ship, talking together in whispers and with dazed expressions. I could see they were in shock, struggling to come to terms with what had happened to them. As I watched, they formed a straggling line and began making their way along the beach and away from the ship. The man in the lead wore a peaked cap and braided jacket, and I thought he was probably the captain. As they filed slowly past me, my eye was caught by the sight of one woman in particular, small and dark, her slim body encased in a backless evening dress of vibrant green. Her silver stilettos kept sinking into the sand. She was leaning on the arm of a man, a well-built, powerful figure of indeterminate age. His jacket was torn in several places, revealing its grey silk lining. I had the feeling I might know him from somewhere, but I didn't know where. The woman was my wife, Eloise. I stared at her, unbelieving, my amazement gradually giving way to a kind of numb horror. I knew the dream had it wrong, you see – my wife had died in an air crash, not in a shipwreck. Then I remembered with an awful lurch that my wife had not died at all.

It was this jolt of realisation that woke me. I lay for some moments without moving, trying to reorientate myself. My heart was pounding with fear, though I could not have said what I was afraid of. When I finally opened my eyes the room was filled with the silvery greyish light of early morning, and when I looked at my bedside clock I saw with surprise that it was after seven. In spite of the dream I felt rested as I had not done in weeks.

A couple of nights later I dreamed the same dream again. I could not say if it was identical in every particular, but the salient features – the beach, the ship, the passengers in evening dress, recognising my wife at the end – were all as before. I had never really believed in recurring dreams. If I held any opinion about them at all I would have said they were induced or engineered by their dreamers, who by dwelling on particular matters in their waking lives somehow willed these repeated visions into being. I had not even thought much about the first dream afterwards, and if it had not repeated itself I would no doubt have forgotten it entirely. As it was, I felt unsettled by its recurrence, and about a week after that something even stranger happened: I dreamed not the same dream exactly but a continuation of it, like the next episode in a television series, or the second part of a film I hadn't had time to watch in its entirety the first time.

I knew at once that something was different. This time I was not merely observing the passengers, I was one of them, the feeling of being at a safe distance from the proceedings replaced by a feeling of panic. I was trapped in a situation I barely understood but felt certain would end badly.

We had left the ship behind, the captain leading us doggedly along the shore. There was a cold wind blowing, and my discomfort was increased by the knowledge that Eloise was somewhere behind me, accompanied by the man in the black tuxedo. We trudged along for a long time without getting anywhere, and gradually I became convinced we had made a terrible mistake, that with every step we took we were becoming more lost. I struggled forward, pushing other passengers aside in my haste to reach the captain. My clothes stank, and I could feel the sweat running off me in rivers. When I finally reached the captain and began to remonstrate with him he seemed not to hear me.

Then, in one of those peculiar non sequiturs that are so common in dreams, I was fighting my way alone across the sand dunes. I felt quite mad, desperate. There was sand in my mouth and the reek and taste of salt were everywhere but in spite of these things I eventually managed to get away from the beach, to reach the upward-sloping pathway I had glimpsed in the first dream.

I felt an immediate relief. The ground was stony underfoot but the path was well-defined and not too steep. Now I was away from the shifting sand I found I could walk easily and made steady progress. The barren coastal landscape had disappeared, replaced by low-lying bushes and scrawny trees. I continued my climb, content at first simply to be away from the beach, but little by little my feelings of unease began to return. I was unable to escape the feeling that I had made a disastrous error, that the path led nowhere, that I was now even more at sea than the passengers who had put their faith in the captain.

When I finally came to a standstill I was gasping, not just from the effort of climbing but from sheer panic. To my left lay a seemingly endless vista of dusty scrub. To my right was a low, stone-built structure that I took to be some kind of animal enclosure. In front of me the path continued, but the gradient was now much steeper, gripping the mountainside in a series of tight hairpin bends, a looping concentric spiral that put me in mind of one of the impossible mountain roadways in children's cartoons.

I took a step forward, intending to begin my ascent, but in the precise instant of doing so I knew with utter certainty that *I must not go up there*, that the top of the mountain concealed something so hideous, so inconceivably awful that even to see it would result in madness. I turned and fled, terrified I would fall and break my ankle. From somewhere behind me there came a dull rumble, as of blasting equipment or giant footsteps, and I knew that I was running for my life.

I woke up bathed in sweat, my heart pounding as if I really had been running. I took slow deep breaths, insisting to myself I was safe yet in some deep part of myself still not able to believe it. In the end I managed to get up and go to the bathroom and after that I felt calmer. By the time I was up and dressed I had dismissed the dream from my mind, telling myself that nightmares were a natural side-effect of trauma and that the important thing was that I appeared to have conquered my insomnia.

The final dream came that same night. In it, I entered the living room of the house in Croydon where I had grown up and found my sister, Milly, watching TV. She was lolling in her favourite armchair, her bare feet resting on the coffee table. It was a bright day outside, but Milly had the curtains closed, a habit of hers that drove our mother mad.

She turned towards me and began to speak.

"Look," she said. "They're about to show that film about the mountain."

I turned towards the screen. The television was the old Ultrabrite portable I had taken with me to university. A grainy black-and-white title sequence showed a barren, hilly landscape of scrub and shale.

"No!" I cried, my mind filling with terror. I made a lunge for the off switch and then woke up. My first thought was to call Milly, but one glance at the clock told me that if I didn't hurry I would be late for work.

I spent the day feeling distracted, as if there was something important I had forgotten to attend to. I telephoned Milly as soon as I got in that evening.

"Hey," she said. "Are you OK?" Milly's given name is Sandra, but if anyone ever called her that I can't remember.

"I'm fine," I said. "I felt like a chat, that's all."

She seemed to accept that all I wanted was a little company, and we had talked for more than half an hour before she suddenly asked me how I'd been sleeping.

"Better," I said. Her question caught me off guard but it shouldn't have. Milly always did have a way of knowing what I was thinking. I couldn't have put into words exactly why I had called her, except that my dream of the night before had made me worry about her, and as the day wore on I felt increasingly anxious to know that she was all right.

Milly never liked Eloise. She told me I was crazy to marry her.

"She'll bleed you dry, Vernon," she said. "I can't believe you don't realise."

"What is there to bleed? I'm hardly a millionaire."

"I'm not talking about money, you know that. What I mean is she's selfish. She's not interested in you, she's interested in the way you feel about her. You make her feel like the most fascinating woman that ever lived and she can't get enough of it."

The truth was that at the time I was so infatuated with Eloise that as far as I was concerned she was the most fascinating woman that ever lived, but I wasn't about to admit that to

Milly. My sister was always civil to Eloise for my sake, but she adopted a policy of having as little to do with her as possible. In the months before my marriage, and for some time afterwards, I told myself Milly was jealous, that it was natural for her to be jealous, and that all I had to do was give it time. I made various efforts to bring the two women together, but after a while even I could see that Eloise disliked Milly almost as much as Milly disliked Eloise.

I think at least some of Milly's dislike really did stem from jealousy. Milly and I were close, a bond made stronger by the fact we had been born just ten months apart. When Eloise's plane went down, Milly behaved with impeccable tact. She expressed horror at the tragedy and sorrow for the victims. She didn't pretend any grief for Eloise personally though, and before many days had passed she stopped mentioning her altogether. It was obvious, at least to me, that Milly believed I would be better off without her.

I think it was Milly's dislike of Eloise, as much as anything, that formed part of the reason I never told her the truth about the plane crash.

Now, speaking to her on the phone, I found myself wishing for the thousandth time that I could find a way of telling her without it seeming to my sister that I had lied. I hadn't called about the crash, though – for the first time since it happened, what happened with Eloise's plane seemed of secondary importance.

"Do you remember a film about a mountain?" I said instead.

"A mountain? Not unless you mean *The Sound of Music*. What on earth are you on about?"

"Don't laugh, this is serious. I mean a weird story about a man who gets lost on a mountain and then goes mad. It was in black-and-white, I think, a horror film."

"I don't think so." Milly paused. "Is it important?"

I sighed. "Not really. It's just that I couldn't remember the title. You know what it's like when that happens."

"I honestly don't think I've seen it. Are you sure you're all right?"

"Don't worry about me, Mil. I'll see you at the weekend, OK?"

We said goodbye and I went to make supper. I poured myself a glass of wine, thinking how bizarre it had been, to question my sister about a film that, so far as I knew, did not exist outside my dream. I began to wonder if the attack of madness that led me to conceal the truth about what had happened to Eloise had not been a one-off incident as I had encouraged myself to believe, but the prelude to a full-throttle dive into insanity.

I thought I would be bound to return to the world of the mountain in my dreams, but I did not go there that night, or the night after that. As the days passed, and then the weeks, the memories and the images began to recede. In the end I put down the episode to shock, a delayed reaction to the loss of my wife. But then something happened that forced me to change my mind.

• • •

At the time I first met Eloise I was working as a sales rep for a publisher and distributor of school textbooks. I had not planned on such a career. Rather, I drifted into it after I left university as a way of staying afloat financially while I worked out what I wanted to do with my life. After a couple of months I began to see that the job had advantages. I was my own boss to an extent, and did not have to put up with the bickering and infighting that goes on in most office environments. I also liked the travelling, the sense of freedom and change that came with being continually on the move. I was constantly busy, and yet able to retain the illusion that I was in charge of my life, that I could change direction whenever I wanted, that my destiny was just around the corner.

Eloise was the deputy administrator of a medium-sized comprehensive in Sidcup. She obviously had her eye on the top job, which at the time I first knew her was in the possession of a pedantic spinster in her late fifties who was secretly referred to as the Dragon.

I was attracted to Eloise the moment I saw her. She was small and slim, with finely made gamine features and flawless ivory skin that flushed a delicate shade of rose whenever she laughed. She had an alluring lilt to her walk that I discovered only later was due to her right leg being very slightly shorter than her left. She had a curious love for all things French. I often saw French books on her desk – everything from Simone de Beauvoir to the Roux brothers. For a long time I supposed this fascination for a foreign country originated with her name, but after we married I learned that she had changed her name to reflect her passion. The name on her birth certificate was not Eloise but Helen.

Each time I called at the school I had to sign in at the administration office, and as I grew familiar with the routines of the various people who worked there I was able to time my appointments to coincide with when I knew Eloise would be alone. We seemed to have much in common, and it was not long before I was dropping in at the school for no other reason than to see her. I started bringing her little presents: a book of poems by Baudelaire, a piece of Roquefort from the cheese stall on Borough Market. She appeared to enjoy the attention and I couldn't believe my luck.

Our marriage lasted just over five years. Milly was right, of course, we should never have been together, but even now I find myself reluctant to blame Eloise for a situation that was as much her mistake as mine. In her mind she had imagined me rising through the ranks of my firm, becoming first an area manager then a director, with my steadily increasing salary finally sufficient to acquire the four-bedroom Victorian semi in Chiswick she had always dreamed of. Imagine her horror when she discovered I was happy coasting along, that I saw no reason why we should not be content with our current station.

"When are you going to grow up?" she yelled at me once, during one of our increasingly frequent arguments. "I'm sick of you bumming around." A somewhat inaccurate description of the forty-hour week I invariably put in at my job, perhaps, though I understood what she meant. I alternated between a kind of frozen, impotent anger and an apologetic, ineffectual grief that made me wish I was anywhere but crammed together with Eloise in our shabby little two-bed in Camberwell, a place I had once been proud of and still loved.

We wanted different things. Our break-up had been inevitable from the start.

I found out my wife was leaving me because she did not die in a plane crash. I already knew that she would leave me eventually – it was simply a matter of when, or rather how soon. When she told me she was taking a trip to Luxor with an old school friend I didn't believe her, but I kept my doubts silent. I wasn't ready for the truth yet, for the tumult of conflicting emotions, the recriminations, the lawyers, Eloise's permanent removal from my life.

"What about our trip to Avignon?" I said. We were due to go on holiday ourselves in just a few weeks. I think I was hoping she might still change her mind.

"That's just an excuse for you to trawl around museums. I want some fun for a change."

I tried not to notice what went into her suitcase. I didn't want to be presented with any clues. The case stood in the hallway overnight. It was enormous, bigger than anyone would have needed just for a week, even Eloise. When she left for the airport by taxi the following morning I pretended to be asleep.

I was in the car when I heard about the crash. The radio was tuned to Radio 4 as usual. I was half-listening, my eyes on the road, my mind partly preoccupied with my next appointment. When the midday news came on, the newsreader announced they were getting reports that a passenger plane had come down somewhere over Egypt. The cause of the crash was not yet known, though it was feared there were no survivors. They gave the number of the flight, another number to call for the relatives of those on board. I swerved over to the side of the road, almost causing an accident myself in the process. I remained where I was for at least fifteen minutes, parked up in a lay-by on the outskirts of Tonbridge, watching the traffic rush past the windows and listening to the rest of the news bulletin: a terrorist bomb in Delhi, the closure of a car plant in Dagenham, a royal visit to a hospital somewhere near Manchester. Then I reignited the engine and drove slowly home. I was still not completely sure it was her plane. But the time was right, and the flight number, which I had seen because Eloise had written it down for me on the back of an envelope, seemed ominously familiar.

I parked outside the house, bemused by the number of free parking places, forgetting it was the middle of the day and most people would be at work. I forced myself to get out of the car and go inside. Then I went upstairs in search of the envelope. It was there on the dressing table, exactly as I remembered, the flight number scrawled in red biro beneath the telephone number of the hotel where Eloise was supposed to be staying. The computer confirmed it was the same number they had read out over the radio.

I sat down on the edge of the bed. I heard the ticking of the clock on the landing, the characteristic double click of the hot water thermostat, a car passing by on the street. I was still holding the envelope, and I could not get past the thought that Eloise had had the same envelope in her hands less than twenty-four hours before. I had been in bed already, fanning her irritation with my immobility, watching her covertly from behind the covers of the book I was reading and trying not to think about where she was going.

Now I was trying not to think about her final moments, trying not to wonder if she had known what was about to happen to her or whether the sudden influx of freezing air and the loss of cabin pressure had made her lose consciousness immediately. I got up from the bed and went into the bathroom, where I crashed to my knees by the basin and vomited into the toilet bowl. After that I went back to the bedroom and called Milly. I knew she would be at work – Milly is a theatrical costumier – but I also knew she would always answer her phone if she knew it was me. She picked up on the second ring. I told her in as few words as I could manage what had happened.

"My God, Vernon, I can't believe it," she said. "Just hang on in there. I'm coming straight round."

"No," I said at once. "Could I come to you?" I wanted to be out of the house. I felt a terror of being there for some reason, a sudden horror of being confronted with Eloise's possessions.

"Of course you can," Milly said. "I'm leaving now. I'll be home in twenty minutes. Be careful how you drive, OK?"

I put down the phone, feeling dazed and ill but aware nonetheless of other thoughts that were beginning to creep in: that perhaps it was better this way, that now I could grieve for Eloise in earnest, that I would be spared the humiliation of her infidelity, the inevitable separation and divorce. I loathed myself for these thoughts and was sickened by them, but still they came. In the wake of them came the outlandish notion that the plane crash was somehow my fault, that I had willed the deaths of all those people just so I could be free of Eloise.

I packed an overnight bag, trying to keep my mind on the practical details. I was halfway out the door when it occurred to me I ought to telephone the number they had given out on the radio, that I should report in, so to speak, find out if there was anything I needed to do to make my new status as a widower official.

I wondered what the legalities were in cases like this, when your wife was dead but there was no body to prove it. Half an hour later my question had become academic. I called the helpline and spoke to a woman, first confirming the flight number then giving Eloise's name. She put me on hold almost at once. I held the phone to my ear, my mind drifting in slow unsteady circles while I waited for something to happen. Finally the woman came back on the line. She told me she had checked the records and her manager had double-checked and there could be no doubt about it: Eloise had not been one of the passengers on board the plane.

I thanked her and put down the phone. No doubt the woman attributed my distractedness to the shock of relief, but in truth my mind had gone blank. I thought of calling Milly, telling her she needn't come home from work after all, then realised that was pointless, she would already be on her way. In any case I needed her now as much as I had thirty minutes ago and perhaps more so. I decided to drive over as planned and tell her the whole story. It would be easier than trying to explain things over the phone.

Unfortunately that wasn't what happened. Milly had arrived home ahead of me and was watching for me out of the window. As I pulled up to the kerb she opened the front door and came running out to the car.

"I've just been watching the news," she said. "Oh, Vernon."

She hugged me right there on the street, and when she finally drew away from me I could see there were tears in her eyes. She already accepted the plane crash as a fact of our lives, a defining moment, as of course it was, just not quite in the way she imagined.

"Is there anything you need me to do?" she said. "Do you think we should phone the airport?"

"I've already done that," I said. "That's why I'm late getting here." There it was, the moment I should have chosen to set the record straight, to tell Milly Eloise was not dead but that she had left me. Somehow – incredibly – I found myself not doing it, and the more time passed – first five minutes, then ten, then half an hour – the more impossible it became. A part of me dreaded the anticlimax, the revelation that I was not the victim of tragedy after all but just another jilted husband. But I can honestly say there were other reasons, too.

I felt positive Eloise wasn't coming home. If the plane crash had not happened she would most likely have returned from her "holiday" and we might have soldiered on together for another couple of months. As it was, I had a deep and certain intuition that she would use the accident as I was using it: as an opportunity to make a clean break. If both of us let things ride the deed was done. I could, if I so chose, let my wife's fictitious death take on the patina of actuality, let it become if not true exactly then true for me, true within the context of my life.

The decision to do that was easier than you might think. Milly quickly cottoned on to the fact that I preferred not to talk about the plane crash directly and seemed content to leave me to get over the tragedy in my own way. The fact she never liked Eloise probably made it easier for her to keep her distance. When, a couple of days after the crash, she asked me gently if I would like her to go to the victims' memorial service with me, I told her I was grateful for her support but that I would rather go alone. When the day came I put on a suit and went up to town, but instead of heading east to Aldgate where the service was being held – I had looked up the details online – I boarded a train at Charing Cross and travelled south to Folkestone, the home of my maternal grandparents and the site of many happy childhood holidays. I had not been back since Granny Tissot's funeral some ten years before and I felt a sudden urge to see the place again. I wandered round the harbour and browsed the second-hand bookshops in the old town, then had lunch in a seaside café along the Leas. I arrived back in London in the early evening and went straight to Milly's. We ate Chinese food and she told me about her day. It felt as if my marriage had never happened.

As the weeks passed and there was no word from my wife I did my best to believe the case was closed. I was unprepared for the sense of dislocation that accompanied my deception, the knowledge that I was inhabiting one reality – a world where Eloise was alive and walking around somewhere and I knew that she was – while everyone else I knew, including my own sister, was existing inside a fantasy I had created for them. This might not have mattered so much had it not been for Milly. I'd never kept secrets from Milly before. We had always shared everything.

Milly might not have known the truth, but she knew there was something. She insisted I had to make a start on rebuilding my life.

"You can't keep moping like this, Vernon," she said. "You're going to make yourself ill." We were having dinner over at her place and were both a bit drunk. "How about buying a painting? You haven't bought a painting in ages."

I made a face. "I'm not sure I want to do that any more."

"Oh come on, you used to love going to auctions. You had a real knack for it, too."

"Do you think so?"

"You know you did. You have a really good eye. You should go to a couple of sales, get your mind on something else. It would do you the world of good."

I had to admit her suggestion sparked my interest. I had always loved pictures. I did not have Milly's practical talent for painting, but I felt strongly drawn to those who did. I made my first art purchase when I was fifteen years old, a set of three pencil sketches of milk bottles by a boy in the year below me. I had neither the budget nor the ambition to be a serious collector, but the artworks I acquired gave me intense pleasure, as well as the sense that the world was a larger and more mysterious place than certain celebrity secularists would have us believe.

The paintings I bought were by artists few people had heard of, either because their careers ended prematurely or because they were overshadowed by some other greater figure of the time. I came to love these painters, not just because they were all I could afford but because of the mystery they presented.

I would gaze at the solemn, odd little works they produced – the still lifes with goats' skulls, the maiden aunts taking tea, the boarding-house living rooms with their monstrous sideboards and embroidered antimacassars – fascinated by their peculiar beauty and secretly hoping that I might one day uncover the work of some lost mad genius.

Eloise never took my art collecting seriously. She dismissed my treasures as so many white elephants, and saw in my taste for the worthless and unfashionable a perverse dilettantism, no doubt just one more aspect of my bumming around. Her indifference discouraged me, and during the course of my marriage I stopped attending auctions more or less entirely.

I knew Milly was right. I needed a focus, an interest that was mine alone and without any association with Eloise.

It was late when I got home, but my talk with Milly had left me feeling wide awake and full of energy. I booted up the computer and began to search the listings for upcoming sales. By lucky coincidence there was one the following day, an auction of paintings and antique furniture at a sales room I had visited once or twice in Muswell Hill. I went to bed just after one and slept soundly, waking at around ten o'clock. I rushed to get dressed, and arrived at the auction house shortly before midday. I had more or less made up my mind not to bid, that it would be enough for me simply to be there, to get my eye in.

I moved slowly around the exhibits, examining each lot with the languid complacency of the casual browser. I had always enjoyed the atmosphere of sales, the smell of dust and antique books and old leather, the furtive faces, the hushed confidences. I felt excited to be immersed in it again. I saw some artworks I liked, but none with the compulsion that tempted me to acquire them. Then I wandered idly into one of the side rooms and came face to face with the painting that would change my life.

It was in oil, some twenty-four inches by eighteen. In the picture, a two-masted sailing ship had run aground on a sandbank, a diagonal ochre band that formed a mainstay of the picture's composition. The sky was heavy, banked with rain clouds. The ship's rigging was badly torn, and what remained of its sails flapped uselessly against the masts in a blustering wind. A dozen or so passengers stood huddled beneath the prow. They were all in evening dress, ball gowns and black tuxedos. One of the women was wearing a green dress. Off to her right and slightly apart from the others stood a man in uniform. His right hand was raised, pointing into the distance and out of the picture.

The painting was called *Wreck of the Julia* and it depicted my dream. It was true that the ship in my dream was a steamer, an ocean liner rather than a sailing ship, but the atmosphere in the painting – that sense of haunted desolation – was identical with what I remembered from when I had dreamed it. The work was beautifully executed, with both the sea and the sky demonstrating a genuine facility. The artist's name was Kenneth Goule. I assumed from the style and the subject matter that he was a Victorian, but when I checked the auction catalogue I saw he had been dead less than ten years. The discovery surprised me. There were plenty of contemporary artists who excelled in pastiche, who made their living from making copies of the masters or from works painted in a deliberately traditional manner, but *Wreck of the Julia* had a quality of passion about it, a vigour, that made it seem authentic.

I knew at once I had to have it. The bond I formed with the painting was so compelling, and so immediate that the thought of seeing it sold to another bidder caused me distress. I think I almost believed it was mine by right. I had no idea how much it might go for. Traditional figurative oils by unknown artists did not often spiral out of control, but you could never tell with auctions. Everything depended on who was there and what they were looking for.

The bidding was due to start at two o'clock. I left the saleroom and went to a pub I knew on Muswell Hill Broadway. Somehow I sat out the hour, picking at a plate of chicken curry and feeling nervous. I set off back to the hall as soon as I could.

When the lot was finally called I felt sick to my stomach. I managed to avoid making the first bid – I knew it was best to hang back a little, to let your enemies come out of the woodwork. Once the first flurry of early, purely speculative bidders had fallen by the wayside I was left with just one main opponent, a woman with a moon-shaped face and short fair hair. She made her bids in a nervous, hand-fluttering manner that made it clear she was not a regular. This was a bad sign, because it suggested her interest in the painting was personal and not professional. Such bidders were always harder to shake off. Strangely enough I felt no animosity towards her, and there was something about her round, open face and tomboyish haircut that I found appealing. But I knew I could not let these sympathies affect me, that it was my purpose to defeat her challenge, and finally I did. I felt exultant, even though I knew I had most likely paid double what the painting was worth.

I glanced towards my rival to see how she was taking it. To my amazement and dismay I saw she was crying. As I watched she wiped her face with the sleeve of her jacket and hurried out of the hall.

It's hard to say what made me follow her. Partly guilt at being the cause of such distress, but also curiosity. I felt I needed to know what made her covet the painting so badly. There was also the simple, insistent fact that I liked the look of her. I wanted at the very least to know her name.

I reached the foyer just in time to see her disappearing into the Ladies. I hovered about by the noticeboard, waiting for her to reappear, but ten minutes passed and there was still no sign of her. I was about to leave, thinking I must have missed her in the crowd somehow, when the door to the toilets opened and there she was. Her moon face looked paler than before and the skin around her eyes was puffy and red. I took a step towards her, hoping I didn't look too threatening and wondering what I would do if she started screaming the place down and calling for help.

"I know this must sound strange," I said quickly. "But I wanted to make sure you were all right."

She gazed at me blankly, her eyes still bright with tears. Then her cheeks flushed a deep shade of pink.

"Oh dear," she said. "It was you that bought the painting, wasn't it? I expect I've made a right fool of myself."

"Not in the least," I said. "But I could see how upset you were. I wanted to say I'm sorry. I'm not used to making people cry." I could feel myself beginning to blush and I knew that in a few seconds my own cheeks would be as red as hers. More from panic than anything else I asked her if she would like to have coffee somewhere.

"I couldn't possibly," she said. "You must think I'm a crazy person." She smiled then. It was the first time I had seen her smile and it lit her whole face. Her moon cheeks and the thatch of bright hair made me think of sunflowers in full bloom.

"Actually I think you could be helpful to me," I said. "I want to know about the picture, and something gives me the feeling that you are the one to ask."

She turned serious again almost at once. "Do you mean that?" she said. "If you do, I can tell you about it. Kenneth Goule was my uncle, you see." She looked as if she might start crying again. I was seized with the impulse to kiss her. I wondered if I was going insane after all.

"There's no way I'm letting you get away now. Not until I know the whole story."

She raised a hand to her face, hesitating, then appeared to come to a decision. "I can't now. I have to be somewhere. But we could meet up next week, if you really are serious about this." She scrabbled about in her handbag, eventually extracting a small spiral-bound notebook. "Write your number in here. Do you have a pen?"

I found I was smiling and so was she. I couldn't help thinking how different this conversation was from my first tongue-tied encounter with Eloise, how strangely intimate. I pushed the thoughts away as far as they would go.

"I don't even know your name," I said.

"Clarissa, but I hate it. Everyone calls me Charlie. Charlie Goule."

"The same surname as the artist?"

She nodded. "Uncle Ken was my father's brother."

"I'm Vernon Reade." I jotted down my telephone number and email address in the back of the notebook, then handed it back to her. We left the hall together, walking the short distance to the bus stop at the bottom end of Colney Hatch Lane.

"This is me," she said. "It was nice to meet you. I'll call you soon, I promise." At that moment a bus pulled up to the kerb and Charlie got on to it. As the bus drove away I found myself wondering if I would ever see her again, and felt a pang of regret. I hadn't even thought to get her phone number. I returned briefly to the auction rooms to pay for the painting and arrange to have it delivered, and then I went home.

In the days following the auction I thought about Charlie constantly. I wondered what she was doing, what she was thinking, whether she was thinking about me. I almost forgot about the painting itself. When it was delivered to my house at the beginning of the following week I was unprepared for the shock of seeing it again. The image of the wrecked ship reared up at me, imprinting itself upon my retinas like a camera flash and reminding me of the panic I had felt in the dreams, my mad flight across the dunes, the acrid scents of seaweed and brine.

I was still contemplating it when the phone rang. I jumped like a rabbit, snatching at the receiver. I thought it was probably Milly calling, wanting to know what my plans were for that evening – we often went to the cinema on Mondays because it was cheaper. It wasn't, though, it was Charlie. I was so surprised to hear her voice I almost dropped the phone.

"Hello. Is that Vernon?"

"Yes, it's me."

"It's Charlie. Are you all right? You sound out of breath."

"I'm fine. The painting's just arrived. I was looking at it when the phone went."

"Oh. You haven't gone off it, have you?"

"Not in the least. It's superb."

She was silent for a moment, and I wondered if I had been tactless. I didn't want it to sound as if I was gloating over my ownership of the painting. But Charlie was the one person in the world I knew would understand what I was talking about. I had said nothing to Milly about the auction. I didn't want to have to explain about the dreams, and I especially didn't want to have to explain about Charlie. Not that there was much to explain, at least not yet.

"How come you're at home now, anyway?" Charlie said. She didn't sound upset. I felt relieved. "It's the middle of the afternoon. I thought you'd be at work."

"I moved my appointments around. I wanted to be here when the picture came." I laughed. "You mean you rang me because you thought I wouldn't be in?"

"I hoped I'd get the machine. I thought it might be easier that way. I don't like using the telephone."

We were both laughing by then and I was relieved to find my nerves beginning to subside.

"Maybe you should pretend I am the machine," I said. "I won't say a word, I promise."

"Oh stop, you must think I'm a right idiot. I was wondering if you're free on Wednesday, that's all. If you still wanted to, I mean. I thought we could meet at the National Gallery. That would help me to explain to you better about Uncle Ken."

"That sounds wonderful," I said, hoping I didn't sound too manic. "Perfect."

We arranged to meet at four, and I tentatively suggested we might go for supper afterwards. I put down the phone feeling elated. I had half-expected Charlie never to call me. The idea of seeing her again, and soon, was very pleasant indeed.

Then, of course, there was the painting. I had searched for Kenneth Goule online, but had been unable to find a single reference to him. I was not entirely surprised – Goule had died before the internet became ubiquitous, and he was not well known enough to feature in articles or critical writing. There were other ways I could find out about him, of course, through newspaper archives and college records and old exhibition catalogues, but such methods were invariably slow, and none would provide me with the kind of personal insight that Charlie possessed by right as part of her background.

I wasn't sure if I believed in such a thing as fate, but I knew that meeting Charlie had been at the very least an extraordinary piece of luck.

• • •

Charlie had said to meet in the gallery gift shop. As I went up the steps and through the revolving doors I had a momentary fear I might not recognise her, but I needn't have worried. The mop of bright blonde hair made it impossible to miss her. She was standing next to the book displays, holding a postcard reproduction of Stubbs's *Whistlejacket*.

I leaned in and kissed her on the cheek. "It's good to see you," I said.

She coloured slightly, but smiled. "Shall we go and have a look at some paintings?" she said.

We spent just over an hour in the galleries. My usual way of looking at paintings was to plot out a course for myself, to concentrate on two or three rooms in particular, but Charlie seemed happier to wander at random.

"Ken loved it here," she said. "He was always dragging me off to galleries. He said it would be good for my education but really it was because he needed to be constantly in contact with art. There are paintings in the National that he almost worshipped. He was always different after we'd been here, quiet and rather sad." Charlie stopped in front of Giordano's *Perseus*, a large canvas depicting a scene from Ovid, in which the hero Perseus turns his rival Phineas to stone by forcing him to look at the severed head of the Gorgon Medusa. I had never paid much attention to the painting before – I preferred the more contemplative atmosphere of the Holbeins, the quiet seclusion of Vermeer's Delft interiors – but seeing it now in Charlie's presence I felt something of its power. Perseus's disgusted expression as he brandished the head made it clear it had begun to stink like rotting offal.

"Ken liked paintings that told stories," said Charlie. "He never had much time for modern art. He used to say most of it was about the painter wanting to take a short cut to greatness. Ken didn't believe in short cuts, he believed in craft."

"But what about his own work?" I said. "He had real talent, I can see that just from looking at that one painting, and yet he seems to have been almost unknown. Why wasn't he more successful? I don't understand."

"You might have understood better if you had known him." Charlie folded and unfolded her hands. "He would never compromise, on anything. He hated being described as a traditionalist. He saw himself as a revolutionary, a kind of neo-Pre-Raphaelite. He did have a gallery once, but he had a bust-up with the owner and refused to show his paintings there again, even when the manager came round to the house to apologise. Sometimes I think he actually enjoyed rubbing people up the wrong way. But he was never like that with me." She paused. "Uncle Ken brought me up, really. My mother died when I was two. My father was a long-distance lorry driver, so he was often away overnight. Ken was always there for us. He moved into our attic after my mother died. He'd just come back from Guatemala and had nowhere to stay, and my father was in a fix because he needed someone to take care of me and my brothers while he was away on the job. It was meant to be a temporary arrangement, but Dad came to rely on Ken. In the end he said he could have the attic rent-free if he agreed to carry on looking after us. The attic was massive and it made a marvellous studio. Ken ended up staying ten years."

"What made him leave?"

"He got married. Everything changed when he met Julia, and when she left him she broke his heart. The picture you bought is named after her. It was one of the paintings Ken did in the months after his marriage to Julia ended. He did some amazing work that year. It was almost as if his grief was feeding him. But then he suddenly packed everything up and went abroad again. We hardly ever saw him after that."

"I thought Julia was the name of the ship." My heart had leapt at the mention of the painting. I suppose I was still hoping Charlie would be able to explain its effect on me, that she would be able to help me unravel the mystery of the dreams.

"That's what he wanted people to think. But the painting was really about Julia herself, a metaphor for the wreck of their marriage. Julia is still alive – she lives near Peterborough somewhere. I always find it strange when I think of that. She's just an ordinary woman, and yet she'll live on after the rest of us are dead because she'll always be alive in that painting, standing there in her green dress like a character in a movie. It was Uncle Ken that gave her that gift, and she threw it back in his face. She invited me to stay with her once, her and her new husband in Peterborough, but I didn't go."

"What went wrong between her and your uncle? Why did she leave?" I wanted to ask Charlie if Julia had been beautiful, but I was afraid the question might upset her or make her angry.

Charlie shrugged. "Julia would deny this like mad but it was basically money. She had imagined herself as the wife of a famous artist and instead she found herself living in three rooms above a newsagent in Camden. She was angry with Ken because he didn't try to get on more, as she put it. Just the usual kind of story, I suppose."

I fell silent. I couldn't help being struck by the similarities between Julia, as Charlie described her, and Eloise. If Kenneth Goule's painting was anything to go by they even looked alike.

"How come the painting was put up for auction?" I said at last. "You didn't want to sell it, that was obvious."

Charlie laughed, but cheerlessly, as if at some bitter memory. "That's all down to my brothers, I'm afraid. John and James are much older than me. They were both in their teens when Mum died and so for them it was a massive event. They were never close to Uncle Ken themselves, but I think they were pretty miffed when they found out he had left me the lease on his flat. He knew I wanted to move out of the Highgate house. Everything else, his letters and paintings and sketchbooks, he left to my father. I don't know why. Dad never showed the slightest interest in Ken's art and had no idea what to do with it all. He insured everything as part of the business – he was running his own haulage company by then. My brothers are partners in the firm, so when Dad died earlier this year everything came to them. They reckon I've already had my fair share of Ken's estate, and that if I want any of the paintings I should have to bid for them like anyone else. Perhaps they're right, I did get the flat. I know they could do with the money."

"I'm sorry about your father," I said.

"I loved my dad but I barely knew him. It's Uncle Ken I miss the most, and that's why I wanted the painting." She spoke quietly, her eyes downcast. "I've always loved that picture, even though Julia is in it, even though I know Ken was unhappy when he painted it. It seems so like him, somehow. So like his life, with all its mysteries and disasters and thwarted ideals.

I've often thought that if only he'd been able to get over what happened with Julia that painting might have been a turning point, and he might have found the success he deserved. Perhaps that's wishful thinking but I wanted the painting anyway. It was something of his at least, something of *him*. I don't really have much else, just a couple of the funny animal sketches he drew for me when I was small."

She looked up at me suddenly, her blue eyes wide. "I don't want you feeling sorry for me, or guilty. None of this is your fault. The painting is yours, fair and square. I'm just glad it's gone to someone who cares about it."

She sounded close to tears. Finally unable to help myself, I reached out and took her hand. I felt at ease with her in a way I never had with anyone, apart from Milly. Even though we had only just met and I still knew so little about her I had the feeling once again that our story was already out there in the universe, simply waiting for the chance to unfold.

"I think we should go," I said. "Do you fancy getting something to eat?"

"I would like that very much," she said. "Paintings always make you hungry, don't you find?"

We laughed in low voices, not wanting to attract the displeasure of the other patrons, and I continued to hold her hand as we made our way out of the gallery and on to Charing Cross Road.

We went to an Italian restaurant on Leicester Square. It was still early, and we were able to find a table by the window. I looked out at the people, passing to and fro on their way to the theatres and cinemas of Shaftesbury Avenue and the

Haymarket, feeling Charlie's knees lightly brushing mine under the table. Happiness was not something I had given much thought to in the wake of Eloise's departure. I had imagined it would be enough simply to feel all right again, to escape the mess of confusion and guilt produced in me by her leaving. The idea that Eloise might cease to matter had not occurred to me. I felt euphoric, giddy with the same sense of unreality that had sometimes come upon me during those early weeks of insomnia. As we waited for our food to arrive I reached across the table and took Charlie's hand once more. I wondered if this might be too much, if she might try to pull away, but instead she smiled and squeezed my fingers. She was so different from Eloise. I wondered what it might feel like to kiss her, to kiss her properly.

"I reckon it's my turn to talk now," I said to her. "I want to tell you about how your Uncle Kenneth's painting appeared to me in a dream."

"What?" Charlie said. "What on earth are you talking about?" She giggled, and I understood at once that she was not laughing at me, she was simply happy like I was, that she would be glad to listen to anything I had to say.

Was I falling in love with her? I supposed I might be. I knew Milly would be horrified, that she would tell me I was on the rebound from Eloise, that it was too soon for me to get involved with anyone else. But Milly was not there, and this was not her business. I began to tell Charlie about my dream of the beached ship, of the passengers in evening dress, the shock of recognition when I had first seen *Wreck of the Julia*. For some reason, perhaps because this was the aspect of the dreams that frightened me most, I did not tell her about my flight across the sand dunes, the nightmarish scenes on the mountain. I also conveniently forgot to mention the woman in the green dress.

"I know how crazy it sounds," I said. "But that's honestly what happened."

"When did you have this dream? How long ago, I mean?"

"About a month ago. Recently, anyway. Is there any possibility I might have seen your uncle's painting somewhere before?" It was the one thing that had occurred to me, that I had seen *Wreck of the Julia* on some previous occasion – at a saleroom or exhibition, say – and that in spite of having no conscious memory of it the image had lodged in my mind. This was the only logical explanation for the dreams that I could think of.

Charlie shook her head. "It's impossible. Uncle Ken put all his paintings into storage when he went abroad and that's where they've been ever since. Most of them, anyway. *Wreck of the Julia* was never on public view. Not before the auction."

"Then how do we explain what happened?"

"I don't know, Vernon. People always think dreams are about the past, but perhaps you were dreaming about the future, have you thought of that? About going to the auction and finding the picture there? Anything's possible."

"Do you really believe in that kind of thing? Precognition and psychic awareness and all that?"

"Not especially. I've never really thought about it. I'll tell you one thing, though – Julia did. It was weird, because on the surface it seemed like all she was interested in was clothes and money and being the centre of attention. But there was this whole other side to her, odd superstitions and elaborate rituals she felt she had to keep up. She hated people knowing about it. But in many ways the rituals controlled her life."

"How strange."

"It was sad, really. She acted so confident, but she couldn't have been, not underneath. I expect I was horrible to her. She'd taken away my uncle and I was jealous. You must think I'm a monster."

I laughed, thinking precisely the opposite, that she was thoughtful and gentle and delightful, and that I could not believe I had known her less than a week. Just then our meals arrived, and for a while we were silent as we concentrated on the food. I thought back over our conversation, fascinated by all I had learned about Charlie and the circumstances of her life, but with the nagging realisation that I was still no closer to solving the mystery of the painting.

If I had left things as they were, put it all down to coincidence, things would have been different. The course of my future was about to be decided, but as with all turning points in our lives, I approached the bend in the road without knowing it was there.

"What gave your uncle the idea for the painting in the first place, do you know?" I said as the waiter cleared our plates away. It seemed an obvious question. I couldn't think why I hadn't asked it before.

"I do, actually. It was something he read, a story about a steam freighter that ran aground off La Gomera in the Canary Islands, right around the end of World War Two. Some of the passengers went missing. One of them was a woman."

"They were drowned in the wreck, you mean?"

"No, that's what's odd about it. Everyone got ashore safely, but there were four people who disappeared later, after they landed on the island. No one ever found out what happened to them. Ken loved stories like that; he saw them as modern myths. I suppose they are, in a way. But that story about the ship gives me the creeps."

"Did you ever try reading up on it?"

"Ken lent me the book he found it in and I read that. The ship was Dutch, but the missing passengers were all German, and one of them turned out to be an ex-SS officer called Martin Foerster. The ship had been on its way to Argentina and people thought Foerster probably had contacts there. Once Foerster's identity was established everyone assumed the Germans were ferried off La Gomera in secret by a Nazi accomplice. But it was never proved, and none of the four was seen again. I don't suppose we'll ever know the truth now."

"Why don't we try to find out?"

Charlie frowned. "Do some more research, you mean? I suppose we could try. I'm not sure where we would start, though."

"I think we should start by going to La Gomera."

"What?" Charlie laughed. It was difficult to tell whether she was horrified by the idea or delighted, or simply making fun of me. I could have drawn back, pretended I was joking, but instead I pressed on, captivated by a notion that had come to me in a flash, in the moment of speaking it aloud almost, born from the simple desire to *be with Charlie*, to spend time with her in a place that was far from here, to strengthen the bonds between us in the pursuit of some common goal. I thought briefly of the holiday in Avignon I had been scheduled to take with Eloise, the plane tickets expired and unused, still in their cardboard wallet in the glove compartment of my car. I think I even had the idea my proposed trip to La Gomera might act as an exorcism.

"Why not? I could do with a holiday." I said. "I've never been to the Canaries. It's supposed to be marvellous."

"Are you serious?"

"I am, actually," I said, realising that I was. "I'd like to get to the bottom of this thing. To try, anyway. I think it would be fun."

"Would you be able to get time off work?"

Her words, which seemed to suggest an acceptance of my scheme, surprised me so much I wondered if I'd misheard her, though her expression was alert and smiling and she seemed completely in earnest.

"I can rearrange my timetable," I said. "What about you?"

Charlie told me she worked as an indexer of scientific textbooks and that she could usually schedule her jobs to suit herself. I was curious about the work, but she said it was dull.

"It's a glorified filing job, really. But at least it means I can mostly work from home."

We were laughing and holding hands, both of us caught up in the excitement and unexpectedness of the moment. I booked our tickets online the next day – we would be arriving on La Gomera in less than a fortnight. I had taken two single rooms, but I could not help hoping this would be a temporary arrangement.

I told Milly I was taking a holiday.

"I think that's great," she said. "It's exactly what you need. Send me a postcard, OK?"

I promised I would. She didn't ask if I was going with anyone and I knew she would assume I was travelling alone. I worked hard to clear my diary, bringing forward the more urgent appointments and rescheduling the less important ones for when I got back. One evening, on my way home from Maidstone, I stopped off at a large electrical store and bought myself a digital camera. I wanted to keep a record of our trip, also of any interesting discoveries we might make. I had a camera at home, an old Kodak, but I had not used it since the early days of my marriage to Eloise and I was unsure if you could still get film for it. I tried out the digital camera at home, firing off a few test shots of the houses opposite, and was surprised at how simple it was to operate. I imagined taking photos of Charlie, freezing her in time as she basked in the golden September sunshine of La Gomera.

Later that evening I dug out some photos of Eloise I had taken with the old Kodak. I thought the sight of them might cause me pain, but already they seemed like fragments of an earlier life. When I thought of Eloise now it was in the context of Julia. In some mysterious way, Eloise and Julia Goule had become synonymous. It was almost as if Eloise had disappeared into the painting.

• • •

Our flight landed at Tenerife at eight in the evening and from there we took the ferry across to La Gomera. There was a tour bus waiting at the harbourside to bring us to our hotel. By the time our luggage had been unloaded and we had checked in it was almost ten-thirty.

"Do you mind if I go straight up?" Charlie said. "I'd like to have a bath and then unpack."

"Of course not," I said. "It's been a tiring day. I'll see you at breakfast."

"Goodnight then."

I moved to kiss her but she had already turned her back on me. In a sense I was relieved. We had spent the past eight hours caught up in the monotonous and exhausting business of travel, and I was pleased to have time alone to find my bearings. No doubt Charlie felt the same. I stepped out of the hotel lobby and on to the terrace. It was dark, but I could hear the sound of the sea, the incessant hush-hush of waves breaking along the shoreline below. I could also smell the island, a mixed aroma of green vegetation and briny ozone. I had a clear sense of vibrant life, of hidden depths, a mysterious secret breathing. In a moment of absolute lucidity I recalled the atmosphere of my first shipwreck dream, its rapt, intense stillness and peculiar light. In spite of the brightness of the hotel lobby, the to-ing and fro-ing of other guests I felt suddenly uneasy. I went back inside. I thought about having a drink in the bar, then decided it would be best to follow Charlie's example and get some rest.

My room was small but pleasant, with a high wooden bed and slatted double doors leading to a narrow balcony. I recognised the night-sounds familiar from a hundred previous hotel visits: the flushing of toilets, the opening and closing of doors, fleeting footsteps along the landing, the muted babble of a TV set in the neighbouring room. The sounds made me feel immediately at ease. I switched on my own television, tuned to a Spanish game show I made no attempt to follow but that gave the illusion of harmless and cheerful company, then showered and got into bed. I began reading the guide to the island I had brought along as part of my luggage. As well as the usual listings of sites of interest and places to stay, the book also contained chapters on La Gomera's history and geography, plus a selection of maps giving details of local walks. The island had the shape of a halved grapefruit, its interior fissured with narrow valleys and steep ravines. The island's chief mountain, Garajonay, was crowned with what was known as the laurisilva, a dense forest of laurel trees that dated back to prehistoric times, unique in Europe.

The landscape sounded fascinating but I was tired. I yawned then laid the book aside and switched out the light. Half an hour later I jerked awake, realising I had forgotten to turn off the television. The room felt occupied somehow, as if someone had been standing watching me as I slept. I dismissed the feeling as groundless, the result of waking suddenly in a strange environment. I slipped back under the covers and fell asleep.

I awoke the next morning to bright sunshine and a sense of well-being. I washed and dressed and went down to the dining room, anxious to reconnect with Charlie as soon as possible. I spotted her at once, sitting alone at a table and reading what also looked like a guidebook. She was wearing a button-up safari dress that ended just below the knee. Her legs were white and straight, but she had neat, delicate ankles, their slimness accentuated by the bulky trainers she had on. I saw she had washed her hair. It stood out around her face, fluffy as feathers. She laid her book aside as I approached.

"Good morning," she said. "Did you sleep OK?"

"Like a log. It must be the sea air." We were both smiling, but I sensed a trace of awkwardness between us, a mutual need to re-establish what we were there for. I sat down opposite her. "Have you had breakfast already?"

"No. I asked them to wait for you. Have a look at this." She passed me her book. "It's a history of wreck salvage. Apparently the waters off the Canaries are famously treacherous."

"Steady on – you'll have wrapped the whole thing up before I'm even awake."

She giggled, that same giggle I remembered from the restaurant after our visit to the National Gallery, and I felt the awkwardness slip away. We drank our coffee and chatted, and decided to spend the morning exploring the town. We set out straight after breakfast. It was a steep climb down to the harbour. The sun had burned away the early morning sea mist, giving a clear view across the water to Tenerife. The sea below us shone like a blue mirror. A ferry had just come in. Groups of passengers stood around on the dockside waiting for their luggage to be brought ashore. It was a tranquil scene, and the town of San Sebastian seemed refreshingly unspoiled. There were some small signs of development along the harbour front, the usual souvenir shops and ice cream stands, but the narrow streets of the town were clean and quiet, while beyond them green tracts of pastureland arched their way upward towards the denser, darker masses of the mountain heights. The soil, where it lay exposed, was a dusty black, the colour of volcanic ash.

We rambled contentedly around the streets, while I took photographs of the pastel-coloured, flat-fronted houses with my new digital camera. After an hour or so we returned to the harbour. I'd come prepared for warm weather but I had expected it to be milder in September and was surprised by how fierce the sun was, glancing off the pale facades in shimmering slivers. I was pleased to get back to the waterside. We ate lunch in one of the cafés – a simple but delicious meal of deep-fried whitebait and avocado salsa – then decided to return to the hotel for a couple of hours. I was sleepy with sunshine and white wine, and the idea of a siesta was wonderfully tempting. Especially wonderful was the idea that Charlie might decide to join me in my room. The morning together and the naturally informal, warmly intimate atmosphere of the island seemed to have dissolved our earlier shyness. We left the café hand in hand. I felt intensely aware of her physical presence – her narrow ankles and dimpled knees, her smooth white arms, still scented slightly with the sunblock she had used – and felt certain she was equally aware of me.

We arrived back at the hotel hot and sticky from the climb. When Charlie said she was going to her room to shower and change I felt a stab of disappointment, fearing I had let some vital opportunity slip past, but I needn't have worried.

"Shall I come down to yours afterwards?" she said. "We could have a look at the guidebooks or something, work out a plan of campaign?"

"That would be lovely," I said, suddenly realising I was just as much in need of a shower myself. Charlie arrived at my door twenty minutes later.

"You have a view of the harbour," she said, looking around the room. "Almost, anyway." She went out on to the tiny balcony. I came and stood beside her, pressing close out of necessity. Without stopping to think or to reason I found myself kissing her hair and then the nape of her neck. Her skin was warm and smooth and smelled of bergamot. Strands of her straw-coloured hair tickled my lips.

"Vernon," she said, turning to face me. "It means 'the place of alders'."

"How on earth did you know that? Did it crop up in one of your indexes?"

"No, silly. I looked it up on purpose."

I kissed her again, this time on the lips.

"I don't mean to be blunt," I said. "But are you involved with anyone? I feel I should know that, before I make a fool of myself. Or more of a fool, should I say."

"There's nothing like that," she said. "I was sort of engaged to a man once, but he decided he wasn't ready to settle down. That's what people say, isn't it, when they realise they don't want to be with you after all? It sounds awful, but I almost hate him now. I can't believe we nearly ended up living together. There was another man too, for a while. His name was Stiva. He had a wife at home in Poland but that was something we never talked about. One day he just disappeared. I presume he went back to Krakow. I suppose he thought it was better for both of us not to have some long drawn-out goodbye scene. I can assure him it wasn't."

She rubbed her eyes with the back of her hand. I felt a surge of rage towards this Stiva who had acted so callously but mostly what I felt was relief that Charlie was free.

"I'm sorry," I said. "I shouldn't have made you talk about it."

"There's nothing to talk about," she said. She wiped her eyes again then smiled. "How about you?"

"I was married, but my wife left me. Just a couple of months ago, actually. Her name was Eloise."

Her question came so swiftly in the wake of my own I had no time to think, to prepare an appropriate answer. Speaking the truth felt strange, but also liberating. Suddenly I felt I could do anything.

"Vernon, I'm sorry, that's awful."

"It was horrible at the time," I said. "But I knew for a long while it was going to happen, and now it has I'm glad it's over. Let's not waste time talking about Eloise."

I cupped her face between my hands and drew her towards me. Now that it was actually happening our lovemaking seemed as natural and inevitable as any of the other things we had done together. Eloise always liked to take the initiative in bed, and this was something I had always found exciting, even at the end when all other connections between us had been eroded. With Charlie it was different, satisfying in ways I could not previously have imagined. It was as if we were making something together, carefully, tenderly, step by step. Her body was larger and heavier than Eloise's, but in some manner I had never known before it defined for me the concept of rapture.

"I can't believe I met you," I said afterwards. "It feels like a miracle."

She was lying on her side, facing me. The room was warm, the air heavy with the mingled scents of our bodies and the musky-smelling island vegetation. Charlie reached out and touched my cheek. Her hair stood out around her head in a golden nimbus, and I was reminded of the laurel wreaths that were used to crown the heads of heroes and poets in ancient Rome. Laurel was plentiful then – most of Europe was covered in laurisilva. I found myself fascinated by this seeming connection between our present on the island and a past that receded almost to infinity, but I must have dropped off to sleep, because the next thing I knew the light in the room was deepening towards twilight and Charlie was in the bathroom taking a shower. A moment later she appeared in the doorway wrapped in a towel.

"Shall we eat here in the hotel or do you feel like going out?" she said. I felt a rush of renewed pleasure in the sight of her, at the confidence in each other's presence that was the first tangible product of our nascent intimacy.

"Let's go to that fish place on the quay," I said. "I like being by the water."

"Sounds good to me."

I showered and dressed, and together we walked down to the quay. The restaurants along the waterfront had put out lanterns, which reflected themselves like kegs of gold upon the rippling indigo waters of the harbour. The heat of the day had dissipated and it was surprisingly chilly. I had hoped we would be eating outside but it was too cold to do that in comfort. Not that I was disappointed for long – the interior of the restaurant was warmly inviting, heated by a wood-burning stove that filled the room with the scent of summer bonfires. We ordered one of the enormous paellas for two, which was brought to our table in the cast-iron skillet it had been cooked in. While we ate we talked over the day. Charlie was keen to see more of the island, and in particular the laurisilva. She had spotted a flyer in the foyer of our hotel advertising excursions up into the mountains, and when she suggested we should make the trip the following day I agreed at once.

"The buses go every two hours," she said. "So we can sleep in late."

She smiled and I touched her wrist. We had coffee, and then went to stand on the quay for a while, looking out across the water and watching the last ferry of the day come into the harbour. As we turned to start back for the hotel I noticed a spin-rack of postcards outside one of the cafés, and for the first time since we landed I thought of Milly. I had promised to send her a postcard. I turned the rack slowly, looking to see if there was anything that might amuse her. Most of the cards showed predictable views of the harbour and beaches, but tucked in behind a stack of images of the square stone tower that seemed to be San Sebastian's chief architectural attraction, I found a couple that looked more interesting. They were photographs of what looked to be an island fiesta, with decorated floats, and men and women dressed in brightly coloured national costumes. One card showed a young woman in a towering headdress formed from a stack of papier-mâché fish. Another pictured a man in a yellow cloak with long silver tassels and strange black protuberances that gave him the appearance of having extra arms. I turned the card over, hoping to get more information, but the caption was in Spanish.

"What have you got there?" Charlie said. "Can I see?"

I handed her the cards. "Just something I thought my sister might like," I said. "She designs theatre costumes. Any idea who they're supposed to be?"

Charlie examined the pictures then turned them over to look at the back. "They represent the Guanche gods," she said. "Orahan and Hirguan. They're good and evil, like God and the Devil. The Guanches were the people that lived here before the Spanish arrived. Some of the islanders still have Guanche blood."

She handed the postcards back to me. I looked them over again with new interest. "Not the kind of characters you'd want to meet on a dark night," I said. "I didn't know you spoke Spanish."

"I don't. I recognise the names from my guidebook. Some of the older islanders still worship the Guanche gods, apparently. They leave offerings for them up on the mountain." She paused. "You never told me you had a sister."

"There hasn't been time, that's all. Milly's great, I know you'll like her. I'll take you to meet her as soon as we get home."

We set off back to the hotel. Our return climb was hampered by a stiff sea wind, damp with spray and suffused with the green aroma of the mountains. Quite suddenly, and for no reason I could name, I found myself missing London. Julia Goule would no doubt have insisted I was experiencing a premonition.

Charlie stayed in my room that night and somewhere around dawn we awoke and made love again. The morning was clear and bright with no trace of wind. I felt glad to be alive, happier perhaps than I had ever been. If anyone had told me that within twenty-four hours my view of the world would be altered for ever I would not have believed them.

• • •

The bus left straight from the quay, an ancient vehicle with its rusted light-blue paintwork coated in dust. Most of the seats were taken up by a party of German tourists, noisily self-absorbed and kitted out in full walking gear. There was also a Spanish couple with their young daughter, and two older people who I thought at first were with the Germans but when I heard them speaking in English I realised I had been mistaken. I moved towards the rear of the bus, wanting to get as far from them as possible. I didn't want them latching on to us as fellow English-speakers. I rolled my eyes, trying to communicate my fears silently to Charlie, but she seemed not to share my concern.

"They're all right really," she said quietly. "They're from our hotel. I said hello to them yesterday at breakfast, before you came down. They're from Huddersfield." She sat down in the seat directly behind them and I had no choice but to follow. I felt a flash of irritation, not understanding why Charlie was willing to risk our day being ruined by having to exchange pleasantries with two elderly busybodies. I did my best to suppress the feeling. There had been many times during our marriage when Eloise had accused me of misanthropy. I spent most of my working life being polite and amusing to strangers, and so felt reluctant to indulge in small talk when I was off duty. But when I tried to explain that to Eloise she said it was this kind of standoffish attitude that had shrivelled my capacity for real friendship. I had occasionally wondered if she was right. Charlie worked from home and spent most of her time alone – she would naturally welcome the opportunity of making new friends. I consoled myself with the thought that the Huddersfield couple looked pretty harmless and in any case we would only have to put up with them for the duration of the bus journey. The old man in particular looked frail, and I couldn't imagine him venturing much beyond the car park.

I took out my camera and began taking photographs – of the Germans, the Spanish family, the bus driver in his Che Guevara T-shirt. I wanted to distract myself from my negative feelings about the old people, but soon found myself becoming absorbed in the activity for its own sake: the people on the bus were no longer troublesome interlopers in my private space but potential subjects. As such they were fascinating. Their clothes and mannerisms and facial expressions began to interest me, as the subjects of a documentary film might interest me. As I turned the camera on the Spanish girl – a fragile-looking child of about six years old – I had a sudden flash of insight that this was how Kenneth Goule must have felt, when he started to get an idea for one of his paintings.

Eventually the bus set off, carrying us first through the streets of the town, and then across the swathe of farmland which formed a cordon between the mountains and the sea. Gradually the fields and the gently sloping wooded valleys gave way to a harsher landscape of dense scrub and rude outcrops of volcanic rock. The road also began to deteriorate. The bus rattled and jounced on the exposed hardcore, clinging to the tarmac by what seemed the narrowest of margins and granting prolonged and dizzying glimpses of the abyss below. The driver, chattering away on his mobile, seemed not to notice the danger. On the one occasion we encountered another vehicle – a battered pick-up truck loaded with timber – he slammed on the brakes, bringing us to a juddering standstill on what looked like the edge of a precipice. Many hundreds of feet below us, the tail-end of the road we were ascending wound its way unconcernedly towards the sea. The driver put the bus into reverse, careering backwards down the slope until eventually we reached a passing-place, little more than a gash in the trees.

"I thought it was illegal to fell trees here," I said to Charlie as the pick-up ratcheted past us at sixty miles an hour. I had long since stopped taking photographs. My stomach was a liquid mire.

"It is," Charlie said. "It's a designated national park." She spoke absently, as if her attention was focused elsewhere, and then I saw she was looking at the Huddersfield couple. The old woman was slumped sideways and her shoulders were shaking. I thought at first she was laughing, but it turned out she was in tears. Her husband was patting her knee, bringing his hand down again and again in a series of short taps. I had a sudden incongruous image of the Dragon, the po-faced head administrator at Eloise's school, banging in drawing pins on the office noticeboard with her ever-ready tack hammer. Charlie leaned forward in her seat, a movement which seemed to place the whole bus in jeopardy.

"Are you all right?" she said. She placed her hand on the woman's shoulder. The woman gasped in fright and turned slightly to face us. Her thin cheeks were shiny with tears.

"It's my wife," said the husband. He rounded on Charlie eagerly, gripping her wrist like a drowning man seizing hold of a rope. "She doesn't like heights. We thought there'd be a proper road, you see. If we'd known it was going to be like this we wouldn't have come."

He spoke quietly with a soft Yorkshire accent. His eyes were the faded turquoise of a thousand seaside watercolours.

"I'm sure there's nothing to worry about," said Charlie. "The driver goes up and down this road a dozen times every day. He must know it like the back of his hand." She spoke in a sweetly encouraging voice I had never heard her use before. The woman tried on a watery smile and a moment later she was telling Charlie her name was Adele Phillotson and that the man in the seat beside her was her husband, Bill.

"William Bevan, he was christened," Adele Phillotson said. "His dad was very big on the unions."

"Is that so?" Charlie replied. "I'll bet he had some stories to tell." They carried on talking, and soon Adele Phillotson was laughing and joking, clearly enjoying herself and with her surroundings of no more concern to her than if we had been cruising along the seafront at Morecambe.

I began to feel irrationally annoyed, jealous of Charlie's concern for the elderly couple. I turned and stared out of the window, stonily fascinated by my own terror. It was not just the awful road, the way the bus lurched sickeningly to one side each time it rounded a bend. More than any of that it was the feeling I had seen all this before, that I had somehow slipped off the map of reality and entered the arid, nightmare landscape of my dreams. I knew this was impossible, and yet the evidence lay all around me. The higher we climbed, the further we progressed from the safety of San Sebastian and its picture-postcard harbour, the more I became convinced that this was not just a mountain but *the* mountain, and that if we went any further we were done for. I wondered vaguely what would happen if I stormed to the front of the bus and demanded to be let off. Would Charlie come with me or would she stay with the Phillotsons? I grappled with the illogical conviction that the Phillotsons were turning her against me.

Finally we reached a plateau. The road levelled off and widened out, and after a further five minutes of driving, the bus ground to a halt on a stony patch of ground signposted as a car park. At the far end under some trees, a pair of motor cycles stood in the shadow of a squat concrete structure that turned out to be a public toilet. We piled out of the bus. Once outside it was easy to see we were not at the mountain's summit at all but a staging post on the way to it, a flattish shelf of land immediately below the high peak which rose up squarely in front of us, its upper slopes clouded with the dense green blanket of the *laurisilva*. The driver announced in halting English that the next bus would arrive at the car park in two hours' time. Then he clambered back into his vehicle and drove away.

A silence descended. The Spanish family made straight for the cluster of picnic tables that lay just below the car park, the woman opening bags and setting out food, the little girl skipping back and forth on the springy grass. The Germans shouldered their rucksacks and moved off in a phalanx along the stony path that branched off by the public toilet and that was presumably the route to the summit. I watched them spread out on the trail, a small column of khaki-coated ants, each with its burden to carry, each with its place in the line. No doubt they would make the round trip to the summit within the two hours recommended by the guidebooks, and be safely back in town enjoying a beer on the quayside as the sun went down.

I envied them. What I wanted more than anything was to confide my fears to Charlie, no matter how irrational, but the presence of the Huddersfield couple seemed to have erected a barrier between us. I excused myself and made for the toilets. The effects of the bus ride on my stomach and bowels had made a rest stop imperative. Entering the mean breeze-block construction was disturbing to me, and felt almost as if I had crawled into some rank-smelling fistula between the real world outside and the dreamland inside my head.

I released a torrent of foul-smelling effluent into the toilet bowl and then just sat there, breathing in shallow breaths and trying to work out what was happening to me. In the end there was no choice but to rejoin the others. The Phillotsons watched as I emerged, seeming to stare in amazement as if they had doubted I would ever come out again. Charlie stood beside them. It was obvious they had been talking together in my absence.

"Here we are then," said Bill Phillotson. "Would you care to join us for a spot of lunch? We've brought plenty. You'd be most welcome."

I saw Charlie hesitate, and my fear was temporarily replaced by something like rage.

"That's very kind of you," I said quickly. "But we were planning to climb to the top. Perhaps we'll see you later, back in town." Without waiting to see if Charlie would follow I stormed off in the wake of the Germans. I was appalled at my behaviour but felt powerless to stop it. Like having a demon on my shoulder, prodding me into action and then laughing at the results. I could not remember feeling so helplessly adrift from myself since my cousin Tim had tried to kiss Milly in the garden of my grandparents' house in Folkestone. I had been ten years old then and so resentful of the intrusion into our hitherto inviolable togetherness I had all but choked with despair and chagrin. I felt the same way now, and about the same age. I walked away quickly, almost running over the rough ground, my eyes stinging with angry tears. It was at least a full minute before I realised Charlie was hurrying to catch up with me.

"Vernon, wait," she called. She was breathless from running. "What on earth's the matter?" She caught at my sleeve, and finally I came to a halt. I was almost afraid to look at her, sensing and fearing her heart was changed towards me, but when I did I saw that she too had tears in her eyes. Her face was deeply flushed. A small scar, the remains of some long-ago pock mark, stood out in the centre of one moon cheek.

My chest felt tight as a drum.

"I'm sorry," I stammered. "I don't know what got into me."

"Are you OK? You look ill." She closed her fingers around my wrist. I wanted to hug her close, to bury my face in her mop of fair hair, to tell her that yes I was feeling ill, that we should go back to the car park and wait until the next bus turned up, that we could even sit and share the Phillotsons' picnic if she wanted.

"It was that awful road," I said instead. "I'm all right now, I promise. Thank you for coming after me."

"You needn't have worried about the Phillotsons. I'd already told them we were going to climb the mountain together. They're sweet people really, they don't mean any harm."

"I know that. I've been behaving like an idiot."

I put both arms around her, drawing her close. To my relief she responded, and in another minute we were both laughing. I felt slightly dizzy, but decided it must be the aftermath of my upset stomach, combined perhaps with the high altitude. We were more than four thousand feet above sea level.

"Are you sure you're OK to go on? We can sit here for a bit if you like, catch our breath?"

"I'm fine," I said. "Let's go." I took her hand, and we carried on up the path. The truth was I still felt uneasy. Left to myself I would have started back down immediately, hiking all the way to town on foot if I had to, but I didn't want to risk another upset. We carried on up the path. It was broad and well-defined, but the ascent was steep and we needed all our energy for the upward journey. After half an hour's climbing we entered the laurisilva. It is difficult to explain how it felt, that profoundly physical moment of crossing over. The change in the terrain was as radical as it was sudden: one minute there was the mountain scrub, the next there was the forest. It was not just the landscape, though. There was a sense also of geological alteration, a fracture in time, of moving from the modern present to the prehistoric past.

The forest was swathed in mist. I knew from the guidebook that the laurisilva experienced a microclimate similar to that of a tropical rainforest, but reading about it had not prepared me for the reality. I was chilly with damp, yet I was also sweating from the humidity. It was like being trapped inside an enormous fermenting vat. The great trees soared upwards, forming a dense green canopy. Umbrella-sized ferns sprouted from the forest floor. The silence was thick and complete, green as the forest, yet it did not seem peaceful to me. In spite of the complete absence of sound and movement I had a strong and uncomfortable sense of being watched. I kept expecting and hoping to see or at least hear the party of Germans up ahead of us but there was no sign of them. It was as if the forest had swallowed them whole.

"What an amazing place," Charlie said. "Don't you think so?" She walked slowly, gazing up at the trees, green shadows criss-crossing her face.

"It feels like another world," I said. "Or our own world, but millions of years in the past."

"Like in one of those films, you mean, where people travel back to the time of the dinosaurs without realising it?"

I caught my breath, not wanting to acknowledge how uncannily her words seemed to capture my fears. "I suppose so," I said. "Don't laugh."

"I'm not laughing. Have you noticed how quiet it is? I wonder where the Germans have got to. They weren't that far ahead of us, surely?"

So Charlie also had noticed their disappearance. This shared perception ought to have been reassuring, though in fact it was anything but. If Charlie also could sense the strangeness of the place, that must mean it was real and not in my head. And yes, I had noticed how quiet it was, the sound of our footsteps muffled as if our shoes were wrapped in wadding. There was also a complete absence of birdsong or animal noises, and I knew that if I shouted or yelled there would be no echo. It was as if the forest was feeding on sound, absorbing its vibrations the moment they was produced.

"Should we go back, do you think?" I felt foolish as soon as I said it, a child afraid of the dark, but the fact remained that I *was* afraid, with that nameless, formless terror that haunts all dark places. My eyes showed me nothing more threatening than a lot of tall trees, yet my nerves kept insisting there was more than that, that the forest held some terrible secret, that we should turn and make our escape while there was still time.

"We can if you like," Charlie said. "But it would be a shame to turn back now, don't you think? We've come so far. And the views from the top of the mountain are supposed to be fantastic." What she said made perfect sense, yet I sensed she was hesitating. The idea came to me that she was as scared as I was, that she was hoping I would insist we abandon our plan to climb to the summit and return to the car park. If only I'd had the courage to admit what I felt. But I didn't want to look like a coward in front of Charlie and so I agreed we should go on.

The view from the summit turned out to be non-existent. When after a further twenty minutes of walking we came out of the forest and emerged on to the exposed ground of the summit approaches, we discovered the visibility was so poor we could barely see the path in front of our feet. The mist, which I had believed would disperse as soon as we left the laurisilva, enveloped the top of the mountain like a cloak.

We stared about us, disappointed.

"Perhaps it's the time of year," Charlie said. She cupped her hands about her mouth and brought forth a long, warbling cry. My taut nerves jangled like coat hangers.

"What's that for?" I said. A ridiculous notion came to me, that something in the mist would hear her and come running.

"I'm seeing if we can find the Germans," she said. "I don't like the look of this fog. It would be easy to get lost. I thought it might be safer if we all went down together."

I could see her idea was a good one, but her call raised no response.

"Perhaps they've gone back already," I said. I knew this was nonsense, that there was just the one main footpath through the forest, that there was no way we could have missed each other, even with the mist as thick as it was. If the Germans had begun their descent we would have seen them. I supposed it was possible they had gone down by another route, but the idea made no sense. They would still have to return to the car park to pick up the coach – straying off the recommended route would mean a long and unnecessary detour. Charlie would know this as well as I did. I saw little sense in pointing it out.

"Come on," Charlie said. "If we get a move on now we'll be down in no time." She smiled and put a hand on my arm. I knew she was trying to reassure me, but nonetheless I felt an urge to pull away. I didn't want her to see how frightened I was. We stood together for a moment in silence then began making our way back down into the forest. As we moved in beneath the trees I experienced the fleeting impression that none of this was happening, that the whole drama was being played out on a vast cinema screen while the real Charlie and Vernon sat in a bar on the harbour front, enjoying ice creams and making jokes about the Germans.

Suddenly I remembered my camera, and how helpful I had found it during the bus journey. I unzipped it from the pouch on my belt and levelled it at Charlie. I fired off three quick shots, one after the other, framing Charlie's shoulders and the back of her head as she moved along the path. Mist blurred her outline and diluted her colours. She seemed almost to be merging with the laurisilva. This time, the act of taking the pictures seemed to intensify my anxiety rather than diminishing it, as if capturing Charlie's image had created a concrete embodiment of my fear. I thought of deleting the photographs but found I was afraid to. I knew it would feel too much like deleting Charlie herself.

I put away the camera and carried on walking. It seemed darker, as if the best of the afternoon was already gone. By my watch it was three o'clock, but it felt much later.

"What time does the last bus go?" I said.

"Not until five-thirty. There's plenty of time." It had taken us perhaps an hour to reach the summit. We should have been quicker going down, but as four o'clock came and went we found ourselves still surrounded by trees. With the onset of dusk the immense laurels seemed to take on a phantom quality, looming in and out of existence, the tendrils of mist drifting in slow eddies about their trunks and lower branches. There was no sign of the car park, no sign of the Germans. Most worryingly of all, the path we were now following seemed different from the path we had followed on our ascent. I knew it couldn't be, but that's how it felt. I sensed panic seeping into my bloodstream like a toxin.

"Where on earth are we?" I said. "We should have been down ages ago."

"The path must have branched off somehow. Perhaps we should try retracing our steps."

"We can't do that – it's almost dark. If we don't find the car park soon we'll miss the bus."

We traipsed on for a while in silence. Several times I thought I heard the road, the faint rumble of a vehicle moving uphill, but each time I was proved to be mistaken. My teeth began to chatter. I had read the nights were cold in the mountains, that once the sun went down the temperatures often dropped below freezing. I knew I should be comforting Charlie, trying to raise her spirits, but I felt locked in a cocoon that was equal parts self-pity and outright fear. It was all I could do to keep walking. In the end it was Charlie herself who suggested we stop.

"This is hopeless," she said. She came to a standstill in the middle of the path. Her hair glowed dimly against the advancing dark. "We're getting nowhere. I think we should find somewhere to shelter until the morning. It's no good trying to do anything until it gets light again. We've missed the bus now, anyway."

I glanced at my watch. She was right. The discovery horrified me.

"I don't want to spend the night out here. All we have to do is find the road. Then we can walk down."

"It's miles back down to the town, and we don't even know where we are. For all we know we could be walking in circles." She paused. "There's really nothing out here that can hurt us."

"I don't know." I knew what she was saying was true, and yet I felt mobbed by fear, tangled in it like a fly in a spider's web. The worst part was not knowing how to explain it, how to tell Charlie that what I was feeling was no ordinary fear of the dark but the increasing and irrational conviction that my nightmare of the mountain was coming true. I remembered what she had said when we first discussed Kenneth Goule's painting, that perhaps one might dream of the future as well as the past. The idea had seemed intriguing then, a quaint diversion, something to amuse ourselves with while we pursued the first delightful stages of our love affair.

Now, with the forest all around us, it felt truer and more terrifying than I could have imagined.

"Don't worry," said Charlie. "Everything will be all right." She moved to put her arms around me, and suddenly I was holding her, my arms gripping her back, my face pressed in tight against her shoulder. I thought at first that she was trembling, then realised it was my own trembling I could feel, a combination of terror and cold. My shirt was soaked with cooling perspiration, and for the first time since the business with the Phillotsons I found myself wondering what she must think of me. I felt certain I deserved her ridicule and not her compassion.

She kissed my cheek, my eyelids, my hair. "You'll see," she said. "We'll be laughing about this tomorrow." She kissed me again, then took my hand and began leading me forward. She moved as if by instinct, heading for a part of the forest where the trees were not so tall but grew thickly together. It seemed slightly less cold, as if the trees had surrounded what remained of the day's warmth and prevented it from escaping.

It was now full dusk. In the encroaching blackness the trees formed darker bands, a ghost-forest. A faint patch of luminescence high in the treetops was all that could be seen of the rising moon. When something huge and black reared up from the shadows I almost cried out in my panic, convinced we were being attacked by a giant. It turned out to be a vast lump of stone, one of the rocky outcrops that were everywhere on the mountainside, a constant reminder of the island's volcanic past.

"Wait a moment," said Charlie, stopping. "I think there might be a place." She moved towards the rock then seemed to vanish. My heart stamped in my chest, certain that the rock had swallowed her. Then I realised there was a cleft in the stone, a narrow jagged fissure that looked like a scrawled letter "J". After a moment Charlie's voice came rising towards me, muffled and disembodied, the voice of a conjured spirit in a horror movie séance.

"It's perfect," she called. "Come on in."

I moved forward cautiously, not liking the idea of being underground as well as in darkness, but in fact what Charlie said turned out to be right. The inside of the cleft formed a natural shelter, a cavern that extended some twenty feet into the rock. There was an odd smell, an acridity I suspected came from sulphurous deposits within the stone, but the floor of the cave was perfectly dry and clean.

"We'll be fine in here," Charlie said. "We can bring in some leaves and bracken, make ourselves more comfortable." She came and stood beside me, where I could see her. Her voice sounded cheerful, and I found I could almost believe she was enjoying herself. We spent half an hour or so snatching up armfuls of the dry vegetation that grew around the cave entrance, then piling it together to form a bed. It was not until we'd finished that I realised how hungry I was. Apart from a fish pasty we had shared on the bus we hadn't eaten since breakfast. We hadn't brought much with us, either. We had planned to eat dinner later, in the town.

"Do you still have the food?" I said. I sank down on the mattress of leaves. I was exhausted.

"I've still got the food," said Charlie. "And I have this, as well." I heard her unzip her rucksack. A moment later she was surrounded by a bright white light. My eyes, which had become accustomed to the darkness, were momentarily blinded. I raised my hand to ward off the dazzle. Charlie was standing in front of me, holding a torch.

"How come you have this?" I said. "Why didn't you say before?"

"I always carry a pocket light, in case of emergency. But there was no sense in wasting the battery, not while we still had some natural light."

She plumped down on the leaves beside me, balancing the rucksack on her knees. She reached inside again, producing a bottle of water and then handing me the cheese and salami we had bought as we walked to the bus stop that morning.

"You have to admit," she said. "This is all quite funny." She took a swig from the water bottle. Her face shone out, moon round, in the light from the torch beam. Now we had food and light I could almost agree with her. I ate some of the biscuits and cheese, trying not to think about the black depths of the forest that surrounded us, nor of how far we might be from the nearest town. I moved closer to Charlie, relishing the warmth of her body. She seemed completely calm, and in her presence I felt the worst of my fear begin to relax its hold. Charlie was right, all we had to do was wait till morning. The island was not large, after all. The simple act of walking in one direction would be bound to bring us down from the mountain eventually.

"Sorry I've been so useless," I said. I kissed her, high up on one cheek, then again on the corner of her mouth. "You've been amazing. How come you're so good at this?"

"It's having two brothers, that's all. You wouldn't believe some of the stuff they got me into when we were kids. Dad would have had our hides if he'd ever found out." She leaned back against the wall of the cave and pulled up some of the bracken to cover her feet. "We're lucky it's September and the nights are still quite short. Perhaps we should tell each other ghost stories, to pass the time."

"Ghost stories?" I said. "You must be joking."

The idea was horrible, and yet it was funny too, funnier than anything I had seen or thought or heard since we had got off the bus. To my amazement I found myself laughing. I folded the paper wrapper around what was left of the food and then I reached out for Charlie. She came into my arms at once, the sticking-out tufts of her hair tickling my face. Her warmth was delicious. I lay on my side in the leaves, holding Charlie and feeling her breathing, the slow, steady beat of her heart comforting as the ticking of the grandfather clock in the hallway of my grandparents' house in Folkestone. The image of the clock would not leave me, and as my own breathing steadied and I drifted closer to the borders of sleep I could not help thinking I was being shown something important, that perhaps there was a way to put the clock back, after all.

"I do know one ghost story," I said at last. "It's a true one. Would you like to hear it?"

Charlie stirred in my arms and I could feel her head nodding against my chest. "I'd love to," she murmured drowsily. "I love ghost stories."

"You might change your mind once you've heard this one. Or change your mind about me."

Then I told her what had happened with Eloise. I told her about the breakdown of our marriage, and the way she had left me. I told her about the plane crash, and how I let everyone believe my wife was dead.

"I never meant to do it," I said. "It just happened."

"And you've heard nothing from Eloise since she left?"

"Not a word. But I know she's alive."

Charlie fell silent. I lay beside her and held her, wondering what thoughts were going through her mind.

"You have to find her and you have to speak to her," she said in the end. "It's the same as with real ghosts. You have to lay your marriage to rest, properly, or Eloise will never stop haunting you. And you have to tell Milly. What other people believe doesn't matter, but Milly is different. You must tell her as soon as we get back to London."

"And you don't think I'm a terrible person?"

"Not at all." She raised my hand to her lips and kissed my bent knuckles. "This could have happened to anyone."

Like the comment about the ghost stories this struck me as both awful and funny. It was also true, though I suspected only someone as perceptive and non-judgemental as Charlie would have seen it that way. Once again I found myself marvelling at her warmth, her generosity of spirit. I hugged her close.

"You are incredible," I said to her. "And I will tell Milly. But Milly never liked Eloise much, you know. I reckon she'd prefer to go on believing she was dead."

I stifled a laugh. Then I buried my face in Charlie's hair and fell asleep. I dreamed I was back at the hotel, and that Charlie was sitting up in bed with her back to me. When I reached for her she turned on me angrily, and I saw it was not Charlie, but Eloise.

What are you doing here, Vernon? I haven't made you any trouble. Why don't you go away and leave me alone?

You made me think you were dead, I said.

No I didn't, that was all in your head. You wished I was dead, that's all. You haven't felt a thing for me in years.

I opened my mouth to protest, then realised it was true. I felt ashamed, and wondered what I could say to make amends.

Then Eloise was gone and in her place was Julia Goule. She was wearing the green silk evening dress, like in the painting. She leaned towards me as if to kiss me. Her breath smelled of the sea, and I knew she was dead. I heard a shot and then a cry and then someone was shouting. I felt convinced it was the old Nazi Charlie had told me about, Martin Foerster, that he was hijacking one of the ferries down on the quay. He was ordering the captain to take him to Argentina.

I jerked awake, my heart racing. Charlie was sitting up with her back to me. The fluorescent beam of the torch had been replaced by the flickering orange glow of a naked flame. The cave wall was festooned with shadows.

"What's going on?" I whispered. "What happened to the torch?" My mouth felt dry and my limbs ached. I wondered what the time was, how long I had been asleep.

"The battery's dead. We forgot to turn it off before we went to sleep." She turned towards me, her face thrown into stark relief by the light of the flame. I stared at her fixedly, still caught in the world of my dream. Part of me was afraid that in a moment she would vanish, leaving me alone in the cave with Julia Goule. But it was just Charlie, her fair hair tousled from sleep. She was holding a gold cigarette lighter in one hand, in the other the lighted stub of a candle.

"Where did you get those?"

"I found them under a stone. Someone must have used this cave once, as a hideout." She paused, inclining her head as if to listen. "I thought I heard something outside."

Her words brought me fully awake, reanimating my terror of the evening before. I stopped to listen also, my nerves taut as wires. At first I heard nothing, just the roaring sound within my own ears. Then outside in the night someone screamed. The sound split the darkness like an axe. A cold hand seemed to clench its bony fingers around my heart.

"What was that?" I gasped. "Did you hear it?"

"That's what I heard before. I'm going to see." Charlie began shuffling towards the cave entrance, the lighted candle stub still in her hand.

"You mustn't," I said. "Stay here." I lunged after her, trying to catch hold of some part of her clothing, but succeeding only in banging my elbow painfully against the wall of the cave. I crawled forward in the semi darkness, feeling for Charlie but finding only empty air. There was a cool breeze against my face, and I realised I must be close to the cave's entrance. A moment later I was fully outside.

The mist had lifted, and the sky above was lustrous with stars. I had never seen a sky so radiant, and my terror was replaced by wonder as I gazed at it. I remembered certain marvellous nights during my childhood, when Grandpa Tissot had taken Milly and me out to the Romney Marshes to watch for owls. The skies had been clear then, too, but there had always been the lights of New Romney and Lydd, gleaming like burned out beacons along the horizon. Here there were no lights, just the stars, and hovering above the treetops the bald-headed moon.

I could have looked at that sky for a long time had it not been for the terrible sounds, rising out of the darkness towards us through the trees. There was a snapping of underbrush, and then a series of hoarse cries, not as loud as the scream I had heard before but somehow worse. Whoever or whatever was making them was clearly at the end of its endurance.

I heard the sound of running footsteps coming closer. I shrank back towards the mouth of the cave but in my confusion and fright I was unable to find the entrance. I became aware that Charlie was somewhere close by, that she was struggling to relight the candle which had blown itself out.

"Don't do that," I said. "Get down." My voice was a cracked whisper. I caught hold of her at last, and tried to pull her down into the bracken, but she slipped free of me and went sprawling against the rocks. I heard a small thump and realised she must have dropped the lighter. She started scrabbling for it amongst the leaves.

"Charlie," I said, but she ignored me. She ignited a flame and lit the candle, thrusting it forward into the darkness. I could see something white, dancing and flapping like a piece of paper caught in the trees. At first I thought it was just my eyes playing tricks on me, a kind of after-image of the candle produced by the sudden transition from darkness to light. Then I saw it was a child, a little girl. She ran haphazardly, swooping from side to side like a panicked bird. The light glanced off the pale-toned fabric of her cotton dress, and I realised it was the Spanish child we had seen on the bus that morning.

Something was chasing after her. I thought at first it was a man, but the way it ran, with its torso held horizontally and its forelimbs scraping the ground, was not remotely human. The creature rushed forward, its spindly arms circling in a liquid over-arm crawl, as if swimming through the air. Its bowed legs were skinny and hairless, the legs of some appalling sculpture by Giacometti. Its long body was naked and pale as a moonbeam, with the necrotic, blue-veined pallor of worms that squirm under stones, emerging only at night.

It flinched away from the light, its spidery limbs bunched and tensed as if confronting an enemy. It was too far away to make out its features, but it seemed to me that I could sense its hatred of us, its inarticulate rage at being disturbed.

I fumbled for the camera on my belt, unzipping it from its case and then firing it repeatedly at the creature like a weapon. White flashes seared through the darkness like emergency flares. The whole forest seemed lit up, as if struck by lightning. My head swam, my emotions directionless and demented as a swarm of bees.

Beside me on the ground Charlie was crying. She had dropped the candle, and some fronds of bracken were already catching alight. I used the flat of my hand to stamp them out. I had heard that if you stifle a flame quickly enough it will not burn you, and there must have been some truth to that because aside from a mild discomfort I was unscathed. As I withdrew my hand my fingers brushed against something solid – the gold cigarette lighter. I slipped it into my pocket.

"It's taken the little girl," Charlie wept. "Vernon, we have to do something."

"There's nothing we can do. It's too late."

The darkness closed in around us. I lay on top of Charlie, holding her head between my hands to keep her still. I shut my mind to everything but her. I prayed that the monster was sated, that it would leave us alone. I had seen how it feared the light, and could only hope the camera flash had scared it away from us. I refused to dwell on the fate of the child.

We lay for some time in the open, barely moving. At some point we crawled back inside the cave. We kept close together, covering ourselves with the bracken. We may even have dozed a little. We left the cave as soon as it was light.

The mist had returned, but was much less dense. We set off through the trees, heading downhill. We found the pathway in less than ten minutes. I noticed one familiar landmark and then another. We had been camped less than a mile from the car park after all.

The sun was up. We sat together at one of the picnic tables and waited for the first bus of the day to arrive. When it came, the driver greeted us cheerfully and Charlie exchanged a greeting with him in Spanish. He seemed unsurprised to see us, and I remembered reading that climbing the mountain to watch the sunrise was something of a popular pastime on La Gomera.

I held Charlie's hand throughout the journey back to town. Neither of us said much. Already the events of the night before had started to feel distant and dreamlike. I looked out of the window at the sunlight slanting through the trees, the dizzying sweeps of countryside below. The driver was smoking a cigarette, flicking ash through the open window on to the tarmac. I noted the casual way he held the wheel, his steady expertise. The bus bucked and jounced on the pockmarked road, its back end veering to the outside edge on the tighter corners, but I observed this with dispassionate interest and little more. After our night on the mountain I felt invulnerable to danger, at least temporarily.

We returned to our rooms to wash and change then agreed to take an early lunch on the hotel terrace. I was ravenously hungry, and demolished my steak and chips in a matter of minutes. Charlie on the other hand seemed to have little appetite. I felt acutely aware of her. I found I was afraid to let her out of my sight – even the brief time we had spent in our separate rooms had made me nervous and anxious to be with her again. I knew we would have to talk about what had happened, and I was trying to think how to begin when the Phillotsons arrived, bustling down the steps on their way into town. They were obviously delighted to see Charlie.

"We missed you on the journey down," said Adele Phillotson. "We were afraid you might have got lost."

"We walked down, actually," I broke in before Charlie could speak. "There's a pathway on the far side of the peak that leads you straight into Garajonay village. There's a walkers' hostel there. We decided it might be fun to spend the night."

My speech was unrehearsed but to me at least it sounded convincing. Charlie remained silent throughout. When I finished speaking she asked Adele if she had been all right on the bus ride down.

"Oh, she's a dab hand at it now, she'd be bombing up and down all day, give her half a chance," Bill Phillotson said. He smiled his broad smile. I noticed that one of his molars was capped with gold. "She's an old soldier, is our Addie. Besides, we've had another drama to contend with, or haven't you heard?"

"What happened?" Charlie said.

"That little Spanish girl. The daughter of the couple who were on the bus with us. She's gone missing up on the mountain. They've got the police out with dogs and everything. They're searching the entire area."

"That's terrible," said Charlie quietly. "Those poor people."

"They think she must have fallen into one of the ravines," said Adele. "The mountain can be a dangerous place, you know, especially for a child."

I felt sick with dismay. I had been harbouring the hope that what I had seen the night before had been a nightmare, the final and most terrible in my sequence of dreams about the mountain. The Phillotsons' words now told me this was not so. I glanced at Charlie but she was turned away from me, listening to Bill Phillotson as he talked animatedly about the particular breed of bloodhound the police were using. I thought she was annoyed with me for having lied, but I realised later she was probably just trying to keep them out of our business. People like the Phillotsons were always on the lookout for some new piece of gossip.

"Well, we'll leave you to your lunch," Adele was saying. "We'll see you both about the place, I'm sure."

"Of course," Charlie said. "Let us know if there's any news."

They moved off down the road, quickly dropping from sight as they descended the slope. Once they were gone Charlie turned to me and told me she had decided to return to London.

"I can't bear to be here, Vernon," she said. She laid her knife and fork on the side of her plate. "I want to go home."

I said I would start packing at once but she would not hear

of it. She said I should stay on by myself, that I should continue with the week as planned.

"There's no reason to cut short your holiday," she said. "I'll see you when you get back to town."

I started to argue but she would not listen and in the end I stopped trying. It was clear to me Charlie was not yet ready or willing to talk about what had happened. No doubt she had her reasons. I hoped she would tell me in time, but I knew that if I persisted in trying to force her she was liable to shut down on me altogether.

We spent most of the afternoon asleep on my bed, then walked down to the harbour for a final meal. We talked of books we had read and films we had seen, nothing that involved the island, or Kenneth Goule. Back at the hotel, Charlie said she was going to her room to pack and I did not see her again that evening. I tried not to let it bother me, fully expecting we would have breakfast together the following morning. But she did not appear in the dining room, and when I asked after her at reception they informed me she had already checked out.

• • •

My first instinct was to go after her, and I did actually start to pack, but before the morning was over I had decided to stay. Charlie had made it clear she needed time by herself and I knew that if we were to have a future I should respect her wishes. I had also made a discovery that made me feel compelled to remain on the island, at least for a time.

While turning out the pockets of my trousers I came across the cigarette lighter, the one Charlie had found in the cave. Seeing it again was like experiencing a flashback. The lighter was proof to me of what had happened, a kind of dark talisman. It was also the first time I had seen it in daylight, and I examined it with some curiosity. It was one of the old kind, a naphtha lighter that required the case to be closed to shut off the flame. It was heavy – gold, I thought, probably of some value.

It was also engraved with two initials: M.F. They meant nothing to me at first. Then I remembered the shipwreck, and Martin Foerster.

I had lunch in the hotel, then walked down to the quay, where I had previously spotted an internet café. After half an hour of searching, I finally found a site put up by diving enthusiasts that gave some details of the incident Charlie had described to me, the shipwreck on which Kenneth Goule had based *Wreck of the Julia*. It seemed that Martin Foerster had boarded the ship under an alias, Anders Volkmann, which was actually the name of a cousin who had been killed on the Eastern Front. The names of the three other missing passengers were Paul Moser, Dietrich Hilfeld, and Lisa von Pelz. Moser and Lisa von Pelz were engaged to be married. No one could say what had caused the four to separate themselves from the other passengers, and there was no record of any of them other than Foerster having been a member of the Nazi Party. I made a cursory search for photos of Foerster but couldn't find any. I decided I would follow it up properly once I got home.

The name of the unlucky freighter was the *Julie ten Berg*. The ship had been the *Julia*, after all.

The search for the Spanish child continued. On the day after Charlie's departure a group of more than a hundred islanders was organised into teams to sweep the mountain. I watched them as they assembled in the coach park, chattering excitedly in Spanish and poring over maps.

They searched for many hours, but found nothing. On their return they looked dispirited and tired. I took some photos of them as they came down the hill to the harbour front, trying to keep a low profile but unable to resist recording the event. My new hobby had become a kind of compulsion, and I realised to my surprise that I meant to keep on with it after I returned to London.

On my last day on La Gomera I took the bus again to the foot of the mountain. I wandered in the fields thereabouts, and as the day began to cool I walked for about a mile up the dusty slope. From time to time I stopped to look upwards, gazing at the distant peak, swathed in its cloak of laurels, enfolded in mist. I did not feel afraid, not with the bright sunshine and the red roofs of the town still clearly in sight, but I did wonder what it was that we thought we had seen.

Was there a monster roaming the mountain, or if we returned to the island next week or next year would we discover that the little girl had been the victim of a common criminal, the kind of lone maniac you seem to read about in the papers every other day?

On my way back to the hotel I stopped outside the café where I had bought the postcards for Milly. There were still some left, the woman in her papier-mâché headdress, the man in his yellow cloak with the strange false arms – Orahan and

Hirguan, God and the Devil. I selected one of the Hirguan cards, then took it inside the café and asked the woman behind the counter if she could tell me anything about it. The woman smiled at me uncertainly, and I thought she had not understood, but then she gave a nervous laugh and stated in halting English that I was too early.

"The fiesta is in October," she said. "You must come back and visit us then."

She held up her hands, palm outwards as if to indicate that I should wait, and then disappeared through a narrow doorway behind the counter. After a minute or so she returned. She was holding a small paperback book, one of the many guides to the flora and fauna of the island. She leafed through the pages until she found what she wanted, then passed me the volume, pointing insistently at one of the photographs inside.

"Hirguan," she said, pointing again. "Only on this island."

The photograph she showed me was of a spider, bulbous-bodied and long-legged, with the Latin name of *Dysdera hirguan*. The text was in English, and informed me that the creature was a nocturnal hunting spider that lived in caves. The species was indigenous to La Gomera. Because it feared the light it was rarely seen.

When I asked if I could buy the book from her the woman seemed concerned that it was not a new copy. I told her it did not matter, and much against her protests paid the full price.

• • •

The London I returned to was cold, the wind with the brittle edge of an early autumn.

"You've caught the sun," Milly said when she saw me. "You look better."

We were having Sunday lunch in a pub close to where Milly lived in West Wandsworth. I had brought a selection of my photographs for her to look at, images of the boats in the harbour and the pastel-coloured town houses, also some of the pictures I had taken of the Phillotsons and the German tourists on the bus.

I did not show her my pictures of Charlie, nor did I show her the photo of the Spanish child. The photos I had taken on the mountain – those wild shots into the darkness – had been entirely blank.

Milly passed quickly over the pictures of the boats and the houses but she examined the photos of the bus passengers for some time, sliding them about on the table like a news editor compiling a storyboard. "These are good," she said. "I didn't know you were into photography?"

"I didn't know I was until now. I bought the camera on impulse. The last photos I took before these were with that old Kodak I had for my birthday when I was fifteen."

"You're joking?"

I shook my head. "Honestly." I was thrilled by her response, though for some reason I tried not to show it. I moved the conversation on to other things.

I had tried calling Charlie from the airport the moment I came through customs but her mobile had been switched off, and all subsequent attempts to contact her had similarly failed. She seemed to have vanished, and as first one day passed and then another I began to despair. I realised I still didn't know her address, only that she lived over a newsagent's somewhere in Camden. I imagined myself combing the streets of Chalk Farm and Kentish Town, mapping the locations of the various newsagents and spying on each of them in turn until I found her. This almost began to seem like a sensible plan. I missed her so much, you see. I kept going over our final conversation, hearing her say she would see me when I got back, then torturing myself with the thought she hadn't meant it, that she had been trying to soften the blow. I now profoundly regretted letting her leave the island before we'd had the chance to talk properly about what had happened. Perhaps she had wanted me to make her stay, and had taken my wish to give her space as a sign of indifference.

I also dwelt increasingly on what she had said to me about Eloise, that I should find my wife and finish things properly, lay the ghost of my marriage to rest. I knew she was right. More than that, I started to believe that the business with Eloise might also be the key to finding Charlie. What if Charlie was determined to wait till I was properly free? I knew such thoughts were ridiculous but it made no difference. In any case, they were all I had to cling to.

The new school term had begun and so for a while I was too busy with work to tease out the practical problem of how I might find my wife, but as autumn strengthened its grip and the first frosts arrived I began my investigations. I sorted through Eloise's things, which I had not touched since the day of the plane crash. I hoped she might have left clues, but there was nothing. When I searched her dressing table drawers, which was where she always kept important documents or ongoing paperwork, I discovered that as well as her passport she had also taken her address book, her birth certificate, her degree qualifications and job references, everything she would have needed to start a new life.

There were friends of Eloise's, people from her job and from college who I presumed must know where she was. I could have tracked one of them down easily enough, but I shrank from doing so. Not just because I balked at the idea of confronting them but also because I knew they would call Eloise and warn her the minute I put the phone down.

I knew I had to take her by surprise, but I didn't know how this could be accomplished. It was out of this frustration that my mind returned eventually to my dreams.

The Freudian faith in the relationship of the dream-life to the waking consciousness had always seemed like so much mumbo-jumbo to me, only a short step away from Julia Goule's convoluted hierarchy of superstitions. Nonetheless when I happened to spot a book entitled *Dream Science* in the window of a bookshop in Chatham I found myself drawn inside. I bought the book, and spent most of that evening reading it. Much of what I read served only to confirm my prejudices, but the book did at least contain one idea that appealed to me – the idea of the subconscious as a crime writer. One of the main satisfactions of a detective story lay in trying to pinpoint which parts of the plot were relevant to solving the mystery and which were red herrings. The author of the book insisted it was the same with dreams.

As I lay in bed that night it came to me I had let myself become distracted by the red herrings – by the grounded ship and the empty beach, the mountain in the distance – while ignoring the clue that really mattered: the identity of the man in the black tuxedo.

Perhaps the answer had been in front of me all along.

Since my return from La Gomera I had barely glanced at Kenneth Goule's painting but now I contemplated it obsessively, returning again and again to the group of huddled figures on the foreshore, the woman in green and her dark-suited partner, his face caught in profile but obscured by shadows. It seemed to me now that his face lay in shadow because I had not wanted to face up to him. Once I put my mind to it, it didn't take me long to work out who he was. I had even met him once, at an end-of-term party at Eloise's school. I couldn't recall his name to begin with, but then I remembered he had had the same surname as a boy I had been at school with, Graham Cleverly, that Eloise had introduced this man as Mark Cleverly. He had longish hair and a serious expression, and had been wearing a black tuxedo.

"Mark's an engineer," Eloise had said. "He gave a talk to some of our students during careers week."

I hadn't noticed anything different about Eloise's behaviour at the time, but the truth was she could have had ten affairs if she wanted to. I was constantly on the road, and Eloise knew my schedule by heart. She could have brought men to the house every day and I would never have known. I remembered she had bought new clothes, something she had done a lot when we were first married but not so much recently, and there had been that weekend she spent in Cambridge, supposedly with a friend she knew from college.

I had no idea where Mark Cleverly lived. I realised the only way to find out would be by contacting the school. I had no idea how Eloise had left things at work. For all I knew she had walked out on her job as suddenly and unexpectedly as she had walked out on me, but I somehow doubted it. She would not have wanted to ruin the chance of getting a reference. She had probably timed her departure to coincide with her notice period.

In the end I called the office and spoke to the Dragon. I pitched my voice a little lower than normal in an attempt to disguise it, and told her I was the deputy head of a school in Gillingham, that I was putting together a series of seminars for an upcoming careers fair.

"One of our teachers mentioned someone you used recently, someone called Cleverly?" I said. "A real hit with the students, apparently. I was wondering if I might trouble you for his contact details?"

"Oh, you mean the young man who works on the oil rigs," said the Dragon. She made the sniffing sound that I knew meant mild disapproval, then gave me Mark Cleverly's mobile number and postal address. It was strange and rather moving to hear her voice again. After Eloise left I had arranged with a colleague to take over her school's account and I had not been there since. It was as if the Dragon was speaking directly out of the past.

• • •

Mark Cleverly lived in Frodsham, a small town on the edge of the Peak District. I drove without stopping, watching the industrial hinterland of the Midlands give way to the greenly undulating landscape of rural Derbyshire. It was cold out, barely two degrees above freezing. The afternoon sunlight was thin and pale, shading to dusk. I found the house easily, a modern semi-detached on the edge of a private estate. There were views of the Peak in the distance.

There was no car in the drive, which I hoped was a sign that Cleverly himself was not at home. I parked my own car a little way along the road and simply sat for a while, staring at a yellowed sycamore leaf that had become attached to one of the windscreen wipers. I wondered what I was going to say if I had been wrong about everything, if the door to the house was opened by a total stranger. In the end I had no choice but to find out for sure. As I walked up the path to the door I remembered that other, somehow similar moment months before, arriving at Milly's place on the day of the plane crash.

I felt something click into place deep inside me as the universe twisted itself back into alignment.

She was wearing navy tracksuit bottoms and a red knitted top. Her hair was longer, scraped back from her forehead in a velvet hair band, making her look at once older and more exotic. Her face was without make-up, something I had rarely seen in the old days.

"What are you doing here, Vernon?" She spoke as if nothing had happened, as if we had parted just a week or a day before. Then she sighed heavily and stepped aside. "I suppose you'd better come in."

The living room of the house was modest but comfortable. I saw plaid rugs and patchwork cushions, a set of three modern oils depicting wild horses, galloping along a beach. Eloise and I sat facing each other on two identical brown corduroy sofas.

"I don't want to fight with you, Vernon, I don't see the point," she said. "I haven't made a fuss over money or anything, have I? You knew things were over between us. They'd been over for ages." She paused. "Mark and I are going to have a baby."

I was momentarily stunned. In all the years of our marriage Eloise had never once mentioned children. I realised how little, after all, we had understood each other.

"I don't want to fight with you, either," I said. "I wanted to make sure you were OK."

She seemed to relax, becoming at once some other person, a lovely young mother-to-be with marginally bitten nails and a model's cheekbones. The stranger I had briefly imagined might open the door.

"I'm fine," she said. "We'll be moving up to Aberdeen once the baby is born. Mark will be able to be at home more. We should talk about a divorce, I suppose."

"That shouldn't be a problem," I said. "We've been living apart for six months already."

I promised I would see about a solicitor and Eloise made tea, serving it with wafer-thin macaroons. She told me she had made them herself. She smiled shyly when I praised them, and for an instant I saw again the woman I fell in love with.

I didn't stay long. I drove along country roads until I was clear of the town, then pulled over into a lay-by and watched the sun go down behind the hills. I wiped my eyes with the back of my hand and then drove on. As I came into the village of Kingsley I saw trailers lining the road, tents pitched in a nearby field, the muddle and paraphernalia of a travelling fair. On impulse I stopped the car. Aside from Eloise's macaroons I had not eaten in several hours, and I hoped I might buy some food at one of the stalls.

I bought a hot dog and a carton of soup. Both tasted delicious, and wandering among the sideshows and rides I remembered the seafront amusements at Folkestone Milly and I had loved so much when we were children. The sky was burnt orange. I munched my food and watched the children queuing up to play a game called Hook, Line and Sinker in which you had to catch a plastic goldfish to win a prize.

I unclipped my camera from my belt and began taking photographs. The light was not good, but I had learned to adjust the meter, and the coloured lanterns and plastic fish appealed to me as subject matter. I noticed that the prizes for the game all had a nautical theme and I photographed these too: pirates' hats, plastic telescopes, snow domes containing models of the *Titanic*. At the back of the stall was a ship in a bottle, a fine square rigger, and with the aid of the zoom lens I was able to capture it quite well.

As I walked back to the car I took out my mobile. This time, when I keyed in Charlie's number it began to ring.

RED QUEEN

The problem with having a story is that everyone starts believing they know it by heart.

As soon as he hears her speak the words, Matthew knows he will steal them. They have the ring of a made phrase, the kind that will be repeated and analysed and learned by schoolchildren. Matthew Cleverly had a career before he wrote *The High Wire*, but it was a small one. His poetry was admired but seldom read. His obscurity did not bother him – in common with most obscure poets, he rather enjoyed it. He taught adult education at various colleges, which paid the bills. He was married to the painter Ruth Annis. They lived in Nottingham with their young son, Mark.

Then Matthew met his muse, and everything changed.

• • •

Ruby always felt safe behind the camera, she told him, because it's the character the audience bond with, not the actor. Zoya Klee in *Scaffold Point* and Balalaika Smirnoff in *The Puppeteer* and Julia Goule in *American Star*. When Ruby Castle strips naked in Charlie Sessions's cabin after the ballroom scene, it is Julia's body they gawp at, as if Julia were the real person, and Ruby her stand-in.

Matthew has watched all Ruby's films multiple times, *American Star* more than any. Movie buffs who know the film well are fond of informing him the ballroom scene, with its two hundred extras and lavish set dressing, cost a quarter of the entire production budget. Anyone complaining about this piece of extravagance would be bound to admit the results are sensational: diamond light streaming from the chandelier and the stained-glass ceiling, the captain and officers raising their glasses as the orchestra strikes up a waltz tune by Johann Strauss. The camera lingers lovingly on the angel–devil features of Maxim Schorr, upright and elegant in his black evening coat, not so different from the SS uniform Schorr will be wearing in flashback just ten minutes later. Our first glimpse of Raymond Latour as Charlie Sessions shows him only in profile – he is arguing with Henri Gaudier about Winston Churchill. Ruby Castle enters the ballroom more or less unnoticed.

In comparison with the elaborate costumes of the supporting cast, Castle's gown seems understated. The most remarkable thing about it is its colour – that intense bottle green – and of course the woman wearing it, Ruby Castle in her career-defining role as Julia Goule. *American Star* is often categorised as a horror movie but Julia Goule, with her dubious background and knife-edge psychology and deadly secret, is classic noir.

A cake
In the shape of a castle
Pink ramparts hot
Glazed buttress
Bright bastion
Spun sugar lattice
Of a gold
Portcullis
Sweetly shining
Stallions prancing
Flags waving hearts drowning

And yet it is not Castle's movies that first enthral him, but a film about her. Matthew doesn't care for horror movies, he prefers Bergman and Tarkovsky and Tarr. A European at heart, his heroes are Apollinaire and Celan. Trash shockers like *The Puppeteer* appal him and when he stops to think about how badly those early films of hers are scripted he still feels angry. *Scaffold Point* is better – a serviceably written, mystifyingly underappreciated spy drama, though Ruby herself is underused, a foil for the two main characters, her death a dramatic catalyst for the bloody denouement.

• • •

When Matthew first sees Ruby, it is winter. Frosty gardens, icicles hanging from pine branches like dragons' teeth, frost crackling on fence posts and the lids of dustbins. Ruth is out teaching her evening class, Mark is sleeping over at a friend's house. Matthew is in bed with the flu and he feels like hell.

The film comes on after the news, a documentary about some actress who killed her lover. *More trash TV*, he thinks; trash TV could become a habit if he's not careful. But his head is clogged with mucus and he can't be bothered to get up and change the channel.

He watches footage of a woman being taken in handcuffs from the back door of a hotel – somewhere in Soho, Matthew thinks – the images so blurred they might have been shot a hundred years ago. "*Ruby Castle was born into a family of circus performers,*" the voiceover informs him. "*She made her debut on the London stage at the age of twenty. Rapidly climbing the ladder of showbiz, she murdered her lover and co-star Raymond Latour when he refused to leave his wife for her. Castle had been in a relationship with Latour for just eleven months. Latour was in London, filming the gangland thriller* Mob Handed. *Latour's role was later reshot by Harry Scott Green.*"

More film of Ruby walking to a police car. A collage of newspaper headlines – *Scream Queen in Real-Life Bloodbath*, *Red Queen Strikes Revenge at Capital Hideaway*, *Movie Actress Stabs Lover in Jealous Rage*. Matthew finds he is interested in spite of himself. He thinks about Ruth Ellis, and then Medea. On the screen they are showing clips from Castle's films, *American Star* and *Scaffold Point*, the scene where Gunther Sternbach pulls a gun from his coat and shoots Castle dead.

She is so young in that scene, so ravishingly alive. Once he is up and about again – jelly-limbed still but not contagious – Matthew goes into town and buys the VHS recording of *Scaffold Point*. He watches it twice, back to back, while Ruth is at work, then shows it to her that evening while they are having supper. He watches her surreptitiously, wonders what she is seeing when she looks at Castle, whether it is possible to look at Castle and not be mesmerised.

So different from the way he looks at Ruth: hands rough from turpentine, that scornful twist of the lips he occasionally hates, her keen intelligence as a painter, her clumsy way of walking, the uncouth desire to fuck her that still persists, the absent expression that comes into her eyes when she stares out from the window of a moving train.

Like the best poems such a gaze is complex, and often tiring. It takes years to get right.

Thumbnail windows
Sherbet miracles
A courtyard
Dim with smoke
Burnings beatings pig roasts
Fireworks and New Year toasts
Hate-fuelled promises
He said she said
Bang bang you're dead
An Englishman's home
Is his Castle

The first face-to-face conversation Matthew has with Ruby is about a cake, how her Aunt Marnie made a cake in the shape of a castle to celebrate her eighth birthday. Her aunt is not a company woman by birth – like Ruby's cousin's wife Mae, she married in. Marnie takes over the python act sometimes, when her husband Marty feels like a break. Mostly she keeps the wagon clean and cares for the children. And she likes to bake. Before she married Marty, Marnie worked as a pastry chef.

"Does that make a difference?" Matthew asks. "whether you're born into the carnival or join later?"

Ruby doesn't even answer, just gives him a look. "It was my cousin I was closest to," she says instead. "Marnie's youngest son Marek. Marek and I are astrological twins. We were born on the same day in the same year, ten minutes apart. We should have had the sense to realise."

"Realise what?"

"That we were better as brother and sister than going off to shag in the hay wagon every moment we could. Lovers that close never stay together, there's something doomed about them. As if the world realises its mistake and tears them apart. It was like we shared a skin, Marek and I. The thought we'd split apart one day no more entered our heads than the thought I'd end up in prison and he'd end up driving around the south of England selling aspirin. I've come to think that's the way life likes to play it, though – to show you the riches of Croesus and then rob you blind.

"My sister Ros still writes to me sometimes," Ruby says, "but it's never the same, is it? I've been away too long. She asks me how I am and I say don't bother with that crap, tell me how things are with you, tell me every detail. Tell me what the air smells like in the morning when you first step outside.

"The company disbanded three years ago," Ruby says. "Ros teaches kids to ride at a stables on the South Downs. She can still do a back flip," she says. "Still likes to do a turn or two riding bareback when there's no one around."

• • •

Matthew and Ruby write letters back and forth for more than two years before Ruby agrees to add Matthew's name to her approved visitors list. By then he is so deeply in love with her the cracks in his marriage to Ruth have started to widen, to go friable at the edges, to seep radioactive dust. It is Matthew who finally walks out – packs a bag and gets on a train to King's Cross. He can barely believe what he has done, the cruelty of it, the rapture. He ends up living in a bedsitter-with-own-bathroom in Hammersmith. It's like he's never been married, like his life has been washed back to bedrock and he's a poet again. How can you be a poet when you have faculty colleagues coming over for dinner and – an appalling cliché but even as he hates himself for thinking it he knows it is true – a pram in the hall?

And does he miss them, Ruth and Mark? Not that first winter. The gas fire purring, the dun-coloured, too-thin curtains pulled half closed, the orange streetlamp outside the window, the rash sounds of the street and he is fully content. It isn't until the following spring that he starts seeing them again.

"What kind of a father are you?" Ruth says, and oh, her scorn. Like ashes, grey and vaguely metallic and hard to shift. Once a fortnight he takes the train up to Nottingham. He gazes from the moving window at the passing gardens, strewn with trikes and disembowelled washing machines and rotary driers. Oh the poignant loneliness of the long-distance father.

The train, heaving itself into St Pancras late at night. The tarnished streets – how else would London's streets be? – Matthew exhausted and filthy with shame, the scent of it so like anger it makes no difference. Piccadilly Line to the blessed bedsit, pour a whiskey – Jack Daniel's Red Label, always, that's what these days reek of – flick on the TV then later once he's in bed wank himself blind.

Tell the truth: has he ever been happier, more like himself? Reading accounts of Ted Hughes's first year at Cambridge, or the Poetry Bookshop meetings in Bloomsbury before the First World War. Reconnecting with the old crowd from Merton, discovering he's done better than any of them, in his own last-ditch way. At least he's still writing seriously, still committed. He lets it be put about that he's working on the collection that will make his name. The kind of work that will be talked about, that will set a new standard.

• • •

He has never met her, yet he possesses her, every night.

In his letters to her, Matthew likes to talk about Ruby's films, describing them back at her frame by frame, showing off his knowledge of her art and what he insists on calling her milieu. Like a lyre bird displaying its plumage – look, mine is bigger. She seems unimpressed.

"I remember when we shot *The Puppeteer*," she writes. "The on-set toilets broke down. There was this awful stink for most of the second week. It wouldn't go, not even when they got the toilets working again. I hated that movie. I hated the way they kept the monkeys in the lock-up overnight. It was pitch black in there, they must have been terrified, you could hear them screaming. I kept thinking I should call the police but I was in a bad place right then. I'd just broken up with Bennie, or he had with me. I'd finish shooting then go back to my shitty bedsit and howl until the walls shook. I was worse than the monkeys.

"It's not so bad in here," she writes. "Not once you're used to it. There were some awful years, before. At least in prison you know what you're getting.

"I love getting your letters," she writes, "even though I don't give a stuff about film theory."

Pain honed sharp
As a guillotine
My queen
In the street
They call for your head
You come forward
To the footlights
Let down your hair
The furious crowd
Smash the diamond sherbet
Windows
The butter cherubs
The bitter chocolate
Nightingale
The sugar swans on their foil lake

The first time Matthew visits Ruby he's nervous as hell. *Pretend it's an interview,* he thinks, *pretend it's anyone.* He has barely slept and he is terrified – that she will be ordinary after all, a woman in a shapeless cardigan and awful shoes – whatever kind of shoes they make you wear in prison – that they'll have nothing in common. At the end of the hour he will go home, whatever. Make his way back through the green-painted corridors, the fireproof doors, past that scabby little patch of garden with the birdbath and the daffodils. Out. Their love is only happening because she cannot escape.

He is so fixated on his own panic he has all but forgotten he will not be the only one from outside going in. He did not expect to see so many visitors: mums and kids mainly, sisters, friends. Almost all of them women. The men must mostly move on, he realises, feeling ashamed. The partners and husbands, pissed off with having to do their own washing and not having sex.

When he arrives in the room she is already seated at the bolted-down table, waiting for him. She is wearing a pair of grey sweatpants and a long-sleeved black top, black plimsolls with a lime-green stripe, the kind of clothes a dancer might wear when she's cooling off. Her wrists are bony, her whole frame skinnier and more depleted-looking than he had imagined. Her hair, he realises with a shock, is beginning to go grey. The kind of woman he is used to seeing at book readings, seated near the exit and looking distracted. She is small, strange, unlike her films, yet there it still is, that lurch in the pit of his stomach that tells him this is it, the moment that will determine who he will become, that will set in motion the spring of talent he always knew was there.

She looks up from the table and sees him. Most people would smile from force of habit but she does not. A frown creases her forehead. If Matthew thinks he was in love with her before, he had no idea.

• • •

More than anything he longs to hold her, scoop her up and carry her, smooth back her hair with both his hands, to kiss first her eyebrows and then her lips, to feel himself falling. Matthew has a hard-on. He wonders again if the storm enfolding his heart has blown up only because he knows he is safe from its implications. Safe from entanglement, safe from more children, safe to come and go.

Eloise and Abelard, he thinks, already imagining the poems that might be wrung from such an allusion. A prison is a kind of nunnery, after all. In spite of the thousands of words they have exchanged by letter there is silence between them. "I didn't want to sound stupid," she tells him, later. "I didn't want my first words to you to be pleasantries," he agrees. They touch fingertips across the table instead – this is permitted, apparently. Matthew remembers his first dates with Ruth – the conversations into the small hours, the ferocious sex – and feels certain this is something different, something epic.

• • •

"You never ask me why I did it," Ruby says, months later. 'All the others did."

"Others?" Matthew says, momentarily aghast, for what could be worse than the discovery that he is not Odysseus, that these fractured, uber-poignant meetings are merely a reprise of other meetings with earlier suitors?

She laughs. "I don't mean that. I mean journalists and people. That TV guy who wanted to make a documentary about me. Them."

"What did you tell them?" Matthew says, knowing the TV guy's name is Simon Tarbet, that the film he eventually made is called *Fallen Angels*, an oddly disturbing piece of work that places Ruby Castle within the context of the femme fatale. "A hallucinatory masterpiece," *Sight and Sound* had called it, "a neon blur of black cabs and rain-slicked cobbles and mirrored cocktail lounges." A smart piece of work – Matthew owns the recording on VHS because of course he does – though he feels reluctant to admit to Ruby that he has even heard of it. He does not want to equate himself with *them* – the grave-diggers, the van-chasers, the zeitgeist commentators who have already moved on because so has the zeitgeist.

He has watched Tarbet's film more times than he cares to remember.

"I didn't tell them anything," Ruby says, and Matthew knows to his dismay that he can never ask her now, that if he does he will reduce himself in her eyes to one of the crowd. The only reason he gives a shit is because of the poems. As a man and as a human being he does not care about what happened to Raymond Latour. "Smooth bastard had it coming," he thinks. Latour played mostly spivs and bank robbers; he had that kind of look. Matthew has sought out all Latour's films also, even the early ones, which has not been easy. Two or three are only available as Japanese imports, and cost a fortune.

He has watched Raymond Latour seduce English roses and French barmaids, befriend and bamboozle a lord, plan a ludicrously complicated robbery on the *Brighton Belle*. Latour's best movie is *Highland Spring*, a cut-price *Phar Lap* in which Latour plays the dastardly owner of a rival racehorse. The film is set on a large estate in Surrey, between the wars. For Matthew, the strangest thing about watching it is knowing that at the time the movie was made, Ruby Castle and Raymond Latour had not yet met.

The role played by Latour in *American Star* – a cheap, louche business tycoon who has developed a lucrative sideline in smuggling war criminals to South America – seems tailor-made for him.

The question Matthew most wants to ask is not what made Ruby kill him – that question has so many feasible answers it seems barely worth asking – but what made her fall for the man in the first place. Matthew cannot imagine her being interested in Latour for more than five minutes.

Perhaps he had a big dick. Do women actually go in for those kinds of comparison? He has no idea.

The art of letting them eat cake
The people say
The people want bread not artists
It's only once artists
Have fed the fire the people concede

Bread
Is only good
For one
Coarse-ground
Thick-sliced
Stone-milled
Variety of hunger

"I was bored and it was winter," Ruby tells him. "Winter always depresses me. It reminds me of what the company used to be like in the off season, the endless freezing months of no money and everyone drinking too much because there's nothing else to do. The dark evenings. The best thing about being in prison is that you don't really notice when it's winter, because you're inside anyway. Ray bought me an antique eternity ring and I liked going to bed with him. I don't think it was even him so much as the part I was playing. I enjoyed the sordidness of what we were doing, the hotel bedrooms, the secret phone calls, the whole clichéd bit. I felt like I was living inside a film script and that was fun for a while. As if suddenly I really was the character audiences think I am – powerful and seductive and a little bit crazy. I liked feeling mad because it felt safer than feeling angry. Does that make sense?

"I'm not sorry he's dead," she says. "I don't mean I wanted him dead, just that I honestly couldn't care less either way. I was furious with Ray for what he said to me and I lashed out. He was a user with a massive ego and no loss to the world. The idea of killing him never occurred to me – I wouldn't have wanted to give him the satisfaction."

The murder happened in less than a second, sweet and dark and heady as a shot of good rum.

• • •

"The worst punishment," she says, "is people believing we were this massive love affair."

• • •

"What did he say to you, then?" Matthew asks, cautiously. He's not sure yet if the question is allowed. "What made you lash out?"

Ruby hesitates. She shakes her head, frowns. "You're not going to write about this, are you? Why do you need to know?"

They have reached an even, tranquil place in their relationship where the past seems irrelevant. Ruby is studying with the Open University. She is reading for a degree in Social History, and they talk about that a lot. Ruby insists she is fed up with the kind of history they teach in schools, all the battles and power struggles and fucked-up debates in Parliament that always seem to end with someone deciding the best way of solving the problem is to drop some bombs.

"I want to understand how people survive," she says. "How they find ways to carry on with their lives in spite of the arseholes." She is interested especially in why so many women end up in prison, also prison reform.

Matthew says he is surprised they allow these kinds of books inside a prison and Ruby just laughs.

"Oh, Matthew," she says. Matthew brings her books, and they talk about those, too. In the beginning he is eager for her to read more poetry – Eliot and Lowell and then, when it's obvious she's never opened them, Plath and Sexton and Carson and Elizabeth Bishop. She doesn't take to those either.

"I'm not that person," she says. "I like Agatha Christie and Virginia Andrews. Don't be disappointed."

"I'm not disappointed," he says, trying not to be. He brings her Margery Allingham instead, Raymond Chandler and Patricia Highsmith, James M. Cain and the other James – Ellroy. Ruby likes James Ellroy best of all. "Because he's such a bastard, she says. He makes me laugh." Matthew starts reading Ellroy, who he has never picked up before. He finds a hypnotic beauty in the work, not just the refinement, the rhythmic perfection of the man's sentences but in the gap between the pathos of his past and his appalling ego. Matthew suspects Ellroy doesn't realise he even has an ego, that he probably believes he is damaged and in need of repair. *Like everyone,* he adds to himself. *Like we all are.*

In any case, he is thrilled to realise the books Ruby prefers have their own poetry, a poetry of accustomed plotlines – regular as verse forms – and occasionally exquisite glissandi of apposite words. Matthew begins to count the beats, shivering in anticipation at the next deft turn from major to minor, the thudding, discordant irruption of an accidental plot twist. Most satisfying and delicious of all, the discussions with Ruby – during their truncated, epiphanic meetings and in their letters afterwards: who did what to whom and why, how did the murderer get away with leaving the gas on, that bastard cop.

The urgency to communicate theory. Matthew realises this must be why so many people enjoy soap operas, and feels faintly sheepish.

"I'm interested, that's all," he finally replies to Ruby's question. "I want to understand. I want to know everything about you."

He does not answer her question about his writing but she is on to that.

"Will you promise me, though? Not to write about it, I mean."

Matthew realises he must either lie to her or risk a reversal in their relationship. A lie would be a reversal in any case, for him as well as her, and so he takes the only course he can take and stays silent. Ruby sighs and shakes her head again and Matthew can almost see the words as she thinks them, appearing on the screen of her eyes like a double negative: *bloody men.*

"I asked Ray if he was going to tell his wife about us," she says. "We were in London because Ray was filming that gangster movie. A long, grey afternoon and I kept thinking about how I didn't have to be there, how I could be in LA. We'd already fucked twice and I was bored senseless but I couldn't be bothered to put on my clothes and leave. Where else was there to go? I didn't feel like getting drunk and there was nothing good on at the pictures. What I wanted was someone to talk to, you know, like I would once have talked to Marek, just to pass the time. The only thing Ray liked talking about was himself. I asked him the question about Verlaine just to see what he'd do."

She is continuing with the story, saying something about how she really does feel sorry about what Verlaine had to go through, only maybe she did her a favour in the long run.

Matthew hangs back a moment, reaching after Verlaine's name as if trying to catch a fountain jet between his fingers. He always thinks of fountains when he hears her name because of *Clair de Lune*, even though he knows it is not the poet Ruby is talking about but Verlaine Preston, the daughter of Ashley Preston, who directed *American Star*. Raymond Latour's wife. Verlaine Preston in the newspaper clippings is small and dark, a screenwriter and good friend of the more famous screenwriter Leigh Brackett. How she ended up with Raymond Latour is even more of a mystery than how Ruby did, although of course it isn't, Ruby has said to him, "not when you think about it. He used her the way he used everyone. How do you think he got that part in Ashley's movie?"

"Anyway," Ruby is saying, "I obviously touched a nerve because his face went bright red and he started swearing at me. 'If you even think of telling Verlaine I'll deny everything,' he said. I could see the sweat standing out on his forehead. 'I'll deny everything and say you're crazy. You'll never make a movie again, or not any worth a damn. Maybe you should think about that before you go shooting your mouth off.'"

• • •

"It was strange," Ruby said. "Surreal. Like someone had pressed a button and turned him into his own evil twin. You know the movie with Bette Davis, *Dead Ringer*? I love that movie. I don't think I understood what hate was like until that moment. I knew Ray never felt a thing for me, not really – he saw something he liked and took it, and he was letting me know he could throw me away again the moment it suited him. But it was the contempt in his voice that got to me – like I wasn't just nothing to him, I was less than nothing, and how dare I even presume to have a point of view. We'd had room service and Ray had ordered steak – he always ordered steak, steak with onions and Portobello mushrooms and pepper sauce. I saw the knife on the side of his plate. There was still a smear of sauce on it. I grabbed it and just went for him. I think in my head I was still playing a part. Do you know how difficult it is to kill someone with a single stab wound? The prosecution used my bad luck as evidence of premeditation. They said the only way I could have been that accurate was if I'd been reading up on human anatomy beforehand.

"The whole thing's crazy," Ruby said. "Even now, it still feels crazy to me. I can't believe it happened."

The problem
With having a story
Is that
Everyone comes to believe
They know you by heart
Where's the ruby castle?
Asks my princess
Can we go there tomorrow?
The fat fortune teller laughs
Astounded that you cannot distinguish
This sugar-pink
Birthday palace
From the familiar humdrum hovel
Of your own red name

The poems come slowly at first. Like itemised receipts, they tell the story of those days, those afternoon bus rides to the dismal waiting room, the years – three of them, four – in which Matthew feels he is touched by magic, singled out for greatness. And of course he is awful to be with during those years. He goes months without seeing his son, without caring much one way or the other that he has a child. Ruth learns a deep contempt for him that never quite subsides. Matthew doesn't care about that either, or not much. What he feels most of all is a giddy gratitude, to be experiencing that state of being a poet he always dreamed of through his teens and into his twenties. The sense there is literally nothing more important than capturing the textures of his thoughts and of his world, encoding them in groups of letters on a white ground. Poets as the world's secret legislators and all that. Like a sidewinder surfing the desert, scouring its sacred patterns on the midnight sand.

"You have no idea what you are talking about," he sneers at Ruth once. "I don't have time for this." She is haranguing him for postponing a meeting, forgetting a birthday, something, whatever. When did she become so small-minded, so interminably fixated on inessentials?

The look on her face, like disappointment only disappointment doesn't cover it. This goes way beyond irritation or anger, as if she's cancelling him out of her thoughts, as if she's suddenly realised the person she thought she knew never really existed.

"You'll regret this one day," she says, and her voice is chilling. "I don't mean because of me, I mean because of Mark. You'll never get these years back. There is no way of making up for what you've done."

He wants to tell her again that she has no idea. He stops himself in time, from saying the words, at least, though not from thinking them. His brain whirrs with half-rhymes, with strange, delirious assonances. For a moment he glimpses an image: Ruth, the year they met, that funny little attic room in Beeston. "You smell like a cat," he had said, "an ocelot." She swipes a pillow at his head, but he means it as an endearment, his whole soul full of her. Her scent, like summer colliding with autumn, that green-tea aroma that really is, though he never tells her, just a little like cats' piss. When she's excited anyway, when she's sweating.

He has never smelled Ruby's sweat, never will, and is this the moment, he asks himself years later, when he first begins to admit that their love is a construct? A door he walked through – as Raymond Latour did – to reach the place he wanted to be?

• • •

On the TV arts show Matthew is asked if he thinks it is immoral to make money from making art about someone's death. "The man's relatives are still alive, aren't they?' the interviewer says. "Don't you find that a problem?"

Matthew leans back in his seat and says readers who interpret his poems too literally are missing the point. "*The High Wire* isn't about Ruby Castle," he says, "it's an extended metaphor. The job of a poet is to write poems, not make moral judgements. Make too many moral judgements and what you end up with is propaganda.

"I was inspired by her films, more than her life story," he says. "The narrow line between fantasy and reality, the dangers that come into play when that line is crossed."

He knows he sounds like a dick – exactly the kind of dick he's supposed to hate – and of course there are those who despise him for what they call his sophistry. Yet Matthew is surprised by how quickly he grows used to being a subject of controversy. *The High Wire* becomes a bestseller and wins three prizes. Matthew no longer has time to worry if anyone would give a shit about his "luminous" collection if its subject wasn't a film star and a murderer.

• • •

He doesn't tell Ruby about the prizes, or the TV interviews. He worries about what this means, whether he knows at a subconscious level that he's becoming a fake. He occasionally thinks about how differently he would be behaving if he and Ruth were still together. How they'd have asked Ruth's friend Kira to babysit Mark then gone out to celebrate. The combination of exhaustion and excitement that made Ruth high and skittish and sardonic and eager for sex.

As a student, Ruth was brilliant, more talented than him maybe. Was he really the kind of man who saw this as a problem?

• • •

He receives a postcard from Ruth. "They're good poems," she writes. Just that. Matthew reads the words twice and then again and his hands are shaking.

Sweet murderess
Did you think
Your glass
Dagger
Would
Melt softly as
Sugar
On his lapping tongue?
The knife that
Skewers his heart
Is grey instead
His thin sweet liquid life
So swiftly out
Scattered rubies
On the ballroom floor
Oh agony
Oh mayhem
Oh sweet
Sweet
Disaster

Out of the blue, his weekly visit to Ruby is refused. He heads home only slightly perturbed, expecting her to call that evening with an explanation. An administrative error, he thinks, some senseless mistake. No call comes. He dashes off a letter, which he posts at six in the morning from outside the tube station. He counts off the hours he knows must pass before she receives it. No answering letter, no phone call, no nothing.

A card arrives the following week, on the morning of the day he would normally visit. The card is made from cheap paper, a picture of yellow roses in a wicker basket. Ruby writes that their meetings have become painful to her, that she thinks it would be better for both of them if they stop. "Sorry," she writes. "This isn't your fault."

Matthew writes again in a panic, begs her to see him once more so they can say goodbye. The banality of his words is shocking to him. He is almost relieved when she does not reply – what such a meeting might have been like, he does not care to imagine, and that is without the dreadful triteness of his own final message.

For six weeks in a row he goes on the days he would have visited to stand outside the prison. He stays for exactly one hour, even when it's raining. When his vigil is over he walks to a café a couple of streets away and orders a pot of tea. He drinks the tea and reads Lowell's *Life Studies*. He finds the routine comforting, and the act of repetition imbues it with meaning. On his way home from one of these pilgrimages, he steps into a bookshop and buys a book about Ruth Ellis. *Her life was so hard*, he thinks. Matthew never knew she had a son.

The prison walls are high, and hard to climb, he thinks. A prison is like a nunnery, after all. He imagines Ruby in her cell, or tries to. He cannot decide if what was between them has ended, or is still going on.

acknowledgements

A thousand thanks to Pete and Nicky Crowther of PS Publishing, who first gave Ruby a home back in 2013. My thanks also to Gary Budden, who set this project in motion, also to Cath Trechman, George Sandison, Craig Leyenaar and the whole of the Titan team, who went the extra mile to bring this book to a wider audience during testing times. Thanks to Julia Lloyd for her arresting and inspiring cover art – I could not have imagined anything more perfect. Thanks as ever to my agent, Anna Webber, for her encouragement and support. A special thank you to Rob Shearman, who was one of Ruby's first readers. His continuing enthusiasm for these stories has, in a strange way, helped to define them.

about the author

Nina Allan is the recipient of the British Science Fiction Award, the Novella Award and the Kitschies Red Tentacle. Her story 'The Art of Space Travel' was a Hugo finalist in 2017 and the original version of *The Silver Wind* was awarded the Grand Prix de L'imaginaire in 2014. Her most recent novel is *The Dollmaker.* Nina lives and works in Scotland, on the Isle of Bute.